"I repeat, what are you ———" keeping my voice low.

"A strange question," the Filly still standing said, peering down his long face and comet-shaped blaze at me. "Surely you know we're here to destroy the Abomination."

"That wasn't the deal we made at Yandro," I insisted. "Or aren't you in the loop yet on that?"

"I'm aware of the agreement," Comet Nose said gravely. "I'm also aware of how badly you've kept other such agreements in the past."

Unfortunately, he had a point. "So what exactly are you planning to do?" I asked.

Comet Nose flipped his head. "I?" he asked, stepping right up to me and resting his hand on my shoulder in classic the-car-salesman-is-your-friend fashion. "*I* will do nothing." He slid his hand off my shoulder and down the front of my jacket.

As he did so, I felt him slip something into my outer jacket pocket. I reached up a hand to see what he'd put there—

"*Everyone freeze!*" a Human voice snapped from behind me.

Instantly, the bar went silent. Keeping my hands motionless, I carefully turned my head.

There were six cops spread out around the wall by the door. All six had their guns out.

All six guns were pointed at me.

————

BOOKS BY TIMOTHY ZAHN

DRAGONBACK SERIES

Book 1: *Dragon and Thief**
Book 2: *Dragon and Soldier**
Book 3: *Dragon and Slave**
Book 4: *Dragon and Herdsman**
Book 5: *Dragon and Judge**
Book 6: *Dragon and Liberator**

The Blackcollar
Blackcollar: The Judas Solution
A Coming of Age
Cobra
Spinneret
Cobra Strike
Cascade Point and Other Stories
The Backlash Mission
Triplet
Cobra Bargain
Time Bomb and Zahndry Others
Deadman Switch
Warhorse

Warhorse
Cobras Two (omnibus)
Conquerors' Pride
Conquerors' Heritage
Conquerors' Legacy
The Icarus Hunt
*Angelmass**
*Manta's Gift**
Star Songs and Other Stories
*The Green and the Gray**
*Night Train to Rigel**
*The Third Lynx**
*Odd Girl Out**
*The Domino Pattern**

Star Wars: Heir to the Empire
Star Wars: Dark Force Rising
Star Wars: The Last Command
Star Wars: Survivor's Quest
Star Wars: Outbound Flight
Star Wars: Allegiance

STAR WARS: THE HAND OF THRAWN DUOLOGY

Book 1: *Specter of the Past*
Book 2: *Vision of the Future*

*Denotes a Tom Doherty Associates Book

odd
girl out

TIMOTHY ZAHN

A TOM DOHERTY ASSOCIATES BOOK NEW YORK

For Eric and Kandi
—may your tribe increase.

This is a work of fiction. All of the characters, organizations, and events portrayed in this novel are either products of the author's imagination or are used fictitiously.

ODD GIRL OUT

Copyright © 2008 by Timothy Zahn

Edited by James Frenkel

A Tor Book
Published by Tom Doherty Associates, LLC
175 Fifth Avenue
New York, NY 10010

www.tor-forge.com

Tor® is a registered trademark of Tom Doherty Associates, LLC.

ISBN 978-0-7653-5670-3

First Edition: November 2008
First Mass Market Edition: November 2009

Printed in the United States of America

0 9 8 7 6 5 4 3 2

ONE :

The first thing I noticed when I opened my apartment door was the woman standing there. She was young, late teens or early twenties, her clothing a conservative dark gray, her hair strikingly blonde. She was slender, nearly gaunt in fact, and her face, while pretty enough, was drawn and taut. The glitter of a silver necklace peeked out from her open collar, with a matching twinkle from a ring on her right-hand ring finger.

All that I noticed peripherally, though. My main attention was on the gun she was pointing at me.

"Easy," I cautioned, my eyes flicking once around the room in case I'd somehow arrived at the wrong apartment door and my key had somehow managed to open it anyway. But it was my furniture, all right: old and mismatched, with a thin layer of dust marking the fact that I hadn't spent a lot of time here in the past year. "Let's not do anything we'll both regret."

"Come in," she ordered. Her voice was cold, a really good match for her face.

Briefly, I considered trying to outrun her reflexes by ducking back outside into the hallway and making a dash for the stairs. But the self-rolling carrybags that had followed me from the elevator were still behind me, and I probably couldn't get out without tripping over them. Besides, even if I could outrun her reflexes, I couldn't outrun a 5mm thudwumper round from her gun.

Possibly *my* gun, actually. It was hard to tell one gun from another when all you could see was the view down the barrel, but that could very well be the Glock I kept holstered under the tea table she was standing beside.

She was still waiting. I took a couple of steps forward, bringing myself and my obedient luggage fully inside the room. Just to prove I knew the routine, I reached behind me and pushed the door closed. "Now what?" I asked.

"First tell me who you are," she said.

"I'm Frank Compton," I said. "I live here."

"Prove it."

Prove it so that she would put away the gun? Or prove it to confirm that I was the guy she'd come here to shoot? I glanced around the room again, looking for some clue as to what was going on.

It was only then that I noticed that the layer of dust that should have been covering everything was not, in fact, actually there. I took a third, longer, look, this time spotting the fact that the stack of magazines and unanswered mail on the tea table had been subtly shifted since my last brief time at home.

Which suggested that the woman facing me hadn't simply nipped in five minutes ahead of me, hoping I'd show up and play skeet for her. She had, in fact, moved in.

"What, you've been here this long and haven't looked through my photo albums?" I asked, focusing on the woman again.

Her lips compressed briefly. "No, I have," she conceded. "Mr. Compton, I need your help."

I shook my head. "I never discuss business when there's a gun pointed at me."

Slowly, she lowered the weapon. It was my Glock, all right. "My name's Lorelei Beach," she said. "My sister's in trouble."

"Sorry to hear that," I said. "What does that have to do with me?"

"She's trapped on New Tigris," she said. "I need your help to get her out."

"How do you get trapped on New Tigris?" I asked, walking over to the couch and sitting down. My carrybags followed, rolling to a halt by the corner of the tea table.

"I mean she can't get out," she said with a flash of impatience. "There are some bad people trying to find her, and they're watching the spaceport."

And New Tigris had only one spaceport, or at least only one place where torchships were legal to land. "She owe them money?" I asked.

"Of course not," Lorelei said, a bit stiffly.

"Then why do they want her?"

"They want to hurt her."

"So call the cops," I said. "How about putting that gun down before someone gets hurt?"

"The police can't help us," she said, some desperation creeping into her voice. The gun stayed where it was, hanging loosely at her side. "You're the only one who can."

"I'm flattered," I said. "I also don't believe it."

"It's the truth," she insisted. "Why else would I have waited for you this way?"

"Free rent?" I suggested.

Her cheeks reddened a little. "It was the only place I felt safe."

"Especially since most New York hotels don't stock guns for their guests?"

She lifted the Glock as if she'd only just remembered she was holding it. "They're after me, too," she said in a low voice.

"I'm sorry to hear that," I said. "Feel free to call the cops on your way out."

"If they catch me out there, they'll kill me," she said.

"Oh, come *on*, Ms. Beach," I growled. "Really. You think I haven't heard *that* one before? It's the last card *everyone* tries when they want to con someone into doing something."

"I'm not trying to con you into anything," she insisted.

"Could have fooled me," I said. "There's an emergency women's shelter right down the block. Feel free to go there and tell them your troubles. Maybe they'll put you up for the night. Maybe they'll even talk to the cops for you."

"The shelter can't help me," she said. "Neither can the police."

"You won't know until you try, will you?"

She took a deep breath. "She should still be in the Zumurrud District of Imani City," she said. "She'll wait for you to contact her. Her name's—"

"Ms. Beach, I already told you I'm not interested," I interrupted, standing up again. "Furthermore, it's been a long day and I'm very tired."

"Her name's Rebekah," she went on, the words coming out in a rush like a countdown sprinter trying to beat the clock. "She's ten years old, blonde—"

"Ms. Beach, do *I* need to call the cops?"

Her throat tightened. "No," she said, finally moving toward the door. "Would you at least think about it?"

"Sorry, but I'm otherwise employed at the moment," I said. "You wouldn't believe how complicated my life is these days."

Her lips twitched. "Actually, I would," she said. "Good night, Mr. Compton. If you change your mind—"

"Good night, Ms. Beach," I said. "Just leave the gun on the side table by the door."

She hesitated. Then, turning her back on me, she set the Glock carefully onto the table. She turned back, her eyes searching my face, made as if to say something else, then nodded silently and left.

For a long time I just sat there, too tired even to get up and double-lock the door. I'd been run through the wringer over the past few weeks, getting chased across half the Twelve Empires by the remnants of the Modhri group mind that wanted to take over the galaxy and everyone in it.

This most recent skirmish, over an obscure set of Nemuti sculptures, had ended more or less all right, though I was starting to realize that victories against the Modhri were seldom really clear-cut. Still, one could only do what one could do.

Especially given the somewhat pathetic state of our side of this undeclared war. About all that stood between the Modhri and his dream of galactic conquest were the seven-legged Spiders who controlled the Quadrail system linking the galaxy's inhabited worlds. Assisting the Spiders from the shadows were the remnants of the Chahwyn, a secretive race who had genetically engineered the Spiders into existence in the first place over a thousand years ago. The rest of the opposition consisted of a few stray individuals like me who had wandered or blundered onto the battlefield.

And neither the Spiders nor the Chahwyn could fight.

My half-glazed eyes drifted to the Glock on the table, and I felt a belated twinge of conscience. I actually could have let her take the weapon—I also had a backup Heckler-Koch 5mm hidden beneath my bed. And if the young lady was really in danger . . .

Impatiently, I shook the guilt away. If she was in danger, she needed to call the cops. That was what they were there for.

Collecting together my last waning bits of energy, I got up and double-locked the door. I turned to the table and reached for the Glock.

And paused. Sitting on the table alongside the gun, nestled between its frame and trigger guard, was the ring she'd been wearing.

I picked it up and took a closer look. It was a silver band, with no stones or other additions. The design was simple, but had a certain elegance to it. It was also clearly handmade.

And the fact that she'd left it behind probably meant she intended to return.

Wonderful.

Dropping the ring in my pocket, I returned the Glock to its hidden holster beneath the tea table. Then, leaving my carrybags where they were, I staggered off to bed. Ten hours of sleep, and I might finally feel Human again.

I didn't get ten hours of sleep. I got exactly four hours before the sound of my door chime dragged me awake again.

I pried my eyes open and focused on the bedside clock. Three-fifteen in the morning. Even teenage clubbers had called it a night by now.

The chime came again. Fumbling for my robe, I worked into it with one hand while reaching under my bed for the Heckler-Koch with the other. There were very few people who paid social visits at three in the morning, and most of the ones who would be interested in my door weren't the type I wanted to meet unarmed.

The Heckler-Koch's holster was empty. Apparently, I hadn't sent Lorelei into the wilds of New York unarmed after all.

The door chimed again. Padding my way silently to the front room, I retrieved the Glock from beneath the tea table and stepped to the side of the door. "Who is it?" I called.

"Frank Compton?" a voice called back.

"Who is it?" I repeated.

"Police, sir," he called back. "Would you open up, please?"

I keyed the viewer. There were two men in uniform out there, all right, one of them pressing an authentic-looking NYPD ID against the plate. Dropping the Glock into my robe pocket, I keyed open the door. "I'm Officer Bagler, sir," the cop said, holding up a reader as he compared my face to the picture on my official government record. "Would you get dressed, please? We need you to come with us."

"What's the problem?" I asked, not moving.

"There's been a disturbance, sir," he said in that official give-nothing-away voice I'd often used myself during my years with Western Alliance Intelligence. "Detective Kylowski needs to see you."

"Then Detective Kylowski can come here," I said.

"Please don't make me insist, sir," Bagler said. His eyes flicked to my sagging pocket. "Just leave the weapon here, of course."

"Can you at least give me a hint?" I asked.

He sighed silently. "A handgun registered to you has been involved in a murder, sir," he said. "Now, will you please get dressed?"

They took me to West Seventy-fifth Street and the familiar blazing lights and yellow tape of a crime scene. A dozen more cops were already on the scene, the uniformed ones guarding the perimeter and directing traffic, the plainclothes contingent milling around in the cold November air, collecting evidence or scanning for clues.

In the center of the stage were the guests of honor: one male, one female. Their torsos were covered by preservation cloths, but I had no trouble recognizing the dark gray clothing the woman was wearing.

Lorelei had said she was in danger. I'd been too tired to care.

A middle-aged man with receding hair and a serious seven-o'clock shadow stepped in front of me. "Compton?" he asked.

I pulled my eyes away from Lorelei's body. "Yes," I said.

"Detective Kylowski," he identified himself, holding out an ID badge. "Sorry to drag you down here at this time of night."

Sure he was. "What happened?"

"I was hoping you could tell me," he said. "Neither vic has any ID, and we haven't been able to track them down."

"The woman came to my apartment tonight," I told him, deciding to skip over the fact that she'd already been there when I'd arrived. "She said she was in trouble and asked for help."

"And you said . . . ?"

"I told her to call the cops or try the women's shelter and sent her on her way."

"After giving her one of your guns?"

"I didn't *give* her anything," I said. "Obviously, she helped herself."

"Without you noticing?"

"I was very tired," I said. "I still am."

"Uh-huh," he said, looking closely at me. "And you're sure this is the same woman?"

"I recognize her clothing," I told him. "I doubt there are two women dressed that way who've had access to my apartment lately."

"Don't you think you should at least take a look at her face?" he persisted, gesturing me toward the bodies. "It'll only take a minute."

"If you insist," I said, frowning as I walked over with him. Usually homicide cops weren't so eager to foist the details of their gory little world on people.

"This might shock you a little," he warned as he crouched

down, his fingers getting a grip on the edge of the preservation cloth, his eyes locked unblinkingly on my face.

"Thanks for the warning," I growled. Did he think the sight of a couple of dead bodies was going to shock an ex-Westali agent? "Go ahead."

He flipped over the cloth.

And I nearly lost my dinner.

Lorelei's face above and in front of her ear was blood-spattered but mostly intact. Her head and neck below the ear, in contrast, were effectively gone, shattered into a mess of blood and shattered bone and pulp.

I twisted my face away from the sight, keeping my stomach under control by sheer force of will. I was still standing there, staring at a storm-sewer grating, when Kylowski took my arm and steered me away. "You all right?" he asked.

"How do you *think* I am?" I managed between clenched teeth. Turning my face away from him, I smiled hard, an old trick I'd learned for suppressing the gag reflex.

"I understand," he said. "Come on—have a seat over here."

I let him sit me down on the curb. "I don't suppose you have any idea why anyone would want to do something like that," he went on, sitting down beside me.

I shook my head. My stomach was starting to recover, but my brain was still reeling with the shock of the mutilation. "Looks like a ritual murder."

"Yeah, that was my first thought, too," Kylowski said. "Trouble is, we don't have any of the other usual trappings. No robes, no weird jewelry or tattoos, no strangled chickens. Not to mention that they were killed and mutilated here on the street and not in some abandoned warehouse or tenement."

"Maybe it's a new—" I broke off as a key word abruptly penetrated the haze of nausea. "*They* were mutilated?"

"That's right," he confirmed. He was back to scrutinizing my face. "Both of them were done the same way."

I hauled myself to my feet, my stomach suddenly forgotten. One mutilation was a sick perversion. Two mutilations was a potentially intriguing pattern. "Let me see," I said.

We retraced our steps to the bodies. Kylowski crouched down beside the man and twitched aside the cloth.

His head behind the ear was a copy of the mess that was now Lorelei's, with the lower part of the skull torn to shreds. But there was one vital difference between his upper face and Lorelei's: right in the middle of his forehead was another thud-wumper hole. "Which of them was shot with my gun?" I asked Kylowski.

"Funny you should ask," Kylowski said. "Both of them."

I frowned at him. "*Both* of them?"

"Near as we can tell," he confirmed. "Kind of a puzzle, isn't it?"

I stepped back over to Lorelei's body and lifted the cloth, searching her torso. This time I spotted what I'd missed on the first go-around: two small wet spots where blood had oozed rather than flowed.

The marks of snoozer rounds. "So much for your big puzzle," I said, pointing to them. "This guy and at least one friend got the drop on Lorelei and got in the first shot. Once she was out, they took her gun and did all this."

"The vic's *friend* did this to him?" Kylowski asked, gesturing to the dead man. "That's one hell of a friend."

"Yes," I murmured, staring at the man's mutilated head as it suddenly made sense. The plane of destruction torn by the thudwumper rounds had sliced right across the lower part of his brain.

Right where the collection of polyps that formed a Modhran colony would have been located.

The men who had assaulted and killed Lorelei were walkers.

I looked at the man's closed eyes, a shiver running through me. One of the creepiest aspects of the Modhri group mind was the way it could infiltrate other living beings, Humans and Halkas and Bellidos, setting up small, sentient colonies within their bodies that could telepathically link with other nearby colonies to form a larger and smarter mind segment.

The puppetmaster scenario was bad enough. What made it worse was the fact that the walkers themselves were completely unaware that they'd been drafted into the Modhri's little war of conquest. Most of the time a polyp colony lay quietly, controlling its host with subtle mental suggestions that the host would usually obey, coming up with the most bizarrely convoluted rationalizations afterward for his or her behavior. Under more extreme conditions, though, the colony could push the host's own mind and consciousness aside and take direct control of the body.

The Modhri hadn't infiltrated the Terran Confederation nearly as extensively as he had most of the other governments and cultures around us, but I knew he had a few walkers down here keeping an eye on things. It was a good bet that Lorelei had somehow wandered into his sights and been eliminated.

But why? The Modhri didn't kill just for the sick fun of it. Had Lorelei known something the Modhri didn't want getting out? Had she been another Spider agent like me, someone the Spiders had neglected to tell me about?

Or was it something to do with her sister? The sister on New Tigris, the girl Lorelei had said bad people were trying to find?

"Well?" Kylowski prompted.

"Well what?" I countered, stalling for time while I tried to think. To me, what had happened here was now obvious. Lorelei had shot and killed the first walker, but had been nailed with snoozers before she could take out his companion. The Modhri, rightly guessing that her gunshot wouldn't go unnoticed or uninvestigated, had had the second walker obliterate the dead man's polyp colony, lest an autopsy discover it. He'd then created the same damage to Lorelei's head to make it look like ritual murder or a psycho killer.

But knowing the truth was one thing. Talking about it was something else. The galaxy at large was unaware of the Modhri's existence, let alone his plans and ambitions and techniques, and for the moment those of us in the know wanted to keep it that way. "Okay, so maybe *friend* was too strong a word," I added. "Either way, there was a third person on the scene."

"Obviously," Kylowski said. "That still leaves us with the question of why he took the time to do all this. Especially since multiple thudwumper shots draw a lot more attention than just one or two."

"I can't answer that," I said, which was perfectly true if slightly misleading.

"Yeah," he said. "You always load your guns with thudwumpers?"

"I load them with snoozers, like my permit specifies," I said. "It doesn't take a criminal mastermind to change clips."

"Assuming he or she can find a supply of thudwumpers for that new clip."

"Finding thudwumper rounds doesn't take a criminal mastermind, either," I said. "I presume some other gun fired the snoozers into Ms. Beach?"

"Small-caliber Colt," Kylowski confirmed. "So her name was Lorelei Beach?"

"That's the name she gave me, anyway," I said. "By the way, did any of your people remove anything from either body?"

"No," Kylowski said. "Why, is something missing?"

"She had a silver necklace when she was at my apartment," I said. "It's not there now."

He made a note on his reader. "Why was she at your apartment?"

I shrugged, running a quick edit on the brief conversation Lorelei and I had had. The fact that her attackers had been walkers changed everything. "Like I said, she told me she was in danger and wanted my help," I said. "That's all."

"And instead of helping you sent her out." He nodded back toward her body. "Into this."

"If I'd known this would happen, I wouldn't have done that," I said stiffly.

"Obviously," he said. "Any idea what she might have been doing this far from your place?"

I shook my head. "None."

"Heading for Central Park, maybe?" he persisted. "Or to see some friend who lived uptown?"

"I said I don't know."

He pursed his lips. "Okay. What did you do after she left?"

"I double-locked the door and went to bed."

"Any way to prove that?"

I grimaced. Here was where it was going to hit the fan. "Not unless we had a cat burglar working the neighborhood who looked in my window."

"Yeah," Kylowski rumbled. "See, here's my problem. Four problems, actually. First, by your own admission you met with one of the vics a few hours before her death. Second, you have no alibi for the time of the murder."

"You must be joking," I said. "Cops and vampires aside, precious few people have alibis for this hour of the morning."

"True enough." Kylowski raised his eyebrows. "Problem number three is that the murder weapon hasn't been recovered."

I frowned. "I thought you said it was my gun."

"Oh, it was," he assured me. "We were able to do a microgroove analysis on a couple of the slugs. Most people don't even know we can do that."

"*I* know it," I said. "So what would be my reason for taking the gun away?"

"Because you also know that the chances of recovering a slug in good enough shape for a positive groove ID are pretty small," he said. "The point is that in my experience there's only one reason why a murderer risks getting caught with the murder weapon on him. Namely, if he knows it can be traced to him."

"I already told you Ms. Beach stole it."

"Did you report the theft?"

"I didn't know it was gone until your buddies came knocking on my door an hour ago."

"Uh-huh," he said. "And that brings us to problem number four. The witness who called it in also reported a man of your general height and build running from the scene."

I sighed. "Is there any point mentioning how many people in Manhattan match my general height and build?"

"Not really," Kylowski said. Half turning, he gestured to a pair of nearby uniforms. "Frank Compton, you're under arrest. For murder."

TWO :

The last place I wanted to go was a little three-by-three holding cell at four in the morning, where all was quiet and private and where I had zero maneuvering room in case of
trouble. In fact, I wanted to go there so little that if there'd
been fewer cops on the scene I just might have tried to make
a run for it.

But there *were* all those cops, and arriving in my three-
by-three in a great deal of pain would leave me even more
vulnerable if the Modhri decided to take a crack at me. In
the end, I went quietly.

The police booking ritual hadn't changed much in the last
century, though the level of technology associated with it had
certainly improved. They took my fingerprints, my biometrics,
my DNA, several photos, and one of the new seven-layer physio
scans that had done so much over the past few years to ruin the
once-booming criminal plastic surgery industry.

The arraignment judge was sympathetic, or else recognized the wobbliness of Kylowski's case. Over the DA rep's protests, she went ahead and set bail instead of remanding me to immediate custody.

Of course, the fact that she set the bail at half a million dollars might have implied not so much sympathy but a macabre sense of humor. She would have had my financials on the screen in front of her, and would have known I couldn't possibly raise that kind of cash.

Fortunately for me, I had a friend in New York who could.

He was there within the hour, arriving by autocab and no doubt striding in like he owned the place. Dressed in a severe dark blue business suit, his currently long hair link-curled in a tight conservative knot at the back of his collar, and with a set of enhancement glasses perched on the bridge of his nose, he would have looked like just another defense attorney pulling the night beat.

He was anything but. Bruce McMicking, a human chameleon who changed his appearance like most people changed music providers, was ex-Marine, ex-bounty hunter, and currently the top troubleshooter for multitrillionaire industrialist Larry Cecil Hardin.

He wasn't nearly as happy to see me as I was to see him. "I trust you realize how far I've stuck my neck out on this one," he said coldly as we walked down the precinct steps. "If Mr. Hardin gets even a whiff of this, there will be six counties of hell to pay."

"I know, and I'm sorry," I apologized. "But I didn't have anyone else to call."

"You need to make friends with a few more trillionaires."

"Oddly enough, I do know one besides Mr. Hardin," I told him. "But he's only a potential trillionaire at the moment. Probate's likely to take a while."

"Doesn't it always." He flagged down a passing autocab and ushered me inside. "This had better be good."

I waited until we were rolling, and then gave him a rundown of my evening. "Interesting," he commented thoughtfully when I'd finished. "What's your read?"

"The male vic was a walker, with at least one other walker present," I said. "They jumped Lorelei, but she got off the first shot and managed to plug one of them in the forehead. They got her with snoozers—"

"Which implies they wanted her alive," he put in.

"Right," I said. "After which—"

"So why did they then turn around and kill her?"

I frowned. With my brain still fatigue-fogged that question hadn't even occurred to me. "Maybe the Modhri realized that one walker couldn't get her away fast enough once her shot woke up the neighborhood," I said. "So he went for the draw instead and killed her."

McMicking shook his head. "I pulled the police report while they were processing you out. The witness said the incident started with a single shot—"

"Presumably Lorelei nailing the first walker."

"—but then that shot was followed by only a few seconds of silence before the barrage started."

I scratched my chin. A few seconds wasn't nearly enough time for a pair of snoozer rounds, an attempt to pick her up, the realization that that wasn't going to work, and settling for murder as Plan B. "How sure is the witness about the timing?"

"Very sure," McMicking said. "He was getting something out of the micro when the first shot sounded, and hadn't even gotten it to the table when he heard five or six more."

"The walker getting his polyp colony shredded."

"But again, the next gap wasn't very long," McMicking said. "No longer than it took him to set down his meal and hit the cop-call button on his comm. Another barrage, again consisting of five or six shots, and it was over."

Just long enough, in other words, for the second walker to turn around and mutilate Lorelei the same way. But not enough time for much of anything else. "Okay, so there was no time for an interrogation," I said. "But there might have been enough time for a quick theft."

"That was my read," McMicking said. "Only I'm guessing it was the walkers who shot first, with the snoozers, and that the woman then managed to get off her thudwumper round before she went under."

"I don't know," I said. "A pair of snoozers are going to take down a woman of her size awfully fast. She'd have been lucky to even get the gun out, let alone aim and fire."

"Unless she was like the man who died outside the New Pallas Towers eleven months ago when this whole thing started," McMicking said. "He had three snoozers *and* three thudwumpers in him and still managed to follow you there."

I gnawed at my lip. Earlier, I'd speculated that Lorelei might have been someone like me whom the Spiders had coopted into their war. It hadn't occurred to me that she might have been an even rarer avis, someone like my partner Bayta.

Especially since neither Bayta nor the Chahwyn had ever mentioned there being any more like her roaming the galaxy. "If she was, she could have saved herself a lot of grief if she'd just identified herself to me," I said.

"Maybe she wasn't allowed to," McMicking said. "Given all I don't know about this game, I *do* know the Spiders like to play their cards really close."

"No kidding," I said sourly.

"Speaking of Spiders and playing cards close, where's Bayta?"

"She's off riding the Quadrails somewhere," I told him. "On our last mission we ran into a large shipment of coral allegedly headed for Cimman space. She and the Spiders are trying to find out where it actually ended up."

McMicking grunted. "Good luck to them." He inclined his head microscopically toward the street behind our autocab. "So you think our tail is a friend of Lorelei's? Or have we found our missing walker?"

Even dead tired, I knew better than to spin around and peer out the rear window. "How long has he been there?" I asked.

"Since we left the precinct house," McMicking said. "Private car, Manhattan registry plate. There could be a second person in the car with him—hard to tell with the light and distance." He cocked an eyebrow. "The other interesting question would be which one of us they're following."

"My guess is it's you," I said. "I'm pretty much a known quantity. You're the mystery man." I cocked an eyebrow.

"I mean, they know about Bruce McMicking, but they don't know about *you*, if you follow."

"Those official photos of me do tend to go out of date pretty fast," he agreed. "Of course, that assumes our friend is a walker and not some other unforgiving leftover from your past."

"Could be," I agreed. "Though I'm guessing you probably have as many of those leftovers as I do."

"Someday we'll sit down and compare notes," he said. "Any preference as to how we work this?"

I watched the streetlights flowing past. "Let's first try to find out which of us he's interested in."

Ten minutes later our autocab pulled to a halt by the curb in front of my apartment building. I hopped out, and as the vehicle pulled back into the sparse predawn traffic I strode quickly across the sidewalk and the thin sliver of open ground to my building's outer door.

No one opened fire before I made it inside, nor was there anyone lurking in the foyer. I skipped the elevator in favor of the stairs and headed up.

Midway up the first flight my comm vibrated in my pocket, and I pulled it out. "Compton."

"Looks like it's me," McMicking's voice came back. "The car didn't even slow down for you. Oh, and I got a clear look as we went around the corner. There are definitely two of them."

"Just doubles the fun of it all," I said. "Are they still following you?"

"Like the golden retriever I had as a kid."

"Good," I said, easing around the last corner of the final landing. There was no one lurking in the hall outside my apartment. "Give me ten minutes and then a two-buzz."

The first thing I did once I was inside was to retrieve my Glock and make sure its clip was loaded with snoozers. I tucked it into my belt, and then added a clip of thudwumpers too, just in case. Feeling marginally safer now that I was armed, I went to the kitchen.

Eggs would have worked best, but I'd come straight home from Sutherlin Skyport and hadn't had a chance yet to stock up on perishables. But I did have a pantry shelf full of canned soup. I decided New England clam chowder would work best, and emptied four cans into a plastic bag. Carefully gathering the top of the bag closed, I headed back out.

The street was momentarily deserted as I emerged again onto the sidewalk. I'd already settled on my spot: a somewhat overelaborate covered doorway a couple of doors down that stretched three meters closer to the street than my building's doorway did. I hurried to it and stepped inside, doing my best to melt into the decorative wrought iron.

In my pocket, my comm vibrated twice and then went still. Peering around the doorway, I saw a pair of headlights turn the corner onto my street two blocks away. It had covered the first half block toward me when a second pair of lights appeared and turned onto the street behind it. The first vehicle—an autocab—passed by my position, and I caught a glimpse of McMicking sitting half turned in his seat, one hand on the door handle and the other holding his gun. He continued on, and the car behind him rolled toward my doorway.

And as it started to pass me, I took a long step out of concealment and lobbed my bag of soup squarely into the center of its windshield.

The car's wipers went on instantly, of course. But they'd

been designed for rain and sleet, not clam chowder. One sweep later the entire windshield was a solid layer of chunky white goo.

The occupants were up to the challenge. Even before the windshield was completely blocked, the man in the passenger seat slid down his window and leaned his head out, the wind whipping through his hair as he peered around the side of the car toward the autocab still rolling on ahead.

Unfortunately for them, with the distraction of the soup bomb neither set of eyes had spotted McMicking's drop and roll out of the autocab door. He came up into a low crouch by the side of the street, and as the car passed he quick-fired a pair of snoozers into the passenger's exposed cheek and neck.

The man reacted instantly, jerking his head back inside. But it was too late. As the car sped up, I saw his sideways movement continue on, sagging his head against the driver's right shoulder.

With his partner's eyes suddenly of no use to him, the driver now had no choice but to open his window as well. I was ready, and uncorked a couple of shots at the back of his head as he stuck it out into the night breeze.

But snoozers were by design a low-speed, low-impact round, and the car already had too much distance on me. A few seconds later the vehicle careened around a corner and vanished into the night.

Gun still in hand, McMicking crossed the street to my doorway. "That was interesting," he said. "You reach any conclusions?"

"Did you hear the passenger calling any directions to the driver?" I asked.

McMicking shook his head. "I didn't see any hand signals or gestures, either."

"Neither did I," I said. "In which case, I'd have to say they were definitely walkers."

McMicking gazed down the street where the car had disappeared. "So what now?"

"We get you out of here before he can reacquire you," I said, looking around. Aside from the cars parked along the far side of the street, there were no other vehicles present. "I don't know whether it would be safer to get another autocab or call a friend to pick you up."

He gave me a lopsided smile. "You really think I know anyone I trust that far?" he asked. "But don't worry about me. I meant what about you?"

I thought about what Lorelei had said about her sister being in danger on New Tigris. I thought about the fact that her murder pretty well proved she hadn't been just blowing smoke. I though about the Modhri, and his obvious interest in whatever the hell was going on here.

And I thought about the fact that the man standing in front of me had just put up half a million dollars of Larry Hardin's money to guarantee I'd stay in New York until the legal system took its crack at me. "First thing I'm going to do is get some sleep," I said. "After that, maybe I'll poke around a little and see if I can backtrack Lorelei's movements."

"Sounds good," McMicking said, gazing a little too intently at me. "I'll keep tabs on the autopsy. I'll also try to see if I can find anything on her from official sources."

"I'd appreciate that," I told him. "And thanks again for

bailing me out. I know the kind of bind you've just put yourself into over this."

"No problem," he said, his eyes lingering on my face another
second before he gave the street another sweep. "Get some sleep.
I'll call you later." Giving me a quick nod, he turned and strode
away down the sidewalk.

I watched him for a moment, wondering if I should offer to
backstop him. But McMicking was a big boy, and quite capa-
ble of taking care of himself. More to the point, I was dead
tired. Turning away, I headed back to my apartment.

It was just before two o'clock in the afternoon when I finally
woke up again. I checked for messages—there weren't any—
and then heated up another of my repertoire of soup cans,
washing down the meal with a glass of sweet iced tea. By the
time I finished I felt more alive and refreshed than I had in days.

Time to get to work.

My first task was to write a brief message for transmission
to the Tube station hanging out there in the outer system just
past the orbit of Jupiter. Unless Lorelei had always been in
Terra system, she had to have come here by Quadrail, which
meant that the Spiders should have a record of her movements.
I asked for that record to be put together for me, and threw in
a request that Bayta be located and notified that I would
shortly be on my way.

Encrypting the whole thing with one of the Spiders' special
codes, I uploaded it to the message center, noted it would be
lasered to the transfer station within the hour, and got busy on
a general computer search.

I'd been at it an hour, and was still sifting through all the un-related information on all the unrelated Lorelei Beaches, when my door chimed.

I approached the door as one might approach a sleeping tiger: quietly, cautiously, and with Glock in hand. Standing well off to the side, I keyed the viewer.

The uniform was that of a package messenger, complete with book-sized package in hand. The hair was that of an aging new-drift klivner trying to relive the glory days of his youth.

The face was McMicking's.

I unlocked the door, and he slipped inside. "Still alive, I see," he said approvingly as I closed the door behind him. "Anything else happen last night?"

"Not to me," I said. "You?"

He shook his head and handed me the package. "Here."

"You get something already?" I asked, frowning as I pulled open the tab. There was nothing inside but a set of official-looking cards.

"Not on the woman, no," he said. "I thought you might need these."

I swallowed hard as I focused on the top card. It was an of-ficial Western Alliance ID card, complete with my face and fin-gerprints and other data.

Only it was made out to someone named Frank Abram Donaldson.

I looked up again to find McMicking gazing at me, an all too knowing look in his eyes. "This is . . ." I paused, searching for the right words.

McMicking, typically, didn't have to search. "This is going

to get my butt in serious trouble," he said calmly. "But this is war. And I owe you. You and Bayta both."

"Mostly Bayta," I said, rubbing my thumb across the ID. It even felt real. "She's the one the Spiders listen to, and mostly obey."

"But you're the one *she* listens to," McMicking pointed out. He smiled faintly. "And mostly obeys."

"I'm not sure I'd go *that* far," I demurred.

"I would," McMicking said. "And one of these days I'm hoping you'll be able to explain just how all of that works."

"Definitely," I promised, though I didn't have the vaguest idea when that day would come. Bayta's close relationship with the Chahwyn and Spiders was a closely guarded secret, but at least it was something I could vaguely understand. Bayta's relationship with me, on the other hand, I was still trying to get a handle on. "Meanwhile, I'll do whatever I can to get back before my court date," I added. "If I do, hopefully you'll be able to sneak the bail money back into your department account with no one the wiser."

"You just focus on figuring out what the Modhri is up to and nail him," McMicking said grimly. "Mr. Hardin can absorb the loss if he has to."

"Mr. Hardin isn't the one I'm worried about," I said, sliding the ID to the back of the stack. Behind it was a torchliner ticket, with the shuttle from Sutherlin scheduled to leave that evening for its long voyage across the inner system to the Quadrail station. "I didn't think I was nearly this easy to read," I commented.

He shrugged. "It's not like the Modhri is doing serious work down here," he said. "At least, I hope not. Therefore, wherever you need to go for follow-up on Lorelei will probably be somewhere out-system. I hope the timing isn't going to be too tight."

"No, it's perfect," I assured him. "The sooner I get out of town, the better."

I rotated the ticket to the back of the stack and thumbed through the rest of my brand-new credentials. There was a universal pilot's license, an import/export license, a rare-collectables dealer's certificate, and a notarized security bond. "No plumber's certificate?" I asked.

"Never hurts to be prepared," he said equably. "You may find the last one particularly useful."

I flipped to it, and stopped cold, about as surprised as I'd been in many a day. It was a card identifying Frank Abram Donaldson as a member in good standing in the Hardin Industries security force.

I looked up at McMicking again. This time there was a puckish smile on his face. "And *that* one's even legit," he said. "I have standing authority to hire any security personnel I want."

"Oh, he's going to be pleased about this one," I said. "What exactly is my salary, if you don't mind my asking?"

"Don't mind at all," he said. "You're on staff at a dollar a year. Don't spend it all in one place."

"Not a problem," I assured him. "It's the prestige of the thing that matters."

"The hell with the prestige," McMicking countered. "What matters is that that ID includes a carry permit."

I frowned down at the card. He was right—the proper legal phrasing was there at the bottom. "The hell with the prestige, indeed," I agreed. "That could come in *very* handy."

"And unlike your residence permit, it doesn't require you to load with snoozers, either," he added, moving back toward the door. "I have to get going—Mr. Hardin's briefing me on a new assignment this afternoon. If I get anything more on Ms. Beach before you hit the Quadrail, I'll send it on ahead."

"Thanks," I said, sliding the stack of documents into my inside pocket. "For everything. I owe you."

"Just let me know how it comes out," McMicking said. He paused with his hand on the knob. "Or at least let me know as much as the Spiders will let you tell me."

"You'll get it all," I promised. "I know how to push the boundaries, too."

He gave me a lopsided smile, then opened the door and checked the hallway outside. With a final glance and nod, he was gone.

I double-locked the door behind him, feeling a not entirely pleasant warmth flowing through me. Sometimes it felt like Bayta and I were all alone in this war, with no one but the Spiders and the Chahwyn even cheering from the sidelines. It was nice to know that McMicking was treating the whole thing seriously, too.

On the other hand, the Modhri had a little trick called thought viruses that he could use to plant subtle suggestions into those who weren't already under his control. And thought viruses transferred best between friends, allies, associates, and compatriots.

It was nice to have McMicking as an ally. It was also potentially very dangerous.

But in a few hours I would be aboard a torchliner, out of

reach of him and anything the Modhri might be able to do to me through him. In this case, at least, having an ally had proved to be a worthwhile gamble.

Setting my Glock on the tea table, I headed to the bedroom to pack.

THREE :

I waited until evening, and then headed outside and caught an autocab. No one was loitering outside my apartment as I left, nor was anyone waiting for me when I arrived at Sutherlin Skyport. I watched my fellow passengers closely as they came aboard, but given that the only view I'd had of the two Modhran walkers had been a nighttime glimpse of heads inside a car, I wasn't really expecting to recognize either of them. Sure enough, I didn't recognize anyone.

We lifted from the field and headed for our orbital rendezvous with the torchliner that would take us to the Tube cutting across the outer solar system. At Earth's current position in its own orbit, the trip would take a little under eight days.

I spent most of those days in my tiny shipboard stateroom, avoiding the rest of the passengers and reading everything I could find on the thriving colony world of New Tigris, the first of the Terran Confederation's four colony worlds as you headed inward toward the center of the galaxy. It was about three hundred light-years away, which translated to a nice comfortable five-hour Quadrail trip from Terra Station.

My research on the place, unfortunately, didn't take nearly all of those eight days. The colony had been officially founded twenty years ago, and in that time the population had grown to nearly two hundred thousand people. That sounded impressive, but I knew the truth: most of that growth had been pushed and prodded and possibly bribed by UN officials desperate to bring Earth to the level of the other eleven empire-sized alien civilizations.

Unfortunately, all that prodding had yet to produce much in the way of tangible results. Of the four colony worlds, all but Helvanti were still little more than charity cases, heavily subsidized by the mother world, with little prospect of ever becoming anything more.

Fortunately for Earth's taxpayers, among whom I was so very honored to count myself, it wasn't only public money that was being poured down the rabbit hole. The UN had managed to persuade a number of corporations, both the superlarge as well as the merely large, to add some of their own cash to the pot.

On the firms' balance sheets they were probably called investments, with an eye toward future advancements or discoveries. A more honest approach would be to write them off as favorable publicity and general goodwill.

More cynically-minded types might even consider the donations as a form of other-directed bribes designed to soothe the UN's regulators into looking elsewhere for someone to scrutinize.

I had to admit, though, that New Tigris's founding fathers had done a decent job with all the money flowing into their coffers. They'd built a single major town, Imani City, for those who liked a variety of restaurants and clubs, plus several smaller outlying towns and rural farming communities for those who preferred their companionship in smaller doses and were more casual about haute cuisine.

But even the colony's relative youth, the constant influx of public money, and the leadership's good intentions hadn't prevented a dark underbelly from forming on their new world. There were a couple of districts in Imani where the poor, the frustrated, and the otherwise disenchanted among the populace had developed a habit of gathering to express their grievances. Many of those malcontents already lived there, and as the like-minded were drawn in the more upstanding citizens had found it advisable to go elsewhere. Slums, in everything but name.

Zumurrud District, where Lorelei had said her sister was hanging out, was naturally one of those garden spots.

It was probably a good thing, I reflected more than once, that McMicking had given me that carry permit.

The permit, of course, didn't extend to the Quadrail station itself. The Spiders didn't allow weapons into their Tube, either obvious weapons or more subtle items that might easily be combined into instruments of mayhem. All such devices had to be put in lockboxes at the transfer station, which the Spiders would carry across in their own shuttles and subsequently stow in special compartments beneath the train cars where they'd be out of anyone's reach during the trip.

Agent of the Spiders though I might be, I still wasn't exempt from those particular rules. Mostly I wasn't, anyway. So I put my Glock in a lockbox as directed, accepted my claim ticket from the Customs official, and headed through the door into the main part of the transfer station and the shuttle docking stations at the far end.

Quadrail passengers had the option of either going directly to the Tube and doing their waiting there, or else staying on the transfer station until their trains were called. Since I wasn't scheduled for any train in particular, I took the first available shuttle across the hundred-kilometer gap. With luck, I could touch base with the Spider stationmaster and use my special pass to book a seat or compartment on the next train for New Tigris.

With even more luck, Bayta would have gotten my message and be waiting for me.

For once, luck was indeed with me.

"I only arrived about two hours ago," Bayta said as we sat down at a table in one of the outdoor cafés. "I wasn't sure when you were due in, so when the stationmaster told me you had a data chip waiting I went ahead and picked it up." She handed me the chip.

"Thanks," I said, taking the chip and pulling out my reader, my eyes tracing the lines and contours of her face as I did so. Sometimes it wasn't until you got something back that you realized just how much you'd missed it.

To my surprise, and maybe a little to my consternation, I suddenly realized how much I'd missed Bayta. She'd become such a permanent part of my life and my work over the past eleven months that it had felt strange to spend a couple of weeks all alone without her.

But only because she was my colleague and ally, I told myself firmly. I needed her, and she needed me, in this shadowy war against the Modhri. There'd been a time once when she might have been drifting toward feeling something more than that for me. But that time was past. We were colleagues and allies. Nothing more.

"You all right?" Bayta asked.

To my embarrassment, I realized I'd been staring at her. "Just a bit tired," I said, lowering my eyes to my reader and plugging the chip into the reader's slot. "First things first. Were you able to figure out where all that coral was going?"

She shook her head. "As far as the Spiders' records go, it looks like no crates of their description ever made it to the Cimmal Republic. I'm sorry."

"Not your fault," I assured her, trying not to be too annoyed. It had been almost a month ago that the Modhri had dangled all that coral temptingly in front of us on the train ride between Ghonsilya and Bildim in the Tra'hok Unity. The choice had been clear: follow the crates and see where he was moving it, or stay with the mission we were already on.

We'd stayed with the mission, and it was probably just as well that we had. Still, I'd hoped we might get to have it both ways. "It was still worth a try," I said, keying the reader. The decryption program had done its magic, and there was Lorelei's Quadrail itinerary.

Some itinerary. Twenty days ago the woman had left New Tigris Station and headed to Earth. Adding in the torchliner trip, it looked like she'd gotten to my apartment only a couple of days before I had.

And that was it. There was no record of her arrival into the New Tigris system, or of her departure from anywhere else in the galaxy. The woman might have been born on New Tigris for all the travel data the Spiders had been able to dig up.

"What is that?" Bayta asked.

"Apparently, a huge waste of Spider time," I said, handing the reader to her. "You ever hear of this woman?"

"Lorelei Beach," Bayta murmured as she glanced over the report. "I don't think so. Should I have?"

McMicking's suggestion that Lorelei might have been another Spider agent flashed to mind. "Just thought you might have met her somewhere," I said. "She was killed in New York a little over a week ago."

"Was she a friend of yours?"

I shook my head. "I met her for the first time a few hours before she died. She was shot with one of my guns, by the way."

Bayta's eyes were steady on me. "I think you'd better start at the beginning."

I laid it all out for her, starting with the gun in my face and pausing only when the waiter brought over our lemonade and iced tea. Bayta listened in silence the whole time, not interrupting even once with a question or comment. Her knack for keeping quiet at the right time was one of her most endearing talents.

"So what are we going to do?" she asked when I had finished.

"Well, *I'm* going to go hunt up this sister of hers," I said. "Not sure what *you're* going to do."

"You don't want me with you?"

Her face was expressionless, the words nearly so. But just the same the hurt behind her eyes managed to make it out into the open. Another of her many talents. "Don't get me wrong," I assured her hastily. "Under normal circumstances I'd love to have you along. But this is likely to be dangerous."

She smiled wanly. "Like everything else we've done together hasn't been?"

"Point," I conceded. "But there's a particular edge of nastiness to this one. You didn't see what they did to Lorelei. I did."

"I thought you'd decided the Modhri did that to cover the fact that he needed to destroy the walker's polyp colony," she reminded me.

"That's one possibility," I said. "Problem is, he's never done anything like that before with any of the other walkers he's had to sacrifice for one reason or another. At least, not with anyone he's sacrificed in our presence. It seems out of character for him, and it's definitely a change of pattern. Either of those alone would be enough to worry me. Both of them together get my shivers up."

"What do you think it means?"

"I don't know," I said. "But I've had a few days to think, and a couple of possibilities have occurred to me."

I drank down half my iced tea in a single swallow. Talking about death and mutilation always made my throat dry. "One: the whole thing could have been staged for my benefit. A ploy to get my attention, but good, and make me curious enough to keep digging."

"Why?"

"I won't know that until I find something," I said. "Scenario two: framing me for a gruesome double murder was intended to put me out of circulation long enough for the Modhri to pull off some other stunt."

"Maybe related to all that coral he was moving?" Bayta suggested.

"Could be," I said. "Of course, that would require Lorelei to also have been a walker who went to my apartment to snag one of my guns. Scenario three is that the whole thing was a setup to get me to flush McMicking out into the open for him."

Bayta took a thoughtful sip of her lemonade. "You *did* say the walkers following you seemed more interested in him than in you."

"True," I agreed. "On the other hand, we could still be on scenarios one or two, and deciding to follow us was just something the Modhri decided on the fly after seeing McMicking bail me out."

"I don't know," Bayta said thoughtfully. "Something about the last two scenarios bothers me."

"Me, too," I said. "Starting with the fact that if Lorelei was a walker there was no reason for her to keep hanging around my apartment after she'd stolen my gun. There was certainly no reason for her to spin me that story about a kid sister in trouble."

"So what you're saying is that, for good or evil, someone wants you to go looking for her," she concluded slowly.

I cocked an eyebrow. "'For good or evil'?"

She colored slightly. "I've been reading Earth literature lately," she admitted. "I thought it would help me to understand . . . all of us . . . a little better."

I suppressed a grimace. Bayta was in effect a hybrid, a Human who'd grown up with a full-blown alien Chahwyn similarly growing up inside her. They shared much the same sort of dual mind as a walker and his Modhran colony, except that in Bayta's case it was a true symbiosis and not simply a parasitical relationship. The Chahwyn part gave her a stamina beyond normal Human capacity, and let her communicate telepathically with the Chahwyn and the Spiders, an ability that came in handy on a regular basis.

If I thought about it too hard, it could become a little unsettling. But for her, obviously, it worked.

But partly because of that, and partly because Bayta had been raised by the Chahwyn, there were certain gaps in her Human cultural understanding. I'd been doing my best to help fill those gaps over the past few months by showing her some of the classic dit rec dramas by Hitchcock and Kurosawa and Reed. Now, it seemed she'd decided to branch out into literature, as well.

Still, there was something vaguely embarrassing about her admission, composed as it was of equal parts childlikeness and the painful awareness that for all her Human appearance she still wasn't fully Human. I turned my eyes away from her, pretending I was just checking out the area around us.

My eyes halted their sweep, Bayta's discomfiture abruptly forgotten. Sitting on a bench fifty meters away, his left profile turned to me, was a Pirk.

There was nothing unusual about that per se. Pirks loved to travel, and were reputed to spend more of their income on that than anything else except housing. This particular Pirk was typical of his people: wiry, covered with goose-like feathers, wearing the simple headdress that denoted modest means and social standing. He was gazing across the platforms that straddled the various four-railed Quadrail tracks running along the inside of the Tube.

But there was something else about him, something that was decidedly atypical of the species. The bubble of empty space that typically surrounded every Pirk wasn't there. Other travelers, Humans as well as non-Pirk aliens, were passing by his bench without veering away, some of them getting as close as a meter before they even seemed to notice he was there.

Either Terra Station was witnessing a mass paralysis of the olfactory organs, or else we'd stumbled across the galaxy's first non-aromatic Pirk.

"Frank?" Bayta asked.

"Take a look," I said, nodding fractionally toward the bench. "The Pirk over there with the yellow-and-pale-blue head-dress."

Lifting her lemonade, she casually looked that direction. "Looks fairly young," she said. "Lower-middle-class, probably, from the headdress. Maybe even a bit lower . . ." She trailed off.

"Yeah, that's what I was thinking," I agreed. "Did the Pirks suddenly discover deodorant when I wasn't looking?

"Deodorants don't do any good," she said, frowning at him. "The distinctive Pirk aroma comes from the food they eat. The by-products are metabolized and excreted through the skin pores—"

"I was being facetious," I interrupted. Cultural gaps aside,

Bayta's general book learning was *very* much up to date. "So does that mean this one's on a special diet or something?"

"I don't know," Bayta said. Her eyes shifted a little to the left. "Do you know those Humans he's staring at?"

Caught up in the novelty of it all, I hadn't even picked up on the fact that he was looking at something across the way. I tracked along his sightlines, and found myself facing a similar bench two platforms over.

There, chatting amiably together, were two men I did indeed recognize. "They're a couple of my fellow torchliner passengers," I said. "I don't know their names."

Bayta tapped thoughtfully on our table. "There's something about them that bothers me."

I took a sip of my tea. Now that she mentioned it, there was something about them that bothered me, too. I watched them out of the corner of my eye, trying to figure it out. They were both in their late forties, with similar bland facial features and rotund physiques that put them halfway to the dit rec cartoon version of Tweedledee and Tweedledum. They were nicely dressed but not ostentatiously so, with none of the look of the superrich that were the Modhri's favored target for planting colonies inside.

Still, I knew that up to now he hadn't launched that kind of campaign against humanity, contenting himself with keeping an eye on us via low- and mid-level governmental functionaries. The two Tweedles could easily fit into that category.

But then, so could any number of other people.

So what was it about them that had caught our attention?

And then, suddenly, it hit me. Since I'd been watching them neither man had checked his watch, or looked up at one of the floating schedule holodisplays, or even glanced down the track whose platform they were sitting beside.

They had, in short, a settled look. Like two men who weren't really anticipating the arrival of their train, but were simply hanging around the station enjoying the ambience.

It was much the same look as our non-stinky Pirk had, now that I thought about it. For that matter, it was the same look Bayta and I probably had. Three sets of travelers, none of whom had anywhere to go.

I lowered my eyes to the luggage nestled beside the two Tweedles. Four reasonably large rolling bags, plus two shoulder bags. Enough carrying capacity for someone who was traveling light to go anywhere in the galaxy. "Do me a favor," I said to Bayta. "Find out when the next train is due to arrive on that track, and where it's going."

Bayta's eyes took on a slightly glazed look as she sent out a telepathic message to the station's Spiders. "It's an express heading outward toward the Bellidosh Estates-General," she said after a moment. "It doesn't arrive for nearly two hours."

"Ah," I said. "Okay. Well, the good news is that your instincts are working perfectly."

I quirked a lip toward the Tweedles. "The bad news is that our friends over there seem to be waiting patiently for us to make our move."

Bayta nodded, a typically calm acceptance. "Do we have one yet?"

I ran a finger idly up the side of my now nearly empty glass. "I think so," I told her. "We're going to need two different trains. The first will be a local going coreward to Yandro and Jurian space."

"Where are we going?"

"Yandro," I said. "The second will be another local passing outward through Yandro back here."

Her forehead creased for a moment as she studied my face. Then the wrinkles smoothed out again. "All right," she said. "Let me see what's available."

Her eyes glazed over again. Her lemonade was also gone, and I wondered briefly whether or not I should get us some food when I ordered refills.

"Got it," she said, her eyes coming back to focus. "The train for Yandro leaves from Platform Seven in forty minutes."

So much for getting food or even more drinks. But there would be plenty of both on the train. "And the other?"

"It'll leave Yandro two hours after we arrive."

"Perfect," I said. "We have compartments on both?"

"Of course," she said, as if I even had to ask.

"Good," I said. Pulling out a cash stick, I plugged it into the payment slot in our table. "Let's go."

"Already?" she asked, frowning. "There's still forty minutes."

"I know," I said. "But our friends over there are going to need time to buy their tickets, too. No point in making them rush."

She gave a quiet sigh. "I suppose not. Oh, and you'll probably want this back." Pulling a folded handkerchief from her pocket, she pushed it across the table toward me.

I closed my hand over it, feeling the reassuring weight of the Chahwyn *kwi* weapon as I picked it up. "Thanks," I said, slipping it into my own pocket. "Did you have to use it?"

She shook her head. "The Modhri seems to be avoiding me."

"I don't blame him," I said. The *kwi* had two basic settings—unconsciousness and pain—both of which worked quite well against Modhran walkers.

Of course, it was anyone's guess as to how long the thing would last. The *kwi* was over a millennium old, a relic from the war that had originally spawned the Modhri in the first place. The Chahwyn who'd dug up the *kwi* didn't know an awful lot about it, including if or when it might suddenly pop a vital circuit and become nothing more than a flexible and rather decorative set of brass knuckles.

Still, for now the thing worked, and it worked well, and the Chahwyn had given me permission—albeit grudgingly—to carry it aboard the Quadrail. For that I was grateful.

Grateful enough that I didn't even resent the fact that Bayta and I seemed to be field-testing the thing for them.

Retrieving my cash stick, I stood up and keyed the leash control inside my jacket. Obediently, the two bags at my feet aligned themselves, ready to roll as soon as I started moving. Bayta also stood up, her bags similarly preparing themselves for duty. "Okay, let's go," I said. "Nice and easy and casual."

"I know the routine," Bayta said. "By the way, Frank . . ."

I looked at her, seeing the sudden discomfort and embarrassment in her face. "Yes?" I asked.

Her lip twitched. "Nothing," she murmured. "Sorry."

"That's okay," I assured her. "I'm glad we're back in the trenches together, too."

A flicker of surprise crossed her face, followed rapidly by relief and then a second surge of embarrassment. "Right," she said. "Me, too."

"So let's get to it," I said, gesturing her ahead of me like a proper gentleman.

As we headed away from the table toward Platform Seven, out of the corner of my eye I saw our settled-looking Pirk get up off his bench. He fussed for a moment with his headdress, then started off in the same direction we were also going. I didn't want to turn around and check on the two Humans, but I suspected they had joined the parade as well.

Fourteen hours to Yandro, another eleven back to New Tigris, then probably five to eight days to get to New Tigris proper via torchliner. Add in the twenty days since Lorelei had left New Tigris Station, plus the five to eight days up from the planet itself, and by the time we reached her kid sister Rebekah it would be a month or more that the girl had been on her own.

I just hoped she wasn't in any pressing hurry to be rescued.

FOUR :

Sure enough, forty minutes later when our Quadrail pulled into the station, Tweedledee, Tweedledum, and the Pirk were all waiting on our platform.

Though at very different positions along that platform. Bayta and I were at the head of the line, where the first-class compartment car would be stopping. The two Humans were farther back in the group waiting for the second-class cars. The Pirk, in contrast, was all the way at the far end of the line, poised for the last of the third-class cars, the one just in front of the baggage cars.

The incoming Terra Station passengers got off the train, we all got aboard, and a few minutes later we were on our way.

The trip proved surprisingly uneventful. Neither the Twee-dles nor the Pirk would have been allowed in first-class territory, of course, not with second- and third-class tickets. But if any or all of them were walkers their colonies would be part of the train's overall Modhran mind segment, and there ought to be at least one walker basking in the luxury of first-class. I half expected to be accosted somewhere along the line by some genteel ultra-rich traveler, probably as Bayta and I were walking back to the dining car.

But there was nothing. A few of the other passengers deigned to glance up as we passed by, but most of them ignored us completely.

Still, that didn't mean the Modhri wasn't aboard, or that he hadn't spotted and identified us. He could easily be playing it coy, waiting to see where we were going before making any moves. Under that scenario, we would probably find a crowd getting off with us at Yandro Station.

This time, I was right. Not only did the two Tweedles join us on the platform, but so did four of our fellow first-class passengers: three Juriani and a Bellido. Yandro was hardly the kind of place to attract that kind of attention, which strongly suggested that all four of the latter had been heading elsewhere when the local Modhran mind segment had changed their plans for them. Idly, I wondered what kind of pretzel logic his unsuspecting hosts would use to rationalize this one.

To my mild surprise, the non-aromatic Pirk didn't join us.

Bayta and I had two hours before we could catch the train heading back again toward New Tigris. With only eight of us getting off, it would have been highly suspicious if she and I had opted to wait at the station while the other six boarded the shuttle and headed across to the transfer station. It might even have induced the Modhri to take charge of his hosts long enough to find out what game I was playing this time.

Fortunately, I had something a little more subtle in mind.

Trying to keep an eye on all six of the others as we trooped across to the shuttle hatchway, I ran the numbers and timings through my mind. It should be just about right.

"You must be joking," I said, leveling one of my best Westali glares at the hapless Customs official on the other side of the counter. "You *lost* my *lockbox*?"

"I'm sure it's not actually *lost*," he assured me, trying to sound calm and confident as he punched keys on his terminal. It wasn't a very convincing act. "It could have gotten mixed in with the crates from the last cargo train—"

"I don't want excuses," I cut him off. My act, unlike his, was superb, if I did say so myself. "I want my lockbox. I'm not leaving here without it."

"I understand, Mr. Compton," he assured me, still poking at his keys. "Fortunately, the torchferry for Yandro won't be arriving until tomorrow. That should be more than enough time to get this sorted out."

"Really?" I countered. "What if it's still aboard the Quadrail? What if it's even now heading for Kerfsis or Jurskala or who the hell knows where? You still going to get it to me by tomorrow?"

"Sir, as far as I know the Spiders have never lost a piece of luggage," he said, his confident tone beginning to fray at the edges.

"That's not much comfort for the person who gets to be the first blot on their record, is it?" I said icily.

"No, sir, not really," he conceded. "Let me call over to the stationmaster and get the Spiders looking for it over there."

Finally; the cue I'd been waiting for. "Don't bother," I growled. "We'll go talk to him ourselves. Is the shuttle still at the docking station?"

"Yes, sir," the clerk said. "But there aren't any outgoing passengers right now."

"It can make a special trip," I said. "You owe me. Where can we leave our luggage?"

"You can't go back to the Tube," the clerk said.

"Why not?" I asked.

For a second he fumbled, the mark of a man who had just said something that surprised even him and was searching madly for the reason why he'd said it. "Well, you're *here*," he said at last. "I mean *here*, on this side of the station. You've already passed through Customs."

"So we'll pass through again," I said. "You don't look all that busy."

"Well, no, sir, but that's not the point. It's just . . ." He trailed off, still looking confused.

No doubt he was, and I could almost sympathize. Clearly, the man was a walker, a leftover from the days when the Modhri had actually cared about what happened in Yandro system. Just as clearly, the mind segment currently consisting of the polyp colonies in him and our fellow travelers didn't want me out of his collective sight.

Unfortunately for him, there wasn't any official reason the official could point to forbidding me to go back to the Tube. And even the Modhri could only push his powers of rationalization so far. He could take over the man's body, of course, but I didn't think he was ready to go quite that far. "So where can we leave our luggage?" I asked again.

The clerk's lip's compressed. "You can leave it here behind the counter," he said, his face still working with the strange internal conflict going on inside him. "There's no secure holding area this side of Customs."

"This'll do fine," I said. Shutting off my leash control, I picked up my bags and heaved them around the end of the counter, stacking them as far to the back as the narrow space allowed. "Give me your bags, Bayta."

Silently, she handed me her bags, and I added them to the pile. "Now you just need to check us back through," I told the clerk.

"Yes, sir." Shutting down his terminal, he came out from behind the counter and crossed to the Customs counter five meters away. "I'll need to see your IDs again."

We showed him our IDs and allowed his body scanner to do its work. "And we'll want a double room when we get back," I added as he reluctantly waved us through. "And sleeping rooms on the torchferry, of course."

"Of course," the clerk said. His expression was mostly neutral, but there was a quiet watchfulness beneath it. Taking Bayta's arm, I steered us through the doorway back into the outbound section of the transfer station.

And as we did so, I threw a casual glance back at our fellow travelers.

All six of them were watching us, their expressions a mix of concern and bemusement and sympathetic outrage for our unheard-of dilemma.

But beneath it all, on every one of those faces, I could see a hint of the Customs official's same quiet watchfulness.

The Modhri wasn't happy with me. Not a bit.

Bayta was obviously thinking the same thing. "He knows what we're up to, you know," she murmured as we headed for the shuttle bay.

"He *thinks* he knows what we're up to," I corrected. "The problem is, right now he can't do anything about it."

"He could send his walkers after us," she reminded me. "They all must have come up with rationalizations as to why they were getting off at Yandro in the first place. Surely they wouldn't have any trouble coming up with equally good reasons to leave again."

"Right, but in order to do that, they'd have to clear their luggage through Customs again," I pointed out. "That'll take time, and we'll be on our way to the Tube long before then."

"Even with another walker in charge of giving them that clearance?"

So she'd noticed that, too. I'd expected she would. "That won't help him any," I said. "Human Customs routines are largely computerized, with no way for a mere clerk to bypass the routine and speed up the process. In theory, he could call in his supervisor for an override, but that would probably take more time than he's got."

"Couldn't they leave their bags here, like we did?"

"Even the Modhri would have a hard time coming up with a rationalization for *that* one," I said. "And I doubt he wants to risk taking over the hosts. Not six of them at once, not for the length of time this would take. If they compared notes afterward and discovered simultaneous blackouts, they might finally start to wonder."

I smiled tightly. "Besides, lurking in the back of his ethereal little mind is probably the thought that I might be goading him into precisely that move. We could be pretending to head back to the Tube, then planning to double back and make off with their luggage when they hurry after us."

She gave me a puzzled frown. "What in space would we want with their luggage?"

"I have no idea," I admitted. "But if the Modhri has learned anything, it's not to underestimate how convoluted our plans can get."

"How convoluted *your* plans can get."

"Whatever."

She glanced back over her shoulder. "He might still think it's a risk worth taking."

"What for?" I countered. "So we're dumping this group. So what? We're probably about to get back on the Quadrail, and he's got eyes all over the Quadrail. He'll just have the Customs agent or one of the passengers send messages both directions down the line to alert other mind segments, and figure he'll pick up our trail again before we get too far."

"Excuse me?" a voice called from behind us.

I set my teeth together and turned around. The Modhri might at least have had the common decency to make his move before I'd gone so firmly on record with my prediction that he wouldn't. "Yes?" I asked, turning around.

It was one of my rotund fellow Humans, the one I'd dubbed Tweedledum. "My name's Braithewick," he said, puffing a bit as he came up to us. His luggage, I noted, was nowhere to be seen. Left behind, as I'd just explained to Bayta wouldn't happen. "I'm an associate negotiations researcher at the UN."

A glorified computer clerk, in other words. "And?" I prompted.

He seemed a bit surprised by my unenthusiastic response. "I work at the UN," he repeated. "I wanted to offer my service in your negotiations with the stationmaster."

"What negotiations?" I said. "I'm going to make him find my lockbox and send it over here, and that'll be that."

He chuckled. "You amateurs," he said with a typical mid-level bureaucratic air of self-importance. "You always think it's going to be that easy."

"Why shouldn't it be?" I asked. "Unless you know something I don't."

He smiled cherubically . . . and suddenly the smile faded, and the flabby skin of his cheeks and throat seemed to sag. "Don't play games, Compton," he said, his voice subtly changed.

"Hello, Modhri," I said, the skin at the back of my neck tingling unpleasantly. No matter how many times I watched a Modhran mind segment take over one of its hosts, it still creeped me out. "If you're still looking for the Lynx, you're out of luck. I haven't got it."

"You know what I seek," the Modhri said. "I offer you a bargain: step back, and allow me to deal with it."

"Is that a bargain, or a threat?" I asked. "What exactly is it you're looking for?"

"You know what I seek," he said again. "The Abomination."

"Ah—that," I said, nodding sagely as I wondered what he was talking about. "And what are you going to do when you find it?"

"It must be destroyed."

"Like you destroyed the Human female back in Manhattan?" I asked. "Why *did* you kill her, anyway? Too heavy to take with you?"

"The Abomination must be destroyed," he repeated, ignoring my questions. "For once, Compton, you and I *will* agree on this. You will want it destroyed as well as I."

Another tingle tickled the back of my neck. False sincerity was a dollar a ton in this business, but there was something about the Modhri's expression that half inclined me to believe him. "An interesting assumption," I said. "You really believe that?"

"I do," he said firmly.

"In that case, let me make you a counteroffer," I said. "*You* back off, and let *me* find it."

His sag-faced expression actually shifted a bit. Surprise? Suspicion? "Why?" he asked.

"For one thing, because I'm the one offering the deal," I said. "For another, I'm better at finding things than you are." I cocked my head. "Or hasn't your particular mind segment caught up with the news of the past few weeks?"

The Modhri shifted his gaze to Bayta. "I am aware of those events."

"Good," I said. "Really does save time when everyone's up to speed. Is it a deal?"

His eyes searched my face, shifted again to Bayta, then came back to me. "It is," he said. "I will accompany you to the Tube and pass on word of our new agreement."

"You can pass it on later, after we're on our way." I gestured back toward the Customs area. "Speaking of being on one's way . . . ?"

"It would be a gesture of good faith," he said, not budging. "On your part as well as mine."

"I said no," I told him, dipping my hand into my pocket and getting a grip on the *kwi*. "Don't make me insist."

"Violence will not help you," he pointed out calmly. "Not now. If you had shot all my Eyes when they stood together by the Customs counter, you might have achieved something. But not now. Not when another of my Eyes can immediately call the pilot and alert him that there is a madman loose in the station."

I grimaced. But he was right. As soon as I realized the clerk was a walker, I should have zapped the whole bunch of them unconscious.

But wild and possibly indiscriminate shooting wasn't a good idea even at the best of times, not even with a nonlethal weapon. Besides, I couldn't have been sure there weren't more walkers lurking elsewhere among the station's personnel and guests.

For that matter, I still couldn't. "So I have to zap the pilot, too," I said, wondering why I was even bothering to run with this bluff. "I can fly the shuttle myself if I have to."

He gave me a faint smile. "Come now, Compton," he chided. "Do you really wish to draw that kind of attention to yourself? Besides, what would it gain you?"

"Apart from the satisfaction, it would let us start our trip with a little peace and quiet," I said.

"Is *that* your concern?" he said. "Very well, then. As I said: a gesture of good faith." He nodded behind him. "Shall I bring you your luggage?"

"If you'd like," I said.

Actually, there wasn't anything in the carrybags except some tablecloths we'd scrounged from the server Spiders in our last train's dining car. Our clothing and other personal items were currently in plastic bags in the stationmaster's office, along with my allegedly missing lockbox.

Still, as long as the play was blown anyway, we might as well have our bags back.

"Frank?" Bayta murmured tautly.

"I don't like it either," I conceded. "But there isn't much we can do about it. The station has a crew of probably twenty or thirty, at least some of whom are probably walkers. We can't take down everyone, and it would be lunacy to try."

"Besides, there's no need," the Modhri added. "For the moment, at least, we have a common goal."

"The destruction of the Abomination."

"Correct." He reached into his pocket. "Oh, and you may find this useful." He opened his hand.

My stomach wrapped itself into a tight knot. Nestled in his pudgy palm was a silver necklace. The match to the ring I was carrying in my own pocket.

The necklace Lorelei had been wearing when she was killed.

"Thanks," I said, forcing my voice to remain calm as I plucked it out of his hand. If the Modhri was looking for a reaction from me, he wasn't going to get the satisfaction.

"You're welcome." He turned his head to look behind us.

And as he did so, the skin of his face tightened up again out of its sag. "Sorry," Braithewick said, his voice back to normal. "Sorry. Zoned out on you there for a minute."

"That's okay," I murmured, slipping the necklace into my pocket. "I wasn't saying anything important."

"At any rate, as I was starting to say, dealing with the Spiders can take a little professional finesse," he said briskly. "I was thinking that it might take some time and—ah; your luggage."

The Customs official came into sight, looking like a dit rec comedy bellhop as he struggled with two people's worth of travel bags. "I took the liberty of suggesting to him that it would look better if you had your bags with you," Braithewick explained, a slight frown creasing his forehead.

To me, that made no sense whatsoever. Judging by Braithewick's frown, it didn't make any sense to him, either. I thought about calling him on it, decided I'd heard enough Modhran pretzel logic for one day, and merely switched on my leash control. Bayta did the same, and as the clerk thankfully lowered the bags to the floor they rolled over to us. "There you go," the clerk said, his own forehead a little furrowed. "Have a good trip."

He turned and walked back around the curve and out of sight. "Shall we?" Braithewick asked, gesturing ahead.

"Certainly," I said. "After you."

We reached the Tube without incident and collected our clothing bags from the Spiders. We couldn't get the lockbox, of course—no weapons allowed in the Tube, and all that—but the stationmaster confirmed that it would be put aboard our next train.

"Well, that went well," Bayta commented evenly as we stood together watching the laser light show playing between our incoming train and the Coreline that ran down the center of the Tube. "Tell me again what this stop at Yandro was supposed to accomplish?"

"Anyone ever tell you that sarcasm ill befits you?" I countered.

"I was just wondering," she murmured. "I was also thinking that if the Modhri hadn't been alerted before to what we were up to, he certainly is now."

"No, all that he knows is that we're on the move," I corrected. "But he knew *that* way back in New York, when those walkers followed me home from the precinct house. Maybe he knew it even sooner, when he saw Lorelei leave my apartment. But none of that means he actually knows what we're up to."

"He will soon," Bayta said, an edge creeping to her voice. Clearly, she was blaming me for this fiasco. "Now, instead of us just slipping away quietly, we'll have an entire Quadrail's worth of walkers watching."

"We'd probably have had that anyway," I pointed out, putting a bit of an edge in my voice, as well. It wasn't *my* fault my gambit hadn't worked. "In case you hadn't noticed, you and I are living in a fishbowl these days."

Bayta sighed. "I know," she said quietly. "I'm sorry."

"I'm sorry, too," I said, glancing back over my shoulder. Braithewick was standing well back from our platform, giving us at least the illusion of privacy. "Don't worry. Whatever he's got up his sleeve, we'll be ready for him."

The train pulled up beside us and came to the usual brake-squealing stop.

And I was treated to the most extraordinary sight I had ever seen.

The train began disgorging passengers. Not just the one or two who might be expected to disembark at a minor Human colony world like Yandro, but an entire stream of them. Passenger after passenger stepped out of the cars, their bags rolling behind them: Juriani, Bellidos, Halkas, even a pair of Shorshians from the far end of the galaxy. Some of them glanced around the station as they stepped onto the platform, but most of them gazed straight ahead as they walked stolidly out into the Coreline's pulsating glow.

And every one of them was coming from the train's first-class cars.

Walkers.

Bayta pressed tightly against me, her hands squeezing my left upper arm in a death grip as the walkers continued to come. My right hand had a similar grip on the *kwi* in my pocket, and I could feel the familiar tingling as Bayta telepathically activated the weapon.

But the walkers merely continued to file past us, none of them so much as looking in our direction as they headed away from the train. Not toward the shuttle hatchways, I noted, or even toward Braithewick, but just away from the train.

Finally, with two minutes left before the train's scheduled departure, the streams slowed to a trickle and then ended. The Juri bringing up the rear paused as he passed us, and for the first time one of them actually looked at me. "You wished to begin your trip in peace and quiet," he said in a flat Modhran voice. "Now you may."

"So I see," I said, the skin at the back of my neck creeping. Had he really just taken all his walkers off this train? For *us*? "I appreciate it."

"Remember our bargain," he said, and walked off to join his fellow walkers.

I took a deep breath. "Come on," I said to Bayta. "Let's get aboard before he changes his mind."

Ninety seconds later, we stood at my compartment's display window, watching the group of walkers standing at their inhumanly stiff attention as the Quadrail pulled out of the station. We continued to watch them as the train picked up speed, until we angled up the far end into the main part of the Tube and our view was cut off by the station's atmosphere barrier.

"I'd say the Yandro stationmaster's got some serious rebooking to do," I commented to the universe at large.

"I don't believe it," Bayta murmured. She was still staring out the window, even though there was nothing to see anymore except the curve of the Tube. "Why would he take all those walkers off the train?"

"You heard him," I said. "A gesture of goodwill."

"Of course," she said with an edge of bitterness. "Like giving you that necklace?"

I felt my throat tighten. "It was Lorelei's," I said briefly. "He probably hoped he could use it to track down her sister."

"Only now he's got us to do that for him?"

"Something like that."

She shivered. "I don't like it, Frank. This isn't like him. *None* of this is like him."

"He does seem to be tweaking his usual style a bit," I conceded. "Maybe this Abomination thing has him rattled."

"You think it has something to do with Lorelei's sister?"

I grimaced. "I wouldn't be at all surprised," I said. "Come

on, I'm hungry. Let's see how many non-walker first-class passengers we have left."

We left the compartment and headed back toward the dining car. Ten minutes ago, I reflected, I'd agreed with Bayta's assessment that the trip to Yandro Station and our failed attempt to lose the Modhri had been a complete waste of time and effort.

Now, I was glad we'd made that effort. Very glad indeed.

Nine hours later, we reached New Tigris Station.

To my complete lack of surprise, Bayta and I were the only ones who got off there. We watched the Quadrail pull out of the station on its way to Earth and the Bellidosh Estates-General beyond, then went to the stationmaster's office to see about getting a shuttle to the transfer station.

Like most other small colony worlds across the galaxy, the low amount of Quadrail traffic at Yandro meant the shuttles worked on an on-demand basis instead of running a continual loop between Tube and transfer station. Here, apparently, demand was so low that the shuttles weren't even left on standby. As a result, it was over two hours before we finally stood at the transfer station's Customs counter, dutifully answering the standard entry questions, and having ourselves and our luggage scanned for contraband.

I still didn't know how my *kwi* looked on a Customs scanner. As long as no one challenged it, I wasn't inclined to ask.

"And that's it," the Customs official said briskly as he handed me my lockbox, the final step in the entry procedure. "Welcome to New Tigris. Are you here on business or pleasure?"

"Pleasure," I said. "A friend told us that Janga's Point has some of the best scuba diving in the Confederation. We thought we'd try it out."

"Excellent," he said, his eyes lighting up. Not only visitors to his modest little colony system, but visitors intent on spending money. "I've heard that, too, though I've never had a chance to go there. Now, you do understand that we have only a weekly torchferry service to New Tigris proper, correct?"

"Yes, we know," I said. Briefly, I wondered how many visitors arrived here expecting the daily service enjoyed by real planetary systems. "According to the schedule we saw, it'll arrive in two and a half days?"

"That's correct," he said. "We *do* have torchyachts for rent, though, if you don't want to wait."

"That's all right," I said. New Tigris's torchferry service was heavily subsidized by the mother world. Torchyacht rentals, unfortunately, weren't. "I assume you have rooms available while we wait?"

"Absolutely," he assured me, pulling out a registration form. "In fact, at the moment we only have one other guest."

"Human?" I asked, snagging a pen from the cup beside the computer terminal.

"A Pirk, actually," the clerk said.

My hand froze midway through writing my name. "A Pirk?" I echoed cautiously.

"Yes, but don't let that worry you." He glanced around and lowered his voice conspiratorially. "This one is actually safe to stand downwind of, if you get my drift."

"Right," I growled.

"No, really—he doesn't smell at all," the clerk insisted.

"Damnedest thing. Kind of like when my sister found the one cat in the entire Western Alliance that didn't trigger an instant asthma attack—"

"Yes, very interesting," I interrupted, laying down the pen. "On second thought, I think we'll take that torchyacht after all."

"Yes, sir," he said, taking the half-completed form from me and blanking it. "He really *doesn't* smell, you know."

"And I'm sure your sister wouldn't mind being locked in a room with a bunch of cats, either," I said. "You have a rental form?"

"Yes, sir," he said, pulling out another form and handing it over.

I glanced at Bayta, noting the stony look on her face, and started filling in the blanks.

An hour later, sitting at the controls of our new torchyacht, I maneuvered us away from the transfer station and turned us toward New Tigris. "I'd been wondering where our Pirk had ended up," I commented as I eased the drive up to full power.

"Now we know," Bayta said, her voice as stony as her expression. "I hope you're not expecting the Spiders to pay for this."

"Why not?" I asked. "Our agreement was salary and expenses. This is an expense."

"We could have waited for the torchferry," she pointed out. "If this girl Rebekah has been all right all this time, another two and a half days probably wouldn't have made a difference."

"Though at some point in every crisis a matter of hours or minutes *does* make a difference," I pointed out. "But that's not the reason I opted for the torchyacht. Or hadn't it occurred to you that by some standards a non-stinky Pirk could be considered an abomination?"

Her eyes narrowed. "You're not serious."

"Deadly serious," I assured her. "After all, we don't really know how the Modhri sees things. What would be a triple-A-rated blessing for everyone else in the galaxy might be complete anathema to him." I shrugged. "And our Pirk *did* seem to be watching Tweedledee and Braithewick pretty closely back at Terra Station."

"You're reaching," she said. But her stony expression had softened into something merely annoyed. Annoyed, and thoughtful.

I thought about pressing the point again about the torch-yacht rental, decided against it. Ultimately, the decision on who paid for that would rest with Bayta's recommendation. If the Modhri was as involved with Rebekah Beach as I suspected he was, there would be no question that this was a legitimate use of Spider and Chahwyn funds. If he wasn't, this might actually end up being a nice relaxing trip for a change.

Like I really believed *that*.

FIVE :

The trip to the inner system and New Tigris proper took five days. Bayta and I spent most of that time eating, sleeping, watching dit rec dramas and comedies from the torchyacht's limited selection, and going round and round on the topic of the Modhri and this Abomination he seemed so eager to wipe off the face of the universe.

We didn't reach any firm conclusions, or even any tentative ones. But we came up with a whole laundry list of options, none of them very pleasant, about what the Modhri might actually be up to.

Which meant that by the time New Tigris Control called us with landing instructions we were about as paranoid as it was possible for two Humans to be.

But that was all right. In this business, too much paranoia might annoy people. Too little could get you killed.

The spaceport was a couple of kilometers north of Imani City. It was a pretty casual affair, as landing areas went, little more than delineated rectangles on a reinforced concrete slab. I put us down on our assigned spot, noting as I did so that there were two other rental torchyachts squatting in various places across the field. Apparently, we weren't the only ones who'd decided not to share the regular torchferry run with even a de-odorized Pirk.

The Customs procedures were a quick and painless formality, partly because we weren't bringing any luggage off our torch-yacht for the moment, and partly because New Tigris needed all the visitors it could get and wasn't about to scare them off with annoying bureaucratic procedures. The official did, how-ever, make a point of carefully scrutinizing my Hardin Indus-tries carry permit before allowing me past his counter with my Glock.

There were two autocabs waiting outside the terminal. We grabbed one, gave it an intersection that my map said was at the edge of Zumurrud District, and headed south.

Imani City, once we were actually traveling its streets, was a pleasant surprise.

I'd seen pictures of the place, of course, and had studied maps of the city and surrounding regions during our torchyacht flight. But most of the reports I'd read had focused on New Tigris's dead-end status. Yet another of Earth's ill-conceived and badly managed colonies, the hand-wringing stories went, that would probably be a drain on the public treasury until the heat-death of the universe.

But someone had apparently forgotten to pass on all that depressing news to the colonists themselves. In the city's center, as well as in most of the neighborhood districts we passed through, the people looked for the most part to be cheerful, optimistic, and showing the kind of energy and dogged determination Human pioneers have always displayed.

I also saw that the private sector had responded to the UN's arm-twisting in spades. Along with their probable cash donations, I spotted the logos of at least five major corporations on various buildings along the way. Small operations, undoubtedly, at this point. Nevertheless, it was a vote of confidence in the colony's future, and a nice psychological boost besides.

The locals had done their part, too. There were all sorts of businesses nestled in among the houses, from bakeries and neighborhood grocery stores to the more homespun sorts of places like leather-workers and pottery makers. I spotted electronics shops, small-engine assembly plants, and even a tool-and-die manufacturer, all the signs of a colony determined to become self-sufficient as quickly as possible.

The colonists' private lives also seemed to have been taken care of. The houses were simple but nice and seemed reasonably well-kept. There was a fair sprinkling of homes that looked unoccupied, but it was possible their owners were simply off at long-term jobs elsewhere on the planet, working the mines or forests or else renting scuba equipment to holiday-makers at Janga's Point. Nowhere in Imani City, not even in those half-empty neighborhoods, did I sense anything remotely resembling an atmosphere of defeat, as one of the more effusive commentators had dubbed it.

Not, that is, until we reached Zumurrud District.

If the reporters had come to New Tigris looking for doom and gloom—and knowing reporters, I had no doubt that they had—this was definitely where they'd spent most of their time. The houses here, which had probably started life as nice as those in the rest of the city, were showing the signs of severe neglect. Worse, there were a surprising number whose broken windows and carved graffiti showed complete abandonment. The handful of shops had security grates on windows and doors, and there seemed to be at least twice as many taverns decorating the street corners as I'd spotted elsewhere in the city.

There were also a lot more people on the streets. Some of them were walking purposefully along, but there were a goodly number who were merely sitting or standing in small groups, clustered together on doorsteps or leaning on lampposts. The groups seemed self-segregated by age, with one block's loiterers consisting of bitter-faced middle-aged men, while the next block's were composed mostly of teenagers.

There were few women in evidence in any of the groups. Possibly they were gathered inside the houses instead, looking as bitter or depressed as the men. Or maybe the majority of the women had long since moved out of the neighborhood.

"All this in only twenty years?" Bayta murmured as we walked past another group, this one composed of bitter-eyed men in their mid-twenties.

"It's actually worse than that," I said. Like the other groups we'd passed, the men here had broken off their conversation as we approached, gazing at us with the odd expressions of people who wanted to be suspicious of the strangers but weren't sure we were worth even that much effort. "It's probably really only ten years of decay, not a full twenty. The first ten years would have been filled with typical mad-dash government activity and excitement. Hordes of new colonists being brought in, buildings and businesses going up, industries started, and everyone as optimistic as hell."

"What happened?"

"What happened was the same thing that happened with all the colonies," I told her, feeling a quiet pang of sympathy for these people who'd been casually brushed aside when the governmental winds changed direction. I knew exactly how they felt. "The initial push wound down, the UN brought all the temporary workers back home, and all the extra torchliners they'd rented for the big push were flown to the Tube, disassembled, and packed back aboard Quadrail cargo cars. Suddenly the colony found itself basically ignored while the UN started pouring its money and attention into the newest rage to catch its eye."

Bayta shivered. "Yandro," she murmured.

"In this case, yes, it was Yandro," I confirmed. "But it could have been anything that caught the bureaucratic imagination. Regardless, New Tigris suddenly found itself in the position of a jilted girlfriend. All alone, the gravy train dried up, and with a couple of wheezing modified torchferries her only contact with her former boyfriend."

"But the colonists must have expected something like that would happen eventually."

"I doubt the plan was any big secret," I said. "And to be fair, most of the people here don't seem to have been all that bothered by it." I looked at a group of four teenagers idly tossing a small ball back and forth by one of the broken-windowed houses ahead. "Unfortunately, others just gave up. Interesting."

"What's interesting?"

"That group propping up the front of the bar," I said, nodding toward a tavern a couple of doors past the four teens where a half-dozen men were idling around the doorway. "Notice anything unusual about them?"

"In this neighborhood?" Bayta countered.

"I'm serious," I said. "Note the age range. Everywhere else it's been teens or middle-aged or whatever. Very age-segregated. But the group up there has a teen, a young adult, two thirty-somethings, and that white-haired man has to be at least sixty."

Bayta digested that for a couple more steps. "And you think that's significant?"

"I have no idea," I said. "But it makes me curious enough to want to check it out. You thirsty?"

She sighed. "Do I have a choice?"

"Sure," I said. "You can wait outside."

"In that case, I'm thirsty."

"Good. Let's get something to drink."

We'd made it two more steps when the four teens between us and the tavern detached themselves from their abandoned house and casually re-formed themselves into a line across the walkway in front of us.

At my side, I felt Bayta tense up. "Just keep walking," I murmured to her, eyeing the youths and shuffling quickly through my options.

I didn't have many, and none of those were particularly attractive. I'd seen enough gangs in my time to know that any sign of weakness, such as turning around or crossing the street, would probably be like throwing raw meat into the shark tank.

On the other hand, showing too much strength, such as drawing my Glock, might easily escalate matters way beyond the point where I wanted them right now.

Which left only one real option: to continue on and hope my diplomatic skills had improved since my days in Westali.

I waited until we were within a few steps of the line and then nodded genially toward them. "Afternoon," I said, smiling pleasantly. "Nice day, isn't it?"

"Depends," one of the two boys in the middle said. His voice had the gruff toughness to it that I'd heard many a time in classic dit rec dramas. "You a cop?"

"Why, you think a cop would be interested in what you and your friends are doing?" I asked, still smiling. "No, we're just tourists."

"Tourists don't come to Zumurrud," he retorted darkly. "Who are you working for?"

The mixed group by the bar, I noticed, had stopped talking and were watching our little drama. "I'm not working for anyone," I said, taking Bayta's arm and bringing us to a halt three meters back from the line. "Like I said, we're just tourists."

The kid said a couple of rude words, again straight out of a dit rec drama. Apparently, when he wasn't hanging around street corners he was loitering in front of his entertainment center. "Yeah, right," he said.

"Fine; you caught me," I said, giving Bayta's arm a gentle but steady push to the side. She took the hint and eased a long step away from me. "I'm a special investigator for the Terran

Confederation Opinion Bureau. Tell me, what do you and your friends like most about living on New Tigris?"

I'd expected that to do it, and it did. Glaring at me, he stepped out of line and threw a punch straight at my stomach.

At least he hadn't learned his fighting technique from the dit rec actioners, with their fondness for fist-to-the-jaw punches that in real life usually wrecked the attacker's knuckles. But he hadn't learned his technique from an actual combat instructor either. Pivoting on my left foot, I swiveled out of his way, catching his fist in my left hand and helping it along a little. As he continued to lunge forward off-balance I bent his arm back at the elbow, pushing his fist over his shoulder and dropping him flat on his back on the walkway.

"I'm guessing it's the opportunity for fresh air and good healthy exercise," I continued, taking a step away from him. "That's probably enough of both for one day, don't you think?"

Apparently, he didn't. Scrambling to his feet, he squared his shoulders and came at me again.

Not in a mad-bull rush this time, but with the slower, warier approach I recognized from the better class of martial-arts dit rec actioners. I held my ground, ignoring the insistent tingling of the *kwi* in my pocket as Bayta kept activating it. Obviously, considering the four-to-one odds I was facing, she thought I should haul out the artillery and put the whole lot of them down for the count.

Under other circumstances, I would probably have agreed with her. But my old Westali combat senses were buzzing with the nagging feeling that something was wrong here. With the casual humiliation of their leader, the other three teens should have waded into the fray, hoping to overwhelm me with sheer numbers.

But they were still standing there in their line, watching the show but making no move to join in the fun. I flicked a glance at the bar, wondering if the crowd there was still watching.

And in that moment of apparent distraction, my attacker struck. Rotating on his right foot, he threw a side kick toward my stomach with his left.

Unfortunately for him, my distraction was indeed only apparent. Even more unfortunately, his kick had enthusiasm going for it but not much more. Again I slid out of the way with relative ease, capturing his leg and locking my arm around it at waist height.

And with that, we suddenly went from a dit rec actioner to a dit rec comedy. There he stood on one leg, making small hops with his remaining foot as he fought desperately to maintain his balance. He swung a couple of times at me, but I was well out of punching range. "Are we finished yet?" I asked mildly, watching the rest of his group out of the corner of my eye.

Again, none of them was making the slightest attempt to back up their leader. There would likely be some unpleasant words passing between them later.

"Enough."

I turned my head. While I'd been preoccupied elsewhere, the white-haired man had left the tavern doorway and come up behind the three teens. Like them, he was watching me, an intent look on his face. "Yes?" I asked, keeping my grip on the teen's leg.

"You armed, friend?" he asked.

"I carry the sword of truth and the shield of virtue," I told him.

His expression didn't even flicker. "I was talking about the gun under your jacket," he said.

"Oh—that," I said. "So why bother to ask?"

"Just wondering how honest you were," he said. "Why didn't you draw it?"

"What, against *these*?" I asked, waving at the line of teens. My gesture shifted the leg I was still holding, forcing its owner to hop a little more if he didn't want to fall over. "Hardly necessary. Besides, guns are dangerous."

"True," he agreed. "That was aikido, wasn't it?"

"There was some of that in the mix," I confirmed, eyeing the old man with new interest. Average citizens, despite the glut of hand-to-hand fighting in dit rec actioners, were generally pretty tone-deaf when it came to distinguishing one martial-arts style from another. The fact that he'd picked my aikido move out of the crowd lifted him somewhere above the average. "My instructors had a kind of grab-bag style."

I dropped the teen's leg, allowing him back some of his dignity. "As I see you've been doing with your bird dogs here. They still need work, though."

"Give them time," he said, a faint smile finally creasing his face. "They've only been at it a couple of months. My name's Usamah Karim. Former sergeant major, Afghan Army."

I inclined my head to him. "Frank Donaldson. Former nothing in particular."

A muscle twitched in Karim's cheek. "Frank Donaldson?" he asked, lowering his voice. "Or Frank Compton?"

Sometimes, I thought I might just as well wear a leather

jacket with my name emblazoned across the back in metal studs. "Whichever," I told him.

Glancing casually around, Karim stepped though the line of teens and walked up to me. "Prove it," he challenged, gazing unblinkingly into my face.

For a long moment, I gazed back at him, searching for any trace of the Modhri behind his eyes. But if there was a polyp colony in there, he was being very quiet. "You want to see my ID?" I asked.

"No," Karim said flatly.

"I didn't think so." Reaching into my pocket, I pulled out Lorelei's ring and necklace. "How about these?"

Karim's hand reached up to mine, closed around the pieces of jewelry. "That'll do," he said quietly. "Let's get inside," he added, nodding back toward the bar. "We need to talk."

At Karim's instruction, the four teens returned to their positions by the abandoned house. The one who'd attacked me nodded gravely at me as I passed, with no hint of animosity that I could detect. He'd done his job of smoking me out; more importantly, he'd done it without taking any of it personally.

The signs of a good soldier. *And* of a good instructor.

The tavern was largely deserted, with three of the small tables occupied by lone patrons. Karim led Bayta and me past the nicked and stained wooden bar at the back of the establishment, nodding once to the scraggly-looking bartender as we passed, and through a door into a small office.

"Have a seat," he said, gesturing to a couple of folding chairs propped against the wall as he circled the paper-strewn desk and sat down behind it. "Afraid I don't have anything more comfortable to offer you."

"This is fine," I assured him, unfolding the chairs and setting them down where we were mostly facing Karim but also had a view of the door.

Under cover of the activity, I also slipped the *kwi* out of my pocket and onto my right hand. It was always possible Karim's reason for bringing us in here was to get rid of us quietly, out of view of potential witnesses. Just because I hadn't been able to sense a Modhran colony behind his eyes didn't mean there wasn't one there.

And even if he wasn't a walker, he might have reasons of his own to seriously dislike me. There were plenty of people like that left over from my Westali days.

"I remember when Oved gave these to her," Karim commented, turning Lorelei's ring over in his fingers. "He was taking classes from the jeweler over on Seventh, and they were the first things he made that actually looked decent."

"Oved was her boyfriend?"

Karim shrugged. "He wanted to be," he said. "Lorelei had that effect on people. There was just something about her that made you like her."

He set the ring and necklace on the desk in front of him and looked up at us. "He's the one who attacked you just now, by the way."

"He shows promise," I said.

Karim nodded agreement. "He was the one who first approached me about getting some sort of paramilitary training. He knew Lorelei was in danger from somewhere, and wanted to be able to help her when she got back here with you." A hint of a frown crossed his face. "She *is* here some-where, isn't she?"

I grimaced. I hated this part. "I'm afraid she won't be com-ing back. I'm sorry."

A corner of Karim's lip twitched. "What happened?"

"Someone caught up with her a couple of hours after she left my apartment," I said, carefully skipping over the fact that she'd left because I'd thrown her out. "A couple of someones, actually."

"She said there were people hunting for her," Karim mur-mured, his eyes drifting away. "Oved volunteered to go with her. So did I. But she said she had to do this alone."

Abruptly, his eyes came back to focus squarely on my face. "Why *you,* Mr. Compton?"

"Good question," I acknowledged. "I wish I had a good answer to go with it."

"You weren't somebody she already knew?" he persisted. "A friend, or the friend of a friend?"

"Not that she ever mentioned," I said. "All she said was that her sister Rebekah was in danger, and that she wanted me to get her out."

"Is Rebekah still safe?" Bayta asked.

Karim's eyes shifted to her, his forehead creasing in a frown. "As safe as we can make her," he said. "And you are . . . ?"

"This is Bayta," I told him, frowning in turn at his reaction. Were we going to get into the royal bugaboo of cultural prob-lems here? "Is it inappropriate for her to speak in our company?"

"No, no, not at all," Karim assured me. But he was still staring at her, that odd look still on his face. "It's just that there's something about her. Something . . ." He shook his head abruptly. "Never mind. Tell me how you plan to get Rebekah off New Tigris."

"Not so fast," I cautioned. "I'm not doing anything until I know more about the situation. Let's start with who exactly was hunting Lorelei, and are they the same bunch who are also hunting Rebekah."

"We don't know who they are, exactly," he said. "The police may be involved—I know Lorelei didn't trust them, and didn't want us to, either. There have also been other people, too, mostly non-Humans, who've come to New Tigris for a week or two at a time."

I thought about the other two torchyachts we'd seen on the field north of town. "Tourists?"

"Some were," he said. "Upper-class ones, who threw a lot of money around traveling out into the wilderness areas. But there were also some who seemed to be here on business. That group stayed pretty much in the city."

I looked at Bayta, saw my same conclusion reflected in the tightness around her lips. Rich non-Human tourists and businessmen were prime candidates for Modhran walkerhood. And, of course, we were assuming Lorelei died in the company of Human walkers.

Which seemed to point to the slightly absurd conclusion that this ten-year-old Human girl was the Abomination the Modhri was so worried about. "Do the police have anything official to do with Rebekah?" I asked. "Any warrants or protection formals out on her?"

"None that I know of."

"How long have all these non-Human tourists been wandering around?"

"They started arriving about three months ago," Karim said. "At first, Lorelei didn't seem to be particularly worried about them. Then, about five weeks ago, she suddenly started getting nervous. She said she needed to go to Earth for help, and asked me to hide Rebekah while she was gone."

"Where's Rebekah now?" Bayta asked.

Karim hesitated, his eyes shifting back and forth between us. "Come on, Mr. Karim," I coaxed. "You either trust us right now, or else you don't trust us at all. There's no way to get you any more proof as to who we are or whose side we're on."

Karim snorted. "My father once warned me never to trust people who urge you to make a quick decision on an important matter."

"Whether to veer left or right as you barrel toward a cliff could be considered an important decision, too," I said. "It's also not one you can afford to ponder too long."

"Point taken," Karim said. But his eyes were still troubled.

"Maybe I can make it easier for you," Bayta offered. "If we were your enemies, we'd thank you for your time and leave. Then we'd come back with reinforcements."

"Reinforcements for what?" Karim asked, frowning.

"To get Rebekah," Bayta said. "She's here in this building."

Karim was good, all right. His face and body language didn't even twitch.

But even through his dark skin, I saw some of the color go out of his face. "Bayta's right," I said, putting a casual confidence in my voice even as I wondered how in hell's name she'd figured that out. "You want to take us to her? Or are

you the sporting type who'd rather make us find her ourselves?"

"No need," he said, his shoulders sagging microscopically in
defeat. Standing up, he moved his chair out of the way and
ducked down to the floor. I was halfway around the side of the
desk when there was a soft creaking sound.

And as I finished rounding the desk, I saw him pulling open
a half-meter-square trapdoor. "She's down there," he said,
straightening up and gesturing down the shaft.

I leaned over for a closer look. The shaft was completely
framed with wood that looked like it had been there awhile.
There was a ladder fastened to one side, disappearing downward into the darkness. I pulled out my flashlight and shone it
into the hole, revealing a dirt floor about four meters down. At
the bottom a passageway led off from the desk side of the
shaft, heading in a direction that would take it under the main
part of the bar. "Interesting accommodations," I commented.

"Part of the storage cellar," Karim told me. "We walled it
off from the main cellar when Rebekah went into hiding."

"How obvious is the dividing wall?"

"Not at all," he assured me. "It also has ten beer barrels
stacked against it." He gestured to the shaft. "Shall I go first?"

There was a subtle challenge to my pride hidden in the
question: the big, bad, former Westali agent afraid that a simple
little colonist might pull a fast one and seal him away down in
the deep, dark hole.

But I was way past the point of letting pride make my deci-
sions for me. "Yes, thank you," I said, gesturing him toward the
ladder.

Without a word he knelt, got a grip on the edge of the hole, and started down the ladder. Motioning Bayta to stand watch, I followed him down.

He was waiting just inside the passageway when I reached the ground. The passageway itself, I saw now, ended at a dark dirt face only a couple of meters away. "What now?" I asked.

"This way," he said, turning and starting down the passageway.

Again, I followed. He reached the end, and as he pushed the "dirt face" aside to reveal a soft light beyond I realized that it was just a light-blocking curtain that had been set across the passageway. He stepped through, holding the curtain open for me. Bracing myself, I stepped through after him into a small, low-ceilinged room.

The furnishings were Spartan in the extreme. There was a cot, a small folding table and chair, and a drying rack that held both neatly folded clothing and a collection of ration bars. In one corner of the room a sink/toilet combination nestled up against a section of the wall that had been gouged out for access to the bar's plumbing system. Stacked neatly along one of the other walls were twenty gray metal containers about the size of standard Quadrail lockboxes, about fifty centimeters long and twenty centimeters high and deep.

And sitting cross-legged in the middle of the cot with her back against the wall, gazing at us with an unreadable expression, was a young girl.

"Hello, Rebekah," Karim said. "How are you doing?"

"I'm fine, thank you," she said gravely, unfolding her legs and standing up. Her voice was definitely that of a ten-year-old, but at the same time there was also something very adult about it.

But then, she was apparently being hunted for her life. That sort of thing could age a person very quickly.

"Are you Frank Compton?" she asked.

"Yes, I am," I confirmed, shaking away my musings and giving her a quick once-over. She seemed healthy enough, though her long confinement had left her a little thin and pale.

Aside from her build and hair color, though, she didn't really resemble Lorelei very much. Still, I'd known sisters who were a lot more dissimilar than this. "You ready to get out of here?" I asked, keeping my tone light.

"Very much so," she said gravely. Her eyes flicked down to the *kwi* still gripped in my right hand, but she didn't ask about it. "Mr. Karim told you about my other needs?"

I frowned at Karim. "What needs are those?"

He winced a bit. "The boxes have to go with her," he said, nodding toward the stack of gray boxes against the wall.

I looked at the boxes and then back at Karim. "You're kidding."

"Neither of us is kidding, Mr. Compton," Rebekah said reprovingly. "It's absolutely vital that those boxes and I leave New Tigris together."

I stepped over to the stack and tugged experimentally on the top box. Ten kilos at least, I estimated, maybe as much as fifteen. With twenty boxes, that made for two to three hundred kilos of dead weight.

There were a dozen ways a ten-year-old girl could be smuggled past Customs and off the planet. Adding in a quarter metric ton worth of metal boxes instantly eliminated at least half of those options. "Can we maybe cut it down to two or three of them?" I suggested. "We can try to get the rest out later."

"No," Rebekah said, her voice leaving no room for argument. Her eyes flicked over my shoulder at the passageway. "Is the other one with you?"

"The other one?" I asked.

"The woman," she said.

"Oh—Bayta," I said. "Yes, she's just upstairs." I raised an eyebrow. "But you won't be able to talk her into this any easier than—"

"A moment," Karim cut me off, pulling out his comm and holding it to his ear. "Yes?"

He listened for a few seconds, and I saw his throat muscles tighten. "Understood," he said, and put the comm away. "We have to get back at once," he said, moving back toward the curtain. "Three police cars are on their way."

I glanced at Rebekah. Her face was tense, but under control. "Looking for Rebekah?" I asked.

"I doubt it," he said grimly. "I think, my friend, they're looking for you."

SIX :

Karim and I were back up the ladder in fifteen seconds flat. "What is it?" Bayta asked.

"Cops on the way," I told her, moving aside as Karim swung the trapdoor shut. "Possibly looking for us."

"We need to get out of here," Karim said as he put his desk chair back into position over the trapdoor. "Meet them out in the bar."

"Wait a second," I said. "Have the cops been in this office before?"

"Yes, several times," Karim said, still edging toward the door. "Quickly, now."

"And they obviously didn't find the secret entrance?" I asked, not moving.

"No, of course not."

"Then let's just sit tight," I told him, circling the desk and sitting down again.

He stared at me as if I were crazy. "But what if they're looking for you?"

"What if they are?" I countered as Bayta sat down as well. "We're honest, upright citizens of the Terran Confederation, here to see the sights of New Tigris."

"In *here*?" Karim asked.

"Okay, so we're also here to sample the drinks," I said. "Look, nothing ramps up a cop's personal radar like people under suspicion hurrying to meet him. All that's happened here is that you took pity on a pair of strangers and invited us in to discuss the best places for tourists to visit. What exactly would those places be?"

"Probably Janga's Point and the Gilcress Mountains," Karim said, reluctantly returning to his desk chair and sitting down.

"Scuba and climbing," I said, nodding as I took the *kwi* off my hand and slipped it back into my pocket. "Good. Now, where are the best places to buy or rent the necessary equipment?"

We were in the middle of a discussion of climbing styles when the police barged in.

They did barge in more or less politely, though, knocking before opening the office door. "Excuse me," their leader said, his eyes automatically checking out each of us before settling on me. "Are you Mr. Frank Donaldson?"

"I am," I confirmed. "Is there a problem?"

"Mr. Veldrick asked us to look for you, sir," the cop said. "Your autocab record showed you were here in Zumurrud District." He looked at Karim. "Mr. Karim will tell you this isn't a particularly safe place for strangers to be, especially with dusk coming on."

"I see," I said, passing over the fact that dusk was at least two hours away. "And who exactly is this Mr. Veldrick who has such interest in autocab records?"

The cop raised his eyebrows slightly. "You don't recognize the name of the man you came here to see?"

"I'm terrible with names," I said. "Remind me."

"Mr. Veldrick is the local administrator of Crown Rosette Electronics," the cop explained. "Which I believe Hardin Industries acquired a few months ago."

I looked at Karim. His expression was studiously neutral, but there was a hint of tension showing beneath the mask. "And one of Mr. Veldrick's duties is to keep track of autocab records?"

"Not all of them," the cop said, smiling. "Just yours. Would you come with us, please? Mr. Veldrick is most anxious to meet you."

"Then by all means let's relieve his anxiety," I said, standing up and gesturing Bayta to do likewise. Without knowing how the police were set up outside the bar, anything short of meek compliance would be potential suicide. Considerations of countermoves would have to wait until we could further assess the situation. "Thank you for your time, Mr. Karim. Perhaps we can pick up our conversation again some other time."

"Perhaps," Karim said, nodding gravely to me. "Good day to you, Mr. Donaldson."

There were five more cops waiting outside, three of them engaged in a sort of pickup staring contest with Karim's bar-door buddies. Three marked patrol cars were lined up at the curb, as well, and I wondered just what percentage of Imani City's police force was represented by this group. Either I was a VIP of the top rank, deserving of an official police escort, or else it was a quiet day down at the station.

Or else the cops preferred to run in convoy when they came to Zumurrud District.

Veldrick lived in one of the areas of the city we hadn't passed through on our way in, and it was clearly yet another neighborhood the doom-and-gloom reporters had ignored. The houses were larger and snootier than most of those Bayta and I had seen up to now, set back from the street across large, manicured lawns. Crown Rosette Electronics, apparently, was doing well for itself.

I half expected a neatly uniformed butler to answer the chime. But the man who opened the door was instead wearing a nicely tailored business suit. He was middle-aged and gray-ing, starting to run a little overweight, but with the piercing eyes of a man accustomed to quick evaluation, analysis, and decision. Veldrick, without a doubt.

His eyes flicked once across my face, then dipped quickly up and down the rest of my body, rather like a laser scanner selecting the grading for a particular side of beef. "You must be Mr. Donaldson," he said in greeting. His eyes shifted to Bayta.

And paused there, taking a second and even a third look, his forehead creasing slightly. "And you are . . . ?" he asked.

"This is Jasmine, my assistant," I told him. "You must be Mr. Veldrick."

He looked back at me, the frown clearing away. "That's right," he said. "Come in—I've been expecting you."

He ushered us inside, dismissing our police escort with a glance, and closed the door behind us. "So I hear," I said. "I must admit to being a bit surprised by that."

"Surprised by my interest in you?" he asked, gesturing us through the foyer toward a decorated archway. "Or surprised I even knew you were here?"

"Mostly the latter," I said. "I'd thought I was keeping a reasonably low profile."

"And so you were," he said as we stepped through the archway into an elegantly furnished great room, complete with an impressive half-wrap wood-burning fireplace. "But one of the necessities of corporate survival is to have as many ears to as much ground as possible. I received private word that Mr. Hardin was sending someone my way, and I've been watching for you ever since."

"With a little help from friends in the police and Customs?" I suggested as Bayta and I sat down on a very comfortable contour couch facing a low serving table.

"Ears to the ground, eyes to the horizon," Veldrick said with a smile as he sat down in a throne-like chair on the opposite side of the serving table from us. He tapped a button, and the table opened up to reveal a variety of drinks and small finger foods. "May I offer you some refreshment?"

"Thank you," I said, looking over the selection. It was a nice middle-of-the-road assortment, neither too extravagant nor too cheap. Just the sort of offering I'd expect from someone who wasn't sure whether the corporate visitor across the table was a potential ally or a potential adversary.

Which led immediately to other questions, such as whether Hardin's takeover had been friendly or hostile. If the latter, how hostile had it been, and how exactly Veldrick was positioning himself to deal with it.

But intriguing though the boardroom stratagems might be, they were far outside the scope of our immediate task. "How long have you been on New Tigris?" I asked, selecting a cola and a cookie sandwich.

"Eight years," Veldrick said. "There are some rich selenium and iridium deposits about fifty kilometers west of the city, and we've been taking advantage of them to get some high-end production going. We've been shipping product for nearly seven years now, and the operation has been showing a profit for the past three."

"Impressive," I said, taking a bite of the sandwich. Shrimp, I decided, or the local equivalent. "I presume you're still shipping mostly to Earth?"

"Mostly, but we've also been working to develop markets with the Juriani and Cimmaheem." He smiled. "I'm guessing that's what caught Mr. Hardin's interest in our little company."

"Probably," I agreed. "Mr. Hardin's very big on extending his markets outward."

"As well he should be," Veldrick said. "That's the direction of the future."

He cocked his head. "But I don't imagine you came all this way just to chat about market conditions."

Clearly, he was inviting me to tell him why Hardin had sent me. Problem was, I didn't have the slightest idea why Hardin would even do something like that. "It's nothing you need to worry about," I assured him, going for the vaguest answer I could find on short notice. "This sort of visit is pretty much routine, at least in certain cases."

"What sort of cases?" he asked.

I gave him the bland formal smile I'd learned at Westali for use against criminal suspects and nosy senators. "I'm sure you understand I can't go into details," I said. "Again, though, it's nothing to worry about."

He held my eyes another couple of heartbeats and then gave a small shrug. "Of course," he said, pretending to be satisfied with my answer. "Where are you staying, by the way? The Hanging Gardens?"

I shook my head. "For the moment, we're just staying aboard our torchyacht."

"The Hanging Gardens," he said firmly. "Third and Chestnut. It's the best hotel in Imani City. All the visiting dignitaries stay there, and it's convenient to both our offices and our assembly plant." He cocked his head again. "Or you could stay here," he added, as if the thought had just occurred to him. "I have a very nice guest suite."

"No, we couldn't possibly impose on you that way," I demurred.

"At least let me show it to you," he said, standing up and gesturing through an archway covered with strings of glittering, diamond-like beads. "It's just on the other side of the meditation room."

He stepped to the doorway and pulled the strings aside for us, the beads making gentle bell-like whisperings as they moved. With Bayta close behind me, I stepped through.

The meditation room was small but nicely arranged. There were four large floor pillows clustered in the middle of the room, surrounded by several candelabra with attached incense burners. Along one wall was another fireplace, much smaller than the one out in the great room. On the wall opposite it was a tiered trough with a miniature stream of flowing water, complete with a couple of small waterfalls and a set of rapids.

And inside the trough, glistening with the water flowing over it, was a long patterned formation of coral.

Modhran coral.

Veldrick had a Modhran mind segment right here inside his house.

I shouldn't have reacted. I should have glanced at the coral, made some nice polite comment about how lovely and peaceful the room looked, and moved on.

But the discovery was so unexpected that I couldn't catch myself in time. Instead, I stopped with a jerk, my torso giving a sharp twitch. "That's—"

I broke off. But it was too late. "It's Modhran coral," Veldrick said, his tone subtly altered as he came up behind me. I twitched again, taking a long step away and turning to face him.

But there was no weapon in his hand. "Come now, Mr. Donaldson," he said with a faintly mocking smile. "It's not *that* impressive."

"It's not the impressiveness that worries me," I said, searching for something else to hang my reaction on. It was still possible the fake Donaldson identity had him fooled. "It's the ramifications," I went on. "Last I heard, it was still illegal to import coral or coral-like substances onto Confederation worlds."

He waved a hand, his nose wrinkling in genteel contempt. "A ridiculous law," he said. "Probably illegitimate, certainly unenforceable. Besides, you've no idea how a gift of Modhran coral helps to grease the wheels of commercial enterprise. Especially with non-Humans."

"Perhaps," I said. There were several arguable points in there, but this wasn't the time to argue them. This was the time to make our farewells and get the hell out of here. "But it's getting late. Perhaps we'll go take a look at the Hanging Gardens."

"But you haven't seen the guest suite," Veldrick reminded me, gesturing toward a doorway on the far side of the meditation room, this one also sporting a shimmering wall of beads. "Right through there."

The guest suite was indeed nice, on a par with a mid-range hotel room. I made the standard comments and murmurs of appreciation, again insisted that I couldn't allow us to be a burden to him, and again attempted to disengage.

This time, it worked. Veldrick escorted us back to the front door, encouraged me to come by the office in the morning, and let us leave.

The cops who'd delivered us were long gone. Getting my bearings, I turned us east toward Broadway, one of Imani City's major streets, where we should be able to find an autocab stand.

Broadway was four blocks away. We'd covered two of them before Bayta finally spoke. "Do you think he knows?" she asked.

"After that two-hundred-twenty-volt twitch of mine?" I growled, feeling disgusted with myself. "If he didn't know before, he certainly does now."

"I don't know," she said thoughtfully. "If showing us the

coral was supposed to confirm who we are, why didn't the Modhri do something with that information?"

"You heard him, back at Yandro," I reminded her. "He's going to leave us alone until we find and destroy the Abomination."

She shivered. "Rebekah?"

"That's the logical assumption," I said. "We know the Modhri was tracking Lorelei, and those offworld searchers Karim mentioned were probably also walkers. Coordinated by Veldrick's meditation-room coral, no doubt." I frowned as something suddenly struck me. "Interesting."

"What is?"

"I was just wondering when the coral was brought in," I said, trying to think this through. "It's possible Veldrick himself isn't actually a walker."

Bayta shook her head. "I doubt the Modhri would set up an outpost without a walker here to watch over it."

"Oh, I have no doubt Veldrick's on his way to becoming one," I said. "But if the Modhri just recently figured out Rebekah is here, he may have brought in the outpost solely to coordinate the search. In that case, Veldrick's polyp infection may not have grown to full colony status yet."

"I suppose that's possible," Bayta said, still sounding doubtful. "Especially if there were other walkers here he could use in an emergency."

"Right," I said. "*My* question is why bother with a coral outpost at all? Why not just use walkers for the search?"

"Shall we go back and ask him?"

"Thanks, but I've had enough socializing for one day," I

said. "Let's go check out this Hanging Gardens place and see what it's like."

Bayta was silent for another half block. "What about Rebekah?" she asked.

"For now, we leave her where she is," I said. "In fact, now that you and I are no longer flying under the radar, we should probably steer clear of the whole Zumurrud District for a few days."

"I suppose," she said. "I wonder what's in all those boxes."

"Probably her shoe collection," I grumbled. "That's going to be a major headache all by itself."

"You'll figure something out."

"I appreciate your confidence," I said. "Speaking of figuring things out, how did you figure out where she was?"

"I don't know," Bayta said, shaking her head slowly. "It just seemed . . . I don't know."

"Oh, well, that clears it up," I said, trying not to be too sarcastic. "Come on—work at it a little. Did you hear her, or smell her, or what?"

"I don't *know,*" Bayta said again, starting to sound a little exasperated.

"Okay, okay, take it easy," I soothed. "But if the details ever surface, be sure to let me know."

We reached Broadway, pausing on the corner as I looked both directions down the street for the traditional green-and-yellow banner of an autocab stand. But there wasn't one in sight. I focused my attention on the traffic flowing briskly along, wondering if autocabs simply roamed the streets like they did in some of the cities I'd visited.

But I couldn't see any of them tucked in among the streams of private cars and trucks, either. "I guess you have to call them," I said, pulling out my comm and punching up the city directory.

"We could just walk," Bayta offered, pointing to our left. "If I remember the map right, Third and Chestnut is only five or six blocks away. Probably be just as fast as calling a cab."

"It won't take long in a city this size," I assured her. I found the number and punched in a request, glancing up and down the street again. A block away to our right, a middle-aged man in a jogging suit trotted to a stop at the corner, peering closely at his reader. Checking the news as he ran, I decided, or else he had a map of the city pulled up and was trying to figure out the next leg of his urban walking adventure.

I frowned, red flags going up in the back of my brain. I'd noticed a man in similar garb a block away in that same direction as we were leaving Veldrick's house. If this was that same man, and if we'd reached Broadway half a minute before he did, he had to be the slowest jogger in the business.

Or else he was making sure he *didn't* get ahead of us.

"On second thought, maybe you're right," I told Bayta, canceling the autocab request. Swapping out the comm for my reader, I punched up a street map.

She was right—the Hanging Gardens was five blocks north and one block east of where we were standing. Between us and it was one of the city's commercial and shopping areas, with most of this section of Broadway lined with shops and restaurants. A number of the businesses on our side of the street, I noted, opened onto service alleys running along behind them.

"Yes, you're definitely right," I went on, shutting off the reader and putting it away. "Besides, it'll be dinnertime soon. A walk will give us a chance to check out the restaurants along the way."

Bayta had a faintly suspicious look on her face, no doubt prompted by my sudden one-eighty on the autocab thing. But she merely nodded, and we set off.

We took our time, strolling at a leisurely pace as we checked out the window displays of the shops along our way and paused at each restaurant to look over its posted menu. I made sure not to check on whether our jogger was still back there, either by looking for his reflection in the windows or by actually turning around. Unless he was a complete amateur he would know all the techniques for clearing a backtrail, plus all the techniques for not getting spotted in the first place.

Two and a half blocks later, we reached the place where I planned to lose him.

It was a hardware supply store, one of the establishments I'd noted that had a service alley running behind it. It was a large place, the sort that would likely have tall display shelves, somewhat winding aisles, and perhaps the occasional blind corner. "In here," I told Bayta, nudging her toward the main door as we started to pass.

Accustomed to taking even ridiculous orders from me, she obediently pulled open the door and headed inside. I followed, and for the first time since we set off on our stroll up Broadway I looked behind me.

The man in the jogging suit was nowhere to be seen. I checked the other side of the street. No jogger. He'd either changed outfits, gotten around in front of us and was lying low, or passed us off to a second tail.

This was possibly going to be more interesting than I'd thought.

The store did indeed have the tall racks and relatively narrow aisles I'd hoped for. Catching up to Bayta, I took her arm and steered her onto a zigzag path toward the rear. "What are we looking for?" she asked as we reached the plumbing section.

"Freedom of movement," I told her. "I think we were followed from Veldrick's place."

She digested that as we passed through Plumbing and reached Storage and Shelving. "All right," she said. "But if we lose him now, won't he just pick us up again at the Hanging Gardens?"

"That assumes we're still going to the Hanging Gardens," I said. "I'm thinking now maybe we won't. In here."

We slipped through a door marked EMPLOYEES ONLY. Beyond it was a typical retail store back area: cluttered and uncarpeted, its walls decorated with notices and inspirational placards and the occasional gouge where someone had missed a turn with a loaded cart. I glanced around, spotted a lighted EXIT sign, and steered Bayta toward it. Reaching under my jacket to my belt holster, I got a grip on my Glock and pushed open the back door.

The service alley was much nicer than I'd expected. There were large bins on both sides, but they were neatly lined up and even looked relatively clean. There were only a few stray papers blowing around loose, with none of the more disgusting debris that had a tendency to collect in out-of-the-way places like this. Apparently, the merchants on this block took pride even in the less public areas of their properties.

"Which way?" Bayta whispered.

I pointed south, the direction we'd just come from. "Let's see how fast they are on the uptake." I turned and started to take a step.

And froze as a soft click came from the far side of one of the bins now behind us. The soft but distinctive click of a gun's safety catch being released.

Bayta heard it, too. "Was that—?"

"Yes, it was," a raspy voice said from the direction of the click. "Just pull your hand out of your coat, friend. Nice and easy. And empty."

Keeping my head motionless, I gave the area around us a quick scan. But there was no cover anywhere, at least nothing Bayta and I could reach fast enough. With a sigh, I pulled my hand out of my jacket, holding it up to demonstrate its emptiness. "You're good," I complimented my ambusher.

"No, you're just predictable," he said. The voice was moving, indicating he'd left his cover and was coming up behind us. "You really should work on that."

"I'll make a note," I said.

"You'd better," he warned. "In this business, when you get predictable, you die."

I frowned. Fatherly advice from a street assailant?

And then, suddenly, it clicked. "Well, you would certainly know," I agreed. Without waiting for permission, I turned around.

It was the middle-aged jogger I'd spotted earlier, all right, his gun in hand but pointed harmlessly up at the sky. His hair was gray and ponytailed behind him, his face was lined and leathery with age and a lifetime of too much sun, and he was sporting a two-day stubble on his cheeks. It was a face I'd never seen before in my life. "Hello, McMicking," I greeted him. "What in the name of hell are *you* doing here?"

SEVEN :

The Hanging Gardens was pleasant, pricey, and seemed to have plenty of rooms available. Bayta and I checked into a two-bedroom suite, got a recommendation for a nearby restaurant from the concierge, and headed back out.

McMicking was already seated when we arrived. "How did you know we were coming here?" Bayta asked as we sat down at his table. "I didn't think Frank had called you yet."

"He hadn't," McMicking said, handing her a menu. "But I got the same recommendation from the concierge last night. Considering the averageness of the food, I'm guessing he's getting a kickback from the management."

I looked around at the low lights and the booths' wrap-around isolation shells. "But the privacy factor is above average?" I suggested.

"Exactly," McMicking aid. "Let's order, and then we can talk."

We ordered a stuffed mushroom appetizer, and as we ate I gave him a thumbnail sketch of our activities since my departure from Manhattan, leaving out only our meeting with Rebekah. Restaurant isolation shells were all well and good, but they could be trusted only so far.

McMicking seemed fascinated by all of it, especially the Veldrick part of the story. "Interesting," he said after the waiter had cleared away the appetizer plates. "So is this a truce you've got going with the Modhri? Or would you consider it more of a full-fledged alliance?"

"I consider it a complete scam," I told him flatly. "The only question is what that scam is, what he's actually going for, and how we stop him."

"Good questions all," McMicking said. "You have any proof it's a scam? Aside from your natural distrust of the universe at large?"

"Sure," I said. "Veldrick. If the Modhri's trying to pretend he's giving us rope to track down the Abomination, why reveal the fact that there's a coral outpost in the neighborhood? Or as Bayta and I were discussing earlier, why bring in an outpost at all?"

"Uh-huh," McMicking said, an odd look on his face. "But of course, if he's running a scam, why tip his hand by showing you the coral in the first place?"

"That one's got me stumped," I admitted. "All I can think of is that word of our so-called truce hasn't made it to the local mind segment yet. But that seems ridiculous. It took five days for our torchyacht to get here from the Tube. Plenty of time for the Modhri to have lasered in a message."

"Unless the Modhri mind segment that made the deal hasn't

figured out that we're here," Bayta said suddenly. "He took all his walkers off the Quadrail, remember, and there wasn't anyone at the New Tigris Station."

"He *may* have taken all his walkers off," I corrected. "We only have his word for that. He could just as easily pulled the old duck-blind trick."

"What's a duck-blind trick?" she asked.

"Three people go into a duck blind; two people come out," I explained. "Since ducks don't count very well, they all relax, thinking they're alone and off the hook."

"There is another possibility," McMicking said thoughtfully. "Is there any way to tell whether or not Veldrick is a walker?"

"Not until the Modhri takes him over," I said. "There are definite changes in face and voice when that happens."

"I was hoping for something a little less drastic," McMicking said. "I was thinking about the fact that the Modhri and the Spiders are all telepathic, and wondering if Bayta might be able to sense his presence."

"I wish I could," Bayta said. "But there's no crossover. Spider and Modhri communications work on—" She looked at me, as if searching for the right word. "I guess you could say we're on different frequencies."

"Though thought viruses prove that—" I broke off at a warning twitch of McMicking's eye. The waiter arrived, and we sat in silence as he laid out our plates. "I was going to say, thought viruses prove there's some telepathic overlap between the Modhri and normal humans," I finished when we were alone again.

McMicking grunted. "The fact that polyp colonies can

whisper suggestions and rationalizations to a host proves *that* much," he pointed out. "Where I was going with this was that Veldrick might not be a walker. If he isn't, then there's no connection between him and the Modhri's truce or scam or whatever."

"Interestingly enough, I was wondering that same thing myself earlier," I said. "But then why did he go to all that trouble to show us the coral? Because he *did* deliberately do that."

"Maybe he was trying to gauge your reaction to it," McMicking said.

I frowned at him. With McMicking, it was as much about what he *wasn't* saying as about what he *was*. "And he would do this because . . . ?" I prompted.

McMicking smiled tightly. "Because I came here to take it away from him."

He pointed at my plate. "But your steak's getting cold. Let's eat."

The dinner had been eaten, the plates cleared away, and we were on coffee and the dessert sampler when McMicking finally picked up the story again. "It started five months ago when Hardin Industries bought Crown Rosette Electronics," he said. "One of the first things Mr. Hardin always does once the papers have been signed is to send someone around to make a survey of local manufacturing centers. About three months ago, the rep got around to New Tigris."

He made a face. "And discovered to his stunned disbelief that the head of the local branch had about a cubic meter of highly illegal Modhran coral in his house."

"I warned Veldrick about that," I said.

"So did the rep," McMicking said. "Unfortunately, it was too late for warnings. The stuff was here, and in the possession of a Hardin Industries subsidiary."

I nodded as the light dawned. "Which means if someone decides to make an issue of it, Hardin is on the hook for the whole list of judgments and penalties."

"Exactly," McMicking said. "Obviously, the fact that Veldrick got it in implies the local Customs officials are pretty casual about that sort of thing. But there's no guarantee one of them might not suddenly get all virtuous and law-abiding."

"Especially now that someone like Hardin is sitting in the crosshairs?" I suggested.

McMicking shrugged slightly. "Mr. Hardin has his detractors," he said diplomatically. "Regardless, things obviously couldn't be allowed to remain as they were."

"So Mr. Hardin sent you here to destroy it?" Bayta asked.

"I wish it was that simple," McMicking said ruefully. "But you know Mr. Hardin. Well, *you* don't. But Frank does."

"All too well," I agreed. I'd briefly worked for Larry Hardin some months back, having been hired to find a way for him to take over the Quadrail system from the Spiders. Our relationship had ended abruptly when I told him it couldn't be done, and then proceeded to blackmail him out of a trillion dollars. The money had gone for a good cause, but Hardin didn't know that. "And I know Mr. Hardin didn't get to be a multitrillionaire by burning up valuable assets," I continued. "A cubic meter of Modhran coral represents, what, about half a million?"

"You're behind the times, friend," McMicking said. "Try about eight million."

I goggled. "*Dollars?*"

"Or more," McMicking said. "Between you drying up the supply on Modhra I and your friend Fayr busy blowing up the Bellidosh Estates-General's current supply, the price has gone through the roof."

"Hence, you?" I asked.

"Hence, me," McMicking agreed. "My job is to get the coral out of Veldrick's house, off the planet, onto the Quadrail, and to a buyer Mr. Hardin's trying to set up."

I exhaled loudly. "Terrific."

"I'm not any happier about it than you are," McMicking said grimly. "All alternative plans will be cheerfully considered. But any such plan absolutely has to start with getting Veldrick's coral off New Tigris."

"Understood," I said, frowning as I visualized Veldrick's meditation room. Something wasn't quite right here. "Well, the bad news is that he now knows—or suspects, anyway—that Hardin's about to lower the boom on him. You might have given me a heads-up on this before I left Manhattan."

"I would have if I'd known about it," McMicking said. "You remember me saying Mr. Hardin was about to give me a special assignment? This was it."

"So how did you get here ahead of me?" I asked. "I thought my shuttle and torchliner were the first ones out."

"Eight million dollars can make a man impatient," McMicking said with a touch of humor. "Mr. Hardin had a private shuttle and torchyacht waiting for me after my briefing. Much faster than commercial travel. I've actually been poking around here a couple of days now."

"Ah," I said. "At any rate, that's the bad news. The good

news is that he thinks Bayta and I are the ones here to do it. Ergo, he's going to be keeping his beady little eyes on us, not middle-aged joggers."

"Well, that's something, anyway," McMicking said.

"Unless someone reports we were together tonight," Bayta warned.

"Not a problem," McMicking assured her. "I won't be wearing this particular face again."

"Wait a second," I said as the nagging feeling suddenly fell into place. "You said Hardin's rep reported a cubic meter of coral?"

"About that, yes," McMicking confirmed.

"All in Veldrick's meditation room?"

"Again, yes," McMicking said. "Why?"

I grimaced. "Because at least a third of it isn't there any-more."

For a long moment McMicking stared at and through me, his eyes narrowed. "Interesting," he said at last, his voice casual. "So Mr. Veldrick's decided to be awkward about this. I don't suppose you were given a tour of the whole house?"

"No, just the great room, the meditation room, and the guest suite," I said. "But just shifting it around the house hardly seems worth the effort."

"But he did say Modhran coral helps grease the wheels of commercial enterprise," Bayta offered. "Maybe that means he's given out pieces as gifts."

"More likely as bribes," I said. "He also went out of his way to mention it worked especially well on non-Humans."

"Clever little man," McMicking mused. "A fair percentage of those offworlders will have diplomatic immunity. Even those who don't are probably covered by trade agreements that limit what local law enforcement can do to them."

"He was probably hoping to scatter most of his collection around Imani City before Hardin made his move," I said.

"With the expectation that he would get at least some of it back at a future date," McMicking agreed. "When his friends at Customs reported Frank Donaldson of Hardin Industries had arrived, he must have been rather annoyed."

"Hence, the invitation to visit his home and see if I reacted with the proper displeasure to his coral," I said. "I wonder what his next move will be."

McMicking's eyes flicked over my shoulder. "I think we're about to find out."

I turned around in my seat. Two Imani City policemen were striding through the restaurant toward us. "You armed?" I murmured to McMicking.

"Of course," he said. "But let's not be hasty."

They came to our table and stopped. "Mr. Frank Donaldson?" the taller one asked.

"Yes," I said. "Is there a problem?"

"I'm afraid so, sir, yes," the cop said. "I'm Sergeant Aksam; this is Officer Lasari. Would you mind coming with us, please?"

"Why?" I asked, making no move to get up.

Aksam glanced around at the restaurant's other patrons. Most of them, I noted, were staring back at us with the morbid fascination people always have for the objects of police interest. "I think this would be handled more pleasantly back at the station," he said, lowering his voice a bit.

"I doubt it," I said. "The seats here are really quite comfortable. Shall I ask the waiter to bring you a couple?"

His face darkened. "Fine," he growled, raising his voice back to its original level and then some. If I was going to insist on embarrassing myself in public, he was going to make sure I did it right. "Frank Donaldson, you're under suspicion of associating with known criminals. Now stand up, please."

"Which known criminals are these?" McMicking spoke up.

Aksam flashed him a look. "This doesn't concern you, sir," he said warningly.

"Oh, I think it does," McMicking said calmly, holding up an ID. "My name's Joseph Prescott. I'm Mr. Donaldson's legal advisor."

Years of playing poker against fellow Westali agents allowed me to keep my bland expression in place as McMicking's verbal grenade rolled into the center of the conversation. Beside me, Bayta stirred but didn't speak, and I had no doubt her own face was equally unreadable.

Aksam wasn't nearly that good. From the way his eyes momentarily widened I guessed that the last thing he'd expected on this little outing was to have to explain himself to a lawyer.

I was rather looking forward to this.

"Well?" McMicking prompted.

Aksam found his tongue. "Mr. Donaldson met this afternoon with a bartender in Zumurrud District named Usamah Karim," he said. "Mr. Karim has a criminal record."

"What sort of record?" McMicking asked. "Overcharging for stale pretzels? Watering the drinks?"

"Selling to minors and obstruction of justice," Aksam shot back.

"Really," McMicking said calmly. "What sort of obstruction?"

Aksam threw a hooded glance around the restaurant. Clearly, this wasn't going the way he'd expected it to. "Mr. Karim's record is not the issue here."

"On the contrary," McMicking said. "If Mr. Donaldson is accused of consorting with criminals, the criminality of the other person or persons is of paramount importance."

He looked sagely at me. "Furthermore, unless New Tigris has local ordinances with which I'm not familiar, the prohibition against association with criminals applies only to convicted felons or former felons still on parole. Does Mr. Donaldson have any such criminal record you're aware of?"

It was definitely not going the way Aksam had hoped. "I have my orders," he said stiffly. "*And* I have a warrant."

"Really." McMicking threw a significant glance at me. I caught the glance and lobbed it back again. If the cop had a viable warrant, he should have mentioned it long before now. "May I see it?"

Aksam looked at his partner, as if hoping for help or inspiration. But there was nothing there but more uncertainty and a clear wish to be left out of this battle. Reluctantly, the sergeant pulled a folded piece of paper from inside his pocket and handed it over.

McMicking unfolded it and ran his eyes down the fine print. I watched, wondering how much of his act was actual legal knowledge and how much was complete blown smoke. With McMicking, one could never be sure.

He took his time, going through the entire document. Aksam was starting to fidget by the time he finally looked up again. "I'm sorry," he said, handing back the warrant, "but this document is completely invalid."

"What are you talking about?" Aksam demanded, frowning at it. "It looks fine to me."

"The alleged crime is far too vague, with no dates or other specifications," McMicking told him. "Furthermore, the authorization signature is illegible, and the four referenced laws aren't tagged with their statute and subsection numbers. Any one of those would be enough to invalidate the entire document."

"It's the same format we always use," Aksam protested, still studying it.

"Which probably means it's never been seen by someone actually familiar with Confederation law," McMicking said. "Perhaps I should drop by the courthouse before I leave New Tigris and have a look at all your other document formats."

Aksam's cheeks tightened. He'd probably seen enough dit rec courtroom dramas to know that invalid documents could be grounds for appeal.

I had no idea whether that was actually true. But in my case, it didn't matter. McMicking's goal was clearly to buy us some time, and he'd already accomplished that.

"But thank you for dropping by," I spoke up. "Now that I know about Mr. Karim's record, I'll be sure to steer clear of him. Do you happen to have a list of other local criminals handy, in case I need to ask anyone for directions again?"

Aksam gave me a look that could kill mildew. But he still had one card left to play. "We'll be seeing you later, Mr. Donaldson," he promised menacingly. "In the meantime, I need to ask you to surrender your weapon."

"I have a valid carry permit," I reminded him.

"You *had* a valid carry permit," he countered. "As local

representative of Hardin Industries, Mr. Veldrick has just revoked it."

I frowned. "That's absurd. Mr. Veldrick isn't connected to
Hardin Industries."

"He's the local head of Crown Rosette, which is now a subsidiary of Hardin Industries," Aksam said. "That makes him
the local Hardin representative."

"Hardly," I said. "And certainly not for this. Even actual,
official Hardin managers have no authority over security personnel."

"You're welcome to come down to the courthouse and argue
your case," Aksam said. He had his hand resting on his own holstered sidearm now. "But until a judge rules on the question,
public safety overrides all such concerns. You *will* surrender your
weapon."

I looked at McMicking. He had a sour look on his face, but
he gave me a small nod. "Fine," I said, pulling out my Glock
and handing it over. "But I'm holding you personally respon-
sible for the safety of this weapon."

"Don't worry," Aksam said, taking the Glock and handing it
to Lasari, who tucked it into the back of his belt. "I understand you're staying at the Hanging Gardens?"

"That's right," I said. "Feel free to drop by when you have
a proper warrant for a proper crime." I raised my eyebrows.
"I'm sorry. *If* you ever have a proper warrant for a proper
crime."

A good dit rec detective would have had a sarcastic riposte
ready. But Aksam must have missed that day at cop school.
Sending a last glower at McMicking, he turned and stalked
out, his partner trailing silently behind him.

"So much for Veldrick's next move," I commented, taking a sip of my iced tea.

"Indeed," McMicking said, stroking his lip thoughtfully. "Offhand, I'd say he's getting ready to move out the rest of his coral."

"Going to be tricky," I said. "The stuff was pretty firmly mounted in his little artificial stream. At eight million dollars for the lot, it won't take much damage to start chewing up the potential profits."

"Better a smaller piece than having the whole pie snatched off your cooling rack," McMicking said. "And if he's making his move, it's about time we thought about making ours."

I looked around the restaurant. With the impromptu floor show over, the rest of the diners had returned to their meals and conversation. "You have a plan for getting to his coral?" I asked.

"I have three," McMicking said. "Unfortunately, all of them assumed only one house that would need to be burgled and several days with which to plan the operation."

"I guess we'll just have to improvise," I said.

He inclined his head. "I guess we will."

"But first we need to get Rebekah off New Tigris," Bayta put in suddenly.

I looked at her in surprise. "Yes, we'll do that," I assured her. "But Veldrick's coral—"

"It can wait," Bayta cut me off tartly. "Rebekah's in danger. We have to get her clear."

I looked at McMicking, saw my same puzzlement reflected there. "Is she in more danger than she was two hours ago?" I asked, looking back at Bayta.

"I don't know," she said. Her cheek and throat muscles were tight as she gazed pleadingly at me. "I just know that we have to get to her. Now."

I looked around the restaurant again. Bayta got worked up like this so seldom that it was always something of a shock.

But when it *did* happen, it was worth paying attention to. "Okay," I said slowly. "We can't make a move against the coral anyway until we know where Veldrick's got the other pieces stashed. McMicking can handle that while you and I sneak Rebekah out of hiding and through Customs onto our torchyacht."

I looked at McMicking. "By then, you should have the coral's locations nailed down. Rebekah and Bayta will lift off and head for the Tube, and I'll come back to town to help you with your burglaries."

"Sounds reasonable," McMicking said.

"Not to me it doesn't," Bayta said. "I don't know how to fly a torchyacht."

"You won't have to," I said. "With the minuscule traffic level around here, I should be able to set up a straight autolift while we're working the preflight. I'll also set your course for a low-speed, leisurely trip to the Tube, which will give McMicking and me plenty of time to catch up to you in his torchyacht. At that point I'll come aboard with you and Rebekah and fly us the rest of the way."

"Of course, we'll also have to deal with Customs once we reach the transfer station," McMicking warned. "They'll certainly have been alerted to the coral theft by the time we get there."

"I'm sure you already have a plan for that part," I said.

McMicking shrugged. "Any suggestions as to how I go about finding the rest of Veldrick's coral?"

"There are a couple of options," I said. "How are your computer hacking skills these days?"

"Adequate."

"Good," I said. "Option one: hack into the Crown Rosette computer system. See who Veldrick's been doing business with since the Hardin rep noticed his coral three months ago."

"Paying special attention to the non-Humans on the list," McMicking said, nodding his understanding.

"Exactly," I said. "That should give you the most likely recipients. Once you've got that, hack into the city's utilities system and find out which of them had their water bills shoot up recently."

McMicking frowned. "Their *water* bills?"

"Modhran coral does best with cold water flowing around it," Bayta told him.

"Right," I said. "For anything long-term you'd normally hook up a closed system to cool and recycle the same water. But I doubt Veldrick's buddies had such gadgetry available."

"And even if they put something together later, there should still be a temporary spike in their water usage," McMicking said. "Sounds promising."

"Option two is we break in on Veldrick and beat the snot out of him until he gives us names and addresses," I said. "We should probably keep that one in reserve."

"Probably," McMicking agreed. "Sounds like a plan. Are you going to need anything from me before I head back to the hotel and get started?"

"Just your comm number," I said. "We'll want to keep in

touch on each other's progress." I cocked my head. "I presume you already have my number?"

"Of course," he said, and gave me his. "You might also need this," he added, shifting slightly in his seat.

Something hard settled onto my lap under the table. I reached down and found myself touching a small handgun. "I might, indeed," I said. "Thanks."

"No problem," he said. "Dual clip; left side is snoozers." Pushing back his chair, he stood up. "Good hunting."

"And to you," I said, slipping the gun into my holster. "I take it I'm paying for dinner?"

"Of course." He gave me a faint smile. "You ever hear of a lawyer who picked up his client's tab? Good hunting to you."

"And to you," I said.

He left. I paid with one of my cash sticks, and then Bayta and I also headed out into the streets. "Is this sudden-danger thing connected with how you knew where she was?" I asked her as we walked.

She shook her head. "I don't know."

"Just a hunch, then?"

She bristled. "*You* have hunches all the time."

She had me there. "Fine," I said, looking around. Night had fallen with a resounding crash while we'd been eating, leaving the sky a star-freckled black above us. But the streetlights were going strong, wrapping Imani City in a deceptively nice homey glow. "Any other thoughts or speculations you'd like to share with the rest of the class?"

A shiver ran through her. "Only that there's something wrong here," she said, her voice graveyard dark. "The Modhri truce—Mr. Veldrick—the coral. It doesn't add up."

"I know," I said grimly. "Let's just hope we can figure it out before we're up to our necks in trouble."

"Or even deeper?"

"Or even deeper," I said. I hated it when she came up with mental images like that. "Come on, let's find an autocab."

EIGHT

This time we had no problem flagging down an autocab.
Apparently, they did most of their grid-roving after dark.

With Veldrick's habit of sifting through autocab records in
mind, I directed the vehicle to an address in Makarr District,
one district over from Zumurrud. When we arrived, I paid the
tab, then doubled the amount and sent the autocab back to the
Hanging Gardens.

It disappeared around the corner, and Bayta and I headed off
on foot for Zumurrud District and Karim's bar.

Makarr, which seemed to be mostly residential, was pretty
quiet tonight. Zumurrud, in contrast, was hopping. The populace was out in force, most of them young, most of them angry
or frustrated-looking, nearly all of them drinking. Judging by
the buzz of conversation leaking out their open doors, the
taverns and gaming rooms were doing a brisk business. So

were the street corners and doorways where we'd seen the kids congregating earlier in the day.

Fortunately, none of the simmering anger beneath the hard drinking seemed directed specifically at the two strangers walking through their midst. Still, we collected our share of curious glances and suspicious glares. Occasionally, I saw one of the youths who'd seen us that afternoon nudge one of his buddies and mutter something under his breath.

Twice, outside the entrances of particularly boisterous taverns, a group of thrill-seekers looked as if they were considering stepping into our path. Both times, I slipped my hand quietly but pointedly beneath my jacket and got a grip on the Beretta that McMicking had given me. The would-be toughs spotted the gun, got the message, and backed off.

The street with Karim's bar was as busy as the rest of the district. Unlike the rest of the neighborhood, though, this particular block came equipped with quiet sentries. The four teens I'd had my brief run-in with had now become two pairs, one set standing casual guard at either end of the block.

The closer pair spotted us as we approached. One of the teens was Oved, the boy I'd had the staged tussle with earlier. He gave us a microscopic nod of acknowledgment as we approached while his partner wandered off toward a quiet alleyway, comm in hand, presumably to call Karim with the news of our arrival.

Behind Oved's grim expression, I noted as we passed, his eyes showed the slight puffiness of recent tears. Karim must have told him Lorelei was dead.

The bar was doing brisk business tonight. I spotted Karim

in the back by the bar, pretending to watch the bartender making the drinks. He caught my eye as we came in and nodded sideways toward the office door.

I glanced over the clientele as Bayta and I headed back. They were for the most part older men, most of them displaying the same simmering frustration that I'd seen in the more teen-intensive parts of the district.

I wondered if there were any police informants among them.

The office was dark except for a small writing light that didn't illuminate much beyond the center of the desk. I closed and locked the door behind us and headed for the hidden trapdoor. "Shouldn't we wait for Mr. Karim?" Bayta asked as I pushed the desk chair out of the way.

"Why?" I asked. "We know how to get in."

"Rebekah might be more comfortable if he came in with us," she said, a little crossly.

I looked up at her. "Would she?" I asked.

Bayta's lips compressed briefly. "I don't know. I just thought . . ." She trailed off.

Another hunch? "Okay, fine," I said, straightening up. "We wait for Karim."

I was only going to give the man two minutes to show before I headed down without him. Fortunately, less than half that time elapsed before there was the click of a disengaging lock and Karim slipped into the office.

"Were you followed?" he asked as he relocked the door behind him.

"Ask your sentries," I said. "They're the ones who know who belongs here and who doesn't."

He grunted as he stepped past me and stooped down to tackle the hidden door. "Anyway, I'm glad you're here," he said. "I think something's happened. Rebekah is frightened. *Really* frightened."

"Did you ask her why?"

"She wouldn't tell me." He looked pointedly up at me. "But she wasn't like this until after you left this afternoon."

"A lot of things happen in a city this size over the course of a few hours," I reminded him. "Not all of them have anything to do with us."

"True," he agreed. But his eyes lingered on my face another moment before he returned his attention to the trapdoor.

A few seconds later, he had it open. "I'll go first," he said.

"No, you'll stay here," I told him. "If there's trouble, we'll need someone to lock down the door."

He snorted. "A futile gesture," he scoffed. "Others will have seen you come in here."

"And tearing the place up while they look for the rabbit hole will take time," I countered. "Time is always a good thing to have."

Again, his eyes searched my face. "As you wish," he said. Stepping away from the shaft, he gestured me toward it.

"Thank you." I gestured in turn to Bayta. "After you."

Silently, she got her feet on the ladder and started down. With one final look at Karim, I followed.

We passed through the curtain and into the hidden room. Rebekah was again sitting cross-legged on the bed, just as she'd been the last time I was here.

Karim was right. In the past few hours something had

definitely happened to the girl. Her face was drawn and even paler than it had been earlier. Her shoulders were hunched, and her throat was tight. "Hello, Rebekah," I greeted her cautiously.

"Hello, Mr. Compton," she said. Speaking to me, but with her eyes locked on Bayta.

I looked at Bayta. Her eyes were locked just as tightly on Rebekah. "This is Bayta," I said, looking back at Rebekah. "You asked about her earlier."

"Yes," Rebekah said, an odd breathiness in her voice. "I'm . . . honored . . . Ms. Bayta."

"Just Bayta," Bayta told her. She had some of Rebekah's same breathiness in her voice, too. "We've come to get you out of here."

To my surprise, a pair of tears trickled down Rebekah's cheeks. "It's too late," she whispered. "I can't go."

"Of course you can," I said, taking a step toward her. "If you're too weak to handle the ladder—"

"Don't *touch* me!" she snapped with sudden fire.

I braked to an abrupt halt. For a second there a real live scared ten-year-old had peeked out through all that unnatural maturity I'd seen in her earlier. "Sure," I soothed, searching her face for some clue to her reaction. "Do you need me to carry you out?" I asked.

"No," she said. "I told you, I can't go. I can't move. If I do, he'll know where I am."

An unpleasant tingle went up my back. "You mean the Modhri?"

She closed her eyes. "Yes."

I touched Bayta's arm, nodded back over my shoulder. Together, we backed out of the room into the passageway, stopping at the curtain. "Okay, I give up," I murmured. "What the *hell* is going on?"

"I don't know," Bayta said, her eyes focused on something about five-sixths of the way to infinity. "But I think she's telling the truth."

"I'm so glad to hear it," I growled. "Are you saying the Modhri's developed his own psychic radar now?"

"It's not radar," Bayta said. "I don't know what it is. But she *is* in danger, Frank."

"Why?" I demanded. "What can possibly be so important about a lone ten-year-old girl? I mean, this isn't—"

"It isn't what?" Bayta asked.

"Never mind," I growled. I'd been about to tell her this simply wasn't how the Modhri did things.

But how the hell did *I* know how the Modhri did things? I didn't even understand how this whole group mind thing worked, let alone what kind of alien thoughts or motivations he might have.

I took a deep breath. Fine. Western Alliance Intelligence had trained me to be a detective. It was about time I did some detecting.

Assume Karim was right, that something new and critical had happened sometime in the past four hours. What could that something be?

Bayta and I had visited Rebekah. We'd been hauled away for a visit to Veldrick. We'd run across McMicking and had dinner with him. Veldrick had tried to have me thrown into jail for a few hours, possibly because he was trying to move more of his coral.

Trying to move more of his coral . . .

"Bayta, we were talking at dinner about telepathic overlap between the Modhri and Humans," I said. "Presumably, Humans can't sense the Modhri—or vice versa—any better than you and the Spiders can. Right?"

"I assume so, yes," she said. "There's certainly never been a case I've heard of where the Modhri and any species had that kind of communication."

"Okay," I said. "But what if the Human in question was herself telepathic?"

Bayta's eyes flicked back toward the room. "*Rebekah?*"

"Why not?" I said. "*You* seem able to sense her, at least well enough to know when she's four meters under your feet. And it's starting to sound like she and the Modhri can sense each other, too."

"Except that Humans aren't telepathic," she said tartly. "I'm not aware of a single documented exception."

"Okay, so that's a soft spot in the theory," I conceded. "But there's a first time for everything. Maybe there's something in the air or water here that switched on a gene."

She shook her head. "There must be a more reasonable explanation."

"Like what?" I asked. "She's afraid the Modhri will detect her if she moves. He's not seeing, hearing, or smelling her." I cocked an eyebrow. "For that matter, neither were *you* earlier today."

Her lip twitched. "Let's assume you're right," she said. "What do we do about it?"

"I'll show you." I pulled out my comm and punched in

McMicking's number. "It's me," I said when he answered. "How's the analysis going?"

"I've got a list of Veldrick's alien contacts," he said. "The hacker program's still working on the city's utilities records."

"Any of the alien data jumping out at you?"

"One bit is, yes," he said. "A group of six Filiaelians showed up on New Tigris about six weeks ago. Since then, they've done some very impressive business with Veldrick."

"How impressive?"

"About ten times that of any other Crown Rosette customer," McMicking said.

I chewed my lip. And Veldrick *had* rather bragged about how gifts of his coral had helped with his business contacts. "Forget everyone else for the moment," I told McMicking. "Concentrate on the Fillies."

There was a short pause. "You once told me the Modhri hadn't penetrated the Filiaelian Assembly," he reminded me.

"That was the information I was given," I confirmed. "It may turn out to have been incorrect. It could also turn out that the Fillies are innocent pawns in the Modhri's scheme."

There was another pause, a longer one this time. "All right," he said at last. "If you're sure you want to start poking sticks that direction."

It was an oddly squeamish comment for a man of McMicking's history and reputation. But I didn't really blame him. The Filiaelian Assembly filled a significant fraction of the far end of the galaxy, with colonized worlds and systems reputed to number in the thousands.

That all by itself put them at the top of the social and economic food chain. Add to that their utter alienness, plus their habit of casual genetic manipulation of their own kind, and you had a group of horse-faced, satin-skinned people you did *not* want to irritate or offend. "We go where the trail leads," I said. "Right now, it's leading to those six Fillies."

"All right," he said again. "But unless there's something solid—"

"Hold it," I interrupted. The curtain beside me had rippled slightly, as if catching a puff of air from the other side.

"Mr. Compton?" Karim's voice stage-whispered from the direction of the shaft. "Mr. Compton?"

"I'll call you back," I murmured to McMicking, and broke the connection. "Stay here," I added to Bayta, pulling the *kwi* out of my pocket and pressing it into her hand. Drawing my Beretta, I slipped past the curtain into the passageway.

I reached the shaft just as Karim made it to the bottom. "There you are," he said. Even in the dim light I could see that his face was pale. "Did you see any police officers on your way in here tonight?"

"No," I said. "Are there police officers out there now?"

He swallowed visibly. "Come and see."

Oved was waiting on the walkway when Karim and I emerged from the tavern. His face was even paler than Karim's. "Over there," he said, pointing toward a service alley leading away into the shadows on the opposite side of the street.

I frowned as I peered down it. The alley itself was unlit, but there was enough backwash from the streetlights and store-fronts that I could just make out the outline of a car halfway back facing my direction. It was hard to tell, but it looked like two men were sitting in the front seat.

Sitting with unnatural stillness.

I looked back at Oved. The boy was trembling slightly, I noticed now. Probably the first time he'd ever seen death up close. "Stay here," I told him and Karim, and headed across the street.

No one attacked me as I approached the car. No one jumped from the shadows, either, yelling bloody murder and pointing accusing fingers in my direction. Whatever had happened here, the goal hadn't been to either lure me in or to frame me. I reached the car and looked in.

The two cops were sprawled slightly in their seats. Not like men who'd been killed where they sat, but rather who'd been killed outside the vehicle and then shoved back in.

There was a marked difference in their expressions, though. Sergeant Aksam looked almost serene, as if death had caught him completely unawares. Officer Lasari, in contrast, had a startled expression frozen on his face.

The cause of death in both cases was probably connected to the wide bloodstains in the centers of their chests.

I studied them from outside the car for a minute, taking in their expressions, positioning, and everything else I could see. Then, using a handkerchief to keep from smudging any fingerprints the killer might have left behind, I opened the driver's-side door.

From the lack of any mention of shots, I had already concluded the bloodstains were the result of stab wounds. Gingerly opening Aksam's shirt, I found my assumption was correct. But it was an odd wound, triangular with smaller tears coming off two of the three corners.

I frowned at the mark for a moment, my brain sifting through mental images as I tried to come up with something that could make a puncture like this.

And then, it clicked. Leaving Aksam's door open, I pulled out my comm and punched in McMicking's number.

The connection clicked. "Is something wrong?" McMicking asked.

"Pretty much *everything's* wrong," I said grimly. "I'm standing beside a car with a couple of dead cops in it. The same two cops, interestingly enough, who tried to spoil our dinner earlier."

"In front of a dozen witnesses," McMicking said. "I hope they weren't shot with your gun."

"No, our murderer was a little more creative than that," I said. "It looks like Aksam and Lasari were stabbed with a Filly contract pen."

I could hear his frown right over the comm. "That makes no sense," he said. "Contract pen ink is genetically linked to its owner. He might as well have left family photos at the scene."

"Which implies the murderer didn't care if he got caught," I said. "Which strongly implies in turn that our information about the Modhri and Fillies not working and playing well together is indeed out of date."

"Indeed," he agreed heavily. "You have a read?"

I looked back down the alley. In general, hanging around a murder scene wasn't the brightest thing a person could do.

On the other hand, I had more privacy here than I was likely to get anywhere else in the neighborhood at the moment. "The killer probably approached the car from the front, from near the tavern I told you about earlier," I said. "Both cops appear to have had time to get out to meet him. He approached them, probably asking for directions or some such, and when he was close enough he stabbed Sergeant Aksam. He then pulled the pen out of Aksam's chest and threw it across the hood into Officer Lasari's."

"Either man draw his sidearm?"

"That's a little hard to tell," I said. "Both their sidearms are missing."

He hissed into the comm. "Wonderful," he said. "You're sure the contract pen was thrown into the second vic?"

"Reasonably sure," I said. "Lasari's wound has the slightly ragged edges of a thrown weapon."

"Which may mean only one of the Fillies is a walker," he suggested. "It would have been safer to send in a pair of them, if he had a pair to work with."

"Possibly," I said. "I wouldn't bet the mortgage on it, though. Anyway, our murderer then shoved the bodies back into the car, retrieved his pen and their guns, and left."

"Any thoughts as to motive?"

"Oh, yes," I said sourly. I leaned back into the car and used my handkerchief to pick up the document sitting on the center console's fax. "They have a warrant here for the arrest of one Frank Abram Donaldson. A new one, with all the proper legal bells and whistles in place."

"That's handy," McMicking said heavily. "I hope you haven't left any evidence behind."

"It's pretty impossible not to leave *something* behind these days," I said. "But I haven't left anything they'll find without a detailed scan and sift. Besides, the pen residue should pretty well prove the killer was Filiaelian."

"No, it only proves the killing *weapon* was Filiaelian," he countered. "You could easily have stolen it from one of these six upstanding citizens."

"There's that," I conceded. "On the other hand, I could argue that neither of these cops would have just let me walk up to them this way."

"Try persuading an arraignment judge of that," McMicking said. "This doesn't make any sense. First the Modhri gives you free rein to track down this Abomination, whatever it is. Then he tries to get you thrown in jail, and now he kills a pair of cops so that they *can't* throw you in jail? How schizoid *is* this Modhri, anyway?"

"As schizoid as only a million different mind segments can get," I said. "But in this case, that's not the problem. I think what we have here is two entirely different entities working at cross-purposes to each other."

"The Modhri and who else?"

"Veldrick," I said. "*His* only concern is to keep Frank Donaldson and Hardin Industries from taking his precious coral away from him. He's almost certainly the one who tried to get me arrested earlier, and probably the one who then pushed for this new warrant. It's the Modhri, through his Filly walkers, who killed the cops."

"But why?" McMicking persisted.

"Because he needs me free to persuade Rebekah to come out of hiding. Any progress on the water records yet?"

"Yes," he said. "There aren't any unexplained spikes."

I frowned. "*None?*"

"None," he confirmed. "Not with the six Fillies, not with anyone else."

"That's impossible," I insisted. "We *know* Veldrick gave away chunks of his coral."

"Maybe the Fillies just dumped the coral in their fish tanks," McMicking suggested. "The coral doesn't need the water to be flowing, does it?"

"Not over the short haul," I said. "But after a while it starts going dormant if it doesn't have flow or at least some tidal fluctuation. It's sure not going to be at its best and brightest sitting in a fish tank."

"Maybe it didn't need its best and brightest to track down a ten-year-old girl."

And then, suddenly, it hit me. "Or else it needed to be mobile," I said. "Do you have access to car purchase or rental records?"

"I've got the city's licensing data," he said. "Looks like . . . huh. All six Fillies have rental cars."

"Do you have the locations of their parking spot?"

"They don't have parking permits here," McMicking said. "But the cars *do* all have locators. Let me pull up a map for you."

I pulled out my reader and keyed for a download. "Ready when you are."

"Here it comes," he said. "You haven't explained yet why the Modhri wants Veldrick to pass around pieces of his coral. Assuming the Modhri *has* a reason."

"Absolutely," I said, looking at the city map he'd just sent. One glance at the current positions of the Fillies' cars was all I needed. "Take a look at the placement of the Fillies' cars. Remind you of anything?"

"You mean like your basic more-or-less circle?"

"Exactly," I said. "Now think back to the search and surveillance classes you took back in your Marine days."

There was another pause. "I'll be damned," he breathed. "A *detector array*?"

"Sure looks like one to me," I said. "And, you'll note, currently centered squarely on Karim's tavern."

"Meaning what?"

"Meaning—I think—that our young friend Rebekah is a telepath," I said. "And that she's broadcasting on a frequency the Modhri can pick up."

"Wonderful," he growled. "And the Fillies? Just along to add cultural weight to the whole thing?"

"Or else it only works with a coral-plus-Filly combination," I said. "Probably Fillies genetically engineered nine ways from Sunday, come to think of it. There certainly would be no reason to drag in aliens from the other end of the galaxy if Halkan or Jurian walkers would work as well. Regardless, bottom line is that we need to eliminate or move either the coral or the Fillies before we can move Rebekah."

McMicking grunted. "The whole thing's crazy," he declared. "But that seems to be about par for this course. What's the plan?"

"Like I said, we have to take out the coral or the Fillies or both," I said. "And we might as well start with Veldrick's stash. Get yourself over to his house and figure out the best way in. I'll meet you there as soon as I can. Don't start the party without me."

"What about the bodies?"

I looked into the car. Ideally, I would have preferred to move the whole mess a few kilometers away from Rebekah's hiding place. But I didn't have the time or equipment to pull that off without leaving bits of my DNA everywhere. Not to mention the instant trouble I'd be in if someone caught me driving a car with two dead cops in it. "We leave them here," I told McMicking. "There's no time for anything else."

"All right," he said. "I'll see you soon. Watch yourself."

"You too."

I broke the connection and put my comm away. I started to close the door, then had a sudden thought. Reaching past Aksam, I forced my hand gingerly behind Officer Lasari's back.

The Glock they'd taken from me earlier was gone.

Gently closing the car door, I headed back down the alley. It was, I reflected, just as well that Bayta and I had had a good dinner. It looked like it was going to be a very long night.

NINE :

Bayta wasn't at all happy with the plan. Neither was Karim. But they weren't in charge here. I gave them their orders, borrowed the keys to Karim's car, and headed out.

The garage behind the building where the car was parked was double-locked. Inside, the car itself was literally chained to the concrete floor. Apparently, auto theft was a major problem in Zumurrud District. Even with all the keys it took me a good ten minutes to get the car ready to go.

Maneuvering my way through streets filled with drunks and loiterers was the next challenge, and it cost me another ten minutes. But there was nothing I could do except ease my way forward through the wandering pedestrians and keep an eye out for drunk drivers. Finally, I was out of Zumurrud and back into the relative calm of Makarr. I picked up speed and headed for Veldrick's upscale neighborhood.

All seemed quiet as I pulled into Veldrick's street. I parked a block from his house and went the rest of the way on foot. Things here were even quieter than they had been in Makarr District. Imani City's rich and powerful were apparently finding their evening's entertainment in the comfort of their own homes.

Veldrick's house was well lit, with lights showing through the curtains in both the great room and one of the back rooms. I eyed the shrubbery and nearby buildings as I approached, but McMicking was nowhere in sight. Strolling past the house like an innocent pedestrian, I keyed my comm.

"Yes?" McMicking answered.

"I'm here," I said. "Where are you?"

"Inside," he said. "Hang on—I'll unlock the front door for you."

He keyed off. Muttering a curse, I reversed direction and went back to the house.

The front door opened as I approached. "About time," McMicking commented in greeting. The middle-aged jogger Bayta and I had had dinner with had been replaced by an elderly Oriental man with a small goatee and hair gathered high on the back of his head. "What did you do, walk the whole way?"

"I had to run the Zumurrud obstacle course," I growled as I brushed past him. "I thought I told you to wait for me."

"I'm on Mr. Hardin's clock here, not yours," he pointed out reasonably as he locked the door behind me. "Come on in and give me a hand."

I walked into the meditation room to find a half-dozen small Quadrail-style cargo crates lined up near Veldrick's artificial stream. On top of one of them were a pair of thick, elbow-length leather gloves. "Where did you get the crates?" I asked.

"Veldrick's storage room," McMicking told me, crossing to the boxes and pulling on the gloves. "I figured that however he moved the stuff in he would probably have kept the transport boxes. Turns out I was right."

"It'll certainly make it easier to move it back out again," I agreed, frowning. Something was nagging urgently at the back of my mind. "You have a story ready in case Veldrick walks in on us?"

"Veldrick won't be walking in on anyone for a while," McMicking said. "He's sleeping off a snoozer in the master bedroom."

"You have any trouble getting in past the alarms?"

"Not a bit," he said. "I shot him as he opened the door for me."

I stared at him. "You knocked on the *door*?"

"Actually, I rang the bell." He gave me an innocent look. "You worried he's going to describe his assailant to the police when he wakes up?"

"That would be amusing," I growled, eyeing his *Seven Samurai* look. "How long have you been here?"

"Here in the house? About twenty minutes."

I frowned. "You made it all the way from downtown that fast?"

"Who says I started from downtown?" he asked, reaching into the flowing stream and working at a piece of coral. "It's as easy to tap into a computer system from one neighborhood as another."

"So you came here directly from the restaurant?" I asked.

The urgent nagging in the back of my mind was getting stronger.

"More or less," he said, lifting out the coral and holding it gingerly at arm's length. "I did have to stop once along the way to change faces. You want to open that first crate for me?"

I moved toward the crate, staring at the coral. He'd been here twenty minutes . . .

And suddenly, the nagging in my mind blew into full-fledged certainty. "You know, these crates are going to be a bear to get out of here," I remarked, keeping my voice casual. "I've got some smaller ones in my car that we won't need a forklift to move."

Behind his makeup, McMicking's forehead creased slightly. "You have a car?"

"A borrowed one, yes," I said. "Smaller boxes will be easier to get through Customs, too."

"You may be right." He set the coral back into the flowing water, his eyes never leaving my face. "Where are you parked?"

"Two blocks away," I said, nodding the opposite direction to where I'd actually left the car. "Come on—you might as well give me a hand with them."

A minute later we were outside the house. "This way," I said, heading off at a fast walk toward my car. "Hurry."

"What's going on?" McMicking murmured as he caught up with me.

"Bayta once told me the polyps in Modhran coral could detect and interpret vibrations when they were underwater," I said. "In other words, the coral can hear."

"Yes, I remember her saying that," McMicking said. "So?"

"So you've been in the house for twenty minutes, getting

ready to carve up the coral," I gritted out. "Not just attacking a major Modhran outpost, but also ruining his detector array. *So why haven't the Filly walkers shown up in force to stop you?*"

"Oh, hell," McMicking said, his voice soft but deadly.

"You got it," I said bitterly. "He doesn't need the array anymore.

"He's found Rebekah."

Ninety seconds later, we were in the car, barreling down Imani City's peaceful streets toward Zumurrud District.

"She says they're all right," McMicking said, his comm still at his ear as I took a corner way faster than either the laws of man or physics would have preferred. By a miracle of engineering, the car stayed on the pavement. "She can hear a lot of commotion going on in the bar, but so far no one's come poking around Karim's office."

I didn't answer, my stomach knotted with fury at my stupidity, my mind fogged with images of Bayta standing alone against the full strength of the Modhri.

"How did he figure it out?" McMicking asked.

"He didn't figure it out," I snarled. "I *told* him."

"How?"

No gasps of surprise, no blank stares, no time wasted with recriminations. Sometimes I forgot what it was like having a fellow professional like McMicking at my side.

And that reminder loosened the knots in my stomach a little. Together, we might still have a chance. "Because I was stupid," I told him. "I even *said* he was putting the damn coral in cars."

"You mean he had some in the police car?"

"Can you think of a better way to keep the local kids from taking it out for a spin than to stash it with a couple of dead cops?" I bit out. "It's either in the trunk or just sitting on the ground underneath the car. I never thought to look either place."

"I thought he also needed a Filly nearby to make this trick work," McMicking said.

"This particular chunk wasn't part of the tracking array," I said, a fresh wave of self-disgust washing over me. "It was put there to eavesdrop when I went to investigate the bodies. And I fell for it. I stood there feeling all safe and secure and unobserved and blabbed my stupid mouth off."

McMicking was silent for a few more blocks. "If you're right about the Modhri eavesdropping on you, he knew I was heading over to Veldrick's," he said at last. "But he *didn't* know what I was going to do to the coral once I got there."

"You're taking it home to Daddy, aren't you?"

"You miss my point," he said. "You and I know that, but the Modhri didn't. Neither of us said anything about it in that conversation, or any other he might have listened in on. For all he knew, I was going to bring a sledgehammer and beat him to death."

He drew his gun and laid it ready on his lap. "But the Fillies still didn't show up," he continued. "That means he was willing to sacrifice an entire coral outpost if necessary in order to get at this girl."

Which was pretty much the same deal he'd offered me a couple of months ago, with those boxes of coral on the train from Ghonsilya to Bildim. He'd been willing to sacrifice all that in order to get his hands on the third Lynx sculpture.

I knew now why he'd considered that trade worth making. What the hell was Rebekah to him that he was offering to make the same trade for her?

I had no idea. I just hoped we would all live long enough to find out.

At first glance Karim's block looked pretty much the way I'd left it. There were still drunks and toughs all over the place, making navigation hazardous as they wandered onto and off of the street.

But on second glance I could see that something about the scene had changed. A lot of the drunks weren't wandering anymore, but were just lying or sitting along the sides of the buildings. Passed out, or else on their way there.

McMicking noticed it, too. "They crash and burn early around here, don't they?" he commented.

"Hardly seems worth the effort of going out," I agreed as I let the car roll quietly to a halt by the curb half a block from the bar. "Snoozers, you think?"

"That would be the simplest conclusion," he said. "But bystanders normally don't hang around when that much shooting starts."

A movement across the street to our left caught my eye, and I looked over to see Oved emerge from a doorway and hurry toward us. "Stay here," I told McMicking, and got out.

"Thank God you're back," Oved murmured tightly as we met in the middle of the street. "They're in there now—six of them—handing out drinks like—"

"Hold it, hold it," I interrupted. "Who is in where?"

"Six Filiaelians are in the bar," he said, stumbling a little over the name. "They came in right after you left and sat down at a couple of the tables. They're offering free drinks to anyone who can beat them at arm wrestling."

I looked toward the bar and the sleeping men piled along the walkway around it. "I gather they've been doing a lot of losing?"

"Yes," Oved said, sounding a little mystified that I'd come to that conclusion so fast. "I don't know what's in those bottles they brought, but one shot and you're done for."

"Dark brown bottle?" I asked. "Triangular base with a short, wide, corkscrew-shaped neck?"

"Yes," he confirmed. "They must have a dozen of them, packed away in wraparound belt bags. But it can't be poison—they're drinking it themselves."

"It's not poison," I said. "It's *dilivin*. A classic Filly drink never intended for Human stomachs. Where's Karim?"

"Behind the bar," the boy said. "Standing on the door to the storage cellar. The main storage cellar, I mean. Not the one—you know. He told me to come out here and wait for you."

I nodded with approval. If the Modhri had figured out Rebekah was underground, he would reasonably assume she was in the cellar. Karim standing defiantly on the access door would add weight to that conclusion, which in turn should have the Modhri working on a way to get him off it.

But even the Modhri wasn't crazy enough to take on an entire bar's worth of Humans with only six Fillies. Hence, the rigged drinking contest to thin out the crowd. "Okay, I'll handle it," I told Oved, and headed back to the car. I would go in alone, I decided, and have McMicking find a nice shadow to hide in as backup. Bending down, I looked into the car.

McMicking was gone.

I straightened up, looking around as I silently cursed the man. But he was nowhere to be seen.

"What is it?" Oved called softly.

"Nothing," I said, turning back toward the bar. The least McMicking could have done was wait for my instructions before deciding to ignore them. "Stay here."

The tavern had been reasonably full before I left for Veldrick's place. Now, it was even more crowded, with wall-to-wall people laughing and hooting and generally enjoying themselves at the tops of their lungs. Clearly, word had traveled about the strangers in town providing free entertainment and free firewater.

Both of which were still going strong. Peering through a narrow gap between the bystanders, I saw two Fillies and a burly middle-aged Human seated at a table in the center of the main room. The Human was arm-wrestling one of the Fillies while the other alien looked on, a *dilivin* bottle and set of shot glasses neatly lined up on the table in front of him. Both Fillies, I noted, had turned their chairs around and were seated on their knees and shins in normal Filly style.

Behind the Human, a third Filly and two more Humans stood watching the action. One of the Humans was holding a notebook and pen, the other was cupping a fist full of coins. Apparently, book was being made on the various contests. All three Fillies were wearing the distinctive layered tunics and flared hats that always reminded me of Genghis Khan's thirteenth-century Mongolian warriors.

Fastened around their waists at their backs were the belt bags Oved had mentioned, five bags per Filly, each long enough to hold a *dilivin* bottle. Clearly, they'd come prepared to make a night of it.

The rest of the tables had been pushed back, leaving a small open area around the main event. I pushed my way through the rows of spectators, ignoring the growls and complaints that followed me, until I reached the inner edge. Just as I eased between the last two men the Human slammed his opponent's hand to the table. Through the mixed roar of triumph from the winning bettors and groans of disgust from the losers, I gave the room a careful scan.

Three of the Fillies, as I'd already noted, were standing prominently in the center of the room. The other three Oved had mentioned were nowhere to be seen.

Were they even now with Bayta and Rebekah?

"There you are," a throaty voice said.

I looked back at the table. All three Fillies had turned in my direction and were gazing at me down their long faces in a way that reminded me of an old man in a dit rec drama peering at fine print through the reading section of his bifocals.

They were definitely Filiaelians. No one else in the galaxy looked even remotely like that. And yet, as I studied the somewhat shorter lengths of their faces, the shapes of their scalloped ears, and the colors of their bristly facial hairs, I was struck more by the differences between them and Filiaelian norm than by their similarities to that standard.

And if there were that many differences showing on the outside, there were probably even more drastic changes on the inside. Clearly, someone had done some serious genetic work on them.

But for this bunch, altered DNA was the least of their problems. As I looked more closely, I could see the slightly unfocused eyes and slackened jaws and the minor darkening of the distinctive blaze marks on their long faces. Changes that had taken place sometime since I'd first seen them thirty seconds ago.

The Modhri had taken over.

"Here I am," I agreed. "Question is, what are *you* doing here?"

The two Fillies seated at the table reached behind them into their belt bags, each producing two more *dilivin* bottles. "For all," the losing arm wrestler said, reaching behind him to hand his bottles to two of the men in the crowd. "Enjoy to the fullest."

There was a fresh roar of appreciation as the second Filly passed his bottles off to his side of the ring. With the free entertainment over, but an even better deal on the free firewater, the audience broke up, the onlookers redistributing themselves into new groups centered around the four bottles.

I waited until their attention was firmly elsewhere, then closed the last couple of meters to the Fillies' table. The winning Human arm wrestler had also joined the rest of the crowd, leaving the half-full *dilivin* bottle behind. "I repeat, what are you doing here?" I asked the Fillies, keeping my voice low.

"A strange question," the Filly still standing said, peering down his long face and comet-shaped blaze at me. "Surely you know we're here to destroy the Abomination."

"That wasn't the deal we made at Yandro," I insisted. "Or aren't you in the loop yet on that?"

"I'm aware of the agreement," Comet Nose said gravely. "I'm also aware of how badly you've kept other such agreements in the past."

Unfortunately, he had a point. "So what exactly are you planning to do?" I asked.

Comet Nose flipped his head. "I?" he asked, stepping right up to me and resting his hand on my shoulder in classic the-car-salesman-is-your-friend fashion. "*I* will do nothing." He slid his hand off my shoulder and down the front of my jacket.

As he did so, I felt him slip something into my outer jacket pocket. I reached up a hand to see what he'd put there—

"*Everyone freeze!*" a Human voice snapped from behind me.

Instantly, the bar went silent. Keeping my hands motionless, I carefully turned my head.

There were six cops spread out around the wall by the door. All six had their guns out.

All six guns were pointed at me.

I took a deep breath. "Is there a problem, Officer?" I called.

"Stay exactly where you are, Donaldson," one of the cops ordered. "You—everyone else—get up and move calmly out of the way. *Calmly,* I said."

I turned back to Comet Nose. "Neatly done," I murmured. "I presume that was the murder weapon you just put into my pocket?"

"Correct," he said. "You now have two choices, Mr. Compton. You may refuse to give up the Abomination, whereupon the officers will take you to prison. They will examine the contract pen in your pocket and discover traces of Human blood on it."

"That would probably be bad," I agreed. "What's option number two?"

"You give up the Abomination, and this Eye will take back the pen," he said. "When asked, he will state you had borrowed it only a moment ago to write a note and forgetfully put it in your own pocket."

"We made a deal," I reminded him firmly. "*I* handle the Abomination. *You* stay out of my way."

"Don't be foolish," Comet Nose said scornfully. "You were allowed here to bring the Abomination out of hiding. Now that you have fulfilled that role, you will step aside."

I could hear boots on wood now as the cops started toward me. "I don't quit in the middle of a job," I said. "You really should know that by now."

"This is not the middle of the job," the Modhri warned. "For you, it is the end."

"Don't count on it," I said, trying not to think of me being in jail and Bayta trying to hold off the Fillies by herself. The Fillies, and whatever else the Modhri might have available to throw at her. "You're not getting the girl, period."

Comet Nose flipped his head again. "The Human female?" he asked. "When did I say I wanted any Human females?"

I stared at him. "You don't want—?"

And then the cops were on me, two of them grabbing my

arms and roughly turning me around. "Easy," I told them. "I'll need those arms later."

"Very funny," a third cop said, opening my jacket and pulling McMicking's Beretta from my holster. He was older than the others, with lieutenants' insignia on his collar. The plate above his right shirt pocket gave his name as Bhatami. "Well, well—what have we here?"

"I have a carry permit," I reminded him.

"I understand Mr. Veldrick has canceled that," Bhatami said as he tucked the gun into his own belt.

"Mr. Veldrick has no such authority," I said.

"Perhaps not," Bhatami said. He gestured to the cops holding my arms. Reluctantly, I thought, they released me. "*We,* on the other hand, have all the authority we need."

"Oh, please," I said with a snort. "This isn't about that bogus warrant Sergeant Aksam tried to spoil my dinner with, is it?"

"This is far more serious," Bhatami said grimly. "A short time ago we received a tip that you were involved with the murders of two of our officers."

I felt sweat gathering beneath my collar, freshly aware of the slight bulge of the contract pen nestled in my jacket pocket. "An anonymous tip, I presume?"

Bhatami shrugged slightly. "True, and we both know the general value of such tips," he conceded. "However, given that we've been unable to contact either of the two officers by comm, we're inclined to take this one a bit more seriously."

I looked past his shoulder at the three cops by the door, their guns now pointed at the ceiling but still ready for action. So

that was where at least one of the three missing Fillies had gotten to. He'd been lurking outside somewhere where he could
spot my return and sic the cops on me. "May I ask who it is
who's missing?"

I looked back at Bhatami in time to catch his flicker of
disappointment. Sometimes murderers gave themselves away
by forgetting to ask the identity of their alleged victim. Obviously, he'd been hoping I would add that indicator to the case
against me. "Sergeant Aksam and Officer Lasari," he said.
"The fact that you had a run-in with them earlier this evening
makes the tip somewhat more credible."

"I didn't have a run-in with them," I explained patiently.
"They tried to serve me with a trumped-up warrant and my
legal representative politely invited them to take a hike."

"So I gather," Bhatami said. "They called in for a new warrant, which was subsequently issued."

"Which I was never served."

"Because both officers subsequently vanished."

"Which I know nothing about," I said. "Allow me to point
out I've been on New Tigris less than a day, hardly enough
time to work up a good grudge against anyone, let alone a pair
of cops just doing their duty. Furthermore, there must have
been twenty people who observed Sergeant Aksam and Officer Lasari accost me in the restaurant. If any of *them* had a
grudge, they would have seen me as a gift-wrapped patsy."

"Facts which also have not escaped my notice," Bhatami
agreed. "But the serious nature of the information requires that
we make inquiries."

"I suppose," I said, looking over his shoulder again as the
door opened and a newcomer shambled into the bar. Caught

up in his own thoughts, or else blurred by his blood alcohol level, he got a full three steps inside before he noticed the cops lining the walls around him.

He jerked in shock and skittered nervously in a wide circle around the two nearest ones, keeping a wary eye on them as he backed hurriedly toward the bar. He looked toward me, his eyes narrowing as he peered at the evident object of the cops' attention. As he did so, he lifted his closed fist, thumb extended upward, toward his face. He dabbed the tip of his thumb at the corner of his mouth, the hand wiggling slightly as he did so.

Only then, as I gazed into his eyes, was I able to pierce the layer of grime and sweat and recognize McMicking's face.

McMicking's face, and a wiggling fist with thumb extended upward. The sign-language symbol for ten.

Ten cops? Ten minutes?

Ten seconds?

McMicking turned away and continued his shambling walk toward the bar. "But there's no reason we can't be comfortable, is there?" I asked, looking back at Bhatami. "Let's sit down."

Before the two cops flanking me could react, I took a step backward to the Fillies' table and sat down in the chair the Human arm wrestler had recently vacated. "Lieutenant?" I invited, gesturing Bhatami to the other empty chair as the two cops hurriedly moved back to my sides.

Bhatami looked pointedly at the two Fillies still seated at the table. "I think we'd do better to have this convers—"

From somewhere outside came the muffled thundercrack of an explosion.

Automatically, every head in the room spun that direction,

every eye probing the half-dozen frosted windows for signs of what had happened.

And with their attention momentarily elsewhere, I pulled the damning contract pen from my jacket and dropped it, point down, into the open *dilivin* bottle.

Quickly but casually I pulled my hand back again, glancing at the two Fillies at the table and the one still standing nearby. If any of them had spotted my gambit and yelled for the cops, there might still be time to retrieve the pen before the witch's brew in the *dilivin* destroyed all traces of the murdered cops' blood and my own fingerprints.

But the Fillies weren't yelling, or even looking accusingly at me. All three of them were staring straight ahead, their necks stiff, their eyes glazed over, their lower jaws trembling in the classic Filly indicator of extreme emotional agitation.

And I suddenly realized what McMicking had done. The explosion that had so neatly distracted the bar's attention had been the car with the two dead cops inside. Probably not coincidentally, the blast had also fried the hidden Modhran coral, creating a surge of pain and shock that had kicked back through the group mind connection into my three agitated Fillies.

I looked at the bar, where McMicking was staring in the direction of the explosion with everyone else. His eyes flicked sideways to meet mine, one eyelid dropping in a sort of half wink.

I inclined my head microscopically. Whether he'd deliberately intended it or not, his stunt had just pulled the other half of my bacon out of the fire. With the car probably now blazing away, any traces of DNA that the contract pen might have left in the cops' chests were rapidly disintegrating into their component atoms.

Bhatami recovered first. "Bomb squad and fire department," he snapped, jabbing a finger toward one of the cops beside me. "You—stay with him," he told the other, the jabbing finger shifting to me. Turning, he raced for the door.

It was the signal for instant mass chaos, with everyone in the bar either shouting, gasping, or clawing their way toward the door to see what was happening out there. A minute later, the only ones left in the bar were me, my police escort, the Fillies, the bartender, Karim, and about a dozen men already slumped in their chairs or collapsed across the bar in *dilivin*-induced slumber.

And, of course, McMicking.

I looked at the Fillies. All three were looking back at me now, their eyes blank in a way that sent a shiver up my back. "I hope that didn't hurt too much," I said.

It was probably the wrong thing to say. Slowly, deliberately, one of the Fillies reached into his tunic and pulled out his contract pen. Staring into my face, he turned it around in his hand, gripping it like a knife—

"Is there a problem?" the cop standing behind me asked.

The color of the Filly's blaze paled a bit, his eyes coming back to normal focus. "Problem?" he asked. He looked at the pen in his hand as if wondering how it had gotten there, and tucked it away again. "No. There is no problem."

"Glad to hear it," the cop said. "Maybe you and your friends should move to a different table."

The Filly looked at me. Then, without a word, he and his companion climbed off their chairs, and the three of them walked over to a table across the room. They settled themselves around it, one of them facing me, the second facing the door, the third watching Karim behind the bar.

"Thank you," I said quietly to the cop.

"Save it," he muttered back. "If I find out you killed Aksam and Lasari, I'll take you apart myself."

I sighed. Clearly, I still had the knack of making friends wherever I went.

Someday, I really should work on that.

TEN :

Over the next half hour or so the bar's patrons dribbled back in, talking in the subdued tones of people who've just seen something horrific. At the same time, though, I could sense the excitement and relief that something had happened to shake up their otherwise boring routines. This evening, I guessed, would be fodder for barroom conversations for months to come.

Still, despite the excitement, the free *dilivin* continued to take its toll. Soon after returning to the bar, most of the patrons began wandering back out again or else joined the ones already snoring away. McMicking was one of the latter group, pillowing his head on his folded arms on the bar.

By the time Bhatami returned, the place was down to the sleepers, the Fillies, me, and maybe four other conscious patrons.

The lieutenant looked tired and angry and bitter. "I take it whatever happened out there wasn't good news?" I suggested as he pulled out one of the chairs at my table and dropped into it.

He tried to glare at me, but fatigue was starting to overwhelm the anger and all that made it out past his eyes was a sort of pensive annoyance. "We found Sergeant Aksam and Officer Lasari," he said, glancing up at the cop still standing guard over me. "Or what was left of them."

"I'm sorry," I said. "I will point out, though, that I was right here when that blast went off."

"Which means nothing at all," Bhatami pointed out grimly. "Actually, it means nothing in two different directions. If the investigators find the remains of a timed fuse, it won't matter where you or anyone else was when the car was actually set on fire."

"True," I conceded. "What's the other direction that it won't mean anything?"

His eyes were steady on me. "We'll have to wait for the full postmortem to be sure," he said. "But the preliminary exam indicates they may both have been killed before the fire started."

I pursed my lips. "Any idea how?"

"Not yet," Bhatami said. "But we'll find out." He cocked his head. "Meanwhile, what exactly are we going to do with you?"

I shrugged. "Well, frankly—and I'd say this even if it wasn't me—I don't see that you have any legal grounds for detaining me."

He snorted. "Please. A good prosecutor can always find grounds to detain someone." He raised his eyebrows. "Such as if you impeded our investigation by, say, refusing to give me the name and whereabouts of the legal representative you mentioned earlier."

With an effort, I managed not to look at McMicking. "His name's Joseph Prescott," I said. "I don't actually know where he is right now."

"What's his number?" Bhatami asked, pulling out his comm.

I gave him McMicking's number. There was no point in stalling or pulling a fake one out of the air—Bhatami could easily confiscate my comm and get the real number from my call record.

"Thank you," he said, punching it in.

There was, of course, no telltale ring from the other end of the room. McMicking was way too professional to walk around with his comm on anything except silent mode. Bhatami listened half a minute, then keyed off and put away his comm. "No answer," he said. "Your lawyer keeps odd hours."

"He's a lawyer," I said, as if that explained it.

He pursed his lips, studying my face. "Let me see that Hardin Industries security card."

I pulled it out and handed it over. For a minute he just sat there, his eyes tracing across every word and copyproof squiggle on the thing. "I don't know much about Hardin Industries," he said at last, handing it back. "But a person doesn't get to be a multitrillionaire without having good people on the payroll."

He looked me square in the eye. "Do you know what happened to Sergeant Aksam and Officer Lasari?"

I hesitated. How much of this mess did I dare tell him?

Not much, I reluctantly decided. "I have a theory," I said. "But I don't have anything solid to back it up."

He cracked about a tenth of a smile. "Don't worry, there aren't any defense attorneys present," he said. "Let's have a name."

Out of the corner of my eye I could see the Fillies had abandoned even the pretense of conversation. "Sorry," I told Bhatami. "I can't throw names around without proof."

"Even under threat of an obstruction charge?"

"Even so," I said.

"Is he a friend, then?" Bhatami persisted.

I snorted. "Hardly."

"An acquaintance? An enemy?"

"He's certainly not a friend," I repeated.

Bhatami's lip twisted. "This is not what I would consider cooperation."

"I know, and I'm sorry," I said. "But right now, this is the best I can do."

He nodded and stood up. "I trust you won't try to leave New Tigris until this matter is settled?"

"Don't worry," I assured him. "I like it here."

He snorted gently at that one. "In that case, I'll say good night." He caught the eye of the cop still standing behind me and nodded toward the door. "One other thing," he went on as the cop headed across the floor. "The two dead police officers in the burned-out car? Their sidearms were missing."

I remembered to demonstrate some surprise and shock. "Both of them?"

He nodded. "And both men's extra clips, too."

"I don't suppose you had security trackers on the guns."

"We did," he said. "They've been disabled." He raised his eyebrows a little. "If you give me a name, I can offer you protective custody. You and any of your associates."

One of the Fillies at the table behind him had a hand in his tunic, his fingers resting somewhere in the vicinity of the tailored pocket where they typically kept their contract pens. Like I'd needed a reminder. "Sorry," I told Bhatami. "Not until I can also hand you some proof."

"Then it appears we're at an impasse," Bhatami said. "Good luck, Mr. Donaldson."

"Thank you," I said. "But I doubt I'm going to have very much of that unless you give me back my gun."

Bhatami shook his head. "Sorry. As I said earlier, your carry permit has been revoked."

"And as *I* said earlier, Mr. Veldrick has no authority to do that," I reminded him.

"You're welcome to argue that in court tomorrow," Bhatami assured me.

"I may not make it to breakfast, let alone judicial office hours," I said. "Besides, if I'm not mistaken, the burden of proof is on Mr. Veldrick to show he can issue such an order, not on me to prove that he can't."

Bhatami eyed me a minute. "You really believe your life is in danger?"

I nodded. "Mine, and the lives of several others. At least two of whom are New Tigran citizens."

Slowly, he pulled the Beretta from his belt. "We have severe punishments here for the misuse of firearms," he warned as he set it down on the table in front of me.

"I'll try very hard to keep innocents out of the line of fire," I promised.

"Nice to know Hardin's employees have a sense of civic responsibility."

"Hardin's employees hate filling out paperwork," I corrected.

That one got me nearly half a smile. "Ex-cop?"

"Ex-Westali," I said. "Same thing, but with a more casual dress code."

He snorted. "Good night, Mr. Donaldson." Turning, he strode to the door and left.

I looked at the three Fillies as I picked up the gun. "Your turn," I invited, nodding toward the door.

"You have this one final chance, Human," Comet Nose said. "Take the female and leave."

"The Abomination is mine to deal with," I told him. "That was the agreement."

"Then you may not live out the night."

"Possibly," I said. "On the other hand, if *I* die there are others who can take my place. What about you?"

All three Fillies smiled, three copies of the same identical expression. "I am everywhere," he said.

"Not on New Tigris you aren't," I reminded him. "If I nail all your walkers, you're out of it."

The smiles vanished. "The Abomination must be destroyed," Comet Nose insisted.

"I'll take that under advisement," I said. "Good night, Modhri. Feel free to never drop in again."

Slowly, the three Fillies stood up. With a final, lingering look at me they walked single file to the door and out into the night.

I took a deep breath. "You okay?" I asked Karim.

"I don't know," he said, his voice dark. "Did I just hear you challenge them to a firefight? In *my* bar?"

"It *did* sound that way, didn't it?" I admitted. "Sorry."

"Sorry?" he demanded. "*Sorry?* Compton, does this place look even remotely defensible?"

He had a point. Except for the office, the bar was a single room, a wide-open floor plan filled with tables and chairs that weren't nearly heavy enough to stop police-caliber thud-wumpers. The only serious cover was the wooden bar itself, and that was all the way at the rear.

There was only the single door, which theoretically was to our advantage. Unfortunately, there were also large frosted windows along that same wall, any one of which could be turned into a brand-new entrance with the application of a single thudwumper round. "It's not as bad as it looks," I lied.

There was a sudden rattling of glassware from the other end of the bar as the bartender tried to juggle the shot glasses he was pretending to clean. "You all right?" I asked him.

"Sure," he said, the word coming out like the air from a popped balloon. "Sure."

"Go home, Dawid," Karim told him. He looked sideways at me. "Unless you think . . . ?"

"No, it'll be all right," I said. "Whatever they're planning, they'll wait until most of the potential witnesses have toddled off to bed."

"I suppose," Karim said. "Go, Dawid. Go now."

The bartender didn't need any encouragement. Dropping his apron on the bar, he headed for the door.

I did, too, getting there before he did. "As long as you're

opening the door anyway, I want a look around," I said, stepping behind him and gesturing him forward. "Go on."

He looked over his shoulder at me, probably wondering if
standing directly in front of the Fillies' prime target in dim light
was something he really wanted to do. But hanging around a
soon-to-be battlefield wasn't much better. Bracing himself, he
pushed open the door.

We were met by silence. "Keep going," I prompted, giving
him a nudge.

Hesitantly, he stepped out of the doorway into the full glow
of the streetlights. If the Fillies were already set up, I knew, this
would be the time for them to try to take me out.

But there was nothing but more silence. The bartender, apparently also noticing the lack of gunfire, got his feet moving
again, and within a few seconds he was out of my line of sight.
I gave the area a quick scan, then closed the door again and
locked it.

"Well?" Karim asked.

"They're not shooting yet," I told him. "Go get Bayta, will
you?"

"All right." He took a couple of steps toward the office
door, then frowned. "What about them?"

"What about who?"

He waved a hand over the slumbering customers. "Them."

"If you want to cart them all outside, be my guest," I said.
"But first go get Bayta."

He glowered, but headed into the office without further
comment. I crossed to the bar beside McMicking and waited
until I heard the creak of the opening trapdoor from the other
room. "You want to be carted outside?" I murmured.

"Not unless he wants to cart me at least a block away," McMicking murmured back, lifting his head from his folded arms. "Lying on open ground in the middle of a firefight is considered unwise."

"So is standing at the business end of a shooting gallery," I said. "What do you think?"

"It could be worse," he said, looking around. "You sure you don't want to just give the Modhri the girl and be done with it?"

"That's the interesting part," I said. "He told me he didn't want, quote, any Human females, unquote."

"Then what *does* he want?"

"I see two possibilities," I said. "One, he's after whatever's in those metal boxes she's hell-bent on taking with her when we leave New Tigris."

"You know what's in them?"

"Haven't a clue," I said. "But that possibility meshes nicely with the fact that Lorelei was apparently able to leave New Tigris without serious trouble. If what he wants is the boxes, then her going off alone wouldn't have been a problem for him."

"Then why did he accost her in New York? To get information on Rebekah and the boxes?"

"Probably," I said. "Possibility two—" I hesitated. This was such a weird thought I wasn't sure I wanted to bring it up.

"Dramatic silences don't become you, Compton," McMicking said. "Spit it out."

"You asked for it," I warned. "We know—well, we assume, anyway—that our six Fillies have undergone some extensive genetic manipulation that somehow enabled them to become ranging antennas for locating Rebekah."

"Right. So?"

"So how far can you manipulate Filiaelian genetic code before the result is no longer Filiaelian?" I asked. "Specifically,
how unlike a Filly can a Filly look?"

He stared at me. "Are you suggesting this girl is a *Filly*?"

"I know, it seems ludicrous," I agreed. "But if it's true, it
would definitely put her solidly into the Abomination category," I said. "And remember the Modhri said he didn't want
any *Human* females."

McMicking exhaled loudly. "That has to be the most insane
idea I've ever heard," he said. "You really think someone could
look Human and actually be Filiaelian?"

"I have no idea," I said. "And we're sure not getting her in
for a full bio-scan any time soon. I just think that until we
know what's going on we should keep our minds as open as
possible."

"Opening them that far is a good way for your brains to
fall out," McMicking warned. "All right, fine—we watch our
backs from all directions. What's your take on our grumpy
police lieutenant? I couldn't hear much of your conversation."

"He doesn't like me, and he still thinks there's a fair chance
I offed his fellow cops," I said. "But he seems willing to be as
fair and objective as he can."

"But you're not expecting him to come roaring to the
rescue if you hit your cop-call button?"

"He might come, but he certainly wouldn't be in a hurry
about it," I said.

He grunted. "Still, as you said, the Modhri will probably
wait until the streets are clear before making his move."

"Yes, well, that could be a problem," I said. "Aside from a scattering of sleeping drunks, the streets are already clear. The police presence of the past hour apparently convinced the locals to go do their drinking elsewhere."

"The firefighters are gone, too?"

"Yes."

McMicking frowned toward the door and row of windows. "We might want to think about setting up a defensive line."

"For all the good it'll do," I said. "Those tables will work against snoozers, but they're not going to stop anything heavier."

"Still, we don't want the Modhri thinking we're not being professional about this."

There was a faint creaking of wood from the office. "Go to sleep," I murmured.

McMicking nodded and put his head down on his arms again. A moment later, Bayta and Karim emerged through the doorway. "You all right?" I asked Bayta, taking a step toward her. I noticed she had the *kwi* gripped ready in her hand. "How's Rebekah?"

"She's frightened, but otherwise all right," Bayta said. "We were starting to get worried about you. What's the situation?"

"Fair to middling bad," I said. "Our six Fillies could be coming through that door any minute now, guns blazing."

Her throat tightened. "They're armed?"

"Courtesy of our late friends Aksam and Lasari," I said. "Not that either of them had any choice in the matter."

Bayta looked across at the door. "What do we do?"

"We set up a layered defense and hope for the best," I said. "Karim, you probably still have time to leave if you want."

"No," he said firmly. "This is my bar, and Rebekah is my friend. What do you want me to do?"

"For starters, we move some of those tables in front of the door," I said, heading across the floor. "No point in making it easy for them."

A few minutes later we had the door barricaded as best we could and had set up some obstacles to anyone who tried coming in through one of the windows. "That won't hold anyone very long," Karim warned as we surveyed our handiwork. "Maybe we should consider calling Lieutenant Bhatami and asking for that protective custody he was offering."

"And what happens to Rebekah while we're sitting around our nice safe jail cell?" I asked.

"Why can't he protect her, too?"

"Where, at his house?" I asked. "The Imani City Police Department isn't running a hotel, you know. Besides, you heard Bhatami—he wants names and evidence. I haven't got the latter, and I'm not ready to give up the former."

"Even if it means getting all of us killed?"

"No one's going to get killed," I said, hoping fervently that it was true. "Go tell Rebekah to get herself ready to travel. If we get an opening, we'll need to grab it."

"What about her boxes?" he asked. "She won't leave without them."

"She may have to," I told him bluntly. "If it comes to her life or—" I broke off, as a sudden thought occurred to me. "Tell her we'll do what we can," I told him. "While she's getting ready, start bringing the boxes up here. You can stack them behind the bar."

"All right." He headed back into the office.

"If it comes to her life or what?" Bayta asked quietly.

I held up a finger, listening. A few seconds later I heard the telltale sounds of Karim heading down into Rebekah's hideaway. "Okay, now we can talk," I said. "By the way, say hello to McMicking."

She jumped as McMicking again lifted his head from his pillowed arms. "Oh," she said. "Hello."

"I suddenly realized something," I told them. "Ever since Yandro the Modhri has been insisting the Abomination has to be destroyed. Right?"

"Right," Bayta said, glancing again at the front door.

"So why hasn't he made his move?" I said. "It's been twenty minutes since Bhatami and the cops pulled out. Why hasn't he had his walkers steal a car, drive it through the front door, unload his guns at anything that moves, and torch the bar and everything in it?"

"I presume you have an answer?" McMicking invited.

"Because he *doesn't* want the Abomination destroyed," I said. "At least, not right away. There's something he needs to do first, and he needs the Abomination intact and unharmed to do it."

"Like they did with Lorelei," McMicking said, nodding. "The walkers started by using snoozers on her."

"Exactly," I said. "He has to handle this with finesse, or the whole thing will have been for nothing."

"Which gives us a lever," McMicking said thoughtfully. "We can threaten to destroy the Abomination and leave him with a draw."

"He'll never believe it," Bayta said. "He knows we'd never hurt Rebekah."

"Which is probably why he offered us the Yandro deal in the first place," I said. "He figured we'd be able to flush Rebekah into the open, but we wouldn't hurt her. At least, not until we'd figured out what kind of Abomination she was."

"She's not any kind of Abomination," Bayta said firmly. "She's a scared little ten-year-old Human girl."

"Is she?" I countered. "Up to now she hasn't looked all that scared to *me*."

"You weren't down there just now," Bayta said coldly. "I don't know what the Modhri wants with her, but that Abomination tag is just an excuse."

"You may be right," I said, sending a warning look at McMicking. Now was not the time to tell Bayta that Rebekah might not be nearly as Human as she looked. "In which case, maybe the Abomination is what's in all those boxes of hers. Either way, it's obvious now why the Modhri's switched from letting me run free to trying to get me arrested for cop-killing. Now that he knows where Rebekah is, he figures that with me out of the picture he can get in here, overpower Karim, and do whatever unseemly things he has in mind."

There was another creak of wood from the office, a louder one this time. I motioned McMicking to go back to sleep as I headed around the end of the bar. Karim was just coming to the doorway as I reached it, one of the boxes cradled in his arms. "Behind the bar, you said?" Karim asked.

"Change of plan," I told him. "We're going to stack them in *front* of the bar."

Karim frowned. "In *front* of the bar?"

"All that metal, you know," I explained, taking the box from him and walking around to the front of the bar. Fifteen kilos, all right, if it was a gram. "Might as well give ourselves as much protection as we can."

Karim was still standing in the doorway. "Rebekah won't like this," he warned.

"I'm more interested in how much the Fillies won't like it," I said. "Go get the rest of them. While you do that, Bayta and I will move your sleeping customers over to the side wall where they'll be as far out of the line of fire as possible."

He still looked troubled, but he nodded and disappeared back into the office. "I take it I'm joining the drunks?" McMicking asked, lifting his head again.

"It's as good a cross-fire position as any," I said. "Grab a drunk and pick out your spot."

There were eleven sleeping men scattered around the room, all of them so drunk they didn't even wake up as we manhandled them out of their chairs and across the bar. That *dilivin* was potent stuff, all right.

We'd moved five of them, and McMicking had settled himself partially behind one where his hands would be out of sight, when Karim returned.

But this time he wasn't alone. "Mr. Compton, you can't put them here," Rebekah insisted, making a beeline for the box I'd set in front of the bar. Her eyes were red and puffy, as if she'd been crying, but the rest of her face was back under firm restraint again. Maybe it was just with Bayta that she let her vulnerable side leak out. "They could be damaged."

"Better them than us," I said, watching her closely. Behind the puffy eyes and controlled expression her concern for the boxes seemed genuine. "Besides, I get the impression the Modhri can't afford to destroy them."

"He can't afford to destroy *all* of them," she countered. "All he needs is to take one of them intact."

"Who is this Modhri?" Karim asked.

"The mastermind behind all of this," I told him, frowning at Rebekah. "Which one does he need?"

"Any of them," she said. With an effort, she lifted the box and staggered back behind the bar with it.

"What are they, duplicate records of some kind?" I asked.

"In a way," she said.

"That's great," I said. I'd never really believed she needed all twenty of the damn things in the first place. "Pick one out for yourself and we'll torch the rest."

"It's not like that," she said, giving me a cross look over her shoulder. "I need all of them."

"That makes no sense whatsoever," I growled. "What the hell's in them?"

"I can't tell you that," Rebekah said. She set down the box and turned back to face me, a stubbornly defiant look on her face.

"That bar may stop police thudwumpers, Rebekah," I said. "But it also might not. Are you willing to risk your life for what's in those boxes?"

"Yes," she said firmly.

"She already *has* risked her life," Karim added grimly. "She and Lorelei both."

I felt my stomach tighten, thinking back to how Lorelei had died. "Maybe I'm not ready to risk mine," I said.

"You're welcome to leave," Karim invited me tartly. Reaching beneath the bar, he produced an old RusFed P11 military handgun.

"We're not leaving," Bayta said firmly. Her face was flushed with emotion, her eyes hard and cold. Whoever Rebekah was, she'd clearly gotten under my partner's skin.

"Fine," I gave up with a sigh. "Maybe we can have it both ways."

Turning, I headed toward the door. "Where are you going?" Karim called after me.

"To plant a few seeds of doubt," I said over my shoulder. "Go bring up the rest of the boxes. Put them wherever Rebekah wants."

It took me a couple of minutes to move enough of the table barricade Karim and I had built so that I could get through. Unlocking the door, I opened it a crack. "Modhri?" I called. "You out there?"

My answer was the muffled crack of a low-power gunshot and the slap of a snoozer cartridge against the door beside my cheek. "I guess so," I said, hastily closing it a couple more centimeters. "I just wanted to tell you that the Abomination is here with us, right in your line of fire. You might want to think about that before you come charging in with guns blazing. Have a nice day."

I closed the door just as another pair of snoozers shattered themselves into shards against the heavy wood. I locked up again and backed out of the passage I'd created in the barricade. Bayta was waiting, and together we put everything back the way it had been. "Let's get the rest of the drunks out of the way," I said when we were finished.

By the time we'd finished and returned to the relative safety of the bar, Karim had finished stacking Rebekah's boxes behind it. Rebekah herself was sitting cross-legged on the floor in front of the boxes, a small carrybag beside her. "How are you doing?" I asked her.

"I'm all right," she said, her voice determined but with a little tremble to it. "That won't stop him, you know. I told you he only needs one of them."

"True, but it might slow him down a little," I said, running my eye over the boxes. "They're not alien sculptures, are they?"

She looked at me in astonishment. "*Sculptures?*"

"Just a thought," I said. "Skip it."

From the other end of the room came a sudden thud. I spun around, yanking my Beretta from its holster. "The window," Karim said. He was standing near the end of the bar, his P11 gripped in his hand. "They're seeing if they can break it without having to shoot it out."

"Can they?" I asked.

There was another thud, a louder one this time. "Probably not," he said. "It's glass, not plastic, but it's tempered."

There was a third thud, this time from one of the windows on the other side of the door. "Can't they just shoot them out?" Bayta asked tensely.

"Can, and probably will," I said. "But guns are noisy things. Not so much with snoozers, but very much with thudwumpers or other killrounds. The Modhri can't afford to draw police attention until he's ready to move."

"When will that be?" Bayta asked. "It's already almost midnight."

"Maybe they're waiting until—" Karim started.

"Shh!" I hissed, holding up a hand.

The room fell silent. Faintly, in the distance, I heard the sound of multiple sirens. "There's your answer," I said grimly. "He's set up a diversion somewhere across town to keep the police busy."

"Sounds like paramed and fire sirens, too," Karim said, cupping his free hand behind his ear. "It's either a fire or a massive accident."

"Either of which would be easy enough for the Modhri to arrange," I said. "I think we can expect some action soon. Karim, better douse the lights in here. Leave any outside lights on."

He reached beneath the bar, and the dim lights around us flicked off. I took a deep breath, letting my eyes adjust to the faint glow coming through the windows and settling into combat mode.

The minutes dragged by. We crouched in silence behind the bar, except for Rebekah, who sat in silence in front of the boxes, and McMicking, who lay in silence at the side of the room. "What's he waiting for?" Karim muttered.

"It'll be at least another ten or fifteen minutes," I told him. "He'll want to make sure the cops are completely engaged in whatever diversion he's arranged for them before he makes his move."

Seconds later, the two windows on the far sides of the wall exploded inward.

ELEVEN :

Reflexively, I ducked low behind the top of the bar. "Ten minutes?" Karim shouted as a shot slammed into the wall above our heads through one of the shattered windows.

"More or less," I shouted back irritably. That was twice now, first Yandro and now here, that the Modhri had casually undercut a plan or prediction I'd just taken pains to explain to someone. If he was going to kill me, the least he could do was have the courtesy not to destroy my reputation first.

Another shot whizzed past overhead, this one coming from the other window. It was followed immediately by a third shot from the first window, then a fourth from the second window.

I frowned as the shots settled into a pattern, one shot at a time through alternating windows, each on the heels of the one before, all of them tearing through the wood and drywall at least half a meter above our heads. What was the Modhri up to?

Karim was apparently wondering that, too. "He must be trying to keep us pinned down," he shouted over the steady blam-blam-blam of the thudwumpers. "Probably trying to infiltrate."

"From both sides at once?" I shouted back.

"Maybe he's got more ammo than we thought."

I looked back and forth between the two windows. Standard infiltration technique was to pin your opponent down along the infiltration line, covering only one line at a time to conserve ammo.

But that was for open ground, not this kind of urban setting where you had buildings and convenient corners to hide around. He didn't need to cover *any* line, let alone two at once, until the infiltrators were ready to move.

And they clearly weren't ready. I couldn't see anyone moving out there, through either window. Was he just trying to spook us, then? Goad us into wasting our own shots firing at shadows and unseen enemies?

The shots continued, a steady blam-blam-blam. A *steady* blam-blam-blam, I noticed suddenly. Not a barrage designed to pin us down. Not even a volley, a group of shots followed by a lull where we were supposed to feel obligated to burn some ammo shooting back. A methodical, *steady* blam-blam-blam.

He wasn't covering up an infiltration. He was covering up something else.

Something he didn't want me to notice.

I fumbled out my comm. The incoming-call light wasn't glowing, or flashing with the message-waiting signal. No one was trying desperately to get in touch with me.

But maybe the Modhri was afraid someone was about to.

"Bayta—kick me if they start coming in," I called to her. Dropping behind the bar, I pulled up the city directory, found Veldrick's number, and punched it in.

He answered on the second ring. "Hello?"

"Mr. Veldrick, this is Frank Donaldson," I called. "I need to talk to you."

The words were barely out of my mouth when the steady blam-blam-blam of the Modhri's guns abruptly turned into a full battlefield cacophony. I was already surging back to my feet when Bayta's kick against my thigh confirmed the enemy was attacking.

I got an eye over the bar just in time to see a Filly leap in through each of the broken windows, their stolen police guns blazing away. For a second they faltered on the upended chairs we'd laid across their path, their shots going wild as they fought for balance.

I raised my gun over the bar to fire, but was forced to duck back down as a pair of shots gouged grooves in the bar and threw a handful of wooden splinters into my face. Before I could get back up into firing position, the entire bar began to come apart as the Fillies regained both their balance and their aim.

"Get down!" I yelled at Karim, ducking a little lower myself. He ignored me, his hand stretched up over the bar as he fired blindly in the general direction of our attackers. Bayta started to lift her hand, probably planning to do the same with her *kwi*. I grabbed her wrist before she could get there and pulled both the arm and Bayta herself low to the floor. The barrage was deafening, the rounds from Karim's military weapon adding a slightly deeper counterpoint to the Fillies' lighter police weapons.

And then, suddenly, Karim's gun was firing alone.

"Hold your fire!" I shouted. "Karim?"

Karim squeezed off two more rounds and then stopped. The silence seemed to ring in my ears as I carefully lifted my head above the bar.

The two Fillies were sprawled unmoving on the floor, bright red blood flowing across the floor from beneath their bodies, their guns still held loosely in their hands.

I looked at the side of the room. McMicking was still lying among the oblivious sleeping drunks, his gun and gun hand hidden behind one of the other men. His half-closed eyes rolled to catch mine, and his head nodded microscopically toward the guns.

I nodded back. "Stay here," I told Karim and Bayta, both of whom had risen cautiously to check out the situation. Squeezing past them, I circled around the end of the bar and headed for the Fillies.

I was still two steps away when the guns and gun hands suddenly twitched upward.

I jerked back, reflexively squeezing off a round into the nearest Filly's torso. But the guns weren't coming up in some last-gasp attempt by the Modhri to nail me. Before I could even shift my aim to the other Filly both guns broke free of their late owners' limp grips and skittered back toward the windows. For a moment the weapons bounced around and through the barricade chairs' legs, giving me just enough time to wonder what would happen if one of them bumped hard enough to go off. Then, with one last bounce, they disappeared out their respective windows into the night.

Behind me, Karim spat something vile-sounding. "Tethered guns," he growled. "The favored ploy of those who value their weapons more than their men."

"That's the Modhri in a nutshell," I agreed. Cautiously, I stepped to the nearest window, hoping to see which direction the tethered guns had gone. But both weapons had vanished. Returning to the relative safety of the bar, I retrieved my comm from the floor where I'd dropped it. "Mr. Veldrick?" I called. "You still there?"

"Donaldson?" Veldrick's voice came back. "What the hell's going on there?"

"The more important question is what in hell's going on *there*," I countered.

There was a short pause. "What do you mean?" he asked warily.

"You know what I mean," I said, putting an ominous edge to my voice. I still wasn't a hundred percent sure I had the situation figured out, but I was sure enough to try playing the odds. "The situation with you and your illegal coral. You want to give me the details, or would you rather deal with the mess on your own?"

My hearing had recovered enough from the gun battle to pick up his long, sibilant sigh. "Someone's been in my house," he said. "He came to the door and shot me—snoozers—and then just walked right in."

"Did he steal anything?" I asked.

"No, but he was going to," Veldrick said grimly. "He had

my shipping boxes out, the ones I used back when I brought in the coral."

"But he didn't actually *take* any of it?"

"You don't get it, do you?" he snapped. "You don't burgle someone's home and not even touch a fortune in illegal merchandise. Not unless you've decided it would be safer to turn in the owner and claim the reward."

"Maybe," I said, appreciating the irony of the whole situation. The last thing this particular home intruder wanted was for Veldrick and his eight million dollars' worth of Larry Hardin's coral to fall into official hands.

"Of course I'm right," Veldrick said. "So what do I do?"

"You start by not panicking," I told him. "For one thing, the police don't usually break their necks rushing to investigate anonymous tips. For another, they're all tied up at the moment with some kind of fire or something."

"An accident, actually," Veldrick corrected me. "At least, that's what *Isantra* Golovek says. He says we should have time to get the coral boxed up and hidden over at his place—"

"Wait a second," I said. "Who's *Isantra* Golovek? One of your Filiaelian business contacts?"

"You know any Juriani with Filiaelian titles?" he countered sarcastically. "He and *Isantra* Snievre are on their way now to give me a hand loading the coral."

A cold chill ran up my back. Earlier this evening, when the Modhri had had a murder frame-up planned for me, he'd been willing to sacrifice the coral outpost rather than risk losing track of Rebekah and her stack of boxes.

So why was he now apparently willing to pull his walkers away from his attack on us in order to protect that same outpost?

Unless protecting the outpost wasn't his plan.

I looked out one of the broken windows. The Modhri's earlier murder frame-up of me had failed, leaving me alive and well and unjailed. And I was likely to remain so for the foreseeable future.

Unless the Fillies were on their way to Veldrick's to arrange another frame-up. Possibly for another murder.

Possibly Veldrick's.

"Listen carefully," I said to Veldrick, pitching my voice low and earnest. "Go lock your doors and windows—right now—and don't let anyone in. Understand? *Anyone.* Not Golovek, not the police—no one."

"What are you talking about?" Veldrick asked, his verbal tension level starting to rise, his voice bouncing a little as he headed off on a jogging tour of his house's entry points.

"I'm talking about barricading yourself inside your house," I said, thinking fast. "Don't you get it? Officially, that coral doesn't exist. They can walk right into your house and take it . . . provided you're not around to squawk to the police afterward."

"You mean . . . they'd actually *kill* me?"

"For eight million dollars in untraceable coral?" I countered, praying he would be too rattled to think straight. Since he couldn't complain to the cops without bringing a mandatory prison sentence down on his own head, there was no reason for a would-be thief to even rough him up, let alone kill him. "People kill for a lot less than that."

"But that's insane," he protested, sounding more bewildered than frightened. "These are well-respected, highly positioned Filiaelian businessmen."

"How do you know?" I asked. "You've only known them a few weeks." And he'd only known *me* a few hours. I hoped he wouldn't remember that. Or if he did, that the Hardin Industries security card I'd come in on would matter more than our length of acquaintanceship.

"You're right," he said, his voice shaking openly now. "All right—I've got everything locked down."

"Make sure you didn't miss any of the windows, even small ones," I warned. "I'll call you when I've figured out what we're going to do. You'd better wait in the meditation room, where there aren't any windows."

"What about the coral?"

"You may have to abandon it," I said.

"No," he said flatly.

I rolled my eyes. People and their possessions . . . "Fine," I said. "Then go ahead and start packing it for travel. Don't touch it, though. I've heard of people getting badly poisoned with scratches from Modhran coral."

"I've got some gloves right here," he said. "But it's going to take a couple of days at least to work up the documentation to get it off-planet."

"Even given the fact you've already got that documentation started?"

There was another short pause. "How did you know?"

"Because you were clearly the one who swore out that arrest warrant for me," I told him. "You were hoping the cops could keep me off your back long enough for you to sneak your coral off New Tigris. How far did you get on the paperwork?"

He sighed. "Not far enough," he said. "It'll still take at least two days."

"Maybe I can come up with a shortcut," I said. "I'll be there to help as soon as I can."

"Make it fast."

"I will," I promised. "Wait a second," I added as a sudden thought struck me. "Before you start packing, go get the biggest hammer you own. If things get too tight, you may have to destroy the coral."

"Are you *insane*?" he demanded. "Do you know how much I paid for the stuff?"

"More than your life is worth?" I asked pointedly. "Remember, if there's nothing in your house worth stealing, there's no reason for anyone to murder you for it."

He hissed out a breath. "You're right," he said reluctantly. "It's just that . . . no, no, you're right."

"We'll try to keep it from coming to that," I assured him. "But you'd best be ready. Just in case."

I broke the connection. "What's going on?" Karim asked.

"Our playmates are trying to change the game," I told him, looking at Rebekah. She was still sitting in front of the boxes, still looking scared but determined. "How are you doing?"

"All right," she said. "He's not going to—"

"What the *frinking*—?" a slurred voice said from across the room.

I looked over the bar. McMicking was staring in feigned horror at the dead Fillies he'd just shot. Before I could say anything, he heaved himself up off the floor and began staggering toward the door.

Leaving his reader lying on the floor. "Karim—stop him," I ordered.

Karim was already hurrying toward the would-be escapee, clearly intent on making sure a paying customer didn't wander outside and get himself killed. Slipping around the end of the bar behind him, I angled over and retrieved McMicking's reader.

McMicking put up a good fight, in a shambling, uncoordinated-drunk sort of fashion, muttering incomprehensibly the whole time. By the time Karim managed to get him turned around and walking toward the relative safety of the bar, I was back in place beside Bayta, checking out the data page McMicking had left for me.

It didn't look good. The real-time locators on the Fillies' six rental cars showed that four of them were traveling across Zumurrud District in the direction of Veldrick's house. The other two cars, presumably those of the dead walkers lying on our floor, were still in their original places in the Modhri's detector array.

Karim reached the bar and started maneuvering McMicking past Bayta and me toward the far end. "Don' wanna be here," McMicking muttered. His eyes caught mine with a look of silent urgency. "Wanna go home. Wanna go home now."

"You can't go home," Karim said. "It's not safe."

"It's not exactly safe here, either," I put in. "Maybe we should just let him go."

"What, through the middle of a fire zone?" Karim countered with a snort.

"They didn't shoot Dawid when he left," I reminded him. "They seem to have a pretty good idea of who their targets are."

"He stays here," Karim said firmly. Brushing past us, he guided McMicking to the other end of the bar.

Bayta moved close to me. "What is it?" she asked quietly.

"The Modhri's doing it again," I told her. "Giving us the choice of sticking with Rebekah or nailing Veldrick's stash of coral."

I tapped the reader's display. "Only this time he's also tossing Veldrick's life into the pot."

Bayta looked at Rebekah. "We aren't abandoning her," she said.

"I wasn't suggesting we do," I said, frowning at the display. On the other hand, if four of our six Fillies were heading for Veldrick's house, and the other two were lying dead at our feet, that ought to mean there was no one out there in the street pointing guns at us.

Unless the Modhri had other walkers on New Tigris we didn't know about.

I looked over at Karim as he settled McMicking onto the floor. McMicking might have a handle on that, if I could get Karim out of earshot for a couple of minutes.

Fortunately, there was an obvious way to do that. "Karim, I need you to go get your car and bring it here," I said, digging the keys out of my pocket. "It's parked about half a block north."

He gave me a disbelieving look. "You want me to do *what*?"

"It'll be all right," I said, showing him the reader. "See? Here are the real-time tracking marks for four of the Fillies' rental cars. That means all the survivors of the group have left."

He peered at the display. "What makes you think they don't have a few other friends?"

"Trust me," I said, trying to sound like I believed it.

He looked at Rebekah, then back at me. "All right," he said. He hesitated a heartbeat, then set his P11 down on the bar. "If they *do* have friends, there's no point in giving them another weapon. Back in a minute."

He skirted the edge of the bar and crossed to one of the broken windows. For a long moment he gazed out into the night. Then, getting a careful grip on the edge of the window, he hauled himself up and over the sill and disappeared out into the night.

"He won't let the coral be destroyed, you know," Rebekah warned quietly.

"Who won't?" I asked, gesturing McMicking over to us.

"The Modhri," she said. "If Mr. Veldrick tries to destroy it, the Eyes will kill him."

"I thought he just needed the coral to find you," McMicking said as he came up to us.

Rebekah shook her head. "He also needs it for . . . what he needs it for."

"Glad we cleared that up," I said, turning to McMicking. "Do you know if there are any other non-Humans on New Tigris at the moment?"

"There aren't," he said. "There were a few groups coming in and out over the past few months, but the last of them left about six weeks ago."

"Just after our Fillies came in?"

"About then," he confirmed.

"What about the other two torchyachts we saw at the space-port?" Bayta asked.

"One is mine, the other is the Fillies'," McMicking told her. "According to the port records, they're still paying rent on it." He looked at Rebekah. "Must have figured that when they left, they'd need to leave in a hurry."

"Then this is our chance," I said, lowering my voice. I didn't know whether or not the polyp colonies inside the dead Fillies could still hear, but I wasn't going to take any chances. "With the walkers on their way to protect Veldrick's coral outpost, we've got a clear shot at the spaceport. I say we load Rebekah, Rebekah's boxes, Bayta, and Karim into Karim's car and send them on their way."

"What about Mr. Veldrick?" Rebekah asked.

"Unless the Modhri gets impatient, I should be able to get there fast enough to get him out," I said, skipping over the fact that McMicking and I had to go there anyway to pick up the coral.

"What about Customs?" Bayta asked.

"Not a problem," McMicking said. "Just have Karim park somewhere outside the spaceport and wait."

There was the hum of a car engine, and I looked through the window to see Karim pull his car to the curb in front of the bar. "Bayta, you're on guard duty," I said, holstering my Beretta. "Shoot anything that moves out there that isn't us."

She nodded and headed to the left-hand broken window, the *kwi* held ready. "Keep an eye on the cars," I added to McMicking, handing him back his reader. "If the colonies in the dead Fillies can still hear, there's no way we're going to be able to hide the transfer from him."

He nodded and staggered his way over to the other of the broken windows, flopping down heavily in one of the chairs where he had a reasonably good view of that part of the street. Picking up one of Rebekah's boxes, I headed for the door.

I had made it through our barricade and was unlocking the door when Karim came in through the window. "What are we doing?" he asked, throwing a frown at McMicking. "And *he's* supposed to be behind the bar."

"We're moving out, and I was curious to see how far he would get," I told him. "Not very, as you see. Grab a box and let's get this show on the road."

Despite my own assurances to the others, I nevertheless half expected the Modhri to have some stunt waiting up his sleeve. But the streets remained quiet as Karim and I loaded the boxes into his car trunk. Things remained equally quiet as we then loaded in Bayta, Rebekah, and Karim. "Remember, find a nice quiet hiding place near the spaceport and wait for my call," I told Bayta as I handed Karim back his P11.

"How long do we wait?" Karim asked. "In case—" His lips compressed briefly.

"In case I get myself killed? Half an hour," I said, picking a number out of the air. I actually had no idea how long it would take for McMicking and me to deal with the four walkers converging on Veldrick's house. "If you haven't heard from me by then, I suggest you head out of town and find somewhere to go to ground until you *do* hear from me."

"I know some places," Karim said, his face grim in the glow of the streetlights. "Good luck."

"You too."

He drove off, leaving me standing in the silence of the street.

"You want me to get us a car?" McMicking asked through the window.

"No need," I said, feeling my throat tightening as I watched Karim's taillights disappear around a corner. Something was wrong here. Something was very wrong. But I couldn't put my finger on it.

"You want us to walk?"

I shook the vague apprehension away. "Of course not," I said, heading back into the bar. "You figure out which of the Fillies' cars is the closest. I'll get the keys to both of them."

A minute later we were striding along the deserted walkway toward one of the encirclement cars the Fillies had left behind a couple of blocks from the bar. "How do you want to work this?" McMicking asked as we walked.

"As quickly and cleanly as possible," I told him, feeling the back of my neck tingling as I threw a careful look into each alley and doorway that we passed. This still wasn't adding up. "We can't afford to let the situation settle into a stalemate."

"Agreed," McMicking said. "So you'll drop me about three blocks from Veldrick's house and go the rest of the way in alone. Hopefully, you can draw the Modhri's attention while I come in from behind."

"His attention *and* his fire?" I suggested dryly.

McMicking shrugged. "Would you rather I go in and *you* play backup?"

"I appreciate the offer," I said. *Backup* . . . "But since he already knows what I look like—"

And suddenly, it clicked. "Oh, *damn*," I muttered, coming to an abrupt halt.

"What?" McMicking demanded sharply, his gun coming up to ready position, his eyes darting around.

"We've been played," I said, my mind spinning with possibilities and implications. "Remember Rebekah saying that the Modhri needs Veldrick's coral for whatever he needs to do vis-à-vis the Abomination?"

"Yes, of course," McMicking said. "That's presumably why the Fillies took off so quickly when you told Veldrick to be ready to hammer it to powder."

"Presumably, yes; actually, no," I said. "If that was the whole story, he should have gone equally frantic when you and I broke into Veldrick's home earlier this evening."

"Good point," McMicking said darkly. "So why didn't he?"

"Because he doesn't need *Veldrick's* coral," I said. "The Fillies have an outpost of their own tucked away."

McMicking swore under his breath. "Aboard their torch-yacht."

"Bingo," I confirmed grimly. "Obvious, in retrospect. The Modhri couldn't have expected to find a ready-to-use outpost waiting for his walkers on a Human world."

"Unless he found out from the other walkers who've been snooping around," McMicking pointed out.

"Right, but by then the Fillies were probably already on their way with their own coral in tow," I said. "It's not like there are a hundred places between the Filiaelian Assembly and New Tigris where you can safely stash a Modhran outpost."

"So why are we breaking our necks to get to Veldrick before he destroys his coral?" McMicking asked.

"It's worse than that," I said, pulling out my comm. "If he's got coral at the spaceport, you can bet he's moving a couple of the Fillies there, too."

"All four cars are headed to Veldrick's."

"All four cars' *trackers* are headed to Veldrick's," I said sourly, punching in Bayta's number. "That doesn't necessarily mean the cars themselves are. How hard would it be to pull the trackers out of the cars and load them aboard a couple of autocabs?"

McMicking's hand closed around my comm, canceling the call. "Don't call her," he said. "One of the walkers might be watching them, and a sudden change of direction would tip him off that we were on to this new wrinkle."

"We have to warn them," I insisted.

"We will," he assured me. "I'll go now."

My first thought was to remind him that Bayta and Rebekah were my responsibility, not his. My second thought was to remember that he knew that. "All right," I said. "You probably shouldn't take the other Filly car."

"I wasn't planning to," he assured me. "Watch yourself." He angled across the street, heading toward a pair of parked cars.

I started walking again toward the Filly car that had been our original goal, resisting the urge to also find an alternative mode of transport. The most important thing I could do right now was keep the Modhri thinking I'd fallen for his trick.

The second most important thing was to get Veldrick out of his mess so that I could get back to the spaceport and get Bayta out of *her* mess. The mess I'd put her into.

I picked up my pace. As I did so, I flipped the Beretta's selector switch to the right-hand half of the clip, the one with killrounds in it.

The Modhri was playing this game for keeps. It was about time I started doing the same.

TWELVE :

Under normal circumstances I would have approached Veldrick's house cautiously, parking a couple of blocks away and moving in on foot. But the circumstances here weren't normal. Veldrick's life was in danger, with Bayta's and Rebekah's about to be. There was no time for skulking around in the shadows.

Besides, since there was probably still a chunk of coral in my borrowed car's trunk, it wasn't like the Modhri didn't already know I was on my way.

I braked to a stop by Veldrick's yard, to find the front door of his house standing wide open. Leaving the engine running, I popped the door and dived out.

I barely made it. From behind a wide, multitrunked tree at the edge of Veldrick's lot line came a muted flash and a thud-wumper slammed into the door a dozen centimeters from my hip.

My momentum was already taking me toward the rear of the

car, so that was where I went, grabbing the end of the bumper as I reached it and pulling myself around behind the trunk. Even as I dropped into a crouch a second shot blew through the driver's window.

I pressed my back against the rear bumper, looking quickly around the rest of the neighborhood as I drew my Beretta and thumbed off the safety. The logical way for the Modhri to have split up his remaining forces, I knew, would have been to send two of the Fillies to the spaceport to intercept Bayta and Rebekah, and the other two here to ambush me.

Unfortunately, that was *my* logic, which wasn't necessarily the Modhri's. I might be facing a single shooter here, or two, or maybe even three, depending on how much trouble he was expecting from me and how badly he wanted to permanently remove me from the game.

The shooter behind the tree fired again, this shot taking out the front left tire. I rose from behind the car high enough to squeeze off a round at him, stayed there just long enough to persuade any second or third shooters that I was presenting a good target, then ducked down again.

But if there were any others, they didn't avail themselves of the golden opportunity. The Filly behind the tree was the only one who fired as I dropped back into cover. This time his shot hit the pavement two meters to the left of the car and ricocheted off into the darkness.

I looked around some more, feeling the clock ticking down with each passing second. Sooner or later, no matter how messy the Modhri's diversion was, the cops were going to free up enough personnel to come find out what all the shooting was about. Even if they didn't, there might be someone in the neighborhood with a hunting rifle. I needed to get into Veldrick's house, and fast.

But I didn't dare try a sprint across that much open ground until I knew how many opponents I was facing and their approximate positions. The shooter fired again, this shot burying itself somewhere in the front of the car. The engine's idle sputtered a bit, then recovered, and I waited for the second shot that would silence it for good.

But the shot never came. Instead, the tree-based shooter fired again to the side, bouncing the shot off the pavement a couple of meters to my right.

It was a shot that made no tactical sense whatsoever. He wasn't trying to kill me—those side shots hadn't even grazed the car. He might be trying to keep me pinned down while a partner worked his way behind me, but even then the shots should have been much closer to me.

Unless he was already shooting as close to me as he dared.

I looked sideways at the trunk I was leaning against. Back in Karim's bar, the Filly walkers had gone paralytic when McMicking torched that police car half a block away, a police car that had contained a chunk of Modhran coral.

The trunk release was inside the car, directly in my attacker's line of fire. Fortunately, a carefully placed round into the trunk's lock worked just as well. The lid popped open, and I caught a glimpse of a metallic box about the size of one of Rebekah's cargo boxes in the center of the trunk.

An instant later, all hell broke loose.

The Filly behind the tree shifted to quick-fire, his shots suddenly screaming past my head with the desperation of someone with nothing to lose. Simultaneously, a second fusillade began, this one coming from inside Veldrick's open door. Forcing back the reflex to throw myself on the pavement and scramble for the safety of the far side of the car, I lifted my Beretta and fired two rounds into the box.

Abruptly, the gunfire stopped. I fired one more round into the box and then took off at full Olympic sprint toward the house, shifting to the snoozer half of the Beretta's clip as I ran. Halfway across the lawn, I came within sight of the Filly who'd been shooting at me from behind the tree, now standing stiff and shaking, his gun clenched uselessly in his hand. I fired two snoozer rounds into him on the fly, and charged full tilt into the house.

The Filly inside the foyer was just starting to recover. I sent another pair of snoozers into his torso, dropping him to the floor before he could get his hand under enough control to bring his gun to bear. I glanced at the door, saw that it was un-damaged, and closed and locked it behind me. Then, striding past the crumpled Filly, I headed into the meditation room.

Veldrick was lying on the floor near his coral display area, marinating in a pool of his own blood. The coral itself was gone, as were two of the six Quadrail shipping crates McMicking had pulled out earlier. The other four boxes were still here, sealed for travel.

I checked Veldrick's pulse, just to make sure, then got out my multitool and pried off the top of one of the crates. There was a chunk of coral inside, resting in a few centimeters of water. That wasn't enough water to keep the coral happy for any serious length of time, I knew, but it would be enough for me to get it to the spaceport and aboard McMicking's torchyacht. Once it was there, he could fill the crates the rest of the way to the top and head out for the Quadrail and, ultimately, his rendezvous with Hardin's buyer.

A quick search of the house took me to Veldrick's garage, where I found a fancy sport van with its rear loading door open and the other two Quadrail crates inside. Returning to the meditation room, I lugged the other four crates to the garage and loaded them aboard. Then, climbing in behind the wheel, I opened the garage and headed into the night.

I waited until I was driving north on Broadway toward the spaceport before I called McMicking. "What's your status?" I asked when he came on.

"No trouble so far," he said. "They've gone to ground and are holding."

"Good," I said, freshly conscious of the crates of coral bouncing along behind me. I didn't know whether the polyp colonies could hear me when the coral wasn't completely submerged, but this was no time to take chances. "I've got Veldrick's coral here in the car with me."

"Good," McMicking said, the subtle change in his voice telling me that he'd caught the implication. "Any trouble?"

"Plenty," I told him. "The good news is that I snoozed both of my Fillies, which should leave us only two to deal with. Have they shown their faces recently, by the way?"

"Not that I've seen," McMicking said. "Probably won't, either. Why scour the countryside when there's a perfectly good choke point at the end of the line?"

"Why, indeed?" I agreed grimly. "The bad news is that they got to Veldrick before I did. He's dead."

There was a soft hiss from the comm. "That's not going to go down well at the head office."

"At this point the head office is the least of my concerns," I said bluntly. "The Modhri's already tried to frame me once for murder. I have a bad feeling this is attempt number two."

"Meaning we need to get you off the planet before the balloon goes up," McMicking said. "Okay. Get to the spaceport as fast as you can and wait there for me. I've got a few resources I can pull together, but it'll take some time."

"Got it," I said, frowning down the softly lit street ahead of me. Did he really have some trick up his sleeve, or had that last comment been solely for the Modhri's benefit?

At this point, though, it hardly mattered. Getting off New Tigris with Bayta and Rebekah in tow was still the plan du jour, and whatever McMicking had planned would have to work around that. "Just make it snappy," I warned. "The time-line is running a little thin."

"I'll be as fast as I can," he promised. "Hang in there."

"Right."

I keyed off, then punched in Bayta's number. "Everything all right?" I asked when she answered.

"So far," she said. "What about you?"

"A couple of small problems, but nothing I can't handle," I told her. No point in telling her about Veldrick now. "I'm on my way. Give me a few minutes to check things out, and I'll let you know when it's safe to come in, the way I did on Veerstu."

"Veerstu?" she asked, sounding puzzled.

"Yes, Veerstu," I said, leaning a little on the last word.

"Oh—right," she said. "Be careful."

"You, too."

I didn't know how sensitive the Modhran coral's hearing was back there in the rear of my van, so just to be on the safe side I tapped the edge of my comm right beside the off button, hopefully making the same sound as I would if I'd actually turned the thing off. Then, with the comm still transmitting, I closed it and put it back into my jacket. On Veerstu, I'd done things a bit differently, but the effect here would be much the same, allowing Bayta to eavesdrop on whatever happened from now on. If and when the Modhri decided to get cute, at least this way she and Karim would instantly know about it.

There were no other vehicles waiting as I pulled into the circular drive in front of the main spaceport building. Through the glassed-in foyer I could see a youngish man at the Customs counter, looking slightly bleary-eyed as he worked. Confederation regs required there be someone on duty or on call at all times, but at this hour I'd expected to have to wake someone up.

I parked Veldrick's van in front of the door and got out, scanning the parking area and the autocab stand as I did so. There was no sign of our last pair of Filly walkers. I turned back to the spaceport door, mentally running through my repertoire of sweet talk, bluster, and threats. It was going to take something unusually impressive for me to talk six crates of illegal Modhran coral past a Customs official at this time of night.

The door had just swung open for me when I heard the sound of approaching car engines. I turned, my hand automatically slipping into my jacket for my Beretta.

And as I did so I was hit by a barrage of lights: the stabbing white of headlights, along with strobing flashes of red and blue.

"Freeze," a voice ordered from behind me.

Carefully, I turned around, my hand still inside my jacket. Lieutenant Bhatami had appeared from some nook or cranny inside the spaceport and was striding through the foyer toward me, flanked by a pair of cops with guns in their hands. Bhatami's own sidearm was still in its holster, but his hand was resting on the grip.

"Hello, Lieutenant," I greeted him, easing my hand out of my jacket and holding it out to demonstrate its emptiness. "What brings you here at this ungodly hour?"

"My job," Bhatami said as the three of them reached me. Behind me, the police cars had braked to a group halt, and I could hear the sounds of multiple doors opening as they spilled their own collection of cops onto the circular drive. "Hands behind your back, please," the lieutenant added as his two fellow cops veered off and approached me warily from both sides.

"What's going on?" I asked, doing as he ordered. One of the cops stepped close and cuffed my wrists together at the small of my back.

"Let's start with what you're doing here," Bhatami said, stepping close to me and pulling my Beretta from its holster. "Odd time of night to be leaving the planet."

"I wasn't leaving the planet," I said. "My assistant and I checked into the Hanging Gardens and I came back here to pick up our luggage."

"In a very nice van," Bhatami commented, running his eye over it. "A rental?"

"No, I borrowed it from Mr. Veldrick," I told him. There was no point in lying—they would have had the tag data before I'd even parked. "He had some equipment he needed to send out to the Tube. Since I was coming out here anyway, I volunteered to bring the crates along and put them into secure storage until the next torchferry run."

"You talked to Mr. Veldrick personally about all this?" Bhatami asked.

"We discussed it earlier this evening, yes," I said, choosing my words carefully.

"It would have to have been earlier, wouldn't it?" Bhatami's gaze shifted to a point over my shoulder. "*Isantra* Golovek?" he invited.

"That is the one," a Filly voice came from behind me.

I turned, squinting at the bright lights of the police cars still pointed in my direction. It was my old friend Comet Nose, striding toward me with a cop on either side of him. "Yes, it is definitely the one I saw," Comet Nose continued. "It was he who murdered Mr. Veldrick."

"Thank you," Bhatami said. "Frank Donaldson, you're under arrest for the murder of Anton Charl Veldrick. Sergeant, take him to the station for booking."

"Wait a second," I protested as one of the cops took my arm and started to pull me toward the assembled cars. "That's it? An uncorroborated accusation from a single alien, and that's it?"

"Patience, Mr. Donaldson," Bhatami said, eyeing me closely. "You're acting as if you've already been convicted and sentenced."

"I'm acting as if I'm sitting in the middle of a massive setup," I countered. "Those crates contain highly valuable equipment. Am I supposed to just trust that your men will resist the temptation of pilferage after I've been hauled off?"

"No need," Bhatami assured me. "Those crates are evidence in an ongoing investigation. As such, they'll be returning to the station along with you and secured in the evidence room." He cocked an eyebrow. "If it'll make you feel any better, I can arrange for you to ride in the van along with them."

"And the rest will also be secured?" Comet Nose put in.

"Yes, as soon as it's been located," Bhatami assured him.

"The rest of what?" I asked.

"The rest of the material you allegedly took from Mr. Veldrick's house," Bhatami said. "*Isantra* Golovek gave us a full description."

I frowned. What was he talking about? The pieces of coral they'd loaded aboard their cars?

And then, suddenly, I understood. "Let me guess," I said. "Several metal boxes the size of Quadrail lockboxes?"

"What makes you say that?" Bhatami asked, eyeing me thoughtfully.

"Because I've recently seen boxes like that," I told him. "Only not at Mr. Veldrick's house. They're the property of someone else entirely."

"If so, the owner has nothing to worry about," Bhatami assured me. "Assuming this person you name can prove title, the boxes will be promptly returned."

I sent a sour look at Comet Nose, noting again the subtle cues of Modhran control reflected in his long face. So that was the new game plan. The Modhri didn't particularly care if the murder frame-up against me worked or not. In fact, he probably didn't even care if Bhatami ultimately returned Rebekah's boxes to her. All he wanted was the chance to get his coral outpost and her boxes all thrown in together in the police evidence room. "And where exactly am I alleged to have stashed these other boxes?" I asked.

"Your assistant was alleged to have driven off with them in another car," Bhatami said. "We're looking for her now."

I looked around at the collection of cops loitering around us. There were eight of them, plus Bhatami and the two who'd been hiding in the spaceport building with him. "That's a neat trick, considering most of your force seems to be right here," I commented.

"We're a larger department than you seem to think, Mr. Donaldson," Bhatami said. "And the group here will be back on patrol duty as soon as you and your cargo have been properly secured." Stepping forward, he took my upper arm at the elbow. "Now, as you'd expressed interest in riding in the van with the crates—"

"Lieutenant!" one of the cops at the edge of the pack cut in. "Car approaching along the south access road."

"Take him," Bhatami ordered, shoving me toward one of the other cops. Drawing his gun, he stepped to the front of Veldrick's van and pressed himself against it, his eyes on the approaching headlights.

This was it—McMicking was finally making his move. I took a casual half step forward, easing a little in front of the cop who now had me in tow. As I did so, my cuffed hands brushed the key ring on his belt, a ring that included the key to my cuffs. If whatever McMicking had in mind was spectacular enough, I ought to be able to get my hands free while everyone else's attention was distracted.

The car was still approaching, running rather faster than

seemed prudent. Was it a diversion, rigged with a tied-down steering wheel and braced accelerator? I glanced surreptitiously around the rest of the spaceport grounds, searching for a sign of the real attack.

But instead of crashing into the parked police cars, the incoming car turned sharply to avoid them and braked to a halt directly behind my van. As it settled into the glare of the police cars' headlights, I saw that it was Karim's car.

"Out of the car," Bhatami shouted. "Keep your hands where we can see them."

"Don't shoot," a female voice called back. The two front doors opened.

And Bayta and Rebekah stepped out into the light.

I shot a look at Comet Nose. Even given his alien physiology, I had no trouble seeing the satisfaction on his face. For over a month he'd been searching for this girl, and now here she was, walking right into his arms.

And because I was watching Comet Nose, I completely missed Bhatami's own reaction. "Rebekah *Beach*?" he demanded, his voice sounding annoyed and stunned and relieved all at the same time.

I switched my gaze to the lieutenant. He'd holstered his gun and was hurrying over to the car, his expression the same combination of annoyed and stunned and relieved that I'd heard in his voice. "Where in h—? Where have you *been*?"

"Hello, Lieutenant Bhatami," Rebekah said, her own voice quiet and subdued. "I know, and I'm sorry."

"Sorry doesn't begin to cover it," Bhatami chided. Giving Bayta a quick, speculative look, he took Rebekah's arm and led her away from the car toward our little group of cops. "The whole department's been looking for you for the past month, ever since your sister left."

"I've been hiding," Rebekah said simply. Her eyes brushed Comet Nose and me and then turned back to Bhatami. "There are people who want to hurt me." She hesitated. "They hurt Lorelei, too. She's . . ." Her voice faded away.

A muscle in Bhatami's cheek tightened briefly. "Yes, I know," he said gently. "The word came in from Earth yesterday afternoon. I'm very sorry."

"Thank you," Rebekah said. "Can I please just leave, Lieutenant? All I want to do is leave."

Bhatami looked again at Bayta. "You have a place to go?"

"We're going to Earth," Rebekah said. "Bayta and Mr. Donaldson have offered to take me to the Tube in their torch-yacht."

"Impossible," Comet Nose put in before Bhatami could answer. "Officer Bhatami, that is the car I saw, and those are the Humans. They helped him kill the Human Veldrick."

"You must be mistaken," Bhatami said, his tone polite but firm. "Ms. Beach and her sister are well known in our community. There's no way she would be involved in theft and murder."

"The evidence will make that decision," Comet Nose said firmly. "I am a ranking citizen of the Filiaelian Assembly. You *will* accommodate my request."

"Maybe we can meet you halfway," I suggested. It was about time I stirred up the mud a little. "Tell us what was stolen."

Every eye turned to me. "You will stay silent, murderer," Comet Nose bit out.

"No, really," I said. "You say you saw Rebekah stealing Mr. Veldrick's stuff. What exactly did you see her stealing?"

"Metal boxes," he said. "Twenty of them, shaped—"

"Yes, we know it was in boxes," I interrupted, looking sideways at Bhatami. But he was showing no signs of cutting me off, and his cop's gaze was focused solely on Comet Nose. Apparently, having Rebekah tacitly vouch for me did more for my credibility with the locals than even my Hardin Security card did. "I want you to tell us what you think was *in* those boxes."

"How would I know?" Comet Nose protested.

"Because Veldrick said you were business associates, which implies you must have spent a fair amount of time in his house," I said. "Surely you have some idea what he owned that might be worth stealing."

Comet Nose looked at Bhatami. "Lieutenant, this is completely improper," he protested.

"It's certainly irregular," Bhatami said calmly. "On the other hand, no one murders a man in order to make off with vacation souvenirs. If you can offer a list of Mr. Veldrick's valuables, and if those same items are actually inside those boxes, it would go a long way toward validating your claim."

"I *saw* him shoot the Human Veldrick," Comet Nose insisted, jabbing a finger at me.

"So you've said," Bhatami agreed. "And if you're right, the investigators on the scene will find evidence of that. But that will take time."

Comet Nose's face had gone suddenly very still. "And?" he prompted ominously.

"And I'm not inclined to hold Ms. Beach without some

kind of solid evidence that she's involved in any of this," Bhatami said. "Ms. Beach *or* her property."

Comet Nose's eyes flicked to Rebekah, then to me, then finally back to Bhatami. He didn't look nearly so self-satisfied now. "Very well," he ground out. "The boxes contain Modhran coral." He stabbed a finger at the van. "As do the so-named crates of equipment this Human carries."

"Really," Bhatami said, his voice darkening as he looked at me. "I presume you realize that importation of alien coral and coral-like substances is a class-B felony on Confederation worlds."

"Yes, and I'm sure Mr. Veldrick knew that, too," I agreed. "I can only assume that someone else must have given it to him. Someone from outside the Confederation, probably, who wasn't familiar with all of our laws and import restrictions."

For a long minute Bhatami locked gazes with me. Then, stirring, he turned back to Rebekah. "Rebekah, will you tell me what's in the boxes?"

A slightly pained look flicked across Rebekah's face. "Siris brandy," she said.

Bhatami blinked. "*Brandy?*"

"Yes," she said, looking even more pained. "Three hundred bottles of it."

He pursed his lips. "I'm afraid that's way beyond personal use limits," he said regretfully. "You need an exporter's license to deal in that much alcohol."

"No problem," I put in. "I have a license. We can take it out under my name."

Bhatami frowned at me. "I thought you worked security for Hardin Industries."

"My duties are flexible."

He gave me a long, speculative look, then turned back to Rebekah. "What's the brandy for, Rebekah?"

She lowered her gaze. "Mr. Karim gave it to me. I was hoping I could sell it for enough money to buy my Quadrail ticket to Earth."

Carefully, I suppressed a frown. A fine story, as far as it went. Certainly New Tigris's home-grown alcoholic beverages had become popular among the galaxy's rich and tipsy. Sold to the right dealer, three hundred bottles of Siris might well have brought in enough for a third-class Quadrail ticket.

The only problem was that there was no reason why the Modhri would knock himself out this way, not to mention murder three people, just to get his hands on a stash of Human liquor.

Which meant Rebekah was lying through her teeth.

The Modhri knew it, too. "Ridiculous," Comet Nose spat. "She carries Modhran coral. I insist you impound it as evidence."

"You can look for yourself," Rebekah offered.

Bhatami looked at Comet Nose. "Thank you, I will," he said. "Perhaps you'd care to join us, *Isantra* Golovek?"

Taking Rebekah's arm again, Bhatami walked her back toward the rear of the car. With only a brief hesitation, Comet Nose followed. I got two steps of my own before the cop on guard-dog duty hauled me to a sharp halt. "Lieutenant?" I called.

"Yes, bring him, too," Bhatami ordered over his shoulder.

The cop and I reached the rear of the car just as Rebekah popped open the trunk. I picked myself a spot where I had a view of the boxes and was also within quick-kick range of Comet Nose, just in case. "You have the keys?" Bhatami asked.

Silently, Rebekah handed them over. Bhatami looked over the boxes a moment, then inserted the key into the rightmost box on the top layer.

There was a teeth-aching screech of metal on metal. "They're a little rusty," Rebekah said apologetically. "Sorry."

"That's all right." With careful effort Bhatami managed to turn the key without breaking it, and with a final squeak the lock popped. Removing the key, he lifted the lid.

There, glinting in the soft glow of the trunk light, were eighteen bottles of Siris brandy.

No one spoke. For once, even the Modhri seemed to be at a loss for words. Silently, Bhatami closed the lid and relocked the box. Brushing past Comet Nose, he went to the other end of the trunk and inserted the key into the box one in from the left. With more of the same effort, and more of the metal-on-metal screeching, he got it open.

Inside was another collection of brandy bottles. "Well?" Bhatami asked, looking at Comet Nose.

"It is there," Comet Nose insisted.

"Yes, I can tell," Bhatami said with only a touch of sarcasm. Closing and sealing the box, he moved the middle box of the top layer aside and opened the box directly beneath it. Still more brandy. "Thank you, Rebekah," he said, closing and sealing the box and replacing the one he'd moved. "Were you wanting to leave right now?"

"Yes, as soon as I can," Rebekah said. "What about Mr. Donaldson?"

"I'm afraid Mr. Donaldson will have to stay with us for a

little longer," Bhatami said. "But you and Bayta can go ahead and load your things aboard her torchyacht if you'd like."

"No!" Comet Nose barked. All the work he'd gone to in order to get his coral and Rebekah's boxes together, and now here they were about to slip out of his grasp. "I protest! You must not allow her to leave."

"Hussin, go get a cart from the port building, will you?" Bhatami ordered one of the cops, ignoring the Filly's outburst.

The cop nodded and headed for the building. He might as well not have bothered. The Customs official had been standing by the open door, clearly eavesdropping on the unfolding drama, and as Officer Hussin detached himself from the group of cops, the younger man ducked back inside and snared one of the three transport carts lined up against the wall. He met Hussin halfway to our group, and as they moved the cart together toward the car I could swear they were actually vying with each other as to which of them was doing the better job. Everyone on New Tigris, apparently, was Rebekah's friend.

Almost everyone, anyway. "Officer Bhatami, I protest," Comet Nose said again as the two men maneuvered the cart to the rear of the car and started loading the boxes onto it. He was right in Bhatami's face now, his voice rising in pitch and increasing in volume. "I intend to lodge a formal complaint with the Filiaelian Assembly—"

And then, one of the cops standing near the front of the van gave a little choke and collapsed onto the ground.

THIRTEEN:

"Incoming!" I barked as the cop next to him also dropped into a heap. The other cops were already on it, snatching out their own guns, their heads jerking back and forth as they searched for the shooter. Beside me, Comet Nose slammed the back of one hand across Bhatami's face as he made a grab for the lieutenant's holstered gun with the other.

Bhatami got there first, and for a second the two of them struggled for the weapon before my double kick into the Filly's knee and low ribs sent him sprawling to the pavement. "Get out of here!" I snapped at the Customs official, crouched frozen at the rear of the car, his eyes wide. "Get them inside."

The official shifted his goggle eyes toward me as a barrage of gunfire erupted from the remaining cops, concentrated on the two autocabs in the shelter fifty meters ahead of us. "I said *move*!" I ordered again.

"You heard him," Bayta urged, taking the Customs man's arm. The *kwi*, I saw, was already in place on her other hand.

"Come on, Mr. Elfol," Rebekah said encouragingly, getting a grip on the cart's bar. "I'll help you push."

The man seemed to snap out of his stunned trance. "Okay," he managed. With Rebekah beside him, he shoved off from the car, pushing for all he was worth.

"Wait a second," I called as Bayta started to follow. "Where's Karim?"

"I don't know," she said. "He said he was going to go find a flanking position. He hadn't returned when Rebekah said we needed to come stop them from arresting you."

I swore under my breath. If I'd known Rebekah was going to go all noble that way, I would never have left my phone on for them to listen to.

On the other hand, if she hadn't insisted on coming to my rescue, all the cops would probably have left when they arrested me, leaving her, Bayta, and Karim to face the Filly shooter alone. "Just get her into the ship and seal up," I told Bayta. "They'll need something stronger than handguns to get through a torchyacht hull."

She nodded and headed off after the other two, sweeping the autocab shelter with the *kwi* as she ran. The shooter was almost certainly out of the *kwi*'s limited range, I knew, but it couldn't hurt to try.

I returned my attention to the main event, to find that two more cops had gone down for the count. So far, fortunately, the shooter seemed to be sticking with snoozers. I wondered if and when that would change.

"Hold still," Bhatami growled in my ear, his voice barely audible over the chattering of the gunfire. I felt his hands at my wrists, and a second later I was free. "Here," he added, pressing my Beretta into my hand.

"Thanks," I said, peering around the side of the car. Three of the five cops still standing had taken refuge behind the van and were pouring a controlled stream of thudwumpers at the autocab shelter. The two cops who weren't busy laying down suppression fire were on the move, running hunched over toward the shelter, veering wide to both sides to keep out of their comrades' line of fire.

I held my breath, waiting for the shooter at the shelter to notice the flankers and open fire on them. But either he'd completely missed their approach, or else the cops' fire had him too thoroughly pinned down. Either way, fifteen more seconds and they would have him.

An unpleasant tingle went up my back. This was too easy. It was *way* too easy. "Call them back," I urged, grabbing Bhatami's shoulder. "It's a trap."

"What kind of trap?" he demanded, throwing a frown at me.

Before I could answer, a car with no lights shot suddenly into view from the parking area to our left, gunning straight for the two running cops.

"Look out!" I shouted. But it was too late. The car slammed into the first cop, probably before he was even aware of its presence, hurling him through the air to skid to a broken halt almost at the feet of his comrade. The second cop had just enough time to brake to a halt and try to get out of the way before he too was run down. The impact threw him into the tall chain-link fence at the spaceport's perimeter. He bounced off the fence and lay still.

The police gunfire had faltered during the attack. Now, with a snarled curse from someone, the barrage began again, this time targeting the car.

Ignoring the hail of thudwumpers hammering his vehicle, the driver backed the car up a few meters. Braking to a halt, he opened his door, reached out to snatch the first dead cop's gun from the pavement, and lobbed it to the Filly hidden at the autocab shelter. With the kind of perfect coordination only the Modhri could achieve, the shooter's hand darted out at exactly the right time to the right spot to catch the weapon. Even before the pass was complete, the car lurched forward again, headed for the other dead cop's gun.

But the brief respite was all the rest of the cops needed to get the range. As the car surged toward the fence, I saw the driver jerk like a broken marionette as multiple rounds hammered his head and torso. He slumped over the wheel as the car rolled to a stop.

And then the driver's-side back door opened, and from my crouching position I saw a hand dart down from the rear passenger seat. It grabbed the remaining gun off the pavement, swiveled it around, and began shooting under the car at us.

"What the *hell*?" Bhatami gasped as one of the three remaining cops gave a choked gasp and sprawled onto the pavement. "He can't shoot that way."

"Tell *him* that," I retorted. Of course the Modhri could shoot blind that way—he had both the other shooter and Comet Nose to triangulate his aim for him.

I frowned as the thought suddenly brought Comet Nose to

mind. I looked over at the pavement where I'd dropped him a minute ago.

He was gone.

"Watch it!" I warned, looking around. There was no sign of him. Had he faded into the night to our rear, heading away from the battle on some other errand? Or had he curved back around to follow Bayta and Rebekah? I looked through the glassed-in front of the spaceport building, but there was no one visible.

And then, with a lurch, Veldrick's van pulled away from the curb. Cutting hard around the group of parked police cars, it roared off across the parking area, leaving the two cops who'd been crouched behind it completely exposed to the two Filly shooters. The cops reacted instantly, scrambling for new defensive positions behind the police cars. But once again the Modhri's group-mind coordination was faster. Before they'd made it even halfway, both of them dropped to the ground.

And our side was now down to two: Bhatami and me. "I think it's time to call in some backup," I told Bhatami.

His reply was lost in a sudden thunder of gunfire from the two Fillies' positions. *Real* gunfire this time, not just snoozers. I ducked lower behind the car, wincing as the thudwumpers slammed into the engine compartment and shattered the windows, showering the two of us with bits of glass. "—the hell are they *doing*?" I heard Bhatami snarl over the racket.

"Keeping us busy," I shouted back, silently cursing my own lack of anticipation. Of course the Modhri had restricted himself to snoozers up until now—with the cops crouched behind the van, his precious crateloads of coral had been in his line of fire. With the van now out of the way, his walkers were free to switch to thudwumpers and do their best to put us out of his way permanently. I glanced at the van, bouncing at full speed across and through the modest landscaping around the spaceport parking area as Comet Nose whisked the coral out of the battle zone.

I caught my breath. No—Comet Nose wasn't driving *away* from anything. He was driving *toward* something. Specifically, toward a shadowy figure running stealthily across the parking area. Was McMicking finally joining the party?

And then the headlights brushed across the figure, and I saw that it wasn't McMicking, but Karim.

The cacophony of shots from the two Fillies was joined by the distinctive bark of Karim's RusFed P11 as he opened fire at the vehicle heading toward him. But for all the effect the shots had he might as well have been throwing confetti. With no need for Comet Nose himself to see where he was going, he could crouch low behind the dashboard with the whole engine compartment to block Karim's shots.

I swiveled my Beretta around, resting it across my left wrist, and opened fire on the van's cargo compartment. If I could put a couple of thudwumpers into the coral, maybe the walkers would go catatonic long enough for Karim to get out of the way.

I was still firing when the van caught Karim a glancing blow, throwing him sideways to the ground and sending his gun spinning off into the night.

I winced with sympathetic pain. The impact had been relatively light, and there was a fair chance Karim had survived it.

But that state of affairs wouldn't last long. All the Modhri had to do was pull the van around in a quick circle and roll over him to finish the job.

I peered helplessly out into the darkness surrounding the spaceport. McMicking had to be here—he was too good to have missed out on the probability that the Modhri would have set up for a full-fledged attack. Not Larry Hardin's top troubleshooter. He had to be lurking somewhere on the fringes of the battle, maybe with a homemade mortar and lob bomb, maybe with a cozy sniper's position and a hypersonic rifle. He was the surprise, last-minute flanking move that the Modhri wouldn't be expecting and would have no way of blocking.

Only our last minutes were rapidly running down, and Karim's absolute last minute was nearly here.

Where the hell *was* he?

The van shifted direction, and I waited tensely for it to circle around and finish off Karim. But instead the vehicle veered in the opposite direction, curving around and heading back toward the spaceport proper. "Looks like he's coming back for his friends," Bhatami said. "We've got one last chance to nail him." Rising from his crouch a few centimeters, he braced his gun hand on the car's trunk, pointing it toward the shelter.

And with a sudden snarl of pain, he lunged forward, slamming his chest against the car's rear bumper, and fell heavily to the ground.

I dropped to one knee beside him. To my surprise, it was his ankle, not his chest, that was busy spurting blood onto the pavement. The Filly in the car had managed to land a shot under not only his own vehicle but also under ours as well.

"Never mind me," Bhatami gritted out between clenched teeth as he clutched at his wound. "Nail the *haramzas*."

"In a second," I said, shoving my gun back into its holster and gingerly pulling back the blood-soaked pant leg. There was a pulsing rhythm to the flow, which meant the shot had nicked an artery. If I went charging off after the Fillies now, Bhatami would bleed to death where he lay. "Where do you keep your med kits?"

"You hear me?" Bhatami snapped. "I said—"

"Never mind—I'll find it," I cut him off, eyeing the nearest police car. It was about four meters away, across the business end of the Modhran shooting gallery. Setting my teeth, I gathered my feet under me and sprinted to the car.

No shots rang out. With my skin crawling in gruesome anticipation, I wrenched the door open and ducked down into its limited protection. "Under the front passenger seat," Bhatami called, his voice already sounding weaker.

I reached under the seat and pulled out the shiny white box. Tucking it under my arm, I turned around and braced myself for the return run across the shooting gallery.

And as I did so, there was a horrendous crash from the spaceport fence.

I looked through the car window. Comet Nose had driven the van through the fence and was now bouncing across the landing area. Behind him, running for all they were worth, were the two remaining Fillies from the shelter and the car.

Suppressing another curse, I ran back to Bhatami's side and popped open the medical kit. The all-purpose emergency bandage was right on top; ripping it out of its sterile plastic envelope, I wrapped it around Bhatami's ankle and squeezed the activation disk. The tiny red lights went on as the catalytic reaction inside the bandage began swelling the material, sealing off the entire area around the wound. "Go," Bhatami breathed. "Maybe you can still stop them."

"Right." Away to the south, I could see the faint flickers of red and blue light that marked the approach of the backup forces that I wished had been here three minutes ago. Pressing a pain-med hypo into Bhatami's palm, I headed for the hole in the fence.

I had just reached it and started through when there was a flat crack from somewhere in front of me and a bullet whizzed past my head.

I threw myself down and to the side, landing painfully on a tangled flap of the fencing that Comet Nose's impact had torn free. Another shot ricocheted off the pavement beside me. This time I spotted the shooter crouched at the corner of the spaceport building. I fired three shots, and had the satisfaction of seeing him jerk violently and then fall to the ground.

But my sense of accomplishment was short-lived. I'd made it to his position and confirmed he was dead when, across the field, one of the torchyachts rose into view on its Shorshic force thrusters. Still lifting, it swiveled ponderously around and headed across the sky.

I raised my gun, then lowered it again, the taste of defeat in my mouth. I'd been able to keep the Modhri away from Rebekah at Karim's bar, and had blocked his effort to bring his outpost and her boxes together in the police evidence room.

But this time he had me. Even if Bhatami was willing to let me go without further investigation—and I was pretty sure he

224 : Timothy Zahn

wouldn't—the Modhri would still get to the transfer station ahead of us. At that point, he would simply arrange for his coral and Rebekah's boxes to be shuttled over to the Tube together. Whatever the Modhri had in mind, a nice little hundred-kilometer trip together in a shuttle's cargo compartment would probably do the trick.

We could, of course, bypass the transfer station entirely by sneaking around behind the Tube and pulling the back-door entry we'd used on a couple of previous occasions. But I doubted that would really help us any. The Modhri could simply split up his own coral boxes between the transfer station and the Tube and be ready to pounce with either the minute we showed our faces.

Besides, once we reached the Tube we still had to actually *go* somewhere, and once in the Quadrail system the Modhri had a very definite edge in numbers. All Bayta and I would have would be the *kwi,* and given the Modhri's obsession with Rebekah I doubted that would be enough.

We would just have to come up with some other clever trick. Unfortunately, at the moment I didn't have the faintest idea what that might be.

And in the meantime, I still had a few other hurdles to clear before we could get off the planet. Holstering my Beretta, I headed back to see how Bhatami was doing.

I had just reached the mangled section of fence when the whole landscape lit up around me.

I spun around, my first reflexive thought that the torch-yacht had somehow exploded. But the light was already fading, and as I squinted through the afterimage I realized that the ship had merely cut in its ion-plasma drive for half a second or so. It was already back on its normal atmospheric thrusters before the rumble of the brief high-energy pulse rolled over me.

I was still wondering what that was all about when I reached Bhatami. The rest of the backup crowd had arrived in my absence, and a pair of medics were getting the lieutenant settled onto a stretcher. A few of the cops eyed me warily as I came up, but no one actually pointed a gun in my direction. "How's he doing?" I asked the medics.

"He's doing just fine," Bhatami said. His voice had that slightly distant quality that often resulted from a system full of pain meds. "I see they got away."

"Only two of them," I said. "What's left of the third is over by the corner of the building."

Bhatami nodded and gestured weakly to one of the cops loitering nearby. "Sergeant, take a couple of men and check it out."

"Yes, sir," the cop said, and headed away.

"We have any police presence on the transfer station?" I asked Bhatami.

He shook his head. "Irrelevant question," he said. "You see that flash a minute ago? No—of course you saw the flash. That was their ion-plasma taking out our communications laser."

I grimaced. "I don't suppose you have a backup."

Bhatami puffed derisively. "On New Tigris?"

"I didn't think so," I said. So our last chance of putting even that much of a roadblock in the Modhri's path was gone. If he'd done the job properly, the laser would be out of commission far longer than the five days it would take the torchyacht to reach the transfer station.

"But at least they didn't get Rebekah," he went on. "Thank you for that."

"You're welcome," I said. The Modhri didn't have her yet, anyway. "She's a popular girl, isn't she?"

"Everyone who knows her likes her," he said simply.

"Really," I said, a wisp of something unpleasant curling through me.

"Absolutely," he said. "Her and Lorelei both."

The medics finished their prep work and rolled the stretcher into position behind the ambulance. "What happens to me now?" I asked.

"Not much," Bhatami said. "You'll need to come down to the station and make a statement about this evening's activities. I understand that along with Mr. Veldrick, we have two more bodies at Karim's bar."

"Those were self-defense," I said, peering across the parking area toward where Karim had been run over.

Bhatami caught the look. "He's already been taken away in another ambulance," he said. "He'll need to make a statement, too, once he's sufficiently recovered."

"Of course," I said, wishing I'd had a chance to work out a common story with Karim. "What about the two murdered police officers?"

Bhatami's gaze hardened. "We'll check the weapon used by the Filiaelian you say you shot just now. If it's one of the ones stolen from Sergeant Aksam or Officer Lasari, you'll be in the clear. If the two that got away took those particular weapons aboard the torchyacht with them—" He shrugged slightly. "Things might take a little longer."

Inside my pocket, my comm vibrated. McMicking, telling

me he'd finally finished whatever puttering he'd gone off to do and was ready to come to our aid? "Hello?" I answered.

"Are you still at the spaceport?" Bayta's voice came.

"They're about to take me downtown," I said. "You and Rebekah all right?"

"We're fine," she said. "You need to come over here before you leave. Rather, you need to come to Mr. Veldrick's van. It's over by where the Filiaelians' torchyacht was parked."

"My hosts may not want me taking a walk just now," I pointed out.

"They will," Bayta assured me. "You'll want a couple of them with you."

I looked at Bhatami. "Bayta has something on the field she wants me and a couple of your officers to take a look at."

He frowned but gestured. "Go ahead. Darrian, Joachem—go with him."

With the two cops in tow, I retraced my steps through the hole in the fence. On the way we passed the three others Bhatami had sent to examine the Filly body I'd tapped on my final futile attempt to stop the torchyacht. "You carry a Glock?" one of them called to me, holding up a familiar-looking gun in his gloved hand.

"Usually," I said. "You'll note I'm not the one who's been shooting that one."

He grunted and dropped the gun carefully into an evidence bag. One of his partners, I noticed, was similarly bagging another sidearm, probably one of the guns appropriated from the dead cops the Modhri had run over earlier. I spotted the nose of Veldrick's van half hidden behind one of the two remaining torchyachts, and my escort and I headed over.

We reached the vehicle to find the rear loading door wide open and the crates of coral gone. Wondering which of those completely unsurprising facts Bayta had found so interesting, I walked around the rear of the van to its other side.

And stopped. There, lying motionless on the pavement, were the two Fillies I'd last seen heading for their torchyacht. Their hands had been strapped securely behind their backs with plastic cargo ties, and in the reflected light from the spaceport building I could see the small wet stains of snoozer wounds.

"What the *hell*?" one of the cops beside me muttered as he caught sight of them.

"You'll want to check those," I said, pointing to the three guns lying by the bodies. "Two of them are probably the ones that were stolen from Sergeant Aksam and Officer Lasari."

Wordlessly, the cops pulled out some evidence bags and set to work. I stepped back out of their way, looking up at the stars in the direction the torchyacht had taken.

So *that's* where McMicking had gotten to.

Three hours later, less than twenty-four since our arrival, I eased our torchyacht into the air and headed for space.

"Just like that?" Bayta asked, sounding like she didn't quite believe it.

"Just like that," I confirmed. Double-checking that we were far enough out from the planet, I keyed in the scoop and the ion-plasma drive. "Besides, what were they going to charge me with?"

"Well, there *were* those two dead Filiaelians in Mr. Karim's bar," she reminded me.

"Killed by an unidentified assailant with an unknown gun," I reminded her. "Not my gun. Not my fault."

"How about the theft of the Filiaelians' torchyacht and the destruction of the planet's communications laser?"

"Again, nothing to do with me," I said. "The Customs official who passed the thief through this evening has the man's name, the security cameras have his face, and neither of them match anyone connected to you or me."

"No, of course not," she murmured. "And Mr. Veldrick?"

I grimaced. Even knowing there was nothing I could have done to stop it, that one still bothered me. "Killed with my Glock," I conceded. "But since the last two Fillies were found with the two murdered cops' guns, and since those selfsame cops had already reported having confiscated my Glock long before Veldrick was killed, it logically follows that all three guns were stolen as a set."

"Logically, but not conclusively," she pointed out. "It would have been better if the two Filiaelians could have been found at the scene of his murder."

"Certainly wasn't from any lack of effort on my part," I said. "Two snoozers each should have put them down for the count. Remind me to be more generous if we run into Filly walkers again."

"Or at least Filiaelians who've been genetically designed for special hunting duty."

I nodded agreement. "Speaking of hunting, where's Rebekah?"

"Asleep in her stateroom," Bayta said. "The poor girl was exhausted."

I looked at the status readouts. We were already nearly a

thousand kilometers out from New Tigris, and adding to that distance with every passing second. A few more minutes ought to be more than enough. "Wake her up," I said.

Bayta's eyes widened. "Wake her *up*?"

"Why not?" I asked. "She's probably had more sleep in the past twenty-four hours than either of us have."

"Which means we need sleep even more than she does," Bayta countered. "Can't whatever this is wait?"

"It could, but it's not going to," I said. "Go on—I'll meet the two of you in the dayroom in five minutes."

She looked as if she very much wanted to say something else. But she just nodded and started to turn to the door. "One more thing," I added, catching her arm. "Let me have the *kwi*."

That earned me a long, speculative look. But again, she merely handed the weapon over without argument and left the cockpit. I rechecked the autopilot, confirmed the long-range scanners were clear of any other ships, and headed back to the dayroom. Picking the chair that faced the door, I sat down at the table and settled in to wait.

I'd told Bayta five minutes, but it was closer to fifteen before she reappeared, a bleary-eyed Rebekah in tow. "Hello, Rebekah," I greeted her. "Sorry I had to wake you."

"That's all right," she said as she and Bayta sat down across from me. "I owe you both a great deal for getting me off New Tigris."

"So it would seem," I said. "*Seem* being the operative word."

"What are you talking about?" Bayta asked, frowning.

"I'm talking about Little Miss Sunshine here, the girl who's everyone's friend," I told her. "I'm talking about the Modhri, and the Oscar-level performance he put on down there."

I lifted my hand from my lap and rested the butt of my Beretta on the table, leveling the weapon at Rebekah's chest. "And I'm talking about fraud," I concluded quietly. "You've been manipulating us ever since Lorelei showed up in my apartment."

"Frank, have you lost your *mind*?" Bayta demanded. "This poor little girl—"

"This poor little girl is a Modhran walker," I cut her off. "And I want to know what the game is."

I thumbed off the Beretta's safety, the click sounding abnormally loud in the sudden silence. "Now."

FOURTEEN :

For a long moment no one moved or spoke. I counted the heartbeats—there were eighteen of them—before Bayta finally broke the silence. "I assume you have some proof of this?" she asked.

"I have enough," I said, watching Rebekah closely. The initial shock of my accusation had passed quickly, leaving a sort of watchful calm in its place. A calm well beyond the capability of any ten-year-old Human I'd ever known. "Pointer number one: the Filly walkers were supposedly able to locate her."

"We discussed that earlier," Bayta said. "You came up with at least two possible theories on that."

"Both of which were incredibly lame," I said. "Pointer number two: the Filly at the spaceport said Rebekah's boxes contained Modhran coral." I raised my eyebrows at Rebekah. "Shall we go take a look?"

"Lieutenant Bhatami did that already," Bayta reminded me.

"Which is what finally clinched it," I said coldly. "The Modhri couldn't care less about smuggled Siris brandy. Ergo, there must be something else of value in the rest of the boxes, with those three just there as decoys."

I cocked an eyebrow. "So how did Bhatami know which three were safe for him to open?"

Bayta caught her breath. "A *thought virus*?"

"Can you think of a more perfect setup for one?" I asked. "Sweet, helpless little girl, who everyone in town is already madly in love with?"

"Maybe Lieutenant Bhatami just knew where the safe boxes were," Bayta suggested.

"How?" I countered. "Karim and I were the ones who loaded them into the trunk, and I guarantee we weren't following any special prearranged pattern. You were with Rebekah every minute after that—you tell *me* when she had a chance to clue our good lieutenant in on the layout."

For another five heartbeats Bayta didn't answer. Then, reluctantly, she turned to Rebekah. "Rebekah?" she asked gently.

"Very good, Mr. Compton," Rebekah said quietly, her eyes on me. "We were right to choose you as the one to help us."

"Flattery noted and ignored," I said. "Just tell Bayta I'm right, and we can move on."

Rebekah pursed her lips. "You're right," she acknowledged. "But you're also wrong."

"Well, that's clear," I said sarcastically, forcing myself to remember this was a deadly enemy who was sitting across from me. The minute I started to think of her as a young Human girl I'd be opening myself up to the same thought-virus attack she'd used on Bhatami. "How about a simple yes or no?"

"This is going to be difficult," she murmured, almost as if she was talking to herself. "All right. I *do* have a polyp colony inside me. That part you were right about. But I'm *not* a walker."

"So you're a soldier?"

"I'm not that, either," she said. "I'm more of a—"

"It is a *Modhran* polyp colony, right?" I asked.

She hesitated. "Technically, also no," she said. "The colony started out Modhran, but it isn't anymore." She looked at Bayta. "Actually, I'm more like Bayta than a walker."

Bayta shot a look at me. "In what way?" she asked.

"I'm a symbiotic pair," Rebekah told her. "Human and polyp intelligences in the same body."

I snorted. "Basic definition of a walker."

"Yes, but in the case of an Eye—what you call a walker— the Modhran mind segment is a parasite, with its host unaware of its presence," the girl said. "I, on the other hand, am completely aware of my symbiont, just as she is of me."

"*She*?" I echoed. "I thought the Modhri only came in a masculine flavor."

"As I said, I'm not part of the Modhri," Rebekah said. "We were an experiment he began about thirty years ago." She gave me a somewhat strained smile. "An experiment that's gone horribly wrong, at least from his point of view."

I ran my eyes over her expression and her minimal body language as she sat quietly at the table. If this was a scam, at least it was a fresh approach. That alone made it worth hearing out. "I think we're going to have to back up and start at the beginning," I said.

Her eyes flicked to the gun in my hand, and I had the distinct impression she was considering asking me to put it away. But if she was, the question remained unasked. Not that I would have, anyway. "As I said, it began about thirty years ago," she said. "The Spiders had tried to close off Quadrail service to the Modhran homeworld, and the Modhri had finally realized that it was the Spiders who had been behind all the efforts to find and destroy him. He started looking for a new way to operate, and came up with the idea of planting polyp colonies into infants, where they could grow up together aware of each other as a symbiotic pair."

I felt my stomach tighten. When I'd first heard about the Chahwyn using this symbiont trick on Bayta it had made me seriously wonder whether or not they truly held the high moral ground in their war against the Modhri. Hearing that the Modhri had pulled the exact same stunt was equally disgusting. "How many did he use?" I asked.

"There were only eight Humans in the project," Rebekah said. "Lorelei and I were the youngest of them. There were also nearly three hundred non-Human symbionts created over the twenty years the project was in operation."

"Why bother with this when the Modhri's walkers already worked fine?" Bayta asked. "Was he afraid the system might break down?"

"The problem is that his Eyes are essentially slaves," Rebekah said. "Slavery has certain advantages for the master, but also carries equally serious risks. For one thing, there's no loyalty or real cooperation between the Eye and the mind segment.

There's also the danger that if the Eye isn't used carefully he could become aware of his condition. That would be disastrous for the Modhri."

"You're amazingly articulate for a ten-year-old," I commented. "I take it this is actually your coral speaking?"

Rebekah reddened slightly. "She's helping me find the right words, yes," she admitted. "But just helping. She's not controlling me, if that's what you're thinking."

I shrugged noncommittally. "So what went wrong? I assume something went wrong?"

"Very wrong," Rebekah agreed. "No one knows exactly how it happened, but one day we all just . . . changed."

For a long moment the word hung in the air like a tethered sports zeppelin. "What do you mean, changed?" Bayta asked at last.

"We weren't connected to the group mind anymore," Rebekah said. "We were our own, brand-new person. Or rather, we were our own *persons,* plural. We were still connected together in a group mind like the Modhri, but at the same time we were also still individuals." She looked at Bayta. "Like you and the Spiders."

"Not exactly," Bayta said. "I'm not connected to the Spiders in any permanent way. I can communicate with them, but we certainly don't form any kind of group mind."

"Oh," Rebekah said, sounding a little nonplussed. "Interesting. The Modhri always assumed the Spiders worked the same way he did."

"They don't," Bayta said. "Actually, it sounds to me like your group—what do you call yourselves, anyway?"

"The Melding," Rebekah said.

"It sounds like your Melding is almost a hybrid in itself," Bayta continued. "Partly like the Modhri, partly like the Spiders."

"Maybe," Rebekah said. "At any rate, as I said, everything's changed for us now. We can't connect with the Modhri, though we can still sense his presence and I'm pretty sure he can sense ours. And of course, we have more personal freedom and individuality than any of his own mind segments."

"The Abomination," I murmured.

"What was that?" Rebekah asked.

"It's the Modhri's pet name for you," I explained. A perfectly reasonable assessment of the situation, too, at least from his point of view. Maybe from ours, too. "So after that happened, you decided to get out while the getting was good?"

"Basically," Rebekah said. "There were only a few normal Eyes in our colony. We overpowered them—I say *we,* though of course I was only a baby at the time—collected everything, and escaped to the Quadrail."

"Taking your coral outpost with you," I said. "That *is* what's in your boxes, isn't it?"

"The last segments of it, yes," Rebekah said. "We've been gradually moving it to our new home." She winced. "We were almost done when the Modhri found us. You know the rest."

"Not so fast," I admonished her. "We're not done with the history lesson yet. How did you come to pick New Tigris?"

"I don't really know why we chose it over the other options," Rebekah said. "It was still a fairly new colony, I know, with a lot of construction still going on and people coming and going, both Humans and work-contracted non-Humans. We knew the Human restriction against importing Modhran coral, but our leaders decided it was worth the risk."

"Your *leaders*?" I asked.

"Yes, of course," Rebekah said. "As I said, we're not a single mind like the Modhri. We all have our individual personalities and talents. Some have the talent of leadership, others don't. I do know that part of their thinking was that a small Human colony would be the last place the Modhri would look for us."

I snorted. "Little did you know."

She winced. "Yandro. That irony wasn't lost on us. Once we realized what he'd done, we knew we had to move again." She swallowed. "As I said, we were almost finished when he found us."

"Using genetically altered Fillies," I commented.

"Yes, and that was a new one on us," Rebekah admitted. "We could detect the presence of his walkers, and certainly knew when Mr. Veldrick brought in his coral. But the Filiaelians were completely unexpected."

"How does that work?" Bayta asked. "They need a piece of coral with them, right?"

Rebekah nodded. "As I said, we don't operate on the same wavelength as the Modhri anymore. Lorelei's theory was that the presence of the Filiaelian walkers was somehow able to shift the coral's frequency enough to be able to get direction instead of just a sense of our presence."

"And they needed to use actual coral because their own internal polyp colonies were too small?" Bayta suggested.

"Probably," Rebekah said. "But that's just a guess. All the others except Lorelei and me were already gone by then, and we didn't have any way of doing any experiments."

"So why didn't you leave when Lorelei did?" Bayta asked. "She seemed to slip out without any trouble."

"It wasn't quite as easy as you make it sound," Rebekah said, a shadow crossing her face. "And the only reason she made it at all was because she didn't have any of our coral with her. I think the coral is what they mostly detect, not us."

Though she hadn't been sure enough of that to move freely around her hideout once the Fillies had zeroed in on Karim's bar. Still, as she'd said, she hadn't exactly been set up for field tests. "So what does he want from you?" I asked. "This seems way too much work just for vengeance."

"Especially since most of the Melding is already gone," Bayta added.

"This isn't about vengeance," Rebekah said soberly. "This is an attempt to learn the Melding's new location from the outpost." Her eyes flicked sideways, in the direction of her cabin. "If he does, *then* he'll move in and destroy us."

I had an odd mental image of a bunch of white-jacketed aliens strapping a chunk of coral to an interrogation chair and trying to find somewhere to attach the thumbscrews. "You think the Modhri can make him talk?"

"Make *her* talk," Bayta corrected me.

"Actually, we still refer to the coral part of the Melding as *he*," Rebekah said. "The shift to female characteristics only happens to the colonies inside female symbionts. And yes, I'm very much afraid the Modhri can get the information if he can move enough of his coral around or near a piece of ours."

"From what, the sheer overwhelming mental pressure?"

"Something like that." Rebekah hesitated. "There's also some thought that if one of us doesn't stay physically close to our outpost it might revert back to being part of the Modhri. In that case, he wouldn't have to use any mental pressure at all. But we don't know that for sure."

"That's what you get for aborting an experiment before it's finished," I told her. "You'll have to do better next time."

Rebekah stared at me. "Are you saying we should have—?"

"He's joking," Bayta assured her. "Where exactly do you need to go?"

For a moment Rebekah didn't answer. "Sibbrava," she said at last. "It's a small colony system in the Cimmal Republic."

"Is that where the rest of your group is?" I asked.

She hesitated just a split second too long. "That's where we need to go," she said.

In other words, I gathered, we were *heading* there but not actually *going* there. "We need to know the truth, Rebekah," I warned her. "*All* of it."

"I know," she said. "I'm doing the best I can."

"That's not an answer," I countered. "If you want our help—"

"Frank," Bayta interrupted quietly.

I looked at her, then back at Rebekah's drooping eyelids. The girl was exhausted, I remembered.

As were the rest of us, I suddenly realized. For the past twelve hours or so I'd been running on pure adrenaline, and I could feel my whole system poised on the brink of physical crash. The rest of the interrogation, I decided, could wait. "We'll talk about this later," I told Rebekah. "Right now, we all need to get some sleep."

"Yes," Bayta agreed. "You'd better get back to bed, Rebekah. Before you fall over."

"I will," Rebekah said gravely as she got a bit unsteadily to her feet. "And thank you. Thank you both. For everything."

She left. Getting up, I crossed to the door and stood just inside the dayroom, craning my ears over the low rumble of the drive. A few seconds later I heard the distinctive double click as she closed her stateroom door and locked it behind her. "Well, that was fun," I said, returning to my chair and dropping heavily into it. Suddenly, I was feeling as drained as Bayta and Rebekah looked. "You want to lay odds on how much of her story was actually true?"

"I believe her," Bayta said. "It all fits what happened back there, as well as what the Modhri told us at Yandro."

I rubbed my fingers thoughtfully across the tabletop. The story wasn't inconsistent with what had happened back there, anyway. Though not being inconsistent didn't necessarily mean true. "It certainly puts an interesting new spin on what happened in New York," I said.

"What do you mean?"

"Think about it," I said. "The walkers wouldn't have destroyed Lorelei's polyp colony that way. For all they knew, they might have been able to pull the location of the Melding's new Fortress of Solitude out of it."

Bayta's eye widened in horror. "You mean she did that to *herself*?"

"It's the only way it makes sense," I said, grimacing. It *was* a pretty gruesome mental image, I had to admit. "She felt herself succumbing to the snoozers and did the only thing she could think of to keep her colony from falling into their hands. At that point the Modhri had to do the same thing to his dead walker in order to confuse the issue."

"Horrible," Bayta murmured.

"Definitely," I said. "Ironically, the whole thing still qualifies as obfuscation, which is what I thought about it from the beginning. I just had it backwards as to which direction the smokescreen was going."

Bayta shook her head. "I still don't understand how the Modhri could suddenly change his basic character just because his polyp colonies were put into these people when they were young."

"Can't help you on that one," I said. "But there actually *is* precedent of a sort. A century or so ago the southern part of the Western Alliance had an invasion of killer bees that had been accidentally brought over from Africa. One of the techniques they used to blunt the species' nastiness was to get it to interbreed with a couple of calmer bee species."

"But that's a physical, genetic change," Bayta pointed out. "This is different."

"Only in that the effects are mostly mental," I reminded her. "The polyps *are* physically present, after all." I shrugged. "And don't forget we haven't actually proved this Melding is any more friendly than the original Modhri."

"Of course it is," Bayta said. "You saw how taken those people were with Rebekah. She has to be something very special for so many people to be willing to put their lives on the line for her."

"Unless it's just a whole mess of thought viruses," I countered.

"No," she said firmly. "Thought viruses use friendship as a conduit, but don't actually create that friendship in the first place."

For a brief moment I considered reminding her about the whole Penny Auslander incident. Fortunately, even my fatigue-numbed mind realized in time that that would just be begging for trouble. "Maybe," I said instead. "You know anything about this Sibbrava system Rebekah mentioned?"

"Not really," Bayta said, pulling out her reader and keying it on. "It's the third system you get to in Cimman space along the Kalalee Branch. It's about six and a half days from Jurskala Station, maybe ten from New Tigris Station." She peered at the reader. "Looks like the planet is mostly subsistence farming, mining, and manufacturing, with a small export trade in rare metals and exotic woods."

"Your basic end-of-the-line sort of place," I said. "Perfect spot for the Melding to take a long vacation from the rest of the universe."

"As long as no one wonders about them on their way in," Bayta warned. "The problem with small worlds is that strangers are easy to spot."

"True," I agreed, frowning as a sudden thought struck me. "What does the place have in the way of icy waters?"

Bayta fiddled with the reader's keys. "Not much," she reported. "Both polar regions are covered by land—glaciers and frozen tundra, mostly. There are a few lakes that are cold enough, but they look pretty small and shallow."

I nodded. With proper safeguards, Modhran coral could live nearly anywhere, but it needed lots of very cold water in order to grow. "Good," I said. "That implies the Melding's not trying to increase their coral outpost, only maintain it."

"They wouldn't want it growing anyway," Bayta pointed out. "Especially if they're afraid it might revert to true Modhran status without their presence nearby. They couldn't risk it growing large enough to outnumber them." She frowned. "If that makes sense."

"It does," I assured her. "Where did her boxes end up, by the way?"

"They're in the stateroom behind hers," Bayta said. "She wanted them with her, but there really wasn't enough room for her and them."

"Wants to be as close to them as possible," I said, nodding. "Sure."

Bayta stirred in her seat. "Are we going to take her to Sib-brava?"

I eyed her closely. "You really do trust her, don't you?"

"Yes, I do," she said, meeting my gaze without flinching. "I know trust is hard for you, especially with something like this. But I *do* trust her."

"Okay by me," I said. This was definitely not the time for an argument, or even a long discussion. Not with our minds and emotions clouded by lack of sleep.

But that didn't mean the subject was closed. Not by a long shot. It might be that the Melding's new telepathic frequency was close enough to Bayta's that she could genuinely sense Rebekah's sincerity. It was also possible that during their long hours together Rebekah had managed to plant a thought virus or two in my partner's brain.

"So that's it?" Bayta asked, frowning at my easy capitulation on the subject.

"For now," I said. "We both need some sleep before we can tackle anything requiring higher brain function." I dug into my pocket and pulled out the *kwi*. "Here," I said, handing it to her. "Keep it under your pillow tonight."

She fingered the weapon uncertainly. "She's not going to attack us, you know."

"Glad to hear it," I said. "Keep it under your pillow anyway."

Bayta hesitated, then slipped the *kwi* into her pocket. "All right," she said. "If it makes you feel better."

"It does," I said, standing up. "And lock your door behind you. I'll see you in about ten hours."

"Maybe even twelve," she said tiredly. "Good night, Frank." With a final weary smile at me, she left the dayroom.

I waited until I heard the double click of her door closing and locking. Then, hauling myself to my feet, I headed back to the cockpit.

The autopilot still had us on the minimum-time course to the transfer station that I'd requested. I checked for nearby ships—there weren't any—and then key-locked the autopilot so that it couldn't be changed by anyone except me. Then I did the same to the engine and environmental settings.

Bayta might trust Rebekah. I didn't.

And with that chore complete, I was finally able to retire to my stateroom. I locked the door behind me, took off my shoes, and flopped onto the bed without even bothering to get undressed.

But before I fell asleep, I did remember to slip my Beretta out of its holster and tuck it under my pillow.

I'd told Bayta I'd see her in ten hours. In fact, I was awake in just under eight. Unable to sleep any more, I got up, showered, and headed out to face the universe.

My first job was to check all the course and systems settings I'd locked in before heading to bed. Everything was just as I'd left it, with no indication that anyone had even tried to fiddle with the controls. I got myself some breakfast, listening for signs of life from the rest of the ship as I ate. Apparently, the two women were still asleep. I finished eating, had a second cup of coffee, and did some hard thinking.

And when I was finished with both the coffee and the thinking, I put the cup away and headed aft.

I found the boxes in the stateroom behind Rebekah's compartment, just as Bayta had said, stacked neatly against the forward wall. If Rebekah couldn't have them in the same room with her, arranging them as close to her as possible was apparently her second choice. The boxes were still locked, but I wasn't expecting that to be a serious problem. Getting out my multitool, I knelt down in front of one of them and got to work.

I was nearly there when through my knees I felt the subtle vibration of the door sliding open behind me. "Morning, Rebekah," I said, not turning around. "Did you sleep well?"

"Very well, Mr. Compton, thank you," she said. "May I ask what you're doing?"

"Just curious," I told her. "I wanted to see what this new improved Modhran coral looked like."

"I see," she said calmly. "Would you like me to get you the key?"

"That's okay—I've got it," I assured her. With a final twist of my wrist, and accompanied by a screech of tortured metal, the lock popped open. Setting the multitool aside, I lifted the lid.

It was Modhran coral, all right, soaking in about a two-thirds depth of gently sloshing water. To me, it looked the same as all the rest of the Modhran coral I'd encountered over the years.

"Were you expecting it to look different?" Rebekah asked.

"I don't know," I said, finally swiveling around to face her. She had on a knee-length nightshirt, and her eyes still looked half asleep. The coral had probably woken her up when I started knocking on his door. "I guess I was," I amended. "Stupid of me, I suppose."

"Not stupid," she said. "When the heart changes, we some-how expect the face to change, too."

"Very insightful," I said. "Especially for a ten-year-old from a backwater world."

That earned me a wry smile. "You don't think we have any culture on New Tigris?" she asked innocently.

"I'm sure you're just dripping with the stuff," I assured her. "And you're right. We *do* expect to see outward signs of in-ward changes."

"With people, I think that's actually required." She gestured. "But you have to remember, this is just a lump of coral."

"So it is," I agreed, looking over my shoulder at it. Time for a little experiment. Half turning back toward the box, I reached a hand toward it.

"Don't touch it," Rebekah said sharply.

I paused with my hand still hovering over the box. "Why

not?" I asked. "I thought this was a kinder breed of Modhran coral."

"No, this is a breed of Modhran coral under Melding control," she corrected me tartly. "I told you I don't know what would happen if it left that control. I *really* don't know what would happen if you took a polyp colony out of it on your own."

"You're probably right," I conceded, withdrawing my hand and swiveling again to face her. Not that I'd actually intended to touch the damn stuff in the first place, of course. "I get the feeling it's kind of like a trained attack dog that only responds to its handler's voice."

"Maybe," she said. "I don't know anything about attack dogs."

"You're not missing much," I said. "So where exactly is it you and your friends are planning to go?"

"I already told you," she said. "Sibbrava."

"A small, underpopulated planet where visitors are noted and endlessly discussed by the locals?" I shook my head. "I don't think so. You wouldn't get to the sunward side of the transfer station before the whole system would be buzzing with news and rumors about you."

"Nevertheless, that *is* where we're going," Rebekah said.

"Even if it ends up being suicide?" I asked bluntly.

Her throat tightened. "I trust my leaders, Mr. Compton," she said quietly. "I don't believe they would take us on a path that they thought would lead to our destruction."

"Trust is fine," I said. "But it should never replace thinking for yourself. Even the best leaders have blind spots, and it's up to their followers to compensate."

"I suppose," she said, staring at me with an uncomfortable intensity. "Does that apply to you, too?"

"You mean do I question authority?" I asked.

"No, do you need someone to compensate for your weaknesses?"

"I have Bayta for that, thanks," I said. "But I appreciate the offer."

For a moment we just gazed at each other. Then, reaching behind me again, I closed the lid over the coral. "You still look pretty tired," I told her as I stood up. "You probably should go back to bed after you get some breakfast."

"Actually, I may just skip breakfast and wait for lunch," she said, yawning widely. "How much farther to the Tube?"

"About four and a half days," I said. "After you and Bayta have caught up on your sleep we'll sit down and discuss how we're going to get your coral through Customs at the transfer station." I lifted an eyebrow. "Of course, given the way you can charm the socks off people, we may not really *need* a plan."

"It never hurts to have several options available."

"Words to live by," I said ruefully. "Go on, scoot."

"Okay. Good night." She smiled. "Again."

She turned and left the room. I looked down at the boxes, wondering whether or not it would be worth checking out any of the others. But I couldn't think of a good reason to do so, and my eyelids were starting to remind me that I hadn't exactly caught up on my sleep, either.

And it was still a long way to the transfer station and the Tube. " 'Sufficient unto the day is the evil thereof,' " I quoted under my breath, and headed back to bed.

FIFTEEN :

The next four and a half days passed slowly. The first twenty-four hours saw us caught up on our sleep and caloric intake, and later in the afternoon Bayta and I spent some time working out contingency plans for getting Rebekah's coral past the transfer station's Customs counter.

For me, at least, that felt more like a training exercise than a real-world problem. Rebekah's innocent smile, along with her new improved Melding thought viruses, would almost certainly breeze us straight through Customs without a ripple.

Certainly there wouldn't be any word from New Tigris itself to put anyone on their guard. I'd made a point of flying over what was left of the communications laser on our way off the planet, and McMicking had definitely done a good job of slagging the thing. It would be weeks before it would be up and running again.

Nor would we face the raised eyebrows that would naturally

occur when two torchyachts came through such a backwater station in rapid succession. McMicking was almost certainly running himself a more leisurely course that would allow us to get to and through the transfer station first, exactly to avoid that sort of problem. It was the kind of courtesy I would expect from the man.

Of course, that meant he would be the one facing those raised eyebrows when he came through Customs a day or two behind us. How he planned to deal with them and get his precious cargo through I didn't know.

But that was his problem, not ours. *Our* problems would start once we got to the Quadrail itself.

Bayta and I talked about that, too. But once again, there was little to actually discuss. It would take around eleven days to get from New Tigris to Sibbrava, during which time the Modhri would either catch on to what we were doing or else would miss us completely. If we managed to stay under the radar, we would get to Sibbrava without trouble and send Rebekah on her merry way.

If we didn't, there would be trouble. Problem was, at this point there was no way of telling how much trouble the Modhri was willing to make and, more importantly, how much of it he would be able to throw together in the limited time available.

Given those uncertainties, there wasn't much point in making any detailed plans. As a result, the torchyacht trip quickly took on the feel of an actual vacation, with our primary occupations being food, sleep, and dit rec dramas and comedies.

Rebekah turned out to be even more culturally deficient in the latter area than Bayta. As soon as we realized that, and to my mild surprise, Bayta immediately appointed herself the girl's guide and mentor. She worked up a program to bring Rebekah up to speed on Human cinematic tradition, then set about implementing it.

Rebekah took to the program like a duck to quack, greeting each new dit rec with wide-eyed excitement. She took to Bayta the same way, and for hours the two of them would sit side by side in the dayroom, chuckling at the punch lines and making quiet comments to each other as they watched.

In retrospect, I shouldn't have been surprised by the obvious bonding that was going on. For Rebekah, Bayta was someone to fill the empty hole in her life that had been left by Lorelei's death. For Bayta, I suspected, Rebekah was the little sister she'd never had at all.

It reached such a level, in fact, that I started feeling like a side dish neither of them had ordered. Often during one of their marathon sessions, I would slip out of the dayroom to check on the autopilot or drive systems or even to take a nap, and return with the sense that neither of them had even noticed my absence.

The whole thing gave me a strange and decidedly unpleasant feeling. Being ignored was nothing new to me, and over the past few years I'd been ignored by acknowledged experts in the field. But this was different. Bayta was a colleague, and ever since we'd embarked on this quiet war together I'd been the biggest thing in her life.

Except for the Spiders and Chahwyn, maybe. But they mostly sat on the sidelines. I was the one Bayta had lived with and fought beside and risked her life for. Not the Spiders. Certainly not Rebekah.

Five days after leaving New Tigris we reached the transfer station. The vacation was over, and the danger was about to begin again.

I was almost glad.

The Customs official on duty was the same one who'd sent us through on our way sunward. Considering the relative trickle of customers who came through here, I wasn't surprised that he remembered us.

"Ah—Mr. Donaldson," he greeted me. "This is a surprise. I had the impression you'd be staying on New Tigris a bit longer."

"That was the plan," I agreed, handing over my ID. "But things fell into place more quickly than I'd expected."

"Ah," the official said, his eyes shifting to Bayta. "Good to see you again, too, ma'am." He looked at Rebekah. "And you are . . . ?"

"This is Rebekah Beach," Bayta told him. "She'll be traveling to the Tube with us today."

"Good day, Ms. Beach," the official said, smiling genially at her.

Rebekah didn't smile back. She'd been pale and jumpy ever since we arrived at the transfer station, actually before I'd even finished the docking procedure. If she was trying to look like someone on the run, she couldn't have done a better job of it. "We'll need a shuttle ride to the Tube," I said, trying to draw the official's attention toward me instead of her.

"I'll call the pilot," he said, his eyes still on Rebekah. "Is this the young lady the gentlemen down the hall have been waiting for?"

An unpleasant tingle ran up the back of my neck. "Which gentlemen are those?" I asked.

"I believe they're from the United Nations," the official said. "They mentioned they were here to escort a young lady back to Earth."

"I see," I said, glancing around. There was no one else in sight, but that could change quickly enough. "And you're supposed to let them know when she arrives, I presume?"

"As a matter of fact, I am," he said, his tone drifting from friendly to guarded. "Why, is there a problem?"

"The polite term is *jurisdictional poaching,*" I said, pulling out my Hardin Security card and handing it to him. "*I'm* the one who's supposed to escort Ms. Beach back to Earth, not some bureaucratic glory-hogs."

"I don't understand," the official said, frowning uncertainly at the Hardin card. "They implied this was a very serious governmental matter."

"They always imply that," I growled, putting on my best professional-versus-amateurs face. "The fact of the matter is that *I* was the one sent to locate this girl and bring her back to Earth. Sent by Mr. Hardin personally, I might add. If the UN wants to interview her, they can ask politely. After *we've* finished talking to her."

"I don't know," the official said hesitantly, gazing at Rebekah as he fingered the ID. "Their instructions were *very* specific."

"Did they have a warrant?" Bayta asked.

The official pursed his lips. "Not that I saw."

"Or any official paper at all?" I added.

"Again, not that I saw," he conceded. "But they *do* have UN IDs."

"Which means what?" I persisted, wishing I could just pull my gun and get us the hell out of here. If the UN flunkies were Modhran walkers, they'd probably sensed Rebekah's renegade coral before I'd even finished docking the torchyacht. God only knew why they weren't here already, flashing IDs and trying to confiscate everything in sight.

I frowned. Why *weren't* they here, come to think about it? "But you're right—maybe we should try to be civilized about all this," I said.

I could feel Bayta's eyes on me at this sudden change in tactics. But the Customs man himself showed nothing but relief. Caught between the UN and a multitrillionaire industrial giant wasn't a comfortable place for a low-level career bureaucrat to be. "I'd appreciate that," he said, reaching for his desk comm.

I caught his wrist before he could pick up the handset. "It might be better if I just go talk to them," I suggested. "Keep you and the transfer-station management out of it, you know."

"If you think that would be best," the official said, looking even more relieved as he withdrew his hand. "They're down the corridor to your left. Room Four."

I looked down the corridor. Room Four was about midway along, in plain view of where we stood in front of the counter. "Wait here," I told Bayta and Rebekah, and headed toward it.

The door still hadn't opened by the time I reached it. Settling my shoulders, reminding myself that on this side of Customs the two of them were likely to be as well armed as I was, I pressed the buzzer.

There was no response. I tried again, then a third time. Nothing.

I looked back at Bayta. I could see her lips moving as she continued to talk to the Customs official, probably working out the details of our cargo transfer to the Tube. The official himself, I noted, was too far back to actually see the door where I was standing. Keeping an eye in that direction, I dug out my lockpick and got to work. A few seconds later, the door snicked open, and I slipped through into the room.

They hadn't been dead long, I decided as I knelt over the bodies lying in the middle of the small room. No more than a couple of hours, probably less. The cause of death was pretty obvious: both men had had their necks broken. On the floor beside one of them lay a handgun with the distinctive aroma of recent firing about it.

The target of that fire was also obvious: a dead Pirk lying a meter behind one of the Humans, probably shot in the act of breaking the man's neck. His chest had the small bloodstains of a pair of snoozer rounds, but there were no other signs of injury I could detect.

Ironically, I noted, he was as lacking in normal Pirk odor in death as he had been in life.

I made a single careful circuit of the room, looking for anything that might give me a clue as to what had happened here. But there were no signs of struggle, no documents lying around in the open that someone might have been looking at. Both victims' IDs were tucked safely away in their jackets, with no indication they were being shown to anyone during their final moments. From all appearances, the Pirk had just buzzed the door, walked in when it was answered, and set about killing the two occupants.

Meanwhile, the gentleman at the Customs desk would be

expecting me to return with glad tidings of jurisdictional agreement. I finished my circuit and headed back toward the door, giving the gun on the floor a final look. It was a Heckler-Koch 5mm, I noted, just like the one Lorelei had stolen from my Manhattan apartment.

I paused, my hand hovering over the doorknob. Then, slowly, I retraced my steps to the group of dead bodies and took a closer look at the gun.

It wasn't just like the one Lorelei had stolen. It *was* the one she'd stolen.

I straightened up again, giving the Human bodies a second look. Detective Kylowski had said someone of my general description had been seen running from the scene of Lorelei's death. Both of these latest vics were about my height and build, with similar dark hair in similar cuts as mine.

Under some sets of circumstances, Kylowski would probably be glad to hear I'd found the killer. Under this particular set, he probably wouldn't.

The Customs man was just closing one of Rebekah's metal boxes when I returned to the counter. From his lack of wide-eyed outrage at the discovery of illegal cargo, I assumed it was one of the three decoy Siris brandy boxes. "We wanted these crated up for Quadrail baggage car transport, didn't we?" Bayta asked me, gesturing to the boxes.

"That's right," I said, forcing my voice to remain steady. Out of the corner of my eye I saw Rebekah open her mouth, then close it again. "Oh, and I'll need a lockbox for my gun, too. Did you need to see my importer's license on the brandy?"

"Yes, thank you," the official said as I pulled out the appropriate card. "Did you get everything settled with the two gentlemen?"

"No problems," I said softly. "It's all fine now."

By the time we got Rebekah's boxes settled inside a large cargo crate and wheeled it across the station the shuttle was ready for us. Half an hour later, we were inside the Quadrail station, our luggage and the crate piled on the Tube floor beside us.

And only then, with the three of us now officially outside Terran Confederation jurisdiction, did I tell the others what I'd found in Room Four.

They listened in silence, Bayta with her controlled shock and thoughtfulness, Rebekah with what I was pretty sure was guilty knowledge. "At least now we know who the walkers were who attacked Lorelei on Earth," Bayta said when I'd finished. "Provided you're really sure that was your gun."

"Trust me, it was," I assured her grimly. "Not that anyone else is likely to arrive at that particular conclusion. The Customs man will certainly testify that I was in the room with them, for a start."

"*After* the killings."

"If anyone bothers to refine the timeline that closely." I turned to Rebekah. "You want to tell us what happened in there?"

She dropped her eyes away from the intensity of my stare. "Probably just what you're already thinking," she said with difficulty. "Drorcro was one of us."

"Drorcro being our non-aromatic Pirk, I gather?"

She nodded. "He was supposed to wait for us at the transfer station and then accompany us to our new home. When the two Eyes showed up . . . he decided to sacrifice himself for me."

"How nice and noble that sounds," I growled. "Much better than that he simply panicked."

"I don't think—"

"You *lied* to us, Rebekah," I cut her off.

She flinched back from my sudden anger. "Frank," Bayta cautioned, starting to take a step in front of the girl.

"Keep out of this, Bayta," I warned, keeping my glare on Rebekah. "A lie of omission is still a lie. Why didn't you tell us about Drorcro before? Like, maybe, back on the torchyacht, when it could have done us some good?"

"I couldn't," Rebekah protested, her voice shaking, her eyes brimming. "I'm sorry, Mr. Compton. He was just trying to protect me."

"By murdering two Humans in cold blood?" I shot back. "Yes, I know they were walkers. So what? I could have dealt with them in any number of other ways. But only if I'd known in time."

"That's enough, Frank," Bayta said firmly.

"What, am I scaring her?" I snapped, throwing her a glare of her own. "Good. It's about time she understood the rules here. She *and* the Melding."

I looked back at Rebekah. She was trying hard to hold on to some shred of dignity, but her expression was nothing short of miserable and the tears were now streaming freely down her cheeks. "You say the Melding picked me to get you off New Tigris and to your new home," I said, notching back the thunder and lightning a little. "Fine—I'm here. But if you want my help, you have to be completely honest with me. And that means telling me everything. You understand? Not everything that's convenient. Not everything you think I need to know. *Everything*. Do I make myself clear?"

She nodded, a pair of jerky up-down twitches of her head. I looked at Bayta, whose own anger at my outburst had now cooled to merely smoldering. Clearly, she wasn't very happy with me right now.

I wasn't particularly happy with myself, for that matter. But Rebekah and the Melding needed to learn this lesson, and they needed to learn it right now. "All right, then," I said, finally letting the storm clouds dissipate. "Dry your eyes, and tell me what this has done to your original plan."

Rebekah sniffed a couple of times, her hands dipping into her pockets as she searched for a handkerchief. Bayta got to her own spare first, handing it to Rebekah and resting her hand reassuringly on the girl's shoulder. "Go ahead, Rebekah," she prompted.

"We were hoping you could arrange to put the coral in the front part of the forward baggage car," Rebekah said, daubing at her eyes. "Drorcro was going to get one of the seats in the far back of the last third-class car."

"So he could keep an eye on it?" I asked.

Rebekah shook her head, sniffing a little more. "I told you we need to stay near it to make sure it doesn't revert to normal Modhri."

"That's not just if there's other Modhran coral around?" I asked.

"We don't know," Rebekah said. "Now that Drorcro's gone, I guess I'll have to do that."

"Out of the question," Bayta said firmly. "You're going to be in a first-class compartment where you'll at least be out of sight."

"But I can't," Rebekah protested. "If he reverts—no, I have to be with him."

I looked around us. The New Tigris Station amenities, as befit the colony's lowly status, consisted of only a single shop/restaurant/visitor center. If there was anyone on duty—and it didn't look like there was—he wasn't visible to us out here. There also were no other passengers hanging around the station. "Luckily for us, in this case we can have it both ways," I said. "Bayta, whistle us up a couple of drudges or drones, will you?"

"All right." She paused, and across by one of the freight tracks I saw a trio of medium-sized Spiders detach themselves from the rest of their work crew and start wending their seven-legged way toward us. "What's the plan?" she asked.

"Luckily, Rebekah's coral carriers are just about the size of Quadrail lockboxes," I pointed out. "Lockboxes get loaded underneath the cars anyway, right? So let's have the Spiders load them into standard lockboxes and make sure to put them right below our compartments."

"Yes, that should work," Bayta said slowly, her forehead wrinkled in concentration. "Of course, that assumes the storage areas under those particular compartments aren't already full."

"If they are, the Spiders can unfill them," I said, running my eye down the schedule holodisplay floating above the station-master building. "A more crucial question is how fast it would take for any walkers aboard to zero in on their location."

"They shouldn't be able to at all," Rebekah said. "The way

we sense ordinary Modhran coral is like—well, think of a low-pitched hum like some machines make. You can hear it a long ways away, but it's really hard to figure out where exactly it's coming from. We could tell if there was an outpost aboard the train, or maybe only that it was just somewhere in the station. But that would be all."

"And that's the way the Modhri would sense your coral, too?" I asked.

Rebekah shrugged helplessly. "We assume so. We don't know for sure."

"But that would make sense," Bayta said. "Why else would the Modhri have needed to bring in specially designed Fili-aelians to find her?"

"That's good enough for me," I declared. Actually, whether it was good enough or not, it was probably all we were going to get. "Bayta, is there room for us on the coreward-bound Quadrail coming through in ninety minutes?"

Her eyes defocused briefly. "Yes, there are two adjoining compartments available," she confirmed.

"Book 'em for us," I ordered. "Then—"

"Wait a minute," she interrupted, frowning in concentration. "The stationmaster says there should be a tender along soon, one that's set up for normal people."

"Really," I said, frowning in turn. Tenders were workhorse trains, typically two or three cars with an engine on each end so they could move in either direction without having to go to a station or siding to turn around. Normally, the cars were stuffed with equipment and spare track and Spiders, without any of the conveniences that Quadrail passengers usually demanded, such as food, restroom facilities, and a constant supply of oxygen.

But the Spiders did have a few tenders that had been tricked out for passengers. Bayta and I had traveled on them a couple of times. If there was one in the vicinity, it would be the perfect way to avoid the Modhri on our way to Sibbrava. "When's it due?" I asked.

"About twenty hours," she said.

I shook my head. "No good. In twenty hours half the transfer station personnel will be over here waving papers calling for my arrest on triple murder charges."

"But they won't be able to arrest you," Bayta pointed out. "Not in here."

"Maybe not, but they'll sure be able to sit on me long enough to get my prints and biometrics and send them to Earth for a solid ID," I reminded her. "The minute all that gets crosslinked to my real name and the circumstances around Lorelei's death in New York come to light, I might as well kiss the Terran Confederation good-bye as far as a retirement home is concerned. Forget the tender—we'll just take the next train."

"All right," Bayta said. She wasn't any happier about the situation than I was, I could tell. But I wouldn't be of any use to the Spiders and the war against the Modhri doing four or five life sentences for a bunch of murders I hadn't even committed. "We're confirmed aboard."

"Good," I said. "By the way, which direction is the tender coming from?"

"From rimward," Bayta said. "It's somewhere in the Greesovra area."

One of the worlds of the Bellidosh Estates-General, and the opposite direction from the way we were going. No chance then of rendezvousing with it somewhere along our way.

Unless we took the next Quadrail headed back in that direction, met the tender at Helvanti or one of the minor Belldic colonies, and switched ourselves and our cargo aboard there.

But a glance at the holodisplay torpedoed that one. The next Quadrail heading rimward wasn't due for another twelve hours, which was no better than the twenty it would take the tender to get here under its own steam. "So that's settled," I said briskly. "Let's get this crate unpacked and send the boxes of coral to wherever the Spiders keep lockboxes until they're ready to be loaded aboard."

"Do we just dump the crate completely, then?" Bayta asked.

I looked at the approaching Spiders. "No, let's leave the three brandy boxes inside and have the crate loaded in the luggage car as Rebekah originally planned. When the Customs man back on the transfer station gets questioned about the murders, he'll probably mention we took a crate out with us."

"He'll also tell them there were just some boxes of brandy inside," Bayta pointed out.

"Which no one will believe," I said, pulling out my reader. "The more eyes pointed at it, the fewer pointed at us. What's a good stop on the Kalalee Branch, something well past Sibbrava?"

Bayta looked over my shoulder. "Benedais would work," she suggested, pointing at a spot on my Quadrail map. "It's reasonably large and quite cosmopolitan."

"Benedais it is," I agreed. "Have the Spiders label the crate for Benedais. While you're at it, have them make us up another half-dozen labels for a few other random locations."

"Which we can put over the Benedais one if we need to?" Bayta asked.

"Exactly," I said. "The more effort we can put into making the crate look vitally important to us, the better our chances of keeping the Modhri focused on it until we're ready to slip Rebekah and the coral off the train."

I looked at Rebekah. She had a rather doubtful look on her face, clearly wondering about the possibility of keeping a group mind focused in only a single direction at all. But she merely nodded agreement. "Whatever you think is best, Mr. Compton," she said.

"That's the spirit," I said. "Okay, then. Let's get to it."

SIXTEEN :

I'd told Bayta that twenty hours was way too long to expect the three bodies on the transfer station to go undiscovered. Privately, I'd suspected even our ninety-minute wait would be pushing it.

So it was to my mild surprise that the Quadrail rolled to a halt at our platform without so much as a fact-finding crew making their appearance. Either the transfer station personnel knew trying to talk me out of my safe haven in Spider territory would be futile, or else no one had wanted to barge in on the men in Room Four to ask if they'd really agreed to let me take Rebekah and fly the coop.

I hoped they would at least find the bodies before the Pirk stopped being non-aromatic.

Whatever the reason for our reprieve, the train pulled in, we got aboard, and it pulled out again. I didn't actually see the Spiders put the crate and lockboxes aboard—that was all handled on the opposite side of the train from the passenger doors—but even before the train started on its way again Rebekah was able to confirm that her mutant coral was snugged in safely beneath our compartments. None of us knew whether or not the crate had been brought aboard as well, but knowing Spider efficiency I had no reason to doubt that it had.

A conductor Spider showed up in Bayta's compartment shortly after the train passed through the atmosphere barrier into the main part of the Tube. A couple of minutes later, he'd folded away the luggage rack above the bed and replaced it with a second bunk, converting the compartment from a single to a double.

We stayed put for the first few hours, lying low against the possibility of being spotted and identified by any walkers who happened to be traveling with us. Midway through the nine-hour trip to Yandro Bayta and I slipped back to the dining car to get something to eat.

Rebekah insisted on staying behind where she could be near her coral, which was fine with me. The less she was out in the open, the better. Bayta and I had a quick dinner, then got a carry-away meal to take back to Rebekah.

Yandro came and went, the last stop in Human space. The next stop, seven hours beyond it, was Homshil, one of the heavily traveled node points that linked up several different Quadrail lines, including a super-express that led across a large span of unoccupied territory to the Shorshic and Filiaelian empires at the other end of the galaxy.

Homshil was usually a stop where a lot of passengers got swapped out, and this time was no exception. Bayta and Rebekah and I stayed in our compartments while the do-si-do was going on, keeping our display window opaqued. The layover complete, we headed out again.

Sixteen hours out, and so far not a peep from the Modhri. But that wouldn't last. McMicking would be holding off on his arrival at the New Tigris transfer station, I knew, giving us as much time as he could to make our escape. But he wasn't exactly out of the woods yet himself, and he absolutely had to get through the station and to the legal protection of the Tube before the techs on the planet fixed the comm laser he'd wrecked and blew the whistle on him.

And of course, the minute he reached the Quadrail and the late Mr. Veldrick's coral got within range of any other Modhran mind segments, the balloon would go up in spades.

We had to be as far away as possible before that happened. Unfortunately, we could only go so fast. Our train was what was informally called a local-express, which had fewer stops than a local but more than a regular express. An extra downside to that fact was that once the Modhri knew Rebekah and her coral were on the run, extra stops meant more opportunities for him to bring additional walkers aboard our train.

But there was nothing I could do about that. New Tigris and Sibbrava were both small enough to be served only by locals and local-expresses. Theoretically, we could switch to a faster express somewhere past New Tigris and then get back on a local as we approached Sibbrava. But that would mean two train changes, and two extra opportunities for walkers to notice and perhaps wonder about a whole bunch of lockbox transfers.

For the moment Rebekah's coral was safely hidden out of the public eye. We needed to keep it that way.

Two hours after Homshil we reached the Jurian regional capital of Kerfsis, and an hour-long stop to transfer passengers and cargo. Once again the three of us spent the entire time in our double compartment with the windows opaqued. Kerfsis held some interesting memories for Bayta and me, and I wondered if she was sifting through them the same way I was.

At one point I considered asking her about it. But Rebekah would just want to know what we were talking about, and I really didn't want to discuss it with her, and so I kept quiet. The stopover ended, and we headed out again, through the atmosphere barrier and back to our usual hundred-kilometers-per-hour, one-light-year-per-minute cruising speed.

By now, the trip had settled into a routine: eat, talk, watch a dit rec drama on one of the two computers in our double compartment, sleep, eat again, talk some more. From Kerfsis it was about a three-day journey to the Jurian capital system of Jurskala, though with the extra stops our train would be making it would probably be more like three and a half days. Somewhere in that time, I fully expected the Modhri to make his move.

We were six hours out from Jurskala when he did.

I was just thinking it was time I strolled back to the dining car to pick up a snack when Bayta suddenly sat bolt upright on her bed. "Frank, there's a report of a fire!" she said sharply.

For a second I just stared at her. Fires and other natural disasters simply didn't happen on Quadrails. And then my brain caught up with me, and I realized who had to be behind it. "Where?" I demanded, rolling off my bed onto my feet.

"Last third-class car," Bayta said. "The Spiders are clearing everyone out now."

The last passenger car, in other words, before the three baggage cars. "Nice," I growled, grabbing my jacket.

"What do you mean?" Rebekah asked anxiously. She was sitting at the computer, her fingers poised tautly over the keyboard, her eyes wide and nervous.

"The Modhri's bought into the idea that your coral is in one of the baggage cars," I told her. "He also knows—or at least suspects—that one of your Melding buddies needs to be nearby to make him behave. He wants to split up the team. Ergo, the fire."

"What are you going to do?" Bayta asked as I keyed open the door.

"I'll figure that out when I get there." I dug into my pocket. "Here," I added, tossing her the *kwi*. "Just in case." Checking to make sure no one was loitering near our compartment doors, I slipped out into the corridor and headed toward the rear of the train at a brisk walk.

I didn't notice any particular excitement or anxiety as I passed through the first- and second-class sections of the Quadrail. Clearly, the Spiders were playing it cool, keeping the trouble as localized and isolated as possible.

Of course, that localization wasn't going to last any longer than it took for the uprooted passengers to start spilling out of their car. Where the Spiders intended to stash them while they dealt with the problem I didn't know, but it wasn't likely to be pretty. Third-class Quadrail cars weren't noted for having a lot of spare room, and second-class wasn't much better. I tried to picture the reaction of my fellow first-class passengers to a flood of refugees from third, but my imagination wasn't up to it.

Fortunately, the Spiders had already come up with a better plan. As I left the last second-class car and headed into the second/third-class dining car I found myself having to push through a mob of milling Humans and aliens. Clearly, the Spiders had directed the evacuees to the dining car, where they would at least have a little elbow room to spare.

Beyond the dining car, the hurried passage of the evacuees had left an atmosphere of frowns and low conversation and craned necks. Every eye seemed to turn to me as I strode past, the lone non-Spider going the opposite direction from everyone else.

A few people seemed to consider asking me what was going on as I passed. Fortunately, my brisk stride and carefully honed question-discouraging scowl kept them silent.

The last passenger car was empty except for a handful of Spiders and an acrid smell of smoke. The focus of the Spiders' attention seemed to be a row of three seats in the middle of the car, and as I moved closer I saw the two Spiders nearest the area were spraying a pressurized stream of thick white mist over the center seat. "What was it?" I asked the room in general as I headed back.

The nearest Spider stepped into the aisle in front of me, blocking my way. He was a stationmaster, slightly bigger than the conductor Spiders gathered in the car, and with an identifying pattern of white dots across part of the surface of his globe. "You must return to the dining car," he said in a flat voice. "It is not safe here."

"No I don't, and yes it is," I said, taking another step forward.

The Spider didn't budge. "You must return to the dining car," he repeated. "It is not safe here."

I stopped and gazed hard at the silvery globe as it hung in the middle of the network of spindly legs. "Do you know who I am?" I asked.

There was a moment of silence. "Frank Compton," he said in the same flat voice.

"Then you know I have authority to go wherever in the Quadrail system I choose," I said. "Please step aside."

For a moment he seemed to think about that, no doubt telepathically consulting with the rest of the Spiders on the train. My mandate from the Chahwyn wasn't nearly as broad as I'd made it sound, and I wondered if he was going to try to split hairs.

Apparently not. His moment of contemplation over, he tapped his way silently into the row of seats beside him, clearing the aisle for me. Nodding to him, I stepped past and made my way to the point of interest. The Spiders with the extinguishers had finished their work, and I peered through the rapidly dissipating white mist.

One look was all I needed. "Offhand, I'd say your sensor mesh needs a little work," I commented.

"Explain," the stationmaster said from behind me.

Pulling out my multitool, I flipped it to needle-nose pliers mode and carefully extracted a thin, pointy-ended plastic tube that had been embedded in the inboard side of the center of the three seats. "It's called a whiffer," I said. "It contains two vials of liquids which, when mixed, create a gas that can smell like pretty much anything you want."

"It is not a weapon?" the stationmaster asked.

"Not really, which is probably why your sensor screen didn't flag it," I said. "But even harmless aromas can make good diversions." I held up the whiffer for emphasis. "As you can see."

"A diversion for what?"

"That's the question, isn't it?" I agreed, sniffing at the air. The smoky smell was all but gone. Whatever was in the Spiders' fire-fighting mist, it was handy stuff. "You can go ahead and let everyone back in," I told him, stepping away from the seat and heading toward the rear of the car. "You'll want to make a note of who belongs in this set of seats, though."

"Where are you going?" the stationmaster asked.

"There," I said helpfully, pointing toward the door leading into the first of the baggage cars. "You just concentrate on getting the passengers resettled."

I had the distinct impression that all of the Spiders were watching me as I made my way to the rear. But none of them interfered as I reached the back of the car and opened the door. I crossed the vestibule and punched the door release, and as the door slid open I stepped into the baggage car.

I'd spent more than my fair share of time in Quadrail baggage cars, and this one was typical of the breed. It was dimly lit, with stacks of safety-webbed crates arranged in seemingly haphazard islands throughout the car, the piles creating a twisting maze of narrow corridors meandering around and between them. Each stack consisted of cargo bound for a particular stop, the island configuration allowing the drudges to quickly extract the proper cargo through the roof at each station along the line.

Our crate was supposed to be at the front of the car, in one of the "special handling" stacks, where we would have easy access to it and could keep up the illusion that it had some actual significance. Flashlight in hand, I went looking for it.

Only to discover that it wasn't there.

I walked twice across the full width of the car, double-checking each crate as I went. After that I moved on to the next row of stacks back. Our crate wasn't in any of them, either. Apparently, the Spiders who were supposed to load the thing aboard had screwed up.

Or else someone wanted me to think they had.

For a long moment I stood in the center of the main aisle, gazing at the intimidating archipelago of cargo stacks stretching to the rear of the car and trying to think. Checking out every crate in here would take hours, and there were two more baggage cars behind this one. I could easily be at this until we reached the far end of the Jurian Collective, which was probably exactly what the Modhri wanted me to do.

"Fine," I muttered under my breath. Quadrail crates were pretty well sealed, which made breaking into one a lengthy proposition. A properly handled multitool on one corner of the lid would allow someone a peek inside, but of course with our crate all that would gain him would be a look at the three sealed metal boxes inside. To get any farther than that would require a crowbar—which he wouldn't have been allowed to bring aboard—or else a lot of time and even more patience.

And he certainly wouldn't want someone like me blundering into him while he worked.

Smiling to myself, I headed back toward the baggage car's rear door. It was, I had to admit, a reasonably good plan for something that had to have been thrown together more or less on the fly. A walker plants a whiffer to clear out the car, including the coral's assumed Melding watchdog. In the confusion, the walker and maybe a friend or two slip through the back door and manhandle the crate one or even two cars back.

It was, from the Modhri's point of view, a win-win situation. If the Melding watchdog realized the coral had been moved and came running to find out what had happened to it, the Modhri would gain instant identification of one of his enemies. If the watchdog *didn't* come charging to the rescue, but tried to get a message to Bayta and me instead, the Modhri would have that much more time to break into the crate or whatever else was necessary to bring the wayward coral back into the happy Modhran family.

What he *hadn't* counted on was that the Spiders would alert Bayta, who would alert me, and that I would be on the scene this quickly. By now he would barely have had time to even get the crate moved, let alone started working on it. If I could catch him in the act, not only would I have a pair of walkers identified, but I could have the Spiders kick them off the train as soon as we reached Jurskala.

I reached the door and punched the release. The door opened, and I stepped through into the vestibule and punched the inner door's release.

Nothing happened.

I hit the release again, and again. But it was no use. The Modhri had anticipated me charging to the rescue, all right. He'd locked me out.

I muttered a curse under my breath. So he wanted to play cute? Fine—I could do cute, too. All I needed to do was get back to the passenger coaches and grab the first conductor I saw. Whatever the Modhri had done to lock the door, I'd simply have one of the Spiders undo it.

I was halfway back toward the front of the baggage car when I came around a curve in the pathway to find myself facing a group of four Juriani moving cautiously through the same pathway in my direction. They caught sight of me, the hawk beaks in their iguana-like faces clicked once in perfect unison, and they broke into a fast jog.

I picked up my pace, too, heading straight toward them. I caught a flicker of uncertainty on their scaled faces at the sight of a clearly insane Human rushing into four-to-one odds, and they reflexively slowed their pace a little.

Their uncertainty lasted exactly as long as it took me to clear the current crate stack I'd been passing and take off at full speed down a weaving cross pathway. I was half a dozen steps down it when I heard the sudden clatter of foot claws as they gave chase.

I made it around the back of the next island before they reached my branch point and came in after me. With my pursuers momentarily out of sight, I got a grip on the safety webbing of the stack I was facing and started to climb.

It wasn't easy. The webbing wasn't really designed for this, and the strands were a little too thin for a comfortable grip. But I was inspired, and up I went. I'd had a couple of serious confrontations in Quadrail baggage cars over the past few months, and neither had exactly ended to my complete satisfaction. My best bet for avoiding a repeat performance was to take the high ground and try to get back to civilization before I got myself surrounded.

I had my fingers on the top crate of the stack and was starting to pull myself up when a clawed hand grabbed my right ankle.

Instantly, I kicked sideways as hard as I could with my left foot, catching the Juri's fingers with the edge of my heel. There was a multiple screech from all four walkers as the pain of the blow shot across and through the entire Modhran mind segment. The Juri let go of my ankle, and I quickly pulled myself the rest of my way up and onto the crate.

The fortunes of necessity, I discovered, had ended up with me on top of one of the shorter stacks, one where I could stand nearly upright without bumping my head on the ceiling. From my new vantage point, I saw now that most of the stacks were a crate or even two crates taller than mine. That meant that some of the stacks had enough clearance between them and the ceiling for me to crouch or crawl, while others had a gap I could barely squeeze my arm into.

Unfortunately, the nature of the room's geography meant that I couldn't see from here which routes would lead me safely back to the car's forward door and which would instead funnel me into cul-de-sacs where the only way out would be to backtrack or drop to the floor. At that point, I'd be back to the same short odds I'd started with.

As I hesitated, a movement to my right caught my eye, and I turned to see one of the Juriani laboriously claw his way up onto the top of the crate two islands down from me. Picking the most likely-looking path forward, I set off.

The trip was like an echo of all those fun times on the Westali Academy obstacle course. Most of the islands could only be reached by a sort of leap/roll maneuver that I had to invent more or less as I did it, a trick which enabled me to land on my back or side instead of arriving with my head against the ceiling and my shins against the edge of the topmost crate. As I'd already noted, many of the gaps were too small even for that trick, and for those I had to jump to the stack's side, grabbing the top edge as I passed, and making my way along by sliding sideways hand-by-hand.

Getting to the next island in line from either of those positions was even more challenging. But I had no choice. From the clattering noises around me, and from occasional glimpses of struggling Juriani, it appeared that the Modhri had assigned two of the walkers to the job of chasing me across the rooftops, while the other two waited below to intercept me in case I dropped back to the floor and made a run for it.

On one level, the whole thing was bizarre. There was, after all, only a single door leading back to the rest of the train. In theory, all the Modhri had to do was position his four walkers at that exit and wait for me to get tired or hungry enough to come down from my perch. Bayta would eventually wonder where I was, of course, but if she didn't want to risk leaving Rebekah alone all she would be able to do would be to send a Spider out looking for me. Given the Spiders' inherent inability to fight, that wouldn't be a big help.

Yet here the walkers were, huffing and puffing their way up crates in a dusty Quadrail baggage car, chasing me to the ends of the earth and then some. All I could think of was that the Modhri—or at least this particular mind segment—must be really furious at me for breaking my promise to destroy the Abomination.

I had made it to within a couple of islands of the front of the car, and was starting to wonder what exactly I was going to do when I got there, when I heard the sound of the door sliding open.

I froze, straining my ears. Besides my current playmates, who from their clothing were obviously third-class passengers, the Modhri undoubtedly had another half-dozen or more walkers up in first. If he'd decided to bring them back here to join in the fun, this was going to get very sticky indeed.

And then, over the sound of wheels on track beneath us, I heard the distinctive click-click-click of Spider legs on hard flooring.

I rolled to the edge of my current stack and looked over the side. It was the stationmaster I'd seen earlier at the scene of the whiffer diversion in the third-class car. He had stepped a couple of meters into the baggage car and then stopped, almost as if he was assessing the situation. Two of the Jurian walkers were standing to either side of him, watching him as warily as I could sense he was watching them.

I didn't hesitate. Bayta could probably recognize individual Spiders—for all I knew she could even call them by name—but to me they were a dime a dozen, and the Quadrail system had a billion of them. If I accidentally wrecked this one, the Chahwyn could take it out of my pay. I got a grip on the edge of my stack and rolled off the edge. As my legs swung around, I pulled up and then let go of the stack, sailing in a short arc toward the door.

To land feet-first squarely on top of the Spider's central metal globe.

I had no idea how strong stationmaster legs were, and I half expected him to instantly collapse under my weight, which would have helped cushion my landing but not much more. To my surprise, his legs instead absorbed the impact with ease, lowering the globe and me maybe a meter and a half before coming to a controlled stop. I had just a glimpse of startled Jurian faces, and then the Spider's legs flexed again, and I found myself being catapulted in another low arc toward the door.

The Modhri finally broke his stunned paralysis and the two walkers lunged toward me. But it was too late. I hit the floor, slapped the release, and was through and into the vestibule before they'd even gotten around the Spider's slightly splayed-out legs. I hit the release on the far end of the vestibule, and a second later was back in the third-class car.

The passengers were still in the process of returning to their seats after the fire scare, and I found myself in the role of a salmon on his annual upstream swim. Fortunately, a lot of the passengers were apparently still in the dining car, and the aisle wasn't nearly as crowded as it could have been. I was out of the car before any of the walkers reappeared from behind me.

To my lack of surprise, I also noted as I passed that the seats where the whiffer had been were still unoccupied.

Bayta was sitting stiffly on the edge of my bed when I finally made it back to our double compartment. "There you are," she said, some of the stiffness going out of her back as I entered and locked the door behind me. "I was starting to worry."

"As well you should have," I said, motioning her off the bed and sitting down in her place. With the adrenaline rush long past, my body was feeling the painful effects of my extended playtime on top of all those cargo islands. "The Modhri's finally made his move. The smoke bomb was just a diversion to let him slip a couple of walkers into the baggage car and make off with our crate."

"What do you mean, make off with it?" Bayta asked. "You mean he opened it?"

"No, I mean he picked the damn thing up and moved it," I said, as I took off my shoes. "Where's Rebekah?"

"Asleep in the other compartment," Bayta said, nodding toward the mostly closed partition. "Where did he move it to?"

"Into the second baggage car, I assume," I said, easing my legs up onto the bed and carefully stretching sore muscles and joints. "At least, that's the one he's locked me out of."

"He locked you—?" Bayta broke off, frowning. "Which door exactly did he lock?"

"Front door of the middle baggage car, like I said," I told her. "Why?"

"Because that's not possible," she said. "There aren't any locks on those doors."

I stared up at her, trying to visualize the way Quadrail doors operated. If there were no actual locks, then she was right—there wasn't any way to simply brace or block or jam the doors closed. "Could the walkers have been physically holding them closed, then?" I suggested doubtfully. "Bracing their hands on the—well, I don't know. Bracing their hands somehow."

"Not unless they had the strength of a drone or drudge," she said. "The door motors are quite strong, and they're sealed where no one can get at them."

"What about a stationmaster?" I asked.

"What about them?" she asked. "I doubt they're strong enough, either. Besides, there aren't any of them aboard."

"Sure there are," I said. "There's one, anyway. He was in the last third-class car, watching the conductors deal with the whiffer."

Bayta's eyes went unfocused for a few seconds. "No," she said firmly. "The Spiders say there aren't any stationmasters aboard."

A chill ran up my back. "You have the *kwi*?" I asked, swinging my legs back over the side of my bed and grabbing my shoes.

"Right here," Bayta said, patting her pocket. "What's going on?"

"I don't know," I told her, putting on my shoes. "Okay, I'll take it," I said when I'd finished.

"Should I wake Rebekah?" she asked, handing me the *kwi*.

"No, let her sleep," I said, sliding the weapon into place around my right-hand knuckles. "Come on."

Bayta's eyes widened. "You want *both* of us to go?"

"I can't fire the *kwi* without you there to activate it," I reminded her as patiently as I could. "Without you, it makes a fair paperweight, but that's about all."

"What about Rebekah?"

"She'll be fine," I assured her. "Just warn the conductors to keep a close eye on our compartments."

"But—"

"Bayta, the Modhri has at least four walkers aboard this train, plus whatever he's got here in first class," I interrupted her tartly. "Rebekah will have a locked door between her and whatever trouble he feels like making. All I'll have is you and the *kwi*. Now, come *on*."

Glaring at me, her lips pressed tightly together, Bayta stepped silently to my side. Giving the corridor outside a quick check, I led the way out.

The Modhri was apparently through making trouble for the day. Bayta and I made it back to the last third-class car without so much as an odd look from anyone. Not even the four Juriani I'd met in the baggage car gave us more than an idle glance as we passed their seats in the last third-class car.

But then, that was how the Modhri worked his magic puppets. It was entirely possible that all four of them thought they'd been dozing in their seats the whole time they were actually chasing me, and were even now sitting there wondering why they felt so tired and achy.

Nowhere along the way did we spot the stationmaster.

We maneuvered through the twisty passageways to the rear of the first baggage car, and I touched the release to open the door into the vestibule. "That's the one," I told Bayta, pointing at the door leading into the next car.

She stepped in for a closer look, putting one hand against the side of the vestibule for balance. "It looks all right to me," she said.

"Except that it doesn't open," I said. Reaching past her, I pushed the release to demonstrate.

And without any fuss whatsoever, the door slid open.

For a long moment we just stood there, side by side in the cramped space of the vestibule, gazing through the open doorway into another maze of safety-webbed crate islands. "It doesn't open?" Bayta asked at last, her voice flat.

"Well, it *didn't* open," I growled as the door reached the end of its timed cycle and slid shut. I reached past Bayta and touched the release, and again the door slid open.

"I'll take your word for it," Bayta said diplomatically. "Now what?"

"First thing we do is find our crate," I said. Sliding past her, I stepped into the car and headed down the twisty path. With only a slight hesitation, Bayta followed.

I'd been wrong. The first thing we found wasn't our crate. The first thing we found, just around the first curve in the pathway, was a pair of Halkas.

Dead ones.

"What happened?" Bayta asked, her voice shaking a little as I knelt beside the bodies. No matter how many times death intruded on our lives, she never seemed to get completely used to it.

"No obvious marks; no signs of a struggle," I said, lifting one of the victims' heads for a closer look at the eyes and mouth. There was some kind of mucus at the corners of his mouth and eyes, I saw, which probably meant something. Unfortunately, I didn't have the slightest idea what. "Hopefully, some doctor at Jurskala Station will have time for an autopsy."

"What do you do here, Humans?" a voice demanded from behind me.

I spun around, jumping back to my feet as I did so. Three of the four Juriani who'd accosted me in the other baggage car were staring down their beaks in obvious horror at the sight before them. "Can I help you?" I asked cautiously.

The one in front snapped his beak a couple of times, then gestured to the Juri to his right. "Bidran, bring the conductor," he ordered. "Tell him what you have seen. Tell him what these Humans have done."

The other gulped something and turned, running with complete lack of normal Jurian dignity toward the passenger section of the train. "So, Humans," the spokesman said, his tone dark and ominous and still clearly shaken. "You do not merely come back here to steal. You come back here to murder."

"It's not what you think," I protested. "We just found them this way."

"That will be for a court of discovery to decide," the Juri said flatly.

The *kwi* tingled in my palm as Bayta activated it. Clearly, she assumed I would want to blast our way out of this.

But I couldn't. For one thing, the Juriani weren't under Modhran control, not this time. They were—or thought they were—just honest citizens who'd accidentally stumbled on a double murder and wanted to help bring the perps to justice.

Besides, it was way too late to cover this up by shooting. From the front baggage car I could hear the messenger screaming for assistance at the top of his lungs. Shooting these two would only give us two more bodies to explain when the mob of curiosity-seekers arrived.

"What do we do?" Bayta whispered tensely.

I grimaced. "We surrender to the Spiders," I told her.

I looked down at the bodies. Apparently, the Modhri *wasn't* through making trouble for the day.

SEVENTEEN :

Four hours later, we pulled into Jurskala Station.

Once in motion along the Tube, there's no way for a Quadrail to send a message on ahead. Nevertheless, by the time I finished giving Bayta her last-minute instructions and stepped out onto the platform, I would have been willing to swear the entire station knew what had happened.

Of course, the rumor grapevine had probably been helped along by the two bodies the drones were carefully lifting up through the baggage-car roof. The fact that there were two grim-faced Jurian officials waiting for me on the platform couldn't have hurt, either.

"You are Mr. Frank Compton?" one of the Juriani asked as I stepped off the train.

"Yes," I acknowledged, noting the polished scales and the subtle markings on their beaks. The one who'd spoken was a

Resolver, while the other was a mid-level government official. "And you?"

"I am *Tas* Yelfro," the Resolver said. "Resolver of the Jurian Collective. This is *Falc* Bresi, governor of Minprov District on Jostieer. We have some unpleasant questions to ask you."

"I see," I said. "May I ask your right of questioning?"

Falc Bresi stirred, either surprised or annoyed by the bluntness of my question. *Tas* Yelfro, in contrast, didn't bat an eye. "You are accused of a double murder in Jurian space," he told me.

"A double murder of non-Juriani, and inside Spider-controlled territory," I reminded him.

"Both true," *Tas* Yelfro conceded calmly. "To the first, I remind you that there were three Jurian witnesses to the crime."

"Witnesses to the discovery of a crime, not to the crime itself," I again reminded him.

"That will indeed be the primary question before the court of discovery," the Resolver said. "As to the second, a request is even now being made to the stationmaster for your release into Jurian custody."

I looked over his shoulder toward the complex of buildings that housed the stationmaster's office. Theoretically, I would be on completely solid ground to tell both him and *Falc* Bresi to take a hike, and all three of us knew it.

Unfortunately, theory didn't always link up with the real world. With rumors sweeping across the station, the Spiders were surely feeling the awkward delicacy of the situation. A pair of Humans found at a Halkan murder scene by Jurian citizenry was an engraved invitation for all three governments to get involved, and I wasn't at all sure how well the Spiders would stand up under the kind of pressure that could be brought to bear on them. Especially with the Modhri busily stirring the pot from the sidelines. "I appreciate your concerns for justice," I told the two Juriani. "I have such concerns myself, though you may not believe that. But I also have duties and obligations to fulfill, and I can't do that from the center of a Jurian court of discovery."

"You should have thought of that before murdering two helpless citizens of the galaxy in cold blood," *Falc* Bresi bit out.

"Please, Governor," *Tas* Yelfro said, holding a calming hand toward the other. "Perhaps, Mr. Compton, we will be able to solve our mutual difficulties before your train departs. I believe it will stay for the next hour."

"If not longer," I conceded, craning my neck to look back along the side of the Quadrail toward the baggage cars. With the bodies now gone, there were Spider drones and drudges swarming all over the crime scene, some of them working to unhook the car so that a fresh one standing by could be brought in to replace it. The rest of the Spiders were busy transferring the stacks of cargo to the replacement car.

"It will leave when scheduled," the Resolver said, a hint of mild rebuke in his voice. If there was one thing in this universe you could absolutely count on, it was that the Spiders would keep their trains running on schedule. "Until then, we would appreciate it if you would accompany us to the stationmaster's office to await his decision."

Leaving Bayta and Rebekah alone and helpless, perhaps? But they were hardly that. Bayta had the *kwi* and a ton of Spiders around she could call on to run interference if needed.

Besides, at the edge of my vision I could see three knots of

Halkas loitering on our platform, their flat bulldog faces turned in my direction, their heads leaning back and forth toward each other as they muttered among themselves. Getting out of the public eye for a while might not be a bad idea. "Very well," I said. "But I accompany you voluntarily, with full freedom to leave whenever I choose."

"That will be for the stationmaster to decide," *Tas* Yelfro said. Taking a step to the side, he gestured me past him. "This way, please."

It was the perfect setup for a good dit rec drama mob scene, as the alleged murderer was led on foot past simmering groups of the victims' countrymen. But the Modhri was apparently not interested in trying to tear me limb from limb today. The two Juriani and I reached the stationmaster's office without collecting anything more dangerous than a few glowers, and we all went inside.

"Mr. Frank Compton," the stationmaster greeted me solemnly.

"That's me," I confirmed, listening carefully to his voice. To my ears, unfortunately, all Spiders sounded alike. "Have we met?"

"No," he said briefly. "Has the current situation been explained to you?"

"I've had the Jurian version," I said. "But it seems to me that the only one I need to concern myself with is yours."

The Spider didn't answer, but merely curled up one of his seven legs from the floor and plucked a reader from the desk.

I studied him as he held that pose, paying particular attention to the scattering of white spots on his globe. It was, I decided, a different pattern from the one I'd seen on the stationmaster aboard our Quadrail.

The stationmaster everyone from Bayta on down claimed hadn't been there at all.

This one held up the reader another moment, then laid it down again. "Very well," he said. "Mr. Compton, you may sit. *Tas* Yelfro, you may speak."

Tas Yelfro's case, as one would expect from a professional Resolver, was lucid, well organized, and delivered with the kind of panache achieved elsewhere only by the lawyers in well-written dit rec dramas. I listened with one ear, most of my attention on our train across the way, watching as the Spiders continued the task of switching out the baggage car.

And wondering why exactly they were going to so much effort to keep the crime scene here.

Because they hadn't been nearly so cooperative with the locals the last time I'd gotten tangled up with a murder aboard a Quadrail. In that case, in fact, I'd had every indication that they'd planned to just move out the victim's effects, clean up the bloodstains, and send the car merrily on its way without so much as a preliminary forensic sweep.

Was it the potential for a three-way political tug-of-war that was making them so cooperative? Or was it merely the fact that this was a baggage car instead of a first-class compartment car, which meant there were no VIPs they would have to shift around?

Or did everyone else know something that I didn't?

Tas Yelfro had launched into his final summing-up when Bayta slipped through the door into the office and sat down beside me. "You all right?" she whispered.

Falc Bresi, listening to the Resolver's speech from the side, sent us an annoyed look. But since neither the stationmaster nor *Tas* Yelfro seemed all that worried about Bayta's quiet interruption, I decided not to be, either. "I'm fine," I whispered back. "What are you doing here?"

"It's all right," she assured me. "Rebekah's in a secure storage area along with our crate."

"What about my lockbox?" I asked, knowing she would pick up on the unasked question. "That's the only gun I've got left, and I don't want it going off on a tour of the galaxy without me."

"Don't worry, it's safe," she said. "The Spiders took it off the Quadrail and set it aside by one of the underfloor hatchways where they're collected for shuttle transport to the transfer station."

An underfloor hatchway near where Bayta had put Rebekah? I didn't dare ask, not with the two Juriani standing right there. But there was enough of a knowing expression on Bayta's face that it was clear we both knew what we were actually talking about. The Melding coral was safe, hopefully close enough to Rebekah to continue behaving itself. "Good enough," I said. "If I end up heading in-system, I'll definitely want it with me."

Bayta looked over at *Tas* Yelfro, who was still holding forth. "If the Juriani allow that," she warned.

I tuned back in to the oratory. To my surprise, somewhere along the way the Resolver had apparently switched from requesting a simple court of discovery to asking for a full-fledged criminal trial. "Uh-oh," I murmured.

"Is there really enough evidence to hold you for trial?" Bayta asked, sounding confused.

"Not even close," I said. "From our noble Resolver's expression, I'd say he doesn't think so, either."

"But then why—?" She broke off.

"Right," I confirmed grimly, studying *Tas* Yelfro's face. Though the polyp colony under his brain was clearly feeding him instructions, the lack of an altered expression and vocal pattern meant the Modhri hadn't yet escalated his control to the point of physically taking over his body. Either he didn't feel it was necessary to go to that extreme, or else he was hoping he could keep the identity of the Resolver's true master under wraps. "What does the stationmaster make of all this?" I asked Bayta.

"He's uncertain," she said. "He's not going to simply turn you over to the Juriani, of course. But he's concerned that letting you go free without an investigation would bring unwelcome attention."

"To us?" I asked. "Or to him?"

"Neither would be a good thing," she said diplomatically.

"I suppose," I said. "Let's see if we can help him out a little." Squaring my shoulders, I stood up.

Tas Yelfro noticed me immediately, of course. But Jurian protocol concerning official presentations required him to finish his current thought before he acknowledged me. I, for my part, had the equally rigid obligation to wait silently until he found that end point and invited me into the discussion.

Two sentences later—two very convoluted sentences, as it happened—he reached his stopping point. "You have something to add?" he asked me.

"Actually, I have a suggestion," I said. "It's obvious now that this matter can't be resolved until long after my train has left the station. Therefore—"

"Do you insult the abilities of a Jurian Resolver?" *Falc* Bresi interrupted.

The scales around *Tas* Yelfro's eyes wrinkled in a grimace. Cutting me off in the middle of my turn was a clear violation of protocol, and I would be well within my rights to demand an apology.

But I was a gracious sort of alien, and I let it pass. "Therefore, I suggest you confine me here on the station," I continued, "under Spider guard and protection, until we have sufficient information to decide how best to proceed."

Falc Bresi opened his beak—"Such information to include a full examination of the bodies and the location of their death?" *Tas* Yelfro asked before the governor could say anything.

"Exactly," I said, watching as *Falc* Bresi closed his beak again without speaking. Either the governor didn't know the first thing about how detailed and time-consuming real-life criminal investigations were, or else he simply didn't believe that upstart aliens like me deserved that kind of consideration. "I wouldn't expect it to take more than three or four days."

"The Juriani have no objections to such a path," *Tas* Yelfro said. "Stationmaster?"

"It will be as suggested," the stationmaster said.

Tas Yelfro bowed. "Thank you."

"I recommend a room at the Eulalee Hotel," I said. "They

have room service, so I won't need an escort to take me to my meals."

"Don't overreach your status," *Falc* Bresi growled. "You are a criminal, and will spend your time in a holding cell at the detention center."

"Stationmaster?" I invited. "This is your jurisdiction and decision, not his."

"He will be placed in the Eulalee Hotel," the Spider said.

"Make it a top-floor room on the west side," I added. "That way I can keep an eye on what the examiners are doing with the baggage car."

"Very well," the stationmaster said. "*Tas* Yelfro, you and *Falc* Bresi may accompany Mr. Compton and his Spider escort to his holding area, if you wish."

"Oh, yes," *Falc* Bresi said, glaring coldly at me over the top of his beak. "We most certainly do so wish."

The Eulalee Hotel was the tallest public building in Jurskala Station, a five-floor showcase of Jurian architectural prowess rising over the mostly single-story cafés and shops around it. The exterior was done up in Neo-Revival, a style I'd always found both pretentious and ugly. One of the minor advantages of staying there was that, once inside your room, you didn't have to look at it.

The hotel's elevators weren't nearly big enough for our entire party to squeeze into together, so *Falc* Bresi insisted we take the stairs. The demand was probably designed to annoy me, but I had more urgent things on my mind than Jurian cheap shots and agreed without complaint.

Still, I couldn't help wondering what the travelers relaxing in the hotel's atrium lobby thought as they watched two Humans, two Juriani, and two conductor Spiders making their way all the way up the wide wrought-iron switchback staircase toward the fifth-floor landing. It just begged for a reference to Noah's ark, but given that our escort probably wouldn't get the joke I decided not to bother.

The stationmaster had sent a message ahead, and two more Spiders were waiting when we reached my assigned room. "I assume you're taking the first shift of guard duty?" I asked them as we approached.

In answer, one of them unfolded a leg he'd had tucked under his globe and produced a key. He stuck it into the lock, and the door popped open. "So you are," I confirmed, looking at the two Juriani. "I guess that means your services will no longer be needed," I added as I pushed the door open.

"Yet we would not wish that the entire burden for your security would rest with the Spiders," *Tas* Yelfro said smoothly. "Therefore, *Falc* Bresi has authorized a Jurian security team to be assembled from the transfer station. It will be here within the hour."

I grimaced. As if I didn't have enough enemies and potential enemies to keep track of. "That's very generous of you," I said, taking Bayta's arm and easing her through the doorway into the room. "We'll speak again when the investigation is finished."

"We'll look forward to it," *Tas* Yelfro promised.

I nodded to him and started into the room. *Falc* Bresi started to walk in behind me, but stopped short as I stood my ground in the doorway. "We'll speak again when the investigation is finished," I repeated, a little more firmly.

For a couple of seconds he just stared at me, as if memorizing the features of my face against the day when he had his people rearrange them. Then, without comment, he turned and headed toward the elevators. *Tas* Yelfro nodded again at me and followed.

I cocked an eyebrow at the four Spiders now grouped around the door. "Your turn," I said.

"They'll be staying for a while," Bayta said quietly from somewhere behind me.

I looked over my shoulder. While I'd been verbally sparring with *Falc* Bresi, she'd made her way across the room and was standing with her back to me, staring out the window. Closing the door on the Spiders, I crossed over to her. "You okay?" I asked.

"This isn't going to work, Frank," she said, her voice almost too soft for me to hear. "Every minute we stay here is another minute the Modhri has to bring in more walkers. In three days—" She shook her head, a shiver running through her.

Unfortunately, she had a point. "It'll work out," I said.

She didn't answer. She didn't have to. Grimacing, I stepped around to her side and put my arm around her shoulders. The muscles beneath my hand tensed reflexively at the touch, then softened again. Lifting my eyes from the colorfully dressed Humans and aliens scurrying among the tracks and platforms below, I focused on our train.

The Spiders had finished transferring the cargo from the old baggage car to the new one, and had maneuvered the new car into position between the other two baggage cars. I wondered briefly why they hadn't just put the remaining two cars together and stuck the new one on the end, decided it probably had something to do with keeping the cargo stacks in the properly positioned cargo cars. Through the open roof of the old baggage car I could see a group of smaller tech-type Spiders, both the knee-high mites and the even smaller twitters, moving slowly along the floor as they searched for evidence of how the two Halkas had died. I looked again at the open roof.

And felt my breath catch in my throat. "Bayta, you told me the Spiders took our crate off the train," I said, forcing my voice to stay casual. "Where exactly was it? Somewhere near where we found the Halkas?"

"No, actually, it was in the third baggage car," she said. "The one at the end of the train."

The tingle running up my back went a little more tingly. "Could they tell if it had been opened?"

"I didn't ask them," she said, frowning at me. Casual tone or not, she knew what it meant when I started asking odd questions this way. "But they must have. Otherwise, why would the Modhri have killed them?"

"Is that what you think?" I asked. "That the Modhri killed his own walkers?"

"I assumed he wanted an excuse to keep us here," she said, frowning a little harder. "It's not like he hasn't killed walkers before when he needed to."

"He certainly made use of the situation to make trouble for us," I agreed. "But I think it was mostly pure luck that things turned out that way for him. Do you know where the autopsy is being carried out?"

"In one of the medical center's operating rooms, I think."

"We need to go talk to the doctors." I turned from the window and started toward the door.

"Wait a minute," she said, catching my arm. "*We're* not going anywhere. You're under arrest, remember?"

"So un-arrest me," I said. "This is important."

"So is your life," she said firmly. "I thought the reason we agreed to this was to keep you away from angry Halkas until we could prove you didn't kill their countrymen. What do you want me to tell the doctors at the autopsy?"

I grimaced, but she was right. "Tell them to check for evidence of asphyxiation."

Her eyes widened. "*Asphyxiation?*"

"And then," I went on, "have the Spiders check all the air seals on that baggage car."

She looked back out the window. "You mean the whole thing was just an *accident?*"

"Well, the Modhri certainly didn't kill them himself," I said, carefully sidestepping her actual question. The deaths hadn't been an accident, not by a long shot. But this wasn't the time to go into that. "You didn't see the way those four Jurian walkers came charging in at me after the Halkas died. The Modhri was mad, way madder than he should have been if he'd snuffed the Halkas himself. I think he was convinced I'd killed them, and was going to make it very clear what he thought of that."

Bayta took a deep breath. "All right, I'll go tell the doctors. What do you want me to do after that?"

"We get out of here as fast as we can, before the Modhri can bring in more walkers," I said. "I don't suppose that tender the New Tigris stationmaster told us about would happen to be anywhere nearby?"

"Actually, I think it's right here," Bayta said, leaning a little toward the window and peering past the passenger platforms and buildings. "Yes, I can see it over there."

I looked where she was pointing. It was there, all right: three windowless passenger cars sandwiched between two engines pointed in opposite directions. It was sitting on the second track past the passenger section, in one of the Spiders' service areas. "Then we're good to go," I said. "As soon as you get me officially cleared of the Halkas' deaths, have the Spiders collect the crate and lockboxes and put them aboard the tender. Once everything's there, you and I and Rebekah will join them, and we'll be out of here."

Bayta's lips puckered. "It sounds too easy," she said doubtfully.

"Well, the first part certainly is," I said. "You said Rebekah's in a secure storage facility, which should include dozens of crates waiting to be transferred to different trains. And of course, the Spiders are always moving lockboxes around. Even if the Modhri's watching like a hawk, it should be no trick to get the Melding coral ready to travel."

"But?" she prompted.

"But getting the three of us aboard won't be nearly so simple," I conceded. "We'll need to come up with a really good diversion to keep all those walker eyes pointed in the wrong direction at the critical moment."

"You have any ideas on how to do that?"

"Not yet, but I will," I said. "You just get me off the hook so that I don't have a mob of Halkas breathing down my neck when we make our break."

"Medical center, stationmaster's office, then back here," she said, heading toward the door. "Anything else?"

"No, that should do for now," I said. "And be careful. Some of the Halkas may have seen us together, and the Modhri certainly has."

"Don't worry," she said, pulling the *kwi* out of her pocket. "I'll see you soon."

She opened the door, and I caught a glimpse of a forest of Spider legs out in the corridor before it closed again behind her. Pulling out my reader, I settled down in a comfy chair by the window and pulled up a station schematic. When setting up a diversion, the first thing to consider was geography.

I'd been working for about half an hour when the door chime sounded.

I looked up, frowning. Bayta wouldn't bother ringing—one of the Spiders out there had a key, and she would have no problem ordering him to open up.

The chime came again. Tucking my reader away, I got up and went to the door.

It was the Jurian Resolver, *Tas* Yelfro. "Mr. Compton," he greeted me solemnly. "May I come in?"

"Certainly," I said, stepping back out of his way and wondering what the Modhri was up to this time. *Tas* Yelfro came in, glancing around as if making sure I was alone.

And as I watched, the scales around his beak seemed to sag a little, and the sweep of his shoulders hunched just a bit farther back, and his head straightened and then settled back into its original position.

The Modhri had taken over.

"Greetings, Mr. Compton," he said, his voice altered as subtly but as indisputably as his appearance. "I bring news and an offer."

"Do you, now," I said. "If it's anything like the last seven or eight offers you've pitched to me, I think I'll pass."

"But first," the Modhri said, ignoring the gibe, "I bring you a conversation piece." Reaching into his tunic, he pulled out something small and lobbed it toward me.

Automatically, I reached out and caught it. It was a *kwi,* just like the one I'd conned out of the Chahwyn.

I felt my breath freeze in my chest. No. It wasn't just like my *kwi.* It *was* my *kwi.*

The *kwi* Bayta had been carrying.

I looked up at the mocking Jurian eyes gazing at me. "Where is she?" I asked, forcing my voice to stay quiet and controlled.

"She is safe," the Modhri said. "There's no need to worry." He cocked his head slightly to the side. "Yet."

I took a step toward him. "Where is she?" I repeated, my voice quavering slightly with black anger. My brain was spinning at Quadrail speeds, trying desperately to come up with a plan.

"I said she is safe," the Modhri said, matching my tone. "For now, that's all you need to know."

"I don't think so," I said, taking another step toward him. Most people, I reflected grimly, would have started backing up about now, possibly doing a quick reevaluation on whether they really wanted to cross me or not.

But the Modhri didn't think like that. To him, *Tas* Yelfro was just another of his slaves, one more disposable body in his collection. If he died at my hand, the Modhri would simply find or make a replacement.

And then, as I continued moving toward him, the germ of

an idea finally surfaced. A risky, shaky idea, way too heavy on speculation and suspicion and way too light on actual fact. But it was the best I had, and it would have to do. "You'll tell me where she is, and you'll tell me now," I continued, taking the one final step that put me within arm's reach of him.

His beak cracked open in a mocking smile. "Really, Mr. Compton—"

The rest of the sentence disintegrated in an explosive gasp of surprise and pain as I drove my fist hard into his abdomen.

EIGHTEEN :

The typical Human response when hit like that would be to fold, jackknife-style, around the point of impact. The typical Jurian response, in contrast, was to go stiff as a board and fall backward. Except for his Modhran polyp colony, *Tas* Yelfro was indeed a typical Juri. He gasped again as he toppled backward like a frozen mannequin, the crash of his fall muffled by the thick carpet.

For a second he just lay there, looking like a molded luge-board, staring at me in disbelief. I knelt down beside him and, just to show it hadn't been an accident, I hit him again in the same spot.

He shook with the impact, his eyes and beak widening with agony and even more disbelief and the beginnings of genuine anger. "I'm going to go find her now," I told him, gazing into his eyes with the most intimidating stare in my Westali arsenal.

"If you try to stop me, I'll just have to hurt more of your walkers."

I lowered my face until it was only a few centimeters from his. "And if you hurt her," I added quietly, "I'll kill every walker in this station. You hear me? Every last one of them."

He was still staring back at me, his eyes still swimming with pain. Only now, I could see the first stirrings of fear, as well. If I really succeeded in killing all his walkers, this particular mind segment would die, vanishing without a trace and leaving the overall Modhran mind to forever wonder what had happened here today.

It wasn't an idle threat, either. I'd done it before, destroying the mind segment on an entire Quadrail train.

Or so he believed.

I held his gaze another couple of seconds, just to make sure he knew I was serious, pushing the bluff to the limit. Then, wrapping the *kwi* around my right hand, I stood up, crossed to the door, and eased it open.

My four Spider guards were still standing out there where I'd left them. Slipping out into the hallway, I closed the door behind me. "Can you locate Bayta?" I asked.

"You are ordered to remain in your compartment," one of the Spiders said.

"I know that," I said. "Can you locate Bayta? Yes or no?"

"No," he said.

I felt my stomach tighten. For one telepath not to be able to locate another telepath meant one of three things: out of range, unconscious, or dead.

Not dead, I told myself firmly. Not dead. The Modhri was

way too smart to throw away his best leverage against me by killing her out of hand. No, she was surely only unconscious.

Unfortunately, she could also be literally anywhere on the station. "Alert the rest of the Spiders to watch for her," I ordered him. "You four start searching the passenger areas between here and the medical center."

None of them so much as budged. "Did you hear me?" I demanded.

"You are ordered to remain in your compartment," the Spider said.

"I have authority in Bayta's name to give you orders," I said, easing myself to the side where I would have a clear shot around his maze of legs. Actually, I wasn't really sure how much authority I had over the Spiders when Bayta wasn't with me.

"You are ordered to remain in your compartment," the Spider said, still not moving.

I grimaced. Apparently, not much. "In that case—" I began.

And right in the middle of the sentence, I ducked past him and sprinted for the stairs.

Spiders being the simple workers that they are, I hadn't expected them to react quickly enough to stop me. I was right, and was halfway down the first flight of the wide flowing staircase before they even made it to the landing.

Unfortunately, the Modhri wasn't nearly so slow on the uptake. I had reached the fourth-floor landing and was rounding the corner onto the next curve of stairs when I heard the sounds of a small crowd further down the stairway on its way up.

I was halfway to the third floor when the front of that wave reached me.

There were four of them, all middle-aged Juriani dressed in quiet, dignified, upper-class clothing, breathing heavily as they bounded up the stairs like children in a hop-clink game. Behind them, just starting up the flight of stairs, were two Halkas wearing the trilayered robes of the Halkan Peerage. Apparently the Juriani were the sacrificial lambs, designed to slow me down as I barreled through them so that the larger Halkas could safely corral me before I did any serious damage.

But I had no intention of playing nicely. I waited until I was only three steps away from the panting Juriani, then veered to the outside of the stairway, grabbed the top of the railing, and flipped myself over the edge. Shifting my grip in midair to one of the railing's vertical supports, I slid down until I was hanging straight over the railing of the next flight down. As my momentum swung me inward, I let go of the support and dropped to the stairs below.

Neatly putting me *below* the Modhri's attack line.

I could hear the sudden flurry of activity above me as the Juriani and Halkas screeched to a halt and reversed direction. But they were too late. I was already on my way down, taking the stairs three at a time. I reached the lobby and charged past the rest of the astonished travelers out into the station.

Jurskala Station was the Quadrail stop for the Jurian home system, and as such was large, elaborate, and teeming with travelers. Despite my desperate hurry, I forced myself to slow to a walk, knowing that nothing drew attention faster than someone running full tilt through a crowd. The Modhri was relying on alien minds and alien eyes, and it was likely that most of the people moving through the station had never bothered learning how to distinguish one Human from another.

Even so, I doubted I could slip past all the walkers, not with the Modhri bending every resource he had here toward locating me. Certainly I'd never stay below the radar long enough to find Bayta.

But then, despite the impression I'd worked so hard to leave with the Modhri up in my room, I had no intention of turning the station upside down until I found her. All I needed right now was to get to the stationmaster and make sure he didn't carry out the arrangements I'd sent Bayta to make.

A chipmunk-faced Bellido stepped into my path, a set of three guns holstered beneath the arms of his elaborately embroidered robe. "Excuse me—" he began.

I shouldered my way past him and picked up my pace, cursing under my breath. I'd hoped to get at least a little farther before I was spotted. Theoretically, I knew, I shouldn't have to physically confront the stationmaster, but should be able to relay my instructions to him via any Spider. But Spiders had varying degrees of imagination and autonomy, none of them very impressive, and I didn't dare risk that my message would get garbled or ignored.

Out of the corner of my eye I spotted two Tra'ho'seej angling toward me. I responded by shifting direction toward a bulky Cimma also coming toward me, did a quick sidestep around him, and headed off in another direction entirely. I ducked behind and around a pair of Halkas, passed by a Human wearing a Sorbonne collegiate scarf and jacket, and made a tight circle to put me again on a path to the stationmaster's office.

And suddenly a pair of metallic Spider legs came angling down from my right, hitting the floor directly in front of me.

I had no chance to sidestep or even stop. I slammed into them, feeling them flex a bit with the impact, and bounced back. Before I could do more than catch my balance the Spider swiveled around behind me and wrapped another of his legs, wrestler-style, around my waist. A second later two more legs lifted from the floor and poked their way horizontally under my armpits, and the damn thing lifted me up like a weightlifter doing biceps curls.

And I found myself staring at my distorted reflection in a shiny Spider globe.

But not just any Spider globe. As I looked at the pattern of white dots beneath my face, I realized this was the same Spider I'd done that trampoline off of in my previous train's baggage car.

Was that why he was here? Looking for payback?

He pulled me higher and closer until my cheek was pressed against his globe. I braced myself, wondering if he was going to try bouncing off of me now, just to show me what it felt like, or whether he'd just settle for playing kickball with me across the station.

But to my surprise, I just heard a quiet Spider voice in my ear, almost too quiet to hear. "What do you do here, friend?"

I felt my chest tighten. I'd never had a Spider call me friend. For that matter, I'd never heard of a Spider calling *anyone* friend.

And in that single numbing second I knew that my earlier speculations and suspicions had been right.

God help us all.

"What do you do here, friend?" the Spider asked again.

I took a deep breath. Whatever else this might mean— whatever the implications for the future—my first priority was to get Bayta away from the Modhri. "I need to get a message to the stationmaster," I said. "Can you do that?"

"Yes," he said.

I gave him the message, keeping it short and clear and as authoritative as I could make it. Hanging a half meter off a Quadrail station floor being stared at by hundreds of bemused aliens was no time to get long-winded. "Can he do that?" I asked when I'd finished.

"He will do that," the Spider said.

I grimaced, the sinking feeling in my stomach dropping another couple of floors. "Then I suppose I need to get back to my prison," I told him.

"Yes," he said.

I frowned, focusing on the station around me. To my surprise, I discovered that we were already in motion, though the Spider was walking so smoothly I hadn't even noticed when we'd started up. The Eulalee Hotel's main entrance was in sight out of the corner of my eye, and I could see the two Halkas who'd tried to corral me on the stairs waiting watchfully off to the side.

Belatedly, I realized I probably looked like an oversized baby in its mother's chest carrier. "I can make it from here, Spot," I told the Spider.

There was a slight pause, as if he was pondering the nickname I'd just given him. "It is ordered that you be delivered to your prison," he told me.

"This is extremely undignified," I tried again. "Dignity is important to Humans."

He didn't answer. He also didn't put me down.

And considering the look on the Halkas' faces as we passed,

maybe it was just as well that he didn't. The Modhri was apparently still mad at me.

The four Spider guards were back in their semicircle around my door when we reached my room. Spot set me down, one of the guards unlocked my door, and I went inside.

Tas Yelfro had managed to pull himself off the floor and drag himself up onto the couch in my absence. "Human fool," he rasped as I closed the door behind me. "Did you genuinely hope to accomplish anything useful?"

The voice was raspy, but the face and tone were still those of the Modhri. "You never know until you try," I said, pulling over a chair to face him and sitting down. "I have a deal to propose."

"What sort of deal?"

"One that'll benefit both of us," I said. "But first we need to clear the air a little. Specifically, I didn't kill your walkers aboard the Quadrail. The baggage car decompressed, and they simply asphyxiated."

He cocked his head to one side, the motion making him look more bird-like than ever. "Yes, I know," he said. "How did you decompress the car?"

"I didn't," I told him. "It was probably some malfunction of the seals—the Spiders are looking into it. The point is that there's no reason to blame me for any of that, or to try to take revenge."

"I never take revenge," he said. "Speak your proposal."

"I want Bayta back," I said.

"I want the Abomination," he countered. "Deliver it, and you may have the Human female."

"Actually, you don't want the Abomination," I said. "You want something far more valuable than that."

"There is nothing more valuable than the Abomination."

"You're confusing means with ends," I told him. "Tell me, if you had the Abomination coral right now, what would you do with him?"

"I would take it through the transfer station to Jurskala," he said. "I have many outposts on that world."

"And then?"

Something cold settled into the Modhri's eyes. "It would reveal to me the location of the others."

"No it wouldn't," I said. "You'll never get that information. Not from the coral."

"Once I surround the Abomination, it will have no choice."

"It'll never happen," I insisted. "The coral will suicide long before he lets you get him to your interrogation chamber. Or hadn't you heard about Lorelei Beach and what her symbiont colony did to itself on Earth?"

The Modhri's eyes might have flashed a little on the word *symbiont*. "The Abomination will not have access to any such convenient means of self-destruction."

"Who says he'll need it?" I countered. "You have your polyp colonies kill their hosts and themselves all the time. Who says the Melding's outpost can't pull the same stunt inside his coral?"

The Modhri clacked his beak. "For a Human who claims cleverness, you quickly argue yourself into your own trap," he said. "If the Abomination will not tell me where the others are hiding, then the only other source of that information is the young female. Do you wish for me to demand her instead in exchange for the Human Bayta?"

"Not at all," I said. "I wish for you to take a wider view of all this. I mean, really, what *is* the Abomination? A couple hundred symbionts and a few chunks of coral. What kind of threat can they possibly be to you?"

He gave a loud, derisive snort. It was followed immediately by a wince of pain from his still-tender abdomen and lung sacs. "Of course the Abomination is not a threat," he said. "This is not about threats."

"No, it's about principle, and cleansing the universe of a crime against nature," I acknowledged. "Believe it or not, I understand the concept. But the Abomination has something far more valuable to you than simple revenge."

"Explain."

"Think about it a minute," I urged. "The Abomination was hidden on New Tigris for close to ten years. In the past few months, he and his symbionts have been moving to some other location. You've probably been hunting him for a lot of that time, with every outpost and walker and soldier you've got." I raised my eyebrows. "And yet, with all those resources, you still haven't got a clue as to where they've all gone."

The Modhri snorted again, more gently and carefully this time. "If you have a point, make it."

"It's very simple," I said. "The Abomination has found a hiding place for his new homeland that no one has been able to find. *Which is exactly what you want for your own homeland.*"

The Modhri made as if to say something, then stopped. "You suggest I destroy the Abomination and use its same location?" he asked at last. "A location which you already know?"

"Actually, I don't already know it," I corrected him, fudging the truth only a little. "And of course that would be silly. What I'm suggesting is that you figure out his method or technique and adapt that for your own purposes. Whether it's a matter of the location itself, or some kind of camouflage, if it works for Abomination coral it should work equally well for you."

"And what then of the Abomination?"

"What of it?" I asked. "We both agree it's no threat to you. Find out how they're doing this, then leave the Abomination to itself and go find a place where you can do the same thing. Live and let live, I always say."

His beak opened in a mocking gesture. "As you and I already do?"

"I offered that option to you once," I said. "I was nearly killed for my trouble." I gave him a tight, slightly mocking smile. "But you probably never knew about that."

"On the contrary, I know about everything," he said coldly. "And your subsequent actions show clearly that your offer was not sincere."

"Actually, it was," I said, feeling a shiver run through me. Bayta, I knew, still thought our brief side trip to the Yandro transfer station on our way to New Tigris had been a complete waste of time. Up to now, I had suspected differently.

Now it was no longer merely a suspicion. "But that's water under the bridge," I went on. "Do we have the makings of a deal here?"

For a few seconds he eyed me in silence. "I will keep the Human Bayta," he said at last. "You will lead my Eyes to this place. When I have seen it and learned its secrets, I will release her."

"You'll release her into my direct custody," I said. "And you'll do it immediately after I've led your Eyes to the Abomination's hideout. If you want to stick around and root out its secrets, you can do it on your own time."

Again, he took a moment to study me. "Agreed," he said. "Which train do we need to take?"

"Whichever the next train is on the Kalalee Branch," I said. There was a fair chance that he'd seen the label on our crate, and I might as well keep my lies consistent and easy to remember. "We're heading to Benedais."

"Benedais," he repeated, his eyes boring into mine. "Be certain you speak truthfully to me."

"*You* be certain you have Bayta ready to hand over to me by the time we reach Benedais," I said. "*And* in mint condition. I presume you'll want to make the travel arrangements yourself. Rebekah and I will need a double adjoining compartment."

"No," he said flatly. "You will stay in a first-class coach car where I can watch you."

"Do you want Rebekah to take us to the Abomination's hideout, or don't you?" I asked patiently. "Because if you do, she has to think that things are back to normal, and normal means a double compartment."

He considered. "And the Abomination?"

"It'll be in the compartment with us," I told him. "Just in case you get the urge to go poking around in baggage cars again."

He took a careful breath. "As you wish. What will you tell the young Human female?"

"I'll think of something," I said. "You just get the tickets for our train. While you're at it, you might want to expedite my getting out of here."

"It will be done." *Tas* Yelfro stood up. "I will take the weapon now," he added, holding out his hand.

I looked at the *kwi* still wrapped around my knuckles. "It's of no use to you," I said.

His beak clacked sarcastically. "While I have it, it's of no use to you, either."

There was no way around it. Slipping the *kwi* off my hand, I tossed it to him. "I'll want it back when this is all over," I warned.

"We shall see," he said, pocketing the weapon and moving toward the door. "I shall let you know which train you will be taking."

He opened the door and paused. "And," he added, "I will be watching."

"Yes," I said. "I'll just bet you will."

Even with the Modhri's assistance, it took nearly four hours for the stationmaster to officially release me from my hotel room. Or maybe the delay was *because* of the Modhri. There would be some preparations he would want to make for our trip, and he probably preferred me kept on ice until they were complete.

I headed down the stairs again to the hotel lobby. *Tas* Yelfro himself was nowhere in sight, but one of the Halkas on his backup team was waiting at the main door with the news that our train would be arriving in two hours. I assured him we'd be ready, then headed across to the Spider storage area where Bayta had said Rebekah was waiting.

I'd told the Modhri I would figure out something to tell Rebekah. Over the long hours of my forced idleness, I had.

I told her the truth.

She listened in silence as I described the situation. "What do you want me to do?" she asked when I'd finished.

"That depends on what you're willing to do," I told her. "Option one is that you put your neck into the noose along with Bayta's and mine. Option two is to say no thanks, and be home in time for dinner."

She wrinkled her nose. "That would be a good trick."

"Actually, at the moment it would be simplicity itself," I said, pointing toward the station's service area. "There's a Spider tender parked right over there, ready to go. Usually Bayta's the one who coordinates these special travel arrangements, but I could probably muddle through the process without her this once. You and your coral could be aboard and out of the station before the Modhri even knows you're gone."

She looked in the direction I'd pointed, as if she could see through the wall by sheer willpower. "What would happen to Bayta if I did that?"

"Do you care?" I asked bluntly.

She looked back at me and smiled, a sad, wistful sort of thing. "This is a test, isn't it?" she asked. "You want to know if I'm willing to risk my life for her. Whether I and the rest of the Melding are truly worth saving."

"It's a fair question," I pointed out. "I do know you're willing to risk your life for your chunks of coral. Otherwise, you could have destroyed it back on New Tigris and slipped away. That kind of loyalty certainly counts for something."

"But the coral is family?" she said.

"The coral is family," I agreed. "It's a different thing entirely to take the same risk for a relative stranger."

"And if I'm not willing, I'm no better than the Modhri?"

"Or you're young and scared, neither of which I could really hold against you," I said. "Besides, in the grand scheme of things, what does it really matter what I think?"

"It always matters what a friend thinks," Rebekah said quietly. "Do you have a plan for us to use?"

"I have the opening moves of one," I said. "The details will depend on what the Modhri decides to do. I'll need Bayta aboard the train with us when we make our move."

"What if he leaves her here instead?"

"Then we'll have to tour around the galaxy for a while until he decides I'm stalling and brings her aboard so he can threaten her to my face," I said.

Rebekah's eyes unfocused. "No, he'll bring her along," she said slowly. "He likes keeping his eggs in one basket."

"Yes, I've noticed that," I said. "Let's hope he stays to form on this one." I looked at my watch. "Our train arrives in just under an hour, with a forty-five-minute layover. Plenty of time for us to make our arrangements. We'll have our usual double compartment, by the way, which we'll be sharing with your supposed crate of Melding coral."

"And the real coral?"

"Don't worry, it'll be right there with us," I assured her, smiling tightly. "Just leave that one to me."

One hour and forty minutes later, our train pulled out of the station.

I stayed in my compartment with my face pressed to the window from the moment Rebekah and I got in until the moment the conductors stepped back inside the train and irised the doors closed. I saw no sign of Bayta.

Nevertheless, half an hour after leaving the station, when I took Rebekah on a brief walking tour up and down the compartment car corridor, she confirmed that Bayta was indeed aboard.

"She's in the first compartment, the one across from the car door," she told me as she sat down on the edge of the bed in her compartment. "I don't know why I couldn't sense her when we first came in."

"She was probably still unconscious," I said, stepping back and leaning an elbow on the crate I'd positioned on the midline between our two compartments. It was a fairly inconvenient place to put the thing, actually, and I anticipated a few stubbed toes and barked shins in my future. But if someone started to break into one of our compartments I wanted to be able to quickly shove the crate into the other one and close the dividing wall. It might only gain us a minute or two, but sometimes that made all the difference. "But at least that explains why the Modhri made sure to drag out the cancellation of my murder charge."

"It does?" Rebekah asked, frowning.

"Sure." I pointed toward the front of the car. "The Modhri wanted Bayta along, but he didn't want us seeing where he'd stashed her. So instead of all of us just boarding the train at Jurskala, he had his walkers put her on a train going the other direction, took her off at the next station, and then loaded her aboard this train when it came through. That way, by the time we check in, she's already in and hidden."

"Only he doesn't know I can sense her," Rebekah murmured.

"There are a lot of things he doesn't know," I said, feeling a little of the worry lifting from my shoulders. All our erudite expectations aside, the Modhri could still have decided not to bring Bayta aboard our expedition until we reached our supposed destination of Benedais thirteen and a half days from now. That would have been awkward, since Rebekah and I needed to get off at Sibbrava a week earlier than that. "Anyway, I'm hungry," I went on. "Let's go to the dining car and get something to eat."

"You think that's safe?" Rebekah asked, looking at the door.

"The Modhri thinks you're blissfully leading him to the Promised Land, remember?" I reminded her. "He won't bother us. Besides, now that Bayta's awake we need a Spider to see us so she knows we're aboard with her."

"Oh. Of course," she said, standing up. "Now that you mention it, I'm sort of hungry too."

"Good," I said, giving the crate a tap as I moved toward her door. "By the way, how's your coral doing?"

She frowned toward the rear of the train. "He's all right," she said.

"It's not going to be a problem, you being this far away from him, is it?"

"It shouldn't be," she assured me.

"Good," I said. "Then let's go eat. By the way, have you ever tried onion rings?"

NINETEEN :

The train the Modhri had chosen for us turned out to be a lo-cal, which meant that as we traveled along we never went more than four or five hours before finding ourselves at yet an-other stop. Occasionally a station's decor and service buildings showed some imagination and originality, at least from what Rebekah and I could see through our compartment windows. But most of the stops were small Jurian colony worlds, and for those a fairly straightforward cookie-cutter design mentality had been at work. By the time I turned in that first night, I was hardly even bothering to look out the window anymore as we rolled to a stop.

The next day dawned—figuratively speaking, of course—looking to be a copy of the first.

It didn't stay that way for long.

———

"What *is* this?" Rebekah asked, peering at the breakfast order I'd brought back to our compartment.

"A Cimman delicacy called daybreak noodles," I told her as I set our plates on top of the crate. With neither of us really comfortable sitting out in the open in the dining car, and with the curve couches of both our compartments unavailable inside the folded-up dividing wall, the crate had naturally evolved into our dining table. "Try it—you'll like it."

"Uh-*huh*," she said, with the kind of knowing look only a ten-year-old can deliver.

"No, really," I insisted, scooping up one of the deep blue noodles from my plate with my fork and folding it into my mouth. "Try it."

"I never heard of anyone eating noodles for breakfast," she said, still looking doubtful as she cut off a small piece of noodle with the edge of her fork. She gave it a cautious nibble, her face screwing up as she did so. "It's kind of spicy."

"Kija spice, to be specific," I told her. Putting another noodle into my mouth, I rolled it over my tongue, mentally gauging it against my personal taste-bud Richter scale. "It's no worse than oreganino, really."

"Which people also don't eat for breakfast."

"You'd be surprised what some people eat for breakfast," I told her. "It's not more than an order of magnitude stronger than cinnamon, either, which people eat for breakfast all the time."

"I suppose," she said, trying another noodle. "It's not so bad once you get used to it."

"That's the spirit," I said approvingly. "Anyway, be forewarned that kija's a staple of Cimman cooking, so you'd better get used to it if you're going to set up shop on Sibbrava."

"I suppose," she said, turning her head to gaze out the window. We had passed through an atmosphere barrier and were angling downward, headed into yet another station. "There are so many things about these peoples I don't understand."

"I would assume a telepath would know everything about everyone," I said. "Especially his fellow telepaths."

"I didn't say I didn't *know* them," she said, taking a larger bite of noodle. She was still chewing cautiously, but at least she wasn't wincing outright anymore. "I do, probably as well as any Human. I just don't *understand* them."

"Ah," I said, not entirely sure I understood the distinction.

"Well, like there," she said, pointing out the window with her fork. "All Jurian architecture involves the image of a key somewhere, either a real key shape or else a stylized representation of one."

"You're kidding," I said, frowning. I'd never even heard of such a thing before.

"No, it's true," she said. "They keep it a dead, dark secret from outsiders—they think it sounds silly, and they're sort of ashamed of it. But they keep doing it."

"It's no sillier than stuff the rest of us do," I said, setting down my fork and stepping over to the window. I'd lost track of exactly where we were, but I could see this was a bigger station than most we'd passed through the previous day. Probably a subregional or maybe even a regional capital. "A lot less harmful, too."

"I know," she said. "But try telling *them* that."

I eyed the buildings laid out between the various train plat-forms. If there was a recurring key motif hidden in there, you sure couldn't prove it by me. Of course, I *was* too far away to see anything subtle.

I lowered my eyes to the thirty or so passengers awaiting us on the platform. Most of them were Juriani and Halkas, but I spotted a pair of slender Tra'ho'seej at the third-class end of the platform and a lone Human at the other end, where our first-class cars would be stopping.

And then, behind me, I heard Rebekah's fork clatter onto her plate. "What is it?" I demanded, spinning around.

Her eyes were wide and horrified, her hands gripping the edge of the crate, her face gone suddenly pale. "There's coral out there," she whispered. "He's bringing *coral* onto the train."

A chill ran up my back as I turned back to the window, cursing silently. I should have guessed the Modhri wouldn't simply wait around and see if I carried out my end of the bargain.

In fact, not only should I have anticipated it, but I'd even had a giant clue practically dropped on my foot. Part of the reason we'd cooled our heels for six hours at Jurskala Station was so that he could shuffle Bayta back and forth between trains. Now I realized he must have also used those hours to get one of his outposts moving down the line where it could intercept our train.

I looked back at the platform, my eyes and brain performing a quick evaluation of each carrybag, shoulder case, and rolling trunk sitting beside or behind the waiting passengers. The hell of it was the coral could be in *any* of them. For that matter, it could be split among several—there was nothing to stop the

Modhri from dividing up the outpost the same way Rebekah had done with her Melding coral.

My gaze reached the lone Human and the large, trunk-shaped box beside him. Rather like a smaller version of our own crate, now that I thought about it. I glanced up at his face.

And froze. It was Braithewick, the minor UN diplomat and Modhran walker who had accosted Bayta and me at the Yandro transfer station. The one who'd offered us free rein in exchange for finding and destroying the Abomination.

For maybe two seconds I just stood there, my brain working furiously. My lurking suspicions about Braithewick . . . but there was no time for that now. We had to get out, and we had to get out now.

With a squeal of brakes the train came to a halt. At the edges of my vision as I gazed out the window I saw conductors step out the door of our car and the door of the car behind us, stiffening to Spiderly attention as a handful of exiting passengers filed past them. The brief trickle ended, and the line on the platform began to come aboard. Braithewick, I noted, was hanging back, courteously allowing his fellow travelers to board ahead of him.

As he might well do if his trunk was especially heavy. Heavy enough with coral and water to roll especially slowly . . .

Abruptly, I stepped away from the window. "Come on," I told Rebekah, grabbing her arm and taking a quick look around as I pulled her toward the compartment door. There was nothing here we couldn't do without.

"Where are we going?" she asked as she stumbled after me.

"Down around and under the ground and out in the rain,"

I murmured, pressing my ear against the door and listening to the faint sound of the newly arrived passengers as they moved down the corridor toward their compartments. The timing here would have to be perfect.

"What?"

" 'The Ants Go Marching,' " I explained. "Children's song. Never mind. Stay close, and be ready to run when I do."

The footsteps faded away. I gave it two more beats, then opened the door and stepped out into the corridor.

At the front of the car Braithewick was halfway onto the train, watching as his trunk rolled slowly across the corridor toward the number-one compartment directly across from him. Standing in the open compartment doorway was a Juri, also watching the trunk's progress. Both he and Braithewick looked up as I walked casually toward them. "Well, hello there, Mr. Braithewick," I said as I came up. "Small universe, isn't—?"

And in the middle of my sentence, I pivoted on my left foot and drove the edge of my right into Braithewick's stomach.

He gave an agonized cough and folded over, the impact of the kick throwing him back to slam into the edge of the car's doorway. The Juri, whom I hadn't touched, gave a pair of jerks in unison with Braithewick as the pain from my attack flowed into his nervous system via the Modhri group mind. "Stay close," I told Rebekah, and without breaking stride sidled past the groaning Juri into the compartment.

Bayta was sitting on the bed, looking pale and disheveled but otherwise unharmed. "Time to go," I said as I crossed to her. Her hands were out of sight behind her back, but from the cuffs glittering on her ankles I could guess her wrists were similarly pinioned. "Where are the keys?"

"I don't know," she said, her eyes flicking to Rebekah peeking out from behind me. "Frank, are you sure—?"

"I'm sure," I cut her off. "Lean forward."

She did so. I ducked down, got my hands under her thighs, and hauled her up onto my left shoulder in a modified fireman's carry, her head hanging down behind me, her legs in front with her upper thighs pressed against my chest. "Feet in close; kick straight out when I say *kick*," I told her as I curled my left hand around her thighs to hold her in place. Without waiting for an answer, I turned back around and headed to the door.

The Juri had moved to block me, his scaled face still screwed up in shared pain. I threw a kick into his upper leg, then scraped the sole of my shoe down along his shin to his three-toed foot. He howled in pain as the leg gave way and dumped him onto the floor. I stepped past his quivering body and out into the corridor.

A handful of other passengers had emerged from their compartments, weaving slightly as they headed toward me with pain and rage in their faces. First in line was one of the new Halkan arrivals, charging forward in a clear attempt to cut us off before we could make it out the door. I turned toward him and loosened my grip on Bayta's legs. "Kick," I said quietly.

Bayta's legs straightened out convulsively, her heels catching the Halka squarely in the upper chest. I added a kick of my own to his lower abdomen, grabbing Bayta's legs as I did so to keep her from rolling off my shoulder. "Rebekah?" I called.

"Here," the girl's voice came from behind me.

"Grab my arm," I said, and turned toward the car door.

Braithewick was still hunched over in the entryway, his face turned toward me, a deadly fury smoldering in his eyes. "You can move, or you can get kicked again," I told him. "You've got two seconds to decide."

He used up both seconds glaring at me. I gave him one more, then kicked him again in the stomach. He folded a little tighter, and I stepped carefully past him. Rebekah held on tight the whole time, gripping my upper arm like it was a life ring and she was adrift in the North Atlantic. "Bayta, get the door closed," I ordered as we reached the platform. "No, leave the Spider out here," I said as the conductor standing beside the door started to move back toward the car. "He can get aboard once we're clear."

Behind me, I heard the door iris shut. "Now what?" Bayta asked, her voice muffled against my back.

I looked around. That was, I realized, a damn good question. On a smaller Quadrail station, where there would be only a few other people around, none of whom were walkers, we could have just left the train sealed and sent it merrily on its way with the Modhran mind segment pounding its collective fists furiously against the windows.

But this was a subregional capital, and there were a hundred or more Juriani and other aliens standing around gawking at us. More importantly, eight of those hundred were already on the move toward us from spots all over the station. Their expressions were hard to make out, but I had no doubt they were alien equivalents of the look I'd just seen on Braithewick's face.

Which left us exactly one option. "Close all the first- and second-class car doors," I ordered Bayta, turning toward the rear of the train and heading off at the fastest jog I could manage.

"What about the Spiders?" she asked. "They have to get aboard before the train leaves."

"They will," I promised.

"That's only five minutes away."

"So keep the doors locked for four," I gritted, peering along the side of the train. The two baggage cars at the rear were about ten cars away, I estimated. At the rate I was going, four minutes was going to be pushing it.

"Mr. Compton!" Rebekah said urgently, her hand tightening on my arm. "They're coming!"

I half turned, swinging Bayta's body out of the way so I could see. The walkers I'd seen moving in our direction earlier had broken into jogs of their own.

And it didn't take a computerized range finder to realize they would reach us well before we made it to the baggage cars. "Bayta, can you slow them down?" I called, turning back around and trying to pick up my pace.

There was no answer. But I wasn't really expecting one. Clenching my teeth, I kept going, wondering how the hell I was going to take on eight walkers all by myself.

And then, with a multiple thunk of expanding car couplings, the Quadrail beside us began to roll forward.

What the *hell*? "Bayta?" I snapped.

"They're moving the train forward for us," she called back.

Thereby shortening the distance I had to run. "Good— keep it up," I told her. "Let me know when the walkers are fifty meters away. Rebekah? You all right?"

"I'm fine," she called bravely. But I could hear the trembling in her voice.

Small wonder. Back on New Tigris, she'd been quietly

terrified at the prospect of falling into the Modhri's hands. Now, with the end of the journey beckoning, that same horrible threat was suddenly looming again.

I blinked the sweat out of my eyes. It wasn't going to happen, I told myself firmly. Whatever it took, whatever the cost, I was going to get her out of this.

We were running alongside the second to the last of the passenger cars when Bayta gave me the warning. "Fifty meters," she called.

"Right," I said, wishing I could look for myself but knowing I didn't dare take the time. "Tell the Spiders to stop the train."

There was a multiple screech as the Quadrail's brakes engaged, followed by another sequential clunking as the couplings recompressed. The door to the last third-class car was just ahead, and with a final lunge I threw myself through it. "Close it!" I snapped. Rebekah was still gripping my arm, and I twisted my torso around a little to make sure she was all the way in.

"They can't stay closed for long," Bayta warned as the door irised shut. "The conductors are still outside."

"Time?" I asked.

"Ninety seconds to departure."

"Keep us locked down another thirty seconds," I told her. Resettling her weight across my shoulder, I started down the aisle.

Travel, according to cliché, broadened the mind, and there was no doubt that the typical Quadrail travelers had had their minds broadened as much as anyone's. Nonetheless, if the stares I collected on my way down the car were any indication, this was a new one on pretty much everyone.

Fortunately for them, none of them made any attempt to stop us.

We were about a third of the way down the aisle when the train again started up, jostling everyone in the car and nearly dumping me on my face. We continued on, and as the train started angling up the slope leading out of the station we reached the car's rear door and slipped through into the first baggage car.

"What do we do now?" Rebekah asked as the door slid shut behind us.

"We get ready for company," I said, gingerly sliding Bayta off my aching shoulder and setting her down on her feet on the floor. "Bayta, turn around."

"There *is* a plan, then?" Bayta asked as she swiveled around to put her back to me.

"There was," I said, pulling out my lockpick. "Unfortunately, it's now been just slightly shot to hell."

Bayta threw a look at Rebekah. "I hope you have a new one."

"In production as we speak," I assured her. "Rebekah, go push on the stacks of crates nearest the door. See if you can figure out which one's the lightest."

"Okay."

Her tour of the stacks took about a minute, the same minute it took me to get Bayta's wrist and ankle cuffs off. "This one, I think," she said, pointing to the stack to the right of the door.

"Good," I said, flipping out my multitool's tiny knife, the only genuine weapon allowed inside the Tube. Stepping to the door side of Rebekah's stack, I reached up and cut a long vertical slit in the safety webbing. I pried the webbing open, then jabbed the knife into the side of one of the crates midway up. "Okay," I said, getting a grip on the multitool. "I'll pull. You two go around on the other side and push."

The stack was a lot heavier than it looked, and it took a good half minute of grunting to get it to tip. But finally, and with a horrible crash, it came down, spreading its constituent crates all across the floor in front of the doorway.

"That won't stop them for long," Bayta warned as she surveyed our handiwork.

"It won't stop them at all," I corrected, hopping up on the nearest of the fallen crates and starting on the webbing of the stack on the other side of the door. "Bayta, can you climb up that stack over there and get ready to push the top of this one?"

"I'll do it," Rebekah volunteered before Bayta could answer. Grabbing a double handful of webbing, she started up.

I returned my attention to my own stack and finished slicing through the webbing. "Bayta, give me a hand here," I called as I again stuck the blade into the side of one of the crates.

"They're coming," Bayta murmured as she got into position around the back side of the stack.

"I know," I said. "Rebekah?"

"Almost ready," she called.

I nodded and got a grip on the multitool. Dropping this stack on top of the first one ought to leave the door properly blocked.

I was still standing there, waiting for Rebekah to get into position, when the door slid open and a large Halka strode though.

For a split second I hesitated, trying to decide if I could take the time to pull my multitool out of the crate so that I would have at least that much of a weapon in hand. Probably not, I concluded regretfully, and started to step away from the stack into the Halka's path.

But to my surprise, I found Bayta was already there. "Stop!" she ordered, her voice bold and menacing, her hands upstretched like a wizard from a dit rec fantasy standing against the oncoming hordes of hell.

It was so unexpected that the Halka actually stopped, the Modhri controlling him apparently as stunned by Bayta's action as I was.

And as he and Bayta stared across the two-meter gap at each other, she with righteous anger, he with utter disbelief, I felt the stack beside me start to tip. Breaking my own paralysis, I threw my full weight against my multitool.

By the time the Halka saw it coming, it was already too late. He leaped into the car, but the top of the falling stack caught him across his upper back, slamming him forward and downward as the rest of the crates fell in a jumble across the doorway.

But he wasn't down and out, not yet. Even as I charged him, he struggled to his hands and knees, his flat bulldog face swiveling back and forth as he looked for a target. He spotted me and reared up on his knees, cocking his arm and closed right hand over his shoulder.

I beat the throw by about a quarter second, sending a

spinning kick to the side of his head that twisted him a quarter turn on his knees before dropping him flat on his face.

And as the thud of his landing echoed across the car, his hand opened and something small and lumpy rolled through the limp fingers onto the floor.

A chunk of Modhran coral.

Beside me, I heard a sharp intake of air, and I turned to find Bayta staring wide-eyed at the coral. "It's all right," I said quickly. "He never got it anywhere near me."

There was a thud from somewhere. I looked over at the pile of crates as a second thud sounded, and saw the box immediately in front of the door quiver. "That's not going to hold him for long," Bayta said tightly.

"No, but at least he can't send more than two walkers at it at a time," I pointed out. "One of the many advantages of doorways."

"I suppose." She looked around the car. "We should probably make the pile bigger."

"Unfortunately, we can't," I said. "The rest of the stacks are too far away to do any good, and most of the individual crates are probably too heavy for the three of us to manually move over to the pile. Time to retreat to the rear car and see what we can come up with there."

"All right," Bayta said. "Rebekah?"

"I'm here," Rebekah called, coming around from the side of the stack I'd sent her to climb.

"We're going back to the next car," Bayta said as I took her arm and started toward the door leading to the next baggage car. "Come on."

"Wait a minute," Rebekah said.

We both turned back to her. "What is it?" Bayta asked.

Rebekah visibly braced herself. "I was thinking maybe I should stay here."

"Don't be ridiculous," Bayta said firmly. "Come on, now."

"I'm not being ridiculous," Rebekah countered. Her voice was trembling, but her tone was as firm as Bayta's. "I mean . . . he doesn't want you and Mr. Compton."

"If you stay, you'll be putting your people at terrible risk," Bayta reminded her. "You can't do that, not even for us."

"She wouldn't be putting them at risk," I murmured.

"If the Modhri gets hold of her—" Bayta broke off, staring at me in disbelief. "Are you suggesting she should—? *Frank!*"

Actually, that wasn't what I was suggesting at all. I opened my mouth to tell her so— "Mr. Compton and I have already been through this," Rebekah said. "I was willing to give up my life for you. I'm even more willing to give it up for the Melding." She looked at me, a silent plea in her eyes.

I grimaced. But she was right. She and I already knew why capturing her wouldn't do the Modhri any good. With Halkan walkers beating on our front door, there was no reason why Bayta needed to know, too. After all, the Modhri might decide he wanted a prisoner or two for questioning. Better if at least one of those prisoners didn't know anything. "Your nobility does you credit," I went on. "But Bayta's right. We're not leaving you behind, which means that all this conversation is doing is wasting time. So get in gear and let's go."

Rebekah hesitated, then seemed to wilt a little. "All right," she said as she finally came over and joined us.

"And don't worry," Bayta assured her, putting her arm around the girl's shoulders. "Mr. Compton will come up with something."

"Actually, Mr. Compton already has," I said. "Come on. You're going to love this."

TWENTY :

Every Quadrail passenger car came stocked with an emergency oxygen repressurization tank, a complete self-contained and self-controlled supply/scrubber/regulator system that was ready to swing into action in the highly unlikely event of a loss of air pressure in the car. The repressurization of the baggage car where the two ill-fated Halkan walkers had asphyxiated indicated that the non-passenger cars probably had the same setup.

We found the large cylinder and its associated control system in the rear car's front left-hand corner. Getting the tank off the wall, we manhandled it into the vestibule between the two baggage cars. Stripping it of its regulators took longer than I'd expected, but at last we were ready.

"I don't understand how this is supposed to work," Rebekah said as I made one last check on the tank's stability as it leaned against the vestibule wall. "I thought these doors only locked when there was vacuum on one side."

"Actually, the Tube isn't quite a vacuum," I corrected. "Seven hundred years' worth of leakage through the atmosphere barriers of multiple thousands of Quadrail stations has left a thin atmosphere out there. Not enough to breathe, but enough to keep your brains from boiling out through your ears."

Rebekah shuddered. "Frank!" Bayta admonished me.

"Sorry," I apologized. "To answer your question, your typical pressure lock doesn't know what the actual air pressure is it's dealing with. It doesn't know, and it also doesn't care. All it cares about is whether one side has significantly more pressure than the other. If and when that happens, a purely mechanical switch kicks in and locks the doors closed."

Reaching to the top of the tank, I opened the valve, sending a hiss of cold oxygen into the vestibule and wafting into our faces. "And as the saying goes, if you can't raise the bridge, lower the river," I added, letting the door slide shut again. "There should be enough air in that tank to raise the vestibule pressure at least fifty percent, probably more. The pressure lock will kick in, and at that point there'll be nothing the Modhri can do but break in the door."

"I see," Rebekah said. "Though once he does that, he'll be able to get through both vestibule doors, right?"

"Actually, once he's got even a small hole or crack to let the pressure out he can get through both doors," I said. "But I figure it'll buy us a couple of hours."

"Meanwhile, he's got a coral outpost out there," Bayta murmured.

"It won't help him any," Rebekah said.

"I don't think Bayta was referring to your coral, Rebekah," I said. "She was thinking about the fact that if this mind segment wants to, he could turn the entire train into walkers."

Rebekah's face went rigid. "Oh, no," she breathed. "But he wouldn't do that. Would he?"

"He did it once before," Bayta said grimly. "It nearly killed both of us."

"But not quite," I pointed out. "But I don't think he will. Not this time. He already has plenty of walkers aboard for what he needs, and creating a bunch of new ones won't really gain him anything."

"Unless he does it just to spite us," Bayta said.

I shook my head. "The Modhri doesn't seem to care that much about spite or revenge. He has a pretty good soldier mentality, actually, which is one of the things that make him so dangerous. He's too focused on his mission of galaxy domination to bother with petty distractions."

"That might be true for the Modhri as a whole," Rebekah said. "But remember, all we have aboard this train is a single mind segment."

"And you hurt him pretty badly back there," Bayta agreed. "The way Mr. Braithewick looked at you . . . Standing orders notwithstanding, he might decide to bend the rules a little."

I hesitated, gazing at their faces, at their eyes filled with fear and compassion for all the innocent people riding our train. In theory, of course, they were right. A single mind segment, especially one that was out of touch with all the other mind segments, had a certain degree of autonomy. If it was out of touch long enough, as it would be on a long Quadrail trip, it could conceivably drift away from whatever the overall Modhran party line was at the moment.

In fact, that could be the very same mechanism that had caused the drastic change in Rebekah's batch of coral when it came under the influence of her group of rogue symbionts. If so, I could see why the Modhri was so afraid of them, and why he was going to such lengths to find and destroy them.

Should I tell them the truth? Bayta would have to be told eventually, I knew. And it might help alleviate at least this one concern for both her and Rebekah.

But this was something the Modhri definitely didn't want getting out . . . and he still might decide to take a prisoner for questioning. "I doubt the Modhri's discipline is nearly that lax," I said instead. "Personally, I think we've got better things to worry about than having the whole train rise up against us."

I turned back to the vestibule. "That should be long enough," I said. "Let's give it a try." Mentally crossing my fingers, I pressed the door release.

Nothing happened. I tried again, and once more just for luck. The door was indeed locked up tight. "Perfect," I said briskly. "That should hold him for a bit."

"We need to hold him longer than just a bit," Bayta warned, giving me one of those thoughtful looks she did so well. She was smart enough to realize I'd deflected her concern without genuinely addressing it, but she was also smart enough to know when I was telling her to drop a subject. "It's still several hours to the next station."

"True enough," I said, looking at the stacks on either side of the vestibule door. Both were composed of oversized crates with machinery labels on them and double layers of safety webbing. Not a chance in the universe the three of us would be able to knock those over. "Scavenger hunt time. What I want is a crate with a vertical side-sliding panel instead of the usual top-opening lid. It also needs to be on the bottom of its particular stack. First one to find me a crate like that wins a prize."

"What kind of prize?" Rebekah asked.

"I'll think of something," I said. "You two head back; I'll check the ones up here."

The crate I'd described for them was important, but it wasn't actually my first priority. As soon as the two of them were out of sight, I headed to the side toward the spot where the Jurskala Spider contingent was supposed to have loaded my special crate.

It was, thankfully, right where it was supposed to be, sitting on top of a short and easily climbable stack of other crates. I pried open the top, made sure my special cargo was inside, then closed it again. The crate had been a vital part of Plan A, and it was going to be an equally important part of Plan B.

It would probably be necessary even if we had to go to Plan C. Whatever Plan C might end up being.

I was back down on the floor, prowling among the crate islands, when Rebekah won the hunt.

"What's in it?" she asked as I worked the safety webbing up and away from the bottom of the crate. It would have been faster to cut it, but this particular webbing I wanted left intact.

"Typically, side-opening crates contain one of two types of items," I told her. "Either machinery designed to be rolled out at its destination, or stuff that'll flow out into a bin or other container when you pull up the panel. Hold this webbing up, will you?"

She reached up and got a grip on the webbing, keeping it out of my way. "Which is it in this case?" she asked.

"No idea, but I'm hoping it's the former," I said. Popping the catches, I got my fingertips under the bottom of the panel and pulled upward.

I would have been happy with pretty much anything. As it was, I was quietly ecstatic. Packed inside its molded foam spacers was a beautifully restored classic Harley-Davidson motorcycle. "Bingo," I said.

"We're planning on riding somewhere?" Bayta asked, looking confused.

"Like where?" I countered, getting a grip on the front wheel and pulling. For a moment the bike resisted, then reluctantly rolled toward me, its spacers mostly coming along with it. "Besides, it won't be fueled up."

"Then why do we want it?" Rebekah asked.

"Because this is no longer a classic motorcycle," I told her as it came free. "This is a neatly organized collection of spare parts."

I gave the clutch grip an experimental squeeze. "A collection of spare parts," I added quietly, "that can be turned into weapons."

Bayta and Rebekah exchanged looks. "I see," Bayta said, her voice sounding uncomfortable.

Small wonder. For seven hundred years the Spiders had gone to extraordinary lengths to keep weapons off their Quadrails. Now here I was, proposing to create an arsenal out of something that had sailed right through their filters. "It's not a big deal," I told her. "In the real world, almost anything can be turned into a weapon if you work at it hard enough."

"I suppose," she said. "It just makes the whole no-weapons thing seem rather futile."

"Hardly," I assured her. "Keeping guns and knives and plague bacteria off the trains is what's kept the peace through the galaxy for the past seven centuries. Let's not throw out the heirloom silver just because there's a little tarnish on it here and there."

"You're right." She took a deep breath. "What do you want Rebekah and me to do?"

"Right now, nothing," I said. "With only one multitool among us, this is going to be pretty much a one-man job. You and Rebekah can go find yourselves a nice place to sit down and relax."

"What about my prize?" Rebekah asked, a hint of the ten-year-old girl once again peeking through. "You said there would be a prize if I found you the right crate."

"That I did," I agreed, bracing myself. Someone was really going to hate me for this.

He would just have to get in line. Reaching to the Harley's right-hand mirror, I snapped it off. "There you go," I said, handing it to Rebekah. "Don't spend it all in one place."

She gazed at it a moment, then looked up at me again. "Thank you," she said gravely.

And with that, the ten-year-old was gone again. "You're welcome," I said. "Now scoot, both of you. I'll let you know when I need you again."

———

I had never taken a motorcycle apart before, and the very first thing I discovered was that my multitool wasn't much of a substitute for a proper mechanic's kit. Many of the parts came off with difficulty, or thoroughly mangled, or both. Other components never did give up their death grip on the bike, despite the force, ingenuity, and threats I threw at them.

One thing was crystal clear, though: this particular bike would never run again. I hoped the owner had popped for the full-coverage insurance.

Somewhere midway through my work, I heard the first faint thudding sounds from the other side of the vestibule. The walkers had made it past our crate barrier and were tackling the pressure-locked door.

Our time was running out.

The rhythmic banging had been going on for probably half an hour by the time I decided I'd stripped everything I could from the bike. The front fork and rear shock absorbers would serve nicely as clubs, the wheel rims could be used as throwing disks, and I'd worked a section of the exhaust pipe into an arm protector for my left forearm. I'd also collected enough bolts and nuts to make for a couple of good barrages with the slings I'd constructed from the rubber of the tires.

As the final touch, I cut some long pieces of safety webbing and attached the remainder of the bike frame to the crate stacks on either side of the vestibule, leveled at the center of the doorway. With Bayta's help, I hauled the machine back and up, securing it high off the floor with more webbing fastened with a quick-release knot. The first walker to come through that door was going to be in for a very unpleasant surprise.

And after that, there was just one more thing to do.

"I can't," Rebekah protested, staring into the now empty crate that had once housed the Harley. "Please don't make me."

"You have to," I told her firmly. I could understand her reluctance—the crate wasn't shaped like a coffin, but it didn't have much more than a coffin's worth of space inside. But it would be light-years better than being out in the open when the walkers broke through the door. "The Modhri wants to get his hands on you. We don't want him to. It's that simple."

"Trust us, Rebekah," Bayta said, her voice low and earnest. "We'll be back to get you. I promise."

I winced. Unfortunately, there were only two ways that we would be able to keep that promise: if we won the imminent fight, or if the Modhri captured us alive and made us talk. I wasn't counting too heavily on the first, and I didn't much want to dwell on the second.

Maybe Rebekah was thinking about the two options, too, and their respective odds of becoming reality. "All right," she said reluctantly. "If I have to." Bending over, she eased herself into the crate.

I gave her a couple of seconds to settle herself in as best she could, then slid the panel down to close her in. "Start moving those foam spacers somewhere else in the car," I instructed Bayta as I smoothed the safety webbing back into place along the side of the crate. "I'll give you a hand as soon as I'm finished here."

The crate's appearance was back to normal, the foam spacers were on the other side of the baggage car, and we were in position at the door when the Modhri finally broke through.

The first in line was a Halka, probably the biggest walker the Modhri had available at the moment. He came charging through the door, faltering a bit in obvious surprise to find the floor in front of him clear of crates or other obstacles. His eyes flicked upward, the Modhri clearly wondering if one of the nearby stacks was about to come down on top of him.

He was still standing like that when the Harley frame swung in from in front of him and nailed him squarely in the chest.

With a grunt of agony he fell backward into the doorway, slamming into the next Halka in line. Before they could untangle themselves I was on them, hammering at both heads and every limb I could reach with my fork club. The longer I could keep them trapped in the vestibule, where they had limited freedom of movement, the better.

But the same lack of space that hampered the Halkas also limited the amount of power I could bring to bear with my club. The Halkas shrugged off my blows with surprising ease, regained their mutual balance, and started back out at me.

"Frank!" Bayta called.

I dropped into a low crouch as a swarm of nuts and bolts came flying into the lead Halka's face. He snarled something, the snarl followed immediately by a bellow as I swung my club backhand across his knees. He fell forward, landing full-length with a resounding thud, and instantly rolled onto his side as he clutched at his knees.

One down. God only knew how many to go.

Bayta's second salvo, and my second kneecapping, took out the second Halka, dropping him on top of the first. But the third walker in line was a much smaller and quicker Juri. Instead of trying to bull his way through the doorway as the first two walkers had, he leaped up onto the suspended bike's front fender, grabbed the safety webbing rope tied to the handlebars, and swung himself onto the floor on the far side of the double heap of Halkas. I jabbed my club at him over the bike's saddle, but I was only able to deliver a glancing blow to his back before he skipped out of range.

I had just slammed my club across the face of the next Juri in line when the escapee ran around the wounded Halkas and hurled himself at me.

I ducked back, swinging furiously back and forth to try to keep him at bay. But this was a walker, and none of the normal instincts for self-defense applied. He took three punishing swipes across the head and torso before I managed to put him down for good.

But by then it was too late. My forced inattention to the doorway had allowed in three more walkers, two Halkas and a Juri.

And in that handful of seconds I was suddenly on the defensive.

"Bayta—retreat!" I shouted as I ducked into the maze of narrow passageways between the stacks. Over the clacking of Quadrail wheels I could hear the thudding of heavy Halkan feet as the walkers took off after me down the passageway. "Rebekah, get on top of the crates and hide!" I added.

There was no reply from either of them. But then, I hadn't expected any. Rebekah was hidden away in her crate, as safe as she would be anywhere, with no reason to go anywhere else. As for Bayta, she knew perfectly well what my coded retreat order really meant. I passed a distinctive pair of stacks and braked to a sudden halt, turning around and raising my club as if I had decided to make my stand right then and there.

And as the line of walkers charged toward me, the first

Halka hit the trip line that had magically snapped up to knee height between the stacks.

He hit the floor with an even more impressive crash than those of the two I'd laid out by the vestibule. The Halka immediately behind him was going way too fast to stop, and landed full-length on his companion's wide back.

The Juri behind them didn't even try to slow down, but merely charged up onto the downed Halkas' backs and leaped at me like a gymnast coming off a springboard. He got a crack across the side of his rib lattice for his trouble, and another across the back of his head as he hit the floor in front of the Halkas. I stepped to the Halkas and gave each of them a crack on the head to keep them quiet.

Bayta was still crouched by the side of one of the crates, gripping the end of the safety webbing trip line. She dropped the line and jumped to her feet as I came up to her, and together we headed off into the maze.

We had just completed the second zig of a planned three-zigzag maneuver when the Modhri nailed us.

It was a well-planned and well-executed attack. The walkers, mostly Juriani and Bellidos, came at us from three different directions, three assault lines of three aliens each, all of them charging ahead with the by-now familiar disregard for their own personal safety. Bayta and I fought them off as best we could, the confined fighting space around us becoming even more cramped with every fresh body that staggered and then fell stunned or unconscious at our feet.

Fortunately, like most of the beings the Modhri had chosen to infect with himself, these walkers were from the upper classes; rich, powerful, up in years, and not in particularly good fighting trim. Even with their numerical advantage Bayta and I held our own, keeping our attackers back as we steadily whittled them down. I managed to clear out one of the lines of attackers, opening up an exit vector, and grabbed Bayta's arm with my free hand. "Come on," I panted, pushing her behind me as I turned to cover our retreat.

And without warning, something slammed into me from above, bouncing the back of my head off the nearest stack of crates and shoving me to the floor.

The next few minutes were a blur of hands and bodies and movement. By the time the haze lifted from my mind, I found myself back in the relatively open area by the baggage car's forward door and the suspended Harley, sitting on the floor with my back to one of the stacks of crates. There was a Juri towering over me on either side, and a line of Halkas and Juriani and Bellidos staring silently down at me from three meters away. Halkas, Juriani, Bellidos, and one lone Human.

Braithewick.

I took a careful breath, checking out the state of my chest as I did so. There was some serious bruising down there, but it didn't feel like anything was broken. "Well, that was fun," I said casually, focusing on Braithewick's sagging face. "Round One goes to you. Shall we set up for Round Two?"

"Where is the Abomination?" he asked.

"That's hard to say," I said. "I think I may have misplaced it."

Braithewick cocked his head, and from my left came a muffled gasp.

I turned that direction, craning my neck to look around the Juri standing guard on that side. Bayta was two stacks down, being pressed against the safety webbing by a pair of seriously bruised Halkas. One of them was gripping her right forearm with one hand and bending her hand back at the wrist with his other. "Leave her alone," I growled. "You want to torture someone, torture me."

"I think not," Braithewick said calmly. "You are a strong Human, Compton. I make you the compliment that breaking your bones will not gain me anything." He gestured toward Bayta. "But you are not strong enough to stand by and watch the slow destruction of the Human Bayta's life. Tell me where the Abomination is, or I'll begin by pulling out her fingers."

Bayta looked at me, her face taut but determined. "There's no need to get melodramatic," I told the Modhri. "Let her go, and I'll tell you."

"Tell me first," Braithewick said.

"Let her go first," I repeated.

Braithewick seemed to consider. Then, almost reluctantly, the Halka holding Bayta's arm relaxed the pressure on her wrist. "Where is the Abomination?" Braithewick asked.

I looked consideringly at the ceiling. "It should be right about . . . there," I said, pointing upward.

Braithewick didn't speak, but Bayta suddenly gasped again in pain. "Stop it," I snapped. "I'm telling the truth."

"The Abomination is not on the roof," Braithewick snapped back.

"I didn't say it was on the roof," I countered. "I said it was out there." I pointed again.

"You lie," Braithewick insisted. "It is here. I can feel its presence."

"Fine—have it your way," I said. "There are probably three

to four hundred crates in here. Go ahead—knock yourself out."

Braithewick eyed me, his expression turning from angry to puzzled. "Why do you play such games, Compton? Do you truly believe I will hesitate to destroy the Human Bayta's life?" He cocked his head. "Or is it that you fear her agonizing death less than you fear the other fate I hold within my power?"

A cold chill ran through me. Other Modhran mind segments over the years had threatened to infect Bayta and me with polyp colonies and turn us into two more of his puppets. It was a possibility that held a special horror for Bayta, one she would gladly and unhesitatingly give up her life to avoid.

When Braithewick had threatened torture, I'd hoped that the far more terrifying scenario had somehow passed him by. But I saw now that the torture gambit had been merely a game, a psychological ploy to progressively raise the stakes of noncooperation.

And with a supply of coral already aboard the train, this new threat was anything but idle. If I didn't give him the Abomination, Bayta could be part of the Modhri within the hour. Probably we both would.

There was just one small problem. The Abomination really *wasn't* aboard the Quadrail.

I was searching desperately for something else to do or say when, behind the line of walkers directing their cold Modhran stares at me, I saw something that made my breath catch in my throat. A shadowy figure was flitting between the stacks of crates, moving in the direction of the forward door.

Rebekah was out of her crate, and making a break for it.

"Turning her into a walker won't do you any good," I

warned Braithewick, raising my voice a bit to try to cover up any noise Rebekah might make. "I already told you the Abomination's not here."

"Then where is it?" Braithewick demanded. He reached into his pocket and pulled out the lump of coral the Halka in the other baggage car had tried to throw at me. "Tell me. Now."

I braced myself. If the Modhri had been angry before, this was going to make him furious. "The fact of the matter is—"

"Bayta!" Rebekah's voice called from somewhere behind the walkers. "Bayta—*catch*!"

The Modhri sprang into instant action, half the walkers turning toward the sound of Rebekah's voice, the other half surging toward Bayta, their eyes angled upward to spot and intercept whatever it was Rebekah was preparing to throw. At my sides, my two Jurian guards each put a hand on my shoulder, pressing me to the floor to prevent me from leaping to my feet and taking advantage of whatever the situation was that was about to unfold.

And as everyone looked and moved in all the wrong directions, an object came sliding across the floor, neatly passing through the gauntlet of shuffling feet, and came to a halt right in front of me.

It was my *kwi*.

The walkers jerked to a halt as one of their number spotted it, the whole bunch swiveling back toward me as my two guards dived simultaneously for the weapon.

But they were already too late. I scooped up the *kwi*, feeling the familiar activation tingle against my hand as I turned it upward and fired at the guard on my right.

I hadn't had time to check what setting the *kwi* was on, but from the violent shudder that arced through the walker's body as he tumbled uncontrollably to the floor across my leg it was clear that Rebekah had put the weapon on its highest pain setting. I fired twice more as I got the *kwi* into proper position on my hand, peripherally aware that all the walkers were shaking and twitching with the shared pain I was pumping into the group mind.

I fired a fourth time as I shoved the Juri off my leg and surged to my feet. I was barely vertical before I had to duck to the side to avoid a Halka who had managed to keep enough control of his body to throw himself at me. He slammed face-first into the stack of crates I'd been seated against, sending another ripple of pain through the mind. I fired one last jolt on the pain setting, then switched the *kwi* to its full knockout setting.

It was, to use the old phrase, like shooting ducks on the water. The walkers tried desperately to scatter, but the pain throbbing through their individual nervous systems had reduced their muscles to twitching jelly and their escape efforts into something halfway between laughable and pathetic. I strode among them, sending them one by one off to dreamland, occasionally shifting back to pain setting just to make sure those still conscious wouldn't recover enough to mount some kind of counterattack.

Three minutes later, it was all over.

Bayta was still standing by the crate stack where I'd left her, her face tight, her right wrist cradled in her left hand. "You all right?" I asked her, nudging back her fingers so I could get a look at her wrist.

"Mostly," she said, wincing. "I think it might be broken."

"Looks more like just a sprain," I said, gently touching the swelling skin. "We'll try to find someone to look at it in the next few hours."

Abruptly, she stiffened. "Frank, there are more first-class passengers coming this way," she said tightly.

"Interesting," I said, handing her wrist back into her care again. "I think that's the first time the Modhri's bothered to keep any of his walkers in reserve. I guess he *can* learn."

"Never mind whether or not he can learn," Bayta bit out. "What are we going to do?"

"Don't worry, we're covered," I assured her, hefting the *kwi*. "Speaking of which." I turned around. "Rebekah? You can come out now."

There was a pause, followed by a slight shuffling noise as Rebekah peered cautiously from around one of the stacks. "He's down?"

"Down and out, and going to stay that way for quite a while," I confirmed.

She breathed a sigh of relief as she came over to us. "Thank you," she murmured.

"Thank *you*," I countered. "How'd you find our *kwi*, anyway?"

"It was in his pocket," she said, pointing to the first Juri I'd clobbered in the Modhri's initial surge through the vestibule.

"How did you know he had it?" Bayta asked.

"I didn't," Rebekah said. "I'd already searched the ones you knocked out just before they caught you." She shivered. "I'm just glad it wasn't on one of the ones still standing."

"That would have been a little tricky," I agreed. "Meanwhile,

Bayta says there are more walkers on the way, which means it's time to think about blowing this pop stand. Any word on when that might be?"

"Five minutes," Rebekah said. "There's a crosshatch just ahead."

"A crosshatch?" Bayta echoed, frowning.

"A section of spiral-laid tracks that allow a Quadrail to quickly switch from one track to another," I explained.

"Yes, I know what it is," Bayta said, a little tartly. "What do they have to do with anything?"

"Because we need the tender that's currently on Track Fifteen to come over to *our* track so it can pick us up," I told her. "The tender that's been paralleling us for the past two days, by the way."

Bayta's eyes flicked back toward the rear of the train with sudden understanding. "You put Rebekah's coral aboard a *tender?*"

"Specifically, the tender the Spiders had on tap when you got snatched at Jurskala," I said. "This way we could keep it close enough for the Modhri to sense it and think it was aboard the train, but at the same time keep it completely and permanently out of his reach."

"Yes," Bayta murmured, staring off into space. "Yes, I can sense the Spiders aboard now." She focused on me again. "There *is* still one problem, though."

"Actually, it's covered," I said. "Three stacks back from the front along the left-hand wall is a crate with three oxygen masks and tanks in it."

"That'll only solve the first part of the problem," Bayta cautioned.

"Trust me," I soothed. "You and Rebekah head to the rear door while I get the oxygen masks. As soon as I've done that—whoa," I interrupted myself. "What have we *here*?"

One of the Jurian walkers, the first one I'd stunned a few minutes ago, was moving. Not very much, more like a person shifting around in a dream than someone clearing the decks for action.

But with a six-hour *kwi* jolt in him, he shouldn't have been moving at all.

"Something's wrong," Bayta murmured.

"Agreed," I said. I double-checked the setting and shot the walker again, and the dream-like movements stopped.

But for how long? "Maybe it's losing its effectiveness," I said, peering at the *kwi*. "It *is* several hundred years old, after all."

"I sure hope that's not it," Bayta said, wincing. "Maybe you'd better give them all another shot, just to be on the safe side. Rebekah and I can get the oxygen masks."

"Okay, if you think your wrist can handle it."

"It can," Bayta assured me. "Three stacks back from the front?"

"Right," I said. "Top crate on the stack, green stripe pattern around the label. I've already loosened the lid."

Bayta nodded and headed off, Rebekah trailing along behind her. I fired another *kwi* bolt into the next walker in line, watching the two women out of the corner of my eye.

As soon as they were gone, I knelt down beside the one I'd just zapped and started going through his pockets.

He didn't have what I was looking for. Neither did the second walker I checked.

The third one did.

I was back on my feet, systematically zapping everything in sight, when Bayta and Rebekah returned with the oxygen masks. "They're here," Bayta announced as she handed me my mask. "As soon as we're ready, they'll open the roof to release the rear door's pressure lock."

I grimaced. Depressurizing the car would of course kill all the walkers lying asleep around us. By most of the galaxy's legal codes, not to mention most of the galaxy's ethical standards, that constituted murder.

But we had no choice. There was no other way for us to escape, and there wasn't nearly enough time for us to first drag all these sleeping bodies back into the other baggage car. Not with more walkers on the way.

Besides, even if we did, the Modhri probably wouldn't let them live anyway. By their very nature walkers had to be kept ignorant of their role, and there was no way in hell that even the most persuasive rationalization would explain away the blank spots or the broken bones. Either he would have their polyp colonies suicide, or he would permanently take them over and turn them into soldiers. The first was death. The second was worse.

But all the cold logic in the universe didn't make it any easier to take. Collateral damage, unavoidable or not, was still collateral damage.

We were waiting by the rear door, our oxygen masks in place, when there was a creaking from above us and the roof began to open.

For a moment we felt some buffeting as the car's air rushed out into the near-vacuum of the Tube. I felt my ears pop; from Rebekah's sudden twitch, I guessed hers had done the same.

Then the mild windstorm dropped away, and the roof closed over us again, and Bayta touched the door release.

We were facing the gleaming silver nose of a Quadrail engine, holding position about half a meter back from the rear of our train. Straddling the gap, with two of his seven legs braced on each of the two vehicles, was a dot-marked stationmaster Spider. Behind him, stretched out in a line all the way back across the top of the engine, were four of the slightly smaller conductors.

Bayta didn't hesitate. She stepped forward, holding her arms slightly away from her sides. The stationmaster got two of his remaining three legs under her arms, holding the third ready in case of trouble, and lifted her across the gap. He passed her off to the next Spider in line, then swung his arms back to Rebekah and me.

I nudged Rebekah and gestured. What I could see of her expression through her mask wasn't very happy, and her grip on my hand as she stepped to the edge of the short baggage-car platform was anything but gentle. But at least she went without having to be pushed. The Spider lifted her up and over, and then it was my turn.

And as he lifted me up, I took a good look at his dot pattern.

The trip over the speed-blurred tracks below us was mercifully short. A few seconds later, the first Spider handed me off to the next in line, and I was bucket-brigaded across to the rear of the engine.

Two more Spiders were waiting there, hanging on to rings set into the side of the first of the tender's three passenger cars. They got their legs under my arms and lifted me over the coupling, maneuvering me through the open door on the side. Bayta and Rebekah were already inside, and as the Spider withdrew his legs the door irised shut and I heard the faint hiss as the car was repressurized.

I watched the gauge on the inside of my mask, wincing as my eardrums again struggled to adjust to the pressure change. The gauge reached Quadrail standard, and I closed the valve and took off the mask.

The air smelled sweet and fresh and clean. I took several deep breaths as Bayta and Rebekah removed their own masks, trying to wash away the emotional grime and sweat and guilt of the battle with the Modhri and his slave warriors.

"Are we safe now?" Rebekah asked.

I gazed at her face, searching in vain for the ten-year-old girl I'd seen only briefly in all our time together. What lofty goal was it, I wondered distantly, that deprived a child of her childhood? "Yes, we're safe," I said. "It's all over." Without waiting for a reply, I turned away.

Because it wasn't over. Not by a long shot.

At least, not for me.

The car was similar to the ones Bayta and I had traveled in a couple of times before. It was laid out like a double Quadrail compartment, only without the central dividing wall and with a food storage and prep area taking the space where the second bathroom would be. There were two beds at each end, and it wasn't long before all three of us had claimed our bunks and collapsed into them. Bayta and Rebekah were exhausted, and it wasn't long before they were fast asleep.

I wasn't in any better shape than they were, and I could feel fatigue tugging at my eyelids. But I couldn't go to sleep. Not yet. I waited until their breathing had settled down into a slow rhythm, then gave it another five minutes just to be sure. Then, getting up from my bed, I crossed to the car's rear door. It opened at a touch of the control, and I stepped through the vestibule into the next car back.

It was a cargo car, unfurnished, unadorned, and mostly empty. The only cargo were the seventeen coral lockboxes we'd spirited off New Tigris, sitting together in the middle of the floor. At the far end was a door leading into the tender's third passenger car.

Standing beside the car's rear door like a Buckingham Palace guard was the white-dotted Spider who had carried us across the gap to safety. The same white-dotted Spider I'd run into before, in fact, the one I'd privately christened Spot.

I walked the length of the car, feeling a creepy sense of unfriendly eyes watching my every move. Spot stirred as I approached the door, moving sideways to stand in my way. "I need to see him," I said, coming to a halt a couple of steps away.

"He will not see you," Spot said.

"I think he will," I said. "Tell him I know everything."

There was a short pause. "He will not see you," Spot repeated.

So he was calling my bluff. I'd expected nothing less. "He has two choices," I said. "He can see me now, alone, or I can walk back to our car and wake up Bayta, and he can see the two of us together."

There was another pause, a longer one this time. I waited; and then, slowly, Spot sidled back to his place beside the door.

Stepping past him, I touched the door release, crossed the vestibule, and opened the door behind it.

"Good day, Frank Compton," a melodic voice called as I stepped into the car.

Melodic, but with an unpleasant edge beneath it. Anger? Annoyance?

Fear?

"Hello, Elder of the Chahwyn," I said, nodding to the slender, pale-skinned being seated on a chair in the middle of the room between a pair of Spiders. "You *are* an Elder, I assume?"

"I am," he confirmed.

Good—someone with authority. "Elder of the Chahwyn, we need to talk," I said.

"About what?"

"About this fraud you've perpetrated on us," I said. "This fraud called the Melding."

There was a stiffening of the cat-like whiskers on the ridges above his eyes. "There is no fraud," he insisted. "The Melding is as Rebekah has described it."

"Except for one small but critical fact," I said. "The small fact that the Modhri didn't create the Melding."

I leveled a finger at him. "You did."

TWENTY-ONE :

For a long minute the Chahwyn just gazed across the room at me. "How did you learn this?" he asked at last.

At least he wasn't going to waste my time with a useless bluff. I had to give him points for that one. "Lots of little things," I said. "In retrospect, I'm surprised it took me as long as it did."

I nodded behind me. "For starters, this business of melding species together is your trademark trick, not the Modhri's. It's the same thing you did with Bayta. In fact, Rebekah even pointed that out. Does she know, by the way?"

"Rebekah does not know," the Chahwyn said. "None of the Melding does."

"Nice to know she's not as accomplished a liar as I was starting to think," I said. "The next clue was that Rebekah told us the Melding had a secret place where they'd all gone to hide. You don't get anywhere in this galaxy, certainly not by

Quadrail, without Spider cooperation. In a case like this, Spider cooperation means Chahwyn cooperation. QED."

His eye-ridge tufts quivered. "QED?"

"*Quod erat demonstrandum*," I explained. "It's from an old Earth language and means *that which was to have been proved*. In this case, Chahwyn knowledge implies Chahwyn complicity." I cocked an eyebrow. "Where exactly *is* the Melding hiding place, by the way?"

"In an uninhabited system near Sibbrava which the Cimmaheem are thinking about developing," the Chahwyn said. "There is a temporary Quadrail stop there which services only their exploration teams."

"But of course there's no official station yet," I said, nodding. "Which means no manned support services, no resident personnel, and no transfer station with its contingent of nosy Customs agents. Give the Melding a transport or two, and they can go anywhere."

"They have such a transport."

"Again, QED," I said. "There was also your rather ham-handed attempt to protect the coral—or what you thought was the coral—from the Modhri on the train into Jurskala. There was no reason for his walkers to have moved the crate all the way to the last cargo car. *You* did that, probably sending your Spiders across from this very tender to get it out of their reach. When the walkers came looking for it, you let them get into the second car and popped the roof."

"Yes," the Chahwyn said. "I did not expect him to blame you for that."

"I'm sure I appreciate the thought." I reached into my pocket and pulled out the *kwi* Rebekah had given me. "But this was the real clincher," I continued, holding it up. "At the critical moment in our fight, Rebekah was able to get this to me. She told me afterward that she'd found it in one of the walkers' pockets."

"You don't believe that to be the truth?"

"I know it isn't." I reached into my other pocket. "Because *this* is my *kwi*."

For a moment he gazed at the two weapons, his eye-ridge tufts again quivering. "What will you tell Bayta?" he asked.

"That depends," I said. "In retrospect, I can see that from the moment Lorelei showed up in my apartment this whole thing was designed to get Bayta and me to help sneak Rebekah off New Tigris and to safety."

"She was trapped and alone," the Chahwyn said, a note of quiet pleading in his voice. "Our Spiders could not help her, not on a Human world far from the Tube. You were the only ones we could turn to."

"In principle, I have no problem with that," I said. "We do work for you, after all." I let my face harden. "But that's hardly the whole story. You wanted us to help Rebekah . . . but yet you *didn't* want us to know you were also involved with her. Still don't, for that matter. I want to know why."

He exhaled softly, a sound that was almost a whistle but not quite. "Because we were afraid," he said, his voice low and earnest and even a little ashamed. "We were afraid of what you would think."

"What *would* we think?" I countered. "That you were trying to find a way to infuse the Modhri with a calmer, gentler, less aggressive form of himself? As a matter of fact, I brought up that exact idea myself."

"Yet you were extremely angry when you first learned what we had done to create the Human/Chahwyn symbiont that is Bayta," he reminded me. "Your anger nearly caused you to turn your back on us instead of choosing to support us."

"I think you're overstating the case just a bit," I said.

"If so, only in degree, not in substance," he said. "But more than that, there were Bayta's feelings to consider. Whatever she may think about herself and her Chahwyn symbiont, would she accept that doing the same with Modhran polyps and other living beings was both acceptable and needful?"

"I don't know," I said. "But considering how close she and Rebekah have become over the past couple of weeks, I don't think she would have a problem with it."

"Perhaps not," the Chahwyn said. "But it was a risk we dared not take." His face elongated slightly. "A risk we are still not prepared to take."

"In other words, you want me to keep my mouth shut about this?"

"We would be most grateful if you would," the Chahwyn said, relief evident in his voice.

"I'm sure you would," I said. "But that's not the whole story, either. And you, Elder of the Chahwyn, are a liar." I stuffed the two *kwis* back into my pockets. "Permit me to prove it." Bracing myself, I started toward him.

His mouth dropped open, his body stiffening with disbelief and probably fear. But the two Spiders flanking him didn't even hesitate. Before I'd made it three steps they had moved in front of their master, each dropping into a low, four-legged stance with his other three legs raised high like a tarantula preparing to strike. I kept coming, feinting right and then ducking left.

And suddenly I found myself wrapped in a cold metallic grip as one of the Spiders snatched me off the floor. A second later my back was slammed none too gently against the top of the side wall.

I looked past the shiny Spider sphere at the Chahwyn still sitting frozen in his chair. "QED," I said quietly. "The Melding experiment isn't just your attempt to create a less dangerous Modhri."

"You're trying to create a Spider army."

"You are a fool," the Chahwyn bit out, his breath coming in short, spasmodic bursts now. "You don't understand your danger."

"Oh, I understand my danger quite well," I assured him, wincing as the Spider's legs dug into my already sore ribs. "The question is, do *you* understand *yours*?"

For maybe a quarter minute no one moved or spoke. Then, slowly, the Spider holding me lowered me back to the floor. "You don't understand," the Chahwyn said again, his melodic voice gone flat and lifeless. "We cannot fight. We cannot defend ourselves. We are helpless before the Modhran onslaught. We had to do *something*."

"You did do something," I told him. "You hired me."

He snorted, a dog-like sound. "Do truly think you can defeat the Modhri alone?"

"I'm not alone," I said. "Neither are you. We have allies all over the galaxy. Not many of them, granted. Not yet. But our ranks are growing."

"Not as quickly as the ranks of the enemy."

"Perhaps," I conceded. "But you can't defeat the Modhri by becoming just like him."

He looked back and forth between the two Spiders. "Then what *do* we become?" he asked. "Or do we simply resign ourselves to defeat and destruction?"

"You never do that," I told him firmly. "As to what you should become, that's a question for people a lot smarter than I am. All I know is that you've kept peace and prosperity throughout the galaxy by being what you are, and by keeping the Spiders what you created them to be. You don't want to be in a hurry to upset that balance."

His eyes were steady on me. "Will you tell Bayta?" he asked.

I thought about it a moment. "No," I told him. "Or at least, not yet. But circumstances may force me to do so somewhere down the line."

His mouth flattened into a wan smile. "As circumstances may likewise force us to do what we would otherwise prefer not to do?"

I grimaced. I hated it when people used my own logic against me. "I never said any of this was simple. I just don't want you to turn a corner you may wind up bitterly regretting later on. Certainly not until turning that corner is absolutely necessary."

"And until then?"

"Stay with what you are," I said. "Hold on to the high ground, and give the less noble people like me time to do our jobs. We can stop the Modhri. I know we can. But I want to make sure that when it's over we all have a safe, nondespotic Quadrail to ride home in."

His eye-ridge tufts twitched. "I will deliver that message," he said. "I do not guarantee the reception it will receive."

"Good enough," I said. "What about this second *kwi*? Do you want it, or does it go back to Rebekah?"

"I will take it," he said. He held out a hand, the hand and arm both stretching fluidly toward me. "She was asked to keep that part of our involvement secret. It would disturb her to learn you had penetrated her deception by returning the weapon to her."

"Which is one more good reason to back off the path you're taking," I pointed out as I dropped the *kwi* into his hand. "If you hadn't been so concerned about Bayta and me finding out about your new class of Spiders, there would have been no need for you to play this whole thing so far under the table. Rebekah could have given me the *kwi* when we first boarded the train and saved us all a *lot* of trouble."

"Yes." The Chahwyn paused. "How *did* you learn of our new Spiders, if I may ask?"

"Basically, because you tried to be clever," I said. "I already knew there was a class of Spider I didn't know about—there'd been a couple of them hanging around every time we were spirited off a train for a chat with one of your people. I saw one of them aboard our previous train—I call him Spot, by the way—who probably came aboard with the group who moved our crate and then came into the passenger part of the train to keep an eye on things. They use a different telepathic frequency than regular Spiders, don't they?"

"They can communicate on both levels," the Chahwyn said. "It is similar to the difference in communication between the Modhri and the Melding."

"Both of which are also different from the Chahwyn's frequency," I said as a stray fact suddenly stuck me. "Rebekah's *kwi* was tuned to the Melding frequency, wasn't it? *She* was the one activating it for me, not Bayta."

"Correct," the Chahwyn said. "Now that it has been returned, it will have to be retuned to the Chahwyn frequency."

"While you're at it, you should probably check the batteries," I said. "The six-hour knockout charge is only lasting a few minutes."

"That is not a problem with the weapon," the Chahwyn said. "It is because the Modhri mind segment had coral nearby."

I frowned. "What does coral have to do with it?"

"When the mind segment includes a coral outpost, the effects of the *kwi* are not as strong or long-lasting," he said. "We believe the polyps in the coral are able to absorb some of the effect and dissipate it more quickly than is possible for a non-coral mind segment."

"Oh, that's handy," I growled. "And when were you planning to tell me this?"

His cheeks puffed out slightly. "We did not know it ourselves until recently."

Terrific. "Anything else you didn't know until recently that you'd like to share with the class?"

"Not as yet," he said. "But you were speaking about the Spiders."

I grimaced. Getting timely and useful information out of the Chahwyn was like pulling teeth with greased fingers. "The problem came when you decided to disguise your special agent by printing—"

"Our defender," the Chahwyn corrected. "We call them defenders."

"Nice name," I said. "It was when you decided to disguise him by putting a stationmaster's dot pattern on his globe. It was reasonable enough in its way, I suppose—the two classes are about the same size, and I assume stationmasters are transferred back and forth on regular passenger trains every now and then. The problem was that when I mentioned him to Bayta, she told me there were no stationmasters aboard."

"She could have been mistaken."

"With a whole trainful of Spiders as her information network?" I shook my head. "No, it was simply that she'd asked the wrong question. If you're in a band, and someone sees the trumpet player carrying a flute case, that person might ask you who the flutist is. You, knowing full well the band doesn't *have* a flutist, would tell the questioner he was nuts. If Bayta had asked if there was a non-standard Spider aboard, they might have told her there was, and we would have figured it out sooner."

"Yes," he murmured. "And indeed, you describe a perfect example of the problem we seek so urgently to overcome. Would a Human have simply answered the question he was asked without also volunteering the bit of information that he *hadn't* been asked?"

"Actually, some Humans probably would," I told him. "We call them bureaucrats and mid-level managers."

"But the best Humans would not."

"Probably not," I conceded.

His eye-ridge tufts twitched. "Best of fortune to you, Frank Compton."

Apparently, the interview was over. But that was all right.

I'd said everything I'd come here to say. "And to you, Elder of the Chahwyn," I replied.

The temporary Quadrail stop was nothing to look at, consisting of a couple of cargo-sized hatches, a single-story storage building, and a loop of track where a tender or small train could pull off the main track for loading and unloading. A passenger staring out his window at the long light-years of Tube could blink at the wrong moment and miss it completely.

Even at that, it had probably cost around a quarter trillion dollars. Building stops along the Tube didn't come cheap. I hoped the Cimmaheem would get more out of their new colony than Earth had out of hers.

There were two figures waiting for us by a corner of the supply building as Bayta and I escorted Rebekah from the tender: a Pirk and a thirtyish Human female. They started walking toward us as we came into sight. "Beheoro and Karyn," Rebekah identified them quietly. "Beheoro was Drorcro's sister."

The Pirk who'd sacrificed himself to protect us from the two walkers on the New Tigris transfer station. Whether we'd actually wanted that protection or not. "Do they know about him?" I asked.

Rebekah nodded. "I've just told them."

"Oh," I said. "Right."

The five of us met in the middle. "Greetings to you, Frank Compton and Bayta," Karyn said, nodding gravely. "We thank you for what you've done for Rebekah." Her eyes flicked over my shoulder. "And for our brother."

I looked back to see the Spiders carrying out the lockboxes full of Melding coral. "We were glad to help," I said, turning back again. "I'm sorry we couldn't do more." I looked at Beheoro. "Especially for those who were lost."

"Drorcro is not truly lost," the Pirk said quietly. "While the Melding lives, so will he."

"Of course," I said lamely. That old funeral eulogy platitude, that the deceased would continue to live on in the hearts of those left behind, had always rather irritated me. But in this case, I had the discomfiting feeling that it might actually be true. "Well, Rebekah, I guess this is it. Take care of—"

The rest of my stock cliché farewell vanished in a puff of air as she threw herself against me in a startlingly strong bear hug. "Thank you," she murmured into my chest. "Thank you."

With only a slight hesitation, I put my arms around her. "You're welcome," I murmured back.

We held the hug another few seconds. Then, disentangling herself from me, she turned and gave Bayta a hug of similar or possibly even greater vigor and earnestness. A few murmured words passed between them, but I never found out what they said to each other.

And with that, it was finally over. For now.

"Come on," I told Bayta as we watched the four of them and the coral-laden Spiders heading for the hatch and the transport waiting outside. "Time to go."

TWENTY-TWO :

After the carnage aboard our last Quadrail, I wasn't looking forward to climbing onto a normal first-class car for the trip back to Earth. Fortunately, the Spiders seemed to understand, and instead gave us a lift back in the tender.

This time around, I made sure to stay put at our end of the train. If Bayta ever realized there was a Chahwyn at the other end, she never mentioned it.

A brief message reached us via Spider telepathy as we slowed down for one of the stations. Via Bayta and our Spiders, I used the same technique to send back a reply as we passed through the next station in line.

Thus it was that we reached Terra Station to find Bruce McMicking waiting for us at my favorite Quadrail restaurant.

"Welcome home," he greeted us, half standing in old-world courtesy as I helped Bayta into her seat. Her wrist was merely sprained, we'd concluded, but it was still a little weak. "I trust your trip went smoothly?"

"As smoothly as could be expected," I told him. "Yours?"

"Spectacularly successful," he said. "I appreciate your help."

"As we appreciate yours," I said. "You didn't happen to peruse the Manhattan criminal court directory while you were waiting here for us, did you?"

"As a matter of fact, I did," he said. "The good news is that you've been cleared of the double murder the Modhri tried to hang you with."

"Really," I said, frowning. "That was quick."

"Straightforward, really," McMicking said. "With the three killings on the New Tigris transfer station—which, timing-wise, you couldn't possibly have been involved with—plus the presence of your stolen Heckler-Koch among the victims, Detective Kylowski realized his case against you wasn't nearly strong enough to continue with. All charges have been dropped, though he got your gun permit suspended for the next year."

"Like I'm going to spend much of the next year in New York," I murmured.

"And your new Hardin Security ID trumps a city permit anyway," he added.

"At least up until the point where Mr. Hardin notices my name on the company roster," I warned. "Which he'll probably go looking for at the very next audit."

"But Mr. McMicking just said you've been cleared," Bayta objected.

"Yes, but I doubt it was before I was declared in violation of my terms of bail," I told her. "The city bureaucrats would have made sure to confiscate that half million before the charges got dropped."

"And they did," McMicking confirmed. "But not to worry. The half million is back in my Security Department account, all safe and sound and no one the wiser."

I frowned at him "What did you do, rob a bank?"

"In a way," he said. "Remember why I was on New Tigris in the first place?"

"To arrange for the disappearance of Veldrick's illegal coral."

"The disappearance *and* subsequent sale," McMicking corrected. "Did you also forget that when I took off in the Fili-aelians' rented torchyacht I had Veldrick's coral *plus* the extra stash the Fillies had brought to New Tigris with them?"

I blinked. With everything else that had happened, I had indeed completely forgotten about that. "And they had half a million dollars' worth?"

"Half a million, plus about two million more," he said with a tight smile. "After deducting a few extra expenditures I thought it best not to list on my expense account, I put the rest in a very discreet Manhattan bank."

"Nice little nest egg," I commented.

"Nice little war chest," he corrected, his smile going grim. "As soon as we get to New York I'll take you and Bayta in and we'll get your names on the account along with mine."

"I appreciate that," I said. "But we're not heading to Earth. Not just yet."

He studied my face. "The Fillies?"

I nodded. "After their performance on New Tigris, I think Bayta and I should take a trip to that end of the galaxy and see what exactly the Modhri's got going over there."

"That's a whole lot of real estate to poke around in," McMicking warned. "A whole lot of distance away, too."

"Nothing we can do about the distance," I agreed. "But backtracking the six Fillies we ran into should hopefully give us a place to begin the search."

"You want me to take a crack at that?"

"We've got the Spiders on it," I told him. "But if you want to take a shot, too, go ahead. One can never have too much information."

"I'll see what I can do," he promised. "Anything else I should know?"

I hesitated. I hadn't wanted to mention this in Rebekah's presence, or when there were Spiders or Chahwyn in earshot, planning to wait instead until Bayta and I were alone. But now that I thought about it, I realized McMicking deserved to know, too. "One other thing," I told them, lowering my voice a little. "This is going to sound crazy, but—" I took a deep breath. "Look. You said it yourself, that the Modhri tried to put me out of action by framing me for Lorelei's murder. Yet by the time Bayta and I got to New Tigris, we essentially had carte blanche to find her and destroy the Abomination."

"Not that it was a genuine offer," Bayta put in. "All the Modhri wanted us to do was get Rebekah out of hiding so he could move in."

"True enough," I agreed. "But the point is that somewhere along the line the plan was suddenly changed. How could that happen?"

Bayta looked at McMicking. "I'm not sure what you're asking," she said.

"Neither am I," McMicking seconded.

"Think about it," I urged. "Bayta, especially—you were right there. We went to the Yandro transfer station to try to lose our Modhran tails and instead were offered a brand-new deal."

I looked expectantly at them. But both faces merely looked blankly back at me. "Don't you get it?" I said. "You aren't going to have a Modhran mind segment at a backwater place like Yandro countermanding a plan the Modhri's been running for months.

"Not unless that's the mind segment that made the original plan in the first place."

And then, abruptly, they got it. "Oh, my God," Bayta breathed, her eyes suddenly wide.

"Son of a bitch," McMicking said, very quietly. "He's back."

"He's back," I said, nodding. "Or at least the top-level decision-making part of him is."

"But that's crazy," Bayta insisted. "After what we did to him there?"

"No, Compton's right," McMicking said darkly. "After what we did there, Yandro's the perfect place for him to move back in and set up shop. Who'd think to go looking for him again there?"

"And you know what else it means," I said. "Not only is he possibly setting up a new homeland, but Yandro also happens to be a perfect location for an all-out assault on humanity. After this last encounter, I'm guessing he's starting to rethink his previous mostly-hands-off policy."

"And so the war comes home," McMicking murmured. For a moment, he gazed thoughtfully across the station. Then, abruptly, he got to his feet. "I know it's bad manners to invite someone to dinner and then leave," he said. "But suddenly I'm feeling like I ought to get back to work."

"We understand," I said. "Good luck."

"Good hunting," he replied, his eyes flicking to each of us in turn. "Oh, and that Beretta I loaned you? Go ahead and keep it."

"Thanks," I said. "Buy yourself a new one out of the war chest."

He smiled faintly. "Thanks," he said. "I may do that."

He headed across the restaurant and out the door. I caught a final glimpse of him as he circled a planter on his way to the shuttle hatches, and then he was gone. "You hungry?" I asked Bayta.

"Not really," she said, her eyes gazing at nothing. "Maybe we ought to get back to work, too."

"And it's a long way to the Filiaelian Assembly," I agreed. "Get us a train, and let's go."

I started to stand up, but she caught my arm. "Frank . . . is that the only secret you're holding on to?"

"What makes you think I'm holding on to any secrets at all?" I countered, reflexively sidestepping the question.

She didn't answer, but just gazed silently into my eyes. I gazed back, wondering again at this strange woman who had become so much a part of my life. Who'd become my ally, and my companion.

And my friend. "There is one more," I admitted. "But I can't tell you about it. Not yet. I promised."

She took it in stride. "Is it something that could mean danger?"

"Not yet," I said. "Maybe not ever. Mostly, it's just a little disturbing."

She gave me a lopsided smile. "You don't have to protect me, you know," she pointed out. "I'm big and strong and not afraid of the dark."

"It's not you I'm protecting," I assured her. "It's the other guy."

For another minute she studied my face. Then, to my relief, she gave a small nod. "All right," she said. "But if I ever need to know . . . ?"

"You'll be the first," I promised.

After all, I decided, as we left the restaurant, the Chahwyn were only my employers. Bayta was my friend.

And it really *was* a long way to the Filiaelian Assembly. Somewhere along the way, we might very well run out of other things to talk about.

You never knew.

Here's an Exciting Glimpse of
***The Domino Pattern*, the Next Book in**
Timothy Zahn's Quadrail Series,
Now Available from Tor Books.

▼

I'd never tried waking a Shorshian from a sound sleep. It was harder than I thought. But I persisted, and eventually *di*-Master Strinni came fully conscious.

He wasn't happy to be awakened. But his annoyance disappeared when he heard the news. [You believe this not merely a random tragedy?] he asked after I'd explained why.

"We're not sure," I said. "That's why we need to test some tissue samples."

[Might there be a Guidesman of the Path aboard?]

"No idea, *di*-Master Strinni," Kennrick said.

"I could ask one of the conductors," I offered.

The inner eyelids dipped down. I was just wondering if he'd gone back to sleep when they rolled up again. [No need,] he said. [If there was one, that truth would have been made known to me.]

Kennrick and I looked at each other. "So is that a yes?" I suggested.

[No,] he said flatly. [You may not cut into Master Colix's flesh.]

I braced myself. "*Di*-Master Strinni—"

[The subject is closed,] he cut me off. He settled back in his seat, and once again the inner eyelids came down.

This time, they stayed there. "What now?" Kennrick asked.

I frowned at the sleeping Shorshian. Without some idea of what had knocked Colix off his unpronounceable Path, our options were going to be severely limited. "Let's go talk to his traveling companions," I said. "Maybe they'll have some idea of who might have wanted him dead."

The crowd in the second/third dispensary had shrunk considerably by the time Kennrick and I returned. Only Bayta, Witherspoon, and Master Tririn were still there. And Colix's body, of course. "Where'd everyone go?" I asked as Kennrick and I joined them.

"Dr. Aronobal—she's the Filiaelian doctor—went off to work up her report on the death," Bayta said. "Master Bofiv wasn't feeling well and returned to his seat."

"Well?" Witherspoon asked. During our absence, he'd laid out a small sampling kit, complete with scalpel, hypo, and six sample vials.

"Sorry," I said. "*Di*-Master Strinni wouldn't give his permission."

[Did you explain the situation?] Tririn asked.

"In detail, Master Tririn," Kennrick assured him.

"Unless there's a Guidesman of the Path around to supervise, we aren't allowed to cut into Master Colix's body," I added.

"Are we sure there *isn't* someone like that aboard?" Witherspoon asked.

"We'd have to ask the Spiders," I said, looking at Bayta.

She gave me a microscopic shrug. "I suppose we could make inquiries," she said.

Translation: she'd already asked. Either there wasn't a

Guidesman aboard or else it wasn't something the Spiders routinely kept track of.

"Speaking of Spiders," Kennrick said, "where's the one that was here earlier?"

"He's gone about other duties," Bayta said. "Did you want him for something?"

"As a matter of fact, I did." Kennrick pointed to the drug cabinet. "I notice that none of those bottles are labeled."

"Actually, they are," Bayta said. "The dot patterns along the sides are Spider notation."

"The Spider prints out a label in a passenger's native language," Witherspoon explained. "Saves having to try to squeeze a lot of different notations onto a bottle that small."

"I'm sure it does," Kennrick said. "But that also means none of the rest of us has any idea what's actually in any of them."

Bayta frowned. "What do you mean by that?"

"I mean we don't actually *know* that the drugs Dr. Witherspoon and Dr. Aronobal injected into Master Colix were actually helpful," Kennrick said. "It could easily have been just the opposite."

"Are you accusing the Spiders of deliberately causing him harm?" Bayta asked, a not-so-subtle challenge in her tone.

"Maybe," Kennrick said. "Or else someone might have sneaked in here while the Spider was absent or distracted and changed some of the labels."

I stepped around the table to the drug cabinet. Experimentally, I gave the door a rap with my knuckles, then tried the latch.

It didn't budge. "That would have to be one hell of a distracted Spider." I turned back to Kennrick. "Besides, wasn't Master Colix showing symptoms before they brought him in?"

"Symptoms can be counterfeited," Kennrick said. He looked at the body. "*Or* faked."

"You mean Master Colix might have faked his own poisoning so as to get brought in here so he could get pumped full of something lethal from the Spiders' drugstore?" I asked.

"Well, yes, if you put it that way I suppose it sounds a little far-fetched," Kennrick admitted. "Still, we need to cover all possibilities."

I turned to Tririn. "Did Master Colix have any addictions or strange tastes?"

[I don't truly know,] Tririn said, a bit hesitantly. [I wasn't well acquainted with him.]

"You *were* business colleagues, correct?"

[True,] Tririn said. [But he had only recently joined our contract team.] He ducked his head to Kennrick. [I would say that Master Kennrick probably knew him as well as I did.]

"And I only met him a couple of months ago," Kennrick put in.

Between *di*-Master Strinni, Kennrick, and Tririn, this was about as unhelpful a bunch as I'd run into in a while. "How about Master Bofiv?" I asked. "Did *he* know Master Colix?"

[I don't know,] Tririn said. [I believe *di*-Master Strinni knew him best.]

I looked at my watch. I'd already had to awaken Strinni once tonight, and I wasn't interested in trying it again. "We'll start with Master Bofiv," I decided. "Where is he?"

"Four cars back," Kennrick said. "I'll take you."

"Just tell me which seat," I said, taking Bayta's arm and steering her toward the door. "You should stay with Master Tririn."

"I'm going too," Kennrick said. "These people are colleagues. Whatever happened, we need to resolve it before it poisons relations between us." He winced at his own words.

"I'll stay here with Master Tririn," Witherspoon volunteered. "There may be a couple of tests I can do that don't involve cutting."

"I'll stay, too, then," Bayta said. "I'd like to watch."

I eyed her. Her face was neutral, but there was something beneath the surface I couldn't quite read. Probably she didn't like the idea of the body being left alone with a couple of strangers. "Fine," I said. "Come on, Kennrick."

We got there fast. "He's down there," Kennrick murmured, pointing.

I craned my neck. Master Bofiv was in one of the middle seats to my right, his seat reclined as far as it would go, his privacy shield open. "I see him," I said. "Quietly, now."

We headed back. Bofiv was lying quietly. One of the passengers three rows up had his reading light on, which threw the Shorshian into deep shadow.

He was asleep. "I woke up *di*-Master Strinni," I whispered to Kennrick. "Your turn."

"But you're so good at it," Kennrick said, gesturing. "Please; go ahead."

"You're too kind," I said, frowning. On Bofiv's left, against the car's side wall, was an empty seat, presumably that of his compatriot Master Tririn.

But on Bofiv's right, where I would have expected to find the empty seat of the late Master Colix, was a closed privacy shield. "Who's that?" I asked, pointing at it.

"A Nemut," Kennrick said. "He's not part of our group."

"Why isn't that Colix's seat?" I asked. "Didn't he want to sit with his buddies?"

"I don't know." Kennrick frowned. "Huh. You think the others didn't like him?"

"Or vice versa," I said, making a mental note to ask Bofiv and Tririn which of the party had come up with the seating arrangements. "So where *was* Colix sitting?"

"There." Kennrick pointed to an empty middle seat not far from where Bofiv slept.

The late Master Colix's seat was flanked by privacy shields. I wondered if one hid an attractive female Shorshian. Maybe that was why he'd chosen to ditch his colleagues.

As if on cue, the aisle shield retracted to reveal a Human female no older than seventeen. Her face was pale, as if she'd gone two rounds with food that didn't agree with her.

Make that three rounds. She was on the move, heading toward the front of the car at the quick-walk of the digestively desperate.

I eyed the last privacy shield in that block. Maybe *that* was the pretty Shorshic female.

"Well?" Kennrick prompted.

"Well, what?" I countered, turning around to watch the girl. She reached the front of the car and disappeared into one of the restrooms.

"Are we going to ask Master Bofiv about Master Colix's habits?" Kennrick asked.

"In a minute," I said. Colix had gotten sick and died . . . and now one of his seatmates had suddenly made a mad dash for the facilities?

Kennrick caught the sudden change in my tone. "What is it?" he asked.

"I don't know," I said. "Maybe nothing."

"Or?"

"Or maybe something," I said, glancing at my watch. Five minutes, I decided. If the girl wasn't back in five minutes I would grab a Spider and send him in to find her.

Three minutes later, the door opened and the girl reappeared. She started a little unsteadily back down the aisle toward her seat, looking even more drawn than she had before.

"Or nothing, I take it?" Kennrick murmured.

"So it would seem," I agreed. The girl's eyes were fixed on me as she came toward us, a wary and rather baleful expression on her pale face. "You all right, miss?" I asked softly.

"I'm fine," she said, clipping out each word like she was trimming a thorn hedge. If my concerned smile was having any effect, I sure couldn't detect it. "You mind?"

I wasn't even blocking her way, but I gave her a little more room anyway. "I just wondered if you were unwell."

"I'm fine," she said again, brushing past me and flopping down into her seat.

"Because your seatmate had a bad attack of something," I went on, kneeling down beside her. "You might have noticed when his friends took him to the dispensary?"

She slid the privacy shield control forward, and the shield started to rotate into its closed position. "The dispensary, where he died?" I finished.

"What did you just say?" the girl asked, her face suddenly tight.

"I said Master Colix is dead," I repeated.